FOG CITY

THE TRILOGY BOX SET

LAYLA REYNE

Fog City: The Trilogy Box Set

Cover Design: The Book Brander

Box Set Formatting: DJW Formatting

Ebook ISBN: 978-1-7373524-3-3

Print ISBN: 978-1-962010-34-4

ABOUT THIS BOOK

An assassin fighting for his empire, his soul, and the last man he should want.

Hawes Madigan haunts San Francisco's criminal underworld.
But the Prince of Killers is haunted too.
By the one kill that never should have been.
It keeps him up at night—and puts him in Dante Perry's path.

Dante has one goal—vengeance.
And Hawes Madigan is a means to an end.
Until he becomes so much more.

Dante offers his help in the streets and in the sheets, giving Hawes permission to let go.

As their alliance strengthens, so does their desire for each other.
And so do the doubts about the future king and the mysterious private investigator.
But the doubts of others are nothing compared to the secrets between them.

Secrets that could cost them their lives and bring down the entire Madigan empire.

This box set contains:
Prince of Killers, King Slayer, A New Empire

PRINCE OF KILLERS

FOG CITY, BOOK ONE

Prince of Killers

Cover Design: The Book Brander

Cover Photography: Wander Aguiar Photography

Editing: Edits by Kristi, Keren Reed Editing, Susie Selva

First Edition

June, 2019

E-Book ISBN: 978-1-7320883-6-8

Paperback ISBN: 978-1-7320883-7-5

Content Warnings: explicit sex including mild kink; explicit language; violence; instances and/or discussion of homophobia; off-page instances and/or discussion of PTSD, drug use, and abuse of minor characters.

ABOUT THIS BOOK

Get lost in the fog.

Hawes Madigan earned his reputation as the Prince of Killers.
Heir to criminal and corporate empires.
An assassin for hire in CEO's clothing.
Every day, he hates the moniker and his fate a little more.

Until sexy mysterious private investigator Dante Perry swaggers
through his door.

Dante tells him what he suspects—there's a target on his back.
And makes him feel the unexpected, wild and free.
Like maybe he can change his fate. Like maybe he can be more.

But such a shift will require Hawes to root out the traitors in his
organization.
And eliminate the one he unwittingly invited into his life.
Assuming his heart and crown can survive the betrayals.
Not to mention the bullets flying at his head.

There's no shortage of twists and turns in this first book of Hawes and Dante's M/M romantic suspense trilogy. Fair warning: buckle up, cliffhangers ahead!

ONE

Hawes clocked him the second he walked through the restaurant door. At first glance, and he was getting plenty of those, the striking man with long dark hair and leather bracelets could easily be mistaken for a rock star. Not uncommon for Restaurant Gary Danko, the local watering hole of San Francisco's elite. In the fog-shrouded hills of Fisherman's Wharf, the Michelin-starred restaurant with its elegant yet laid-back vibe attracted athletes, entertainers, tech kings, and financial wizards, as well as the city's political players and old-money families. Mr. Double Denim Rock God, with his long legs, windswept hair, and studded leather belt fit right in.

He carried himself like a rock star too, all loose-limbed and casually confident. All that was missing was the instrument, but a guitar slung over his back would be awfully inconvenient if Mr. Not A Rock God had to draw his real instrument of choice—the pistol tucked at the small of his back. Underneath a black tank and denim jacket, its impression was hardly noticeable, unless you were looking.

Hawes was always looking.

As was the chief of police sitting at the corner of the bar closest to the door. Braxton Kane moved quickly and discreetly, rotating on his stool and placing a hand on the stranger's right forearm, playing the odds that the man was right-handed. His bet was correct. The man instinctively jerked back with his dominant hand, but then he settled just as fast, his casual air returning in a blink. He exchanged a few words with Kane and withdrew a small leather case from his jacket pocket. He pulled out what looked like a business card—from Hawes's distance across the dining room—and handed it to Kane. The chief glanced at the card, and the wiry muscles of his army-honed body relaxed. He nodded toward Hawes's table, apparently giving the stranger the go-ahead.

Cop.

Hawes dismissed the thought as quickly as it had come. That gorgeous hair was the antithesis of regulation, his carriage was all wrong, and Kane hadn't recognized him. Neither had Hawes, and he made it a habit to regularly review the rosters of the local law enforcement agencies, SFPD and FBI included. The last thing he wanted to do was kill a LEO and upset the balance he'd spent the past five years rebuilding.

Merc was Hawes's next best guess, the same conclusion reached by the man and woman on either side of him, judging by the flash of metal barrels under the table.

"Safeties on," Hawes ordered, voice low. There was a crowded dining room full of innocents between the door and their corner booth. And Kane wouldn't have sent Canadian Tuxedo in his direction if he'd thought a shoot-out would ensue.

The man's long limbs remained loose as he approached; his core, however, did not, the gun against his spine a steadying rod. Or were his abs just that tight? Hawes could see their defined ridges through the fitted tank as the stranger drew near. He stopped on the other side of the table and braced his hands on top of the lone chair there. The lighter ends of his hair draped over his shoulders, and Hawes wanted to run his fingers through the strands. Wanted to curl them around his fist and see if all the shades of brown in his hair matched the many shades of rain-soaked earth in his eyes.

Hawes wanted a lot of things he didn't often get.

A name and explanation, though, he demanded. "Who are you?" No sense mincing words or introducing himself. The man obviously knew who Hawes was and had come here looking for him.

"Dante Perry." No Canadian accent to go with the double denim. Fucking shame. Though the rest of it made sense. Dark hair and eyes, long face, olive skin, and a pronounced Roman nose. Italian descent to go with the Italian name, and judging by his lack of accent, local. Or if he'd had an accent at one time, he'd since lost it or otherwise trained it out.

"What can I do for you, Mr. Perry?"

Dante pulled out the chair but paused before sitting, his keen eyes darting between the table and Hawes's companions, as if he could see what their hands held beneath the white linen and lacquered wood. He shifted his gaze back to Hawes. "I don't plan to draw mine."

"Plans," Hawes said, skeptically. "All I've got is your name, Mr. Perry. I don't know that I trust you and your *plans*." He trusted Kane more, but better safe than sorry.

And he also demanded the show of respect. Commanded it.

Dante obliged. Hands on the table, where everyone could see them, he lowered himself into the chair. "I'm trusting you."

Hawes's gut clenched.

He ignored it and spread his arms over the back of the booth. A display of ease and confidence for their visitor, Kane, and anyone else watching. A signal for his associates to stand down, for the time being. Leverage, if Hawes needed to lift a leg and kick the table over, which would be another fucking shame. He hoped he wouldn't have to mess up Dante's handsome face. "All right, Mr. Perry, state your business."

Dante leaned forward, forearms resting on the table, and

lowered his voice. "Someone in your organization wants to kill you."

Is that all?

Hawes laughed out loud, drawing curious looks from the nearby tables. Dante's eyes flashed with frustration, his scruff-covered jaw tightening to match.

"Not *my* organization," Hawes said, even as he mentally heard his sister chide, *Trap!* Their family hadn't survived at the top of the food chain for three generations by disclosing the full scope of their operations. Madigan Cold Storage was a legit business. They sold and shipped refrigeration units and frozen goods for more Bay Area restaurants, businesses, and fisheries than Hawes could count. It was also a legit euphemism.

"Not *yet*," Dante said. "How is Papa Cal?"

Hawes dropped his arms, and the safeties-off *snick* was unmistakable.

Dante raised his hands. "Don't shoot me for reading the news."

Fair point. Hawes's grandfather's declining health had first made news five years ago, when Callum Madigan's Alzheimer's had advanced enough to force him to step down as CEO of the family company, as well as from the various charities and local boards he sat on. Hawes had stepped into his shoes at twenty-eight, two years before he could even access the trust fund his deceased parents had left him. Reporters had come back around last month, when news had leaked that Pacific Heights's much beloved—and to a different segment of San Francisco, much feared—Papa Cal had been moved into a local hospice house for end-of-life care.

A leak, the origin of which Hawes's brother still couldn't hack.

"You know my family's business?"

Dante's eyes flicked again to the table and back up. Evidently so.

"Given the nature of our work," Hawes said, "I expect a disgruntled employee from time to time."

Translation: Running an organization of assassins, Hawes expected murder to cross the minds of his associates. That's what they were paid well for with respect to their contracted targets. With respect to Hawes, thinking about or wanting to kill him, their boss, was a natural hyperbolic gripe of any employee. Actually trying to kill him was a very different matter. There'd been no whiff of discontent arising to that level.

But the leak, of a fact known only among the top levels of the organization at the time, still rankled.

Dante drummed his fingers on the table. "I wonder if one of those disgruntled employees knows what really happened to Isabelle Costa."

Hawes's blood ran cold. "Leave us," he ordered his associates. He braced a foot on the stand beneath the tabletop, flip ready.

"No, don't." Dante stood, slowly, no sudden movements, and reached into his jacket pocket. He withdrew the card case Hawes had seen him handle earlier.

This close, Hawes could read *Dante* pressed into the leather on one side, and a time stamp—*23:01*—pressed into the other. The precise time was familiar, but Hawes couldn't place it, not when his attention was focused on the two business cards Dante placed on the table. He slid the first one to Hawes, thumb and index finger pressing firmly on the corners. *Dante Perry, Private Investigator*, the plain ecru card read, with a local post office box, phone number, and email address.

"Run my prints, check me out, then call me when you're ready to talk human resources." He pushed the second card across the table. "Call her if you need more than your brother's exhaustive background checks. She'll vouch for me."

Hawes forced himself not to react. *This* card had no doubt been the one Dante had given Kane. It was a card Hawes carried in his own wallet.

"I'll look for your call." Confident, Dante turned and swaggered toward the exit like a rock star, as if he didn't know two pistols were aimed at him. But the private investigator did know, and he didn't care. He knew Hawes would call.

And he was right. No matter the background checks or references, Hawes would make contact. Because Dante Perry had walked into this restaurant tonight, into Hawes's life, and resurrected his worst nightmare.

HAWES KEPT HIS FOOT BRACED ON THE POLE BENEATH THE TABLE until Dante cleared the door.

"Follow him," he ordered Jodie. "But be back in ten. We're on the clock."

She nodded, slipped out of the booth, and glided across the dining room on silver stilettos, a flash of violet lamé hustling the same direction Dante had departed.

"Can I put a soufflé in the oven for you, Mr. Madigan?"

Hawes's attention snapped to the waiter approaching his table and to Kane passing behind him. Catching Hawes's eye, Kane tilted his head toward the restrooms and continued walking in that direction.

"Not tonight, thank you," Hawes answered the waiter. He hoped his smile didn't look as forced as it felt. Everyone here was always so good to him, but his mind was now a million miles away from the dinner he'd enjoyed. And he was expected elsewhere. Yet courtesy was still owed, as his grandmother had drilled into him. "Cheese course did me in," he added with a pat to his belly. A compliment for all involved. "I think the check is all I have room for."

The waiter smiled, pleased. "Right away, sir."

Hawes tossed his napkin onto the table and fished out his wallet. "Pay the check and bring the car around," he said to Ray, his other associate, as he shoved a stack of bills into his hand.

Ray cut his eyes to the restroom hallway, reading Hawes's intent. "It's not wise."

"I didn't ask you."

"At least let me go with you. It's my job."

"Your job is to be my backup on the contract we're executing tonight. You are not here for my protection, which in any event, is unnecessary where Kane is concerned." Hawes pocketed his wallet, pulled out his phone, and carefully tucked the two cards Dante had left behind into the card compartment on the back. "Text me when the car is out front. I don't want to be late."

He slid out of the booth before Ray could object further. Hawes was confident in his hand-to-hand abilities against Kane, and he was equally confident it would never come to that with the chief.

Kane was waiting for him inside the otherwise empty men's room. Wise choice; no cameras or recording devices in here. Being seen dining at the same establishment or exchanging pleasantries at a charity or veterans' event was one thing; secret meetings were another. Potentially damning, for both their reputations.

"You didn't know him?" Hawes asked without preamble.

"I didn't." Kane flashed the same card Hawes now had in his pocket. "But he checks out with Cruz."

Saved Hawes the call, but he'd still have Holt run the background checks and Dante's prints. He'd dropped too big a bomb to ignore. "Have you heard of him *at all*?"

Kane shook his head. "He wasn't on my radar." He dug a caramel candy out of his pocket, peeled off the golden wrapper, and popped it into his mouth. "You gonna tell me what he wanted?"

"He told me someone wanted to kill me."

Kane laughed, same as Hawes had. "Is it a day that ends in *y*?"

"Exactly."

"But that only explains your bark of laughter." Kane leaned back against the vanity, hands braced on either side of his narrow hips, fingers curled around the sink's porcelain lip. "Perry said something else that made you and your fire team go on alert. You gonna tell me what that was?"

Of course the top cop had picked up on the abrupt change in mood.

"No," Hawes answered. Not until he knew more about Dante's motives and his connection to Isabelle. No sense unleashing that ghost on anyone else if it turned out to be just that —a ghost, whose haunting was limited to Hawes. A specter that had reared its head periodically over the past three years but never gained form enough to torture anyone but him.

"Didn't figure you would." Kane hung his head, and Hawes wondered how much one Madigan or another had contributed to the chief's thinning hairline. His high and tight buzz cut disguised it from most, but Hawes had seen pictures of the before and the reality of the after.

"Safer for you, Brax."

The chief lifted a hand, then his hazel eyes. "I know the drill. Just give me a warning if things are about to go tits-up."

Hawes cringed. "You know I hate that saying, right?"

"You know I spent two decades in the military, right?"

The heavy mood eased with their laughter. Kane's sense of humor, his sass, and his loyalty when it mattered most—a promise he'd never wavered from—were the underpinnings of this unlikely alliance. That and his willingness to look the other way as long as Hawes kept his promises too. "Yes, Chief Kane, I will let you know if the shit is about to hit the fan."

Kane rolled his eyes. "Because that phrase is so much better." He pushed off the sink and started for the door. "Keep me posted, and stay safe." Hand on the knob, he paused and glanced back. All trace of humor was gone from his eyes. "All of you."

TWO

Hawes didn't have time to linger on Kane's words, as his phone vibrated with a text from Ray. **At the curb.**

On my way, he texted back.

But first, he tipped Dante's business card out of his phone case and into his other palm. Handling it carefully, he snapped a couple of quick photos and shot them off to Holt with a message to commence digging.

Copy that, his twin replied.

Hawes tucked the card back into the case, pocketed his phone, and headed for the exit. Outside, Jodie was standing next to the idling Benz.

Shit. She'd lost Dante.

"Sorry, boss," she said as Hawes slid into the back seat. "He made a loop around the block and hopped on the fucking cable car."

No way would she have made it back in the ten minutes Hawes had allowed if she'd followed Dante onto one of those. Also, "fucking cable car" was right.

"It's fine," Hawes said. "Holt's on him."

That would have to satisfy, including Hawes's mind, if he was going to be sharp for the job ahead. Granted, all he had to do was press a button, but he could never be too careful, especially when explosives were involved. There was only one other method of assassination Hawes hated more, but while he was confident foregoing a pistol, he wouldn't ask that of his operatives. "Are we set?" he asked.

Jodie nodded. "Lucas texted. All wired up."

Tension rippled through Hawes, tightening his insides. He didn't let it show. "The area is clear?"

"Pier's deserted except for the warehouse." The derelict pier was set to be demolished later that month. They were doing the city a favor, taking down the largest of the remaining structures on it, but they had to be sure no one was in it.

"You're certain the women are out?"

"All of them." Ray shifted in his seat and passed a tablet to Hawes, two windows open on-screen. "The left one is the security loop Holt hijacked." Everything looked normal in that window. Two guards sat at a card table eating soup out of sourdough bread bowls. "The right window is the real footage from an hour ago." The guards' faces were planted in their food. "Avery got the women out and onto the boat while Lucas wired the place."

"Reno will be by for his nightly check-in at ten," Jodie said, "and find his precious 'merchandise' gone." She sneered at the term the cartel transporter used time and again to refer to the trafficking victims he regularly traded in. The warehouse was a layover stop. The only one Reno had left after Jodie and Ray had taken out a winemaker who was letting Reno use his cellars to hide women awaiting transport.

Hawes scrolled through the live surveillance feeds. No sign of activity inside or outside the warehouse. "Only two guards?" Hawes expected more firepower after the winery incident last week.

"Reno thinks he's flying under the radar with this one," Ray said. "Doesn't want to draw attention to it."

Clearly, neither Reno nor his guards knew Holt had tapped into their webcam. Served them right for broadcasting the "fun" they had with their victims. Not that the trafficking alone hadn't earned them vetted status. These were the kind of contracts Hawes wanted for the organization. Gray areas and despicable human beings the law couldn't reach or catch—the Madigans could.

Jodie turned the car down the road to the pier. The street was almost pitch-black toward the end, the city no longer maintaining the doomed stretch. It was a perfect, under the radar hideout for the cartel's trafficking operation, until they'd been put on Hawes's radar. The tablet vibrated in his hands, indicating they were within range for the remote detonation app. Jodie wheeled the car around and backed it into a narrow alley between two smaller, boarded-up structures, out of sight for when Reno drove past.

"We should be good to go," Jodie said.

Hawes's insides went from tight to knotted as his mind flashed back to another dark night three years ago. To the unintended death precipitated by the weapon of destruction he wielded tonight. He had to be sure.

He cycled through the surveillance feeds one more time. All clear. He moved the monitoring window to the side of the tablet and brought the detonation app to the front. Thumb over the Activate trigger, he'd hit it as soon as Reno was inside. Far enough in to guarantee his death, but before he realized something was amiss.

Motion in the other window caught Hawes's eye.

"Shit!" He dragged that window back to the center and zoomed in. There, on the edge of view, a man crouched and peered into one of the compartments where Reno had hidden the women. "There's still someone inside. Looks like he's checking for the women."

He flashed the tablet at Ray, who likewise muttered a curse.

"He's probably one of Reno's men."

"*Probably* isn't good enough," Hawes said, even if the man did have a gun holstered on his hip. Hawes had been wrong before;

he wouldn't risk it again. Those were the rules now—his rules. He dialed Holt from the tablet.

It rang once through the car's speakers before Holt picked up. "I see him too. Facial recognition is running."

"Call Lucas," Hawes told Ray. "Have him walk you through *exactly* what he did to clear the building."

Ray shoved open the door. "On it."

Phone to his ear, he paced in front of the Benz while Hawes and Jodie waited for Holt's update. On-screen, the man in the warehouse gave the two dead men a wide berth as he continued to check the holding cells.

"Scout for Reno?" Jodie asked.

"Possibly," Hawes said. "Or for a rival cartel, or a fed. Coast Guard has both been snooping around this case too."

"Strike out here," Holt said. "Facial recognition didn't ping."

Ray braced a hand on the frame of the open car door. "Lucas is certain there was no one else in or around the warehouse when he and Avery cleared out with the women."

"Reno's five minutes out," Holt said, adding to their mounting complications.

The biggest one was in that warehouse. They needed to flush him out and confirm who he worked for. "Holt, activate the comm devices. Give us Reno's location every ninety seconds." Hawes lowered the armrest between the back seats and opened the custom-built, foam-lined "tool case" inside. "Ray, you take the north entry. Jodie, you've got the south side." He handed each operative an over-ear comm and hooked on his own. "I'll come through the front. We herd him toward the center, then out the back."

"Toward the water?" Jodie said. "We'll be cut off too if we don't get him out before Reno gets here."

"There's enough of the promenade left for you to skirt around the building," Holt said. "Security feed shows it's clear. As soon as you get out of the blast radius, I'll detonate the explosives from here."

Assuming they booked it fast enough to do so before Reno caught on to the trap. This was risky, but risking an innocent life was unacceptable. Hawes untucked the garrote from the case's foam and lowered the lid with a *snap*. "We wait for Reno and kill him if we have to. So long as the explosion goes off in the end, the evidence will be destroyed and it'll be linked to the winery explosion, as intended." It would look like the cartel was cleaning up their own mess.

"Worse comes to worst," Hawes added, "we'll have the water."

"That water's freezing," Ray protested.

"Better than burning alive."

And better than living with more innocent blood on his hands.

"Reno's two blocks out."

Holt's report came just as their hiccup stepped into Hawes's reach. The man had been so busy yammering on his phone about the *merchandise*—a scout, then; not an innocent—that he hadn't realized he'd been expertly redirected by Ray and Jodie, who'd been locking some doors and opening others. Or that Hawes was hiding in the shadows right behind him.

"He's all yours, boss," Jodie spoke quietly from her position on the other side of the main room's entry door. Ready to round it at any second.

Hawes slowly separated the two ends of the garrote, minimizing the *hiss* of the wire as he unfurled it. No dramatics needed. He inched a wingtip out of the shadows and shifted his weight to step forward.

The scout spoke a name, and Hawes immediately retreated.

"Fuck!" Holt murmured, having heard the same thing. "Stay right there and keep him close. I'm tapping into his wireless signal. I'll check it against their list."

"What's going on?" Ray whispered.

"Rival cartel," Holt answered, since Hawes could not.

"Acceptable collateral," Jodie said.

No such thing.

And the rival cartel was not their target. This was not a war Hawes wanted to set off. Yes, war was likely inevitable if the rival cartel was willing to consider such a rip-off, but for Kane's sake, Hawes wouldn't be the one to start it. Didn't mean he'd let this guy get away, or not get his actual target.

"Confirmed," Holt said. "Abort?"

"No," Hawes said, at full voice, intentionally. "Capture."

"What?" The scout whipped around. "Who's there?"

Hawes lunged out of the shadows. "Bad night to plan a rip-off."

The scout reached for his gun, but Hawes, moving faster, flung one end of the garrote toward the crook of the scout's right elbow. The wire looped around, hooked, and Hawes yanked, stopping the scout short of grabbing his weapon. The man cocked back his left arm, preparing to swing. Hawes ducked, and Jodie swept in from the scout's blindside, grabbing his raised elbow and his gun.

"Good luck with that," she said with a lethal smile.

She jerked the scout's arm the opposite direction as Hawes, who was still holding his right arm trapped in the garrote. The *pop* of dislocating shoulders made Hawes cringe. Add to that the *thump* of knees hitting concrete—Ray kicking the scout's legs out from behind him—and even Holt groaned in sympathy over the comms.

Victory, however, was short-lived. Holt turned serious again in an instant. "Reno's at the gate."

The scout gasped and grunted as Jodie finished trussing him up. "Who the fuck are you guys?"

Hawes knelt and got in his face, making sure the man got a good look at him. "They call me the Prince of Killers." He hated the moniker, whispered through the foggy underbelly of San Francisco's disreputable elite. Hated how it came to be and what it implied, but there was no denying its implication was useful in certain circumstances. Like now, as fear widened the scout's eyes. Hawes also needed deterrence to penetrate his brain. "Remind your cartel boss who keeps the order in Fog City. Don't fuck with it. And *you* remember who saved your life tonight."

"Saved my life?"

"I'm not leaving you here for Reno to find, or to die. That's a war none of us needs." He stood and turned to Jodie and Ray. "Toss him in the Bay."

"I'll drown like this," the scout hissed.

"Better hope you float," Ray said as he hefted him over his shoulder.

The scout continued to struggle as they exited via the promenade. When the inky water of the Bay was in sight, he tried bargaining. "I'll tell you whatever you want to know."

"I'm not interested in anything you have to say." But Hawes did know a certain Bureau AD who was investigating the cartel's trafficking operations. A little goodwill could go a long way. "But I know someone who might be."

THREE

An hour later, the waterfront was still alight, the fire from the explosion raging, and the fleet of emergency vehicles casting their bright lights on the scene. A stark contrast to the occasional car that passed by Hawes in the midtown residential neighborhood where he'd arranged the hand-off of the scout. Hawes dragged his gaze from the fiery sight, the last such explosion he ever intended to set, and hoofed it up the hill. As much as he would have liked to call it a night, he needed to return to the family fort and debrief with his brother and sister. Needed to find out what Holt, now freed from mission-comm duty, had dug up on Dante Perry.

Ray stood at the mouth of an alley half a block up the hill, backlit by the glare of headlights, fog swirling around his legs. Jodie edged the Benz's nose out from between the two structures on either side of the narrow street.

"Take me to the house," Hawes said, turning into the alley.

Mind whirring over Dante, Hawes almost missed the car reversing direction, the taillights reflecting brighter off the house at the other end of the alley, the side-view mirror appearing on the edge of his periphery, the rear door handle moving out of his reach.

Ray's footsteps closed in fast and loud behind him.

Hawes spun, expecting to see someone chasing them into the alley, only to find Ray's pistol raised and aimed directly at him. Hawes stumbled back a step, struggling to put the pieces together. "What the fuck?"

Ray's eyes held his. They were not the eyes of an ally. Not those of the man who'd fought by Hawes's side just an hour ago. They were cold, intent on death. What the hell was going on?

Hawes patted his pocket for the garrote. Empty. His stomach sank.

Ray grinned menacingly. "Missing something?" The garrote dangled from the fingertips of his free hand.

"Have you lost your mind?"

"Better question is, have you?" Ray tossed the garrote behind him, toward the street, then charged forward.

Hawes didn't have time to think. Didn't have time to dwell on the boulder of betrayal threatening to flatten him. All he had time to do was react. He ducked, and Ray's gun crashed into the driver's-side window. Glass rained down onto the pavement, crunching under Hawes's feet as he spun and rammed a shoulder into Ray's middle.

"So much for doing your job," Hawes said. "You call this protection?"

"Not my job," Ray grunted. "Said it yourself."

"Neither is killing me."

"Except it is." Ray brought the butt of his gun down on Hawes's back, dead center and hard as hell, two hundred pounds of muscle behind it.

A spike to his spine, the hit sent waves of pain radiating out to all of Hawes's limbs. He let loose a shout, then gritted his teeth against the agony, against the urge to drop to the ground and curl into a ball. That would only lead to death. He was sure of that. Dante's earlier prediction echoed loudly in his head. Fighting through the pain with a roar, he shoved Ray with all his strength, enough to get a foot of separation. Enough to avoid another pistol whip, hike up his elbow, and ram it under Ray's chin. With his attacker's head flung back, Hawes kicked a leg up between Ray's spread ones, foot aimed directly at the traitor's crotch.

Ray howled, bent forward, and struggled to right himself, hands coming down to shield himself from another kick. Hawes got there first, landing a second kick to his middle. "Consider that your severance pay," he said, as the traitor stumbled backward out of the alley. A blaring car horn warned of Ray's impending fate if he didn't regain his balance soon.

But Ray was no longer the focus of Hawes's attention.

The driver's-side door was flung open and jammed against the siding of the adjacent house, the rest of the broken glass from the window—and from Jodie's skirt—tinkling to the asphalt. It crunched under her heels, but not as ominously as the safety-off snick of her gun or the whoosh of air around the knife she flipped in her other hand.

Not just a single boulder—a fucking landslide of betrayal walloped Hawes. He fought to remain standing. Forced himself to shake out his limbs and prepare for round two. "You too? Did you even bother to follow Perry earlier?"

"Perry's not my concern."

"I can see that." Hawes could also see, with one quick glance at the car, that he was trapped. The Benz was practically parked on the opposite curb, making too narrow an opening for even Hawes to squeeze through. He could use the bars on the left building's subfloor windows to vault onto the trunk, then scramble over the top of the car, but Ray was still stumbling around on the sidewalk and Jodie would land a shot before Hawes could finish executing those maneuvers.

Through it was, then, and since Hawes wouldn't carry a gun and Ray had thrown his best weapon the opposite direction, speed, distraction, and sharp elbows were the only options he had left.

"Were you and Ray planning to make your move tonight, or did Perry accelerate your timeline?"

"Got orders to let you burn," Jodie said. "Turns out that scout saved you too. For an extra hour."

She and Ray had been doing a job. They'd been hired to kill him. Someone hadn't merely wanted to kill him. They'd enacted a plan to do just that. Dante had been more right than he probably knew.

"Orders from whom?" he asked Jodie.

He didn't expect an answer, but with each word he spoke, Hawes stepped closer to where three wires broke off from the dozen or so cables running horizontally along the building's exterior. He couldn't yank the whole bunch off the wall, secured as they were by bolted-in loops, but he could rip free those three vertical-running cords.

More weapons.

"Not to sound arrogant," Hawes said, inching closer, "but I find it hard to believe you found a better boss."

"You do sound arrogant." Jodie spun the hilt of the knife in her hand, her hold loose and flexible. Ready to grip and throw in an instant, like Hawes's sister had taught her.

Panic streaked through Hawes, sudden and breathtaking.

If Jodie and Ray had moved on him tonight, was someone else moving on Helena? On Holt and his wife and daughter? Was this a coordinated attack on the family? A coup? Or was he the only target? Whipping out his phone and calling home wasn't an option. Neither was asking the question. He didn't want to put that idea, if it wasn't already there, in the head of whoever was behind this.

"Can't say I'm not disappointed. You were one of the best, Jodie."

"I am the best."

She proved it the next second, catching the knife mid-spin and hurling it at him, the action practiced and deadly. His quick reflexes and slender frame saved him from a direct hit, the knife slicing through the gray silk of his suit sleeve and flying past his rotated shoulder. She didn't wait to attack, following directly in the knife's wake, aiming to take advantage of Hawes's momentary distraction and open body position. He shot out his left hand, yanked the wires off the wall, and spun into her charging body, forcing her to try to wrap herself around him. He jammed his elbow into her side, and the slight bend in her stance was enough for Hawes to loop the wires over her head and around her neck. She flailed, limbs trying to land a strike, but she'd already used her best weapon for that. The knife was a good two feet away on the ground, and the gun in her other hand was too much of a risk given their close quarters. Cables still clutched in his hands—ignoring the sting of the wires digging into his palms—Hawes used the window bars to vault up onto the trunk of the car and jump back down behind Jodie, his legs tucked for maximum momentum on his way to the ground.

Jodie's neck snapped, her gun clattered to the ground, and her body followed with a muffled *thump*.

"Madigan, get down!" came a shout from the far end of the alley.

Hostile or friendly, Hawes couldn't say, but he didn't think twice about heeding the warning. He snatched up Jodie's knife, stepped back, and yanked open the rear door, crouching between it and the open driver's door. A bullet whizzed overhead, and Hawes whipped around, staring through the frame of the broken window. An apparently recovered Ray was recovered no more. Blood bloomed from a bull's-eye hit to his chest. He crumpled to the ground on the other side of the car door Hawes knelt behind.

Light flooded the alley from the direction the warning had come, and Hawes spun again. On the second-level porch of the house at the end of the alley, Dante stepped into the glow cast by the porch light. He was the last person Hawes expected to see again tonight, and gun in hand, stance professional, he looked as far from Mr. Rock God as possible. "This way!" he shouted, waving Hawes in his direction.

"What the fuck are you doing here?"

Dante's eyes flickered to Jodie. "When she didn't tail me past the corner, I knew something was off."

"Have you been following us all night?"

"Most of it, yes. Now let's fucking go!"

Go where? "It's a dead end that way."

"It's not." Dante raised his firing arm, and Hawes flipped the knife in his hand, ready to throw, but Dante's next words made it clear he was gesturing toward the street. "But that way is. Between the car horns and the gunshot, SFPD will be here any minute."

Hawes glanced at the two bodies on the ground. "I can't just leave them here." And he couldn't leave with a stranger he hardly knew, no matter who vouched for him. But could he stay?

"You were last seen alone," Dante said. "No one knows you met back up with them." He gestured at Ray and Jodie. "When the cops come calling, claim it was a dispute between them, or with a third-party who got away."

"My prints are all over the place."

"On your car, that's expected. Are you hurt? Bleeding?"

Hawes checked himself over. His back hurt like a bitch, but he hadn't been shot or nicked. He flipped over his hands. The wires had left deep grooves in his palms. He didn't think the skin was broken, but he couldn't be sure, as red as they were. "Maybe these," he said, holding up his hands. While they were lifted, he checked the area around him. No blood on the ground or elsewhere. "Would just be on the wires."

"Use the knife to cut the portion—"

"Don't tell me how to do my job," Hawes said, already hacking through the cables. He pocketed the cut portions and used his sleeve to wipe down the dangling ends and the wall, removing any fingerprints. "The bullet from your gun?"

"Won't be traced."

Car tires squealed close by, accompanied by sirens.

"Madigan!" Dante shouted. "We gotta go. Now!"

This was not the best idea, but as the sirens grew louder,

Hawes was out of options. He jumped over Jodie's body and sprinted for the stairs at the end of the alley, taking them two at a time. At the top, Dante grabbed his hand…and dragged him over the wooden stair rail.

The free fall didn't last more than a couple of seconds, but it felt like the longest two seconds of Hawes's life. He'd almost died in that alley—twice—but aside from his initial second of surprise, at no other time had the situation been out of his control. Falling through the dark night, Dante's hand the only thing holding him to reality, was not being in control. It was further from control, and reality, than Hawes had been in a long time.

At three seconds, his back hit canvas. He dipped, then was flung back in the air, his hand ripped from Dante's. A smaller fall followed, then another, before Hawes realized they'd landed on a trampoline.

"Let's go!" Dante whisper-shouted as he scrambled off.

Hawes followed, hopping off the trampoline and onto the ground in what appeared to be a shared backyard. "You could have told me before we jumped that I wasn't going to die."

"Can't make that promise yet." Gun drawn, back pressed against the closest building, Dante peeked around the corner.

Blue lights flashed down the narrow exit walk, and sirens screamed by on the street as police cruisers sped to the alley on the opposite side of the yard. They had to move, now.

Hawes snatched up the knife he'd dropped mid-fall and followed Dante, the two of them creeping down the dark walkway. A few feet shy of the street, Dante paused and tucked his gun back into his waistband where Hawes had first noticed it earlier that night. Not more than two hours ago, and yet the world had turned upside down in that short amount of time.

And it kept turning. Dante rotated to face him and held out his hand expectantly. "The knife," he demanded. "You can't go running out into the street with it, and as attractive as that fitted suit is on you, there's nowhere to hide that blade that won't be obvious."

Hawes hesitated, unwilling to give up his sole tactical weapon to the man with a gun and a good thirty pounds on him.

"I trusted you at the restaurant earlier," Dante said, as if reading his thoughts. "And I gave you information that proved to be true. Now I need you to trust me." Here in the shadows, his big dark eyes were bottomless black holes. Dangerous celestial objects with enough gravitational force to draw Hawes in and snuff him out for good. Hawes already felt the pull to this stranger who'd told him the truth and saved his life.

He handed over the knife. "I need to get to my brother and sister."

Dante strapped the knife into an ankle holster under his pant leg next to another blade. "I can get you there." He righted himself and led them out of the shadows and onto the sidewalk. "But there's a catch."

"What kind of catch?" Hawes asked, walking close at his side.

"How do you feel about riding tandem?"

Hawes followed the direction of Dante's fond gaze to a rainbow parade of fiberglass crotch-rockets. Surely not. No—there, right at the end, pearlescent midnight-blue and gleaming chrome... "The Harley?"

Dante smirked. "The Harley."

Hawes's gut clenched, again. Damn, this was gonna be a thing.

FOUR

Hawes had grown up in San Francisco, had been born and bred in its hills and valleys. He'd learned at an early age how to turn a car's wheels when parked on a slope and how to perfectly time the release of the clutch and the press of the gas so as not to roll the wrong way down Jones Street. He would never, however, get used to cruising his hometown's hills on a motorcycle, not his sister's and certainly not Dante Perry's. And he most definitely would not get used to riding tandem, when one wrong bump could jostle him loose and send him flailing to his death.

By the time they rumbled onto the stone drive of the sage-green Victorian with its high-pitched roofs and bright-white trim, Hawes had mentally uttered more Hail Marys than he had the Sunday after he'd blown the homecoming king. He wished he could say he'd been holding tight to Dante as an excuse to map out every nook and cranny of his ripped torso, but regrettably, he hadn't thought beyond a death grip for survival until after he'd climbed off the bike. At which point, managing to stand on his embarrassingly unsteady legs took precedence.

Assassinate people for a living, no problem. Run a multimillion-dollar company before age thirty, can do. Ride a motorcycle in San Francisco, fuck no.

He gingerly curled one hand into a fist and leaned with his knuckles against the knotted cypress next to the driveway. By contrast, Dante the Confident dismounted the bike with the same casual ease he'd displayed all night. Hawes admired and hated him. The latter was easier to speak too, sarcasm as good a weapon as any. "Did you really think a Hog was the best idea here?"

"It was my dad's," Dante said, stealing another of Hawes's weapons. "He taught me to ride a bike on these hills long before I learned to drive a car on them." He slid a hand over Hawes's lower back, the weight more steadying than it had any right to be. "Never been on a bike?"

"I have," Hawes answered. "Sister's Ducati. Not my favorite thing."

"You don't say." There was humor in Dante's eyes, and also heat, same as in his touch. If Hawes didn't know any better—

"Take your hand off him."

Dante instantly dropped his hand. Hawes felt the loss almost as keenly as the earlier blow to his back, which was making itself known again now that fear and adrenaline were wearing off.

"You good?" Dante asked, not touching him but remaining close.

"Yes." *No*, but it was better to lie than agitate the owner of the cool, crisp voice that had sliced through the darkness. "I'm fine, Hena," Hawes called up toward the house. He didn't need to look to know his sister was waiting on her perch, back to one of the porch columns, legs stretched out in front of her, tonight's weapon of choice—Ka-Bar or Sig Sauer—resting on her thigh. Hawes hoped her fingers hadn't twitched too much at the slip of her nickname.

"You can leave now," she said to Dante.

"I'm not leaving until he's home safely."

"He is home."

Hawes cleared his throat. "I don't think that's what—" His interjection was cut off by a flash of black leather, pale skin, and long blonde hair as Helena vaulted off the porch and landed in front of them.

"I know what he meant, Big H." Barefoot, knees absorbing the minimal impact her petite frame made, Helena had landed quiet as a cat, barely making a sound. She rarely ever did. Silent and deadly was her specialty, and right then, her ice-blue eyes were glaring daggers at Dante. "And he's not your concern." She spun the knife in her hand, like Jodie had earlier, and a shiver raced up Hawes's spine.

"Go," he said to Dante, sensing Helena on a precipice. She'd obviously gotten wind of what had happened in the alley, no doubt also knew about the complication at the warehouse, and had gone into hyperprotective mode. "Go," he repeated when Dante hesitated. Dark eyes swung to his, and Hawes held his gaze, projecting the confidence that tonight's events had dulled. Now at home, or rather, the home he'd grown up in, he was determined to wrestle things back under his control. "I've got this, and I've got your number."

"Use it." Dante pivoted and swaggered back to his bike.

In the restaurant earlier, when Dante had walked away from his table, Hawes had been distracted by unknowns, debating whether the PI was friend or foe. He still wasn't sure, but this time, it didn't distract Hawes from checking out Dante's ass. It filled out a pair of Levi's nicely, no debate there. Dante threw a leg over the bike, straddling the seat, and Hawes cursed himself again for not enjoying the ride more.

"Nine out of ten," Helena whispered at his side. "Grabbable for sure." She bit her bottom lip, humming with approval, and made a squeezing motion with her free hand.

Hawes breathed easier. "What's it take for a ten out of ten?"

"Need to see it out of the jeans." She bumped his shoulder. "But I'm guessing you're calling dibs on that."

The Harley roared to life, and Dante shot him a parting smirk. He was sexier than he had any right to be in double denim, that rock-star hair streaming in the wind behind him. Yeah, Hawes called dibs.

And besides… "What happened to Danielle?" Hawes asked as they started up the steps.

Helena shrugged one shoulder.

"Or Eric?"

She shrugged the other.

No one was ever good enough for his little sister. Or maybe she didn't think she was good enough for them. Though that would be ridiculous. She was gorgeous, a talented lawyer by day, and there was no one Hawes would rather have by his side in a fight at night. Anyone would be lucky to have her, but whoever that person was, they'd never have all of her.

Something Hawes understood all too well. Not everyone got lucky like their parents and grandparents, or like Holt and Amelia. His own bedmates had come and gone, frustrated that Hawes was holding back. For their protection, and his family's. But there was always a red line that separated him from his lovers. He hadn't bothered to toe that line recently, staying far away from it by sticking to one-night stands and club hookups. Dante, however, knew who he was, knew about their family and the business behind their business.

"Brax called," Helena said, confirming the heads-up Hawes had suspected.

"And?" Hawes prompted.

"Told him you were already home." She grinned over her shoulder as she pushed open the front door. "Better go get our stories straight before he gets here to see for himself."

Hawes hissed through clenched teeth as the cold lidocaine cream tickled the abraded skin of his palms. The wires hadn't broken the skin, just left deep, angry grooves, but professional examination, treatment, and bandaging by their very own surgical nurse was insisted upon. He grunted his displeasure all around.

"Oh, come on." His sister-in-law's green eyes twinkled. "I've patched you up from far worse injuries."

"Like that knife wound to your left shoulder," Helena said from where she sat across the table.

Hawes flinched in remembered pain, then flinched again as very real pain rippled out from his throbbing back. "The knife wound *you* gave me?"

Helena paused in her petting of the family's giant Siberian cat to blow him a kiss. Amelia's demeanor, however, was no longer joking. She rested a hip against the dining room table next to him. "Fess up, Big H. Where else are you injured?"

He contemplated lying, but this was the person who, when she wasn't on duty at the hospital, tortured answers out of the organization's targets. Who eight months ago had pushed a ten-pound baby out of her willowy, five-foot-eight frame. Amelia scared him almost as much as Helena did.

"Took a pistol whip to the back." He held out his index finger, pretending it was his spine, and with his other fist, mimicked Ray bringing the gun down on it.

Cringing, Helena shifted in her chair, and Daisy skittered off her lap, joining the tabby, Tulip, in the corner to play.

"I'm going to need to check your back," Amelia told him.

He nodded and tried to extricate himself from his jacket, cursing as he made his back ache worse.

"Easy," Amelia said. "Let me help."

Out of his jacket, Hawes unbuttoned his wrinkled dress shirt far enough to lower it to his elbows, exposing most of his back.

Amelia rotated him sideways on the chair and stepped fully behind him. "Ouch!" she rightly assessed. "That's gonna hurt like a bitch tomorrow." Again, spot on, Nurse Madigan.

As her fingertips gently probed the injured area, Hawes distracted himself with the purpose Helena had mentioned on their way up the steps outside. "Basics," he said, holding up his bandaged hands. "How do I explain these to Kane?"

Helena reached into Amelia's toolbox full of medical supplies and took out a roll of bandages. She tore off two strips and wrapped one around each of her hands, tucking the loose ends under her palms. "Combat practice."

"Or you were amusing Lily," Amelia said. "Baby girl got a cut on her hand today."

Hawes whipped his head around. "She okay?"

"She's fine. Just a scrape." Amelia swatted his shoulder. "Stop being the overprotective uncle."

Chuckling, he looked down again at his hands, then over at Helena's. "As likely an excuse— *Fuck!*" Hawes cursed as Amelia prodded the exact right—or wrong—spot on his back. "I'd say you found it."

"Stay," Amelia ordered him, like she would her crawling daughter, and disappeared into the adjacent kitchen.

Left alone in the dining room with Helena, Hawes bore the full brunt of his sister's icy-eyed glare. "I'm waiting for an explanation," she said.

"I'd prefer to give it just once."

"Fine. I'll holler for Holt to come down."

"No, you won't," Amelia said, reentering the room. "He's in the zone."

"Lily's knocked out, then?" Hawes said.

"Like a light." Amelia smiled the smile of a happy mother. It grew wider as she showed off her bounty—a Ziploc of ice and a baby sling. "We'll go to them."

Ten minutes later, the bag of ice strapped to his back with the bright pink sling, Hawes followed Helena and Amelia upstairs. At the second-floor landing, he noticed only one side of the floor was lit, the multicolored glass from Helena's Tiffany lamps casting a kaleidoscope of color on the common area walls and luring the cats away from their feet. His grandparents' master on the opposite end of the floor was dark.

"Rose?" he asked after their grandmother.

"With Papa Cal," Helena said.

Hawes had figured as much. They hadn't seen much of Rose since they'd moved Cal into hospice. Hawes made a mental note to stop by tomorrow. They continued on to the third floor—Holt's family's domain—and from the seating area there, up the spiral staircase to Holt's lair.

And *lair* was the right word for it.

At the very top of the house, in the peaks of the roof, the attic bonus room stretched the length of the structure. During the day, sun streamed in through the arched front window and overhead skylights. At night it was just as bright, owing to the tech-geek wall of wonder. Across the long, uninterrupted wall, LCD screens were stacked three high and four wide and served as monitors for Holt's bank of computers and surveillance feeds. Each of their family's homes and all their business operations, the legal and illegal ones, could be observed from this perch. It was everything Holt needed to be the eyes and ears of the organization and to do what he did best—digital assassination: financial, social, and otherwise. All from the comfort of home so he could spend time with his daughter.

And that's where this perch diverged from the one Holt had at the company's headquarters. Lily's presence here couldn't be missed—from the wooden crib beneath the front window, to the golden bear mobile twirling above it, to the rocking chair in the corner. It destroyed the typical hacker vibe, but it also humanized the place, more than Holt's wall of monitors and old military-style cot ever had.

Amelia crossed the room to her husband, gave him a kiss on the cheek, and peered into the crib, which had been rolled closer to Holt's seat at the computers. The *tap-tap-tap* of his rapid-fire typing was the best trick they'd discovered for getting Lily to sleep. If he was in the zone, Lily was lightly snoring, dead to the world.

Not wanting to wake his niece, Hawes followed Helena to the

seating area in the opposite corner. Helena collapsed on the couch, and Hawes started for one of the two armchairs before remembering the ice pack on his back. He grabbed the chair from the other paper-strewn desk, rolled it over, and turned it so he could straddle it, arms folded on top.

"Any blowback on the warehouse?" Hawes asked.

"We're clear," Helena said. "Local station got a tip that the cartel was cleaning up its own mess. And the feds?"

"Happy to have a new cartel informant."

"Nice save there." Amelia stepped away from the crib, shook out her long brown hair, and squeezed Holt's arm. "You can stop, babe. She's out cold."

"Just finishing this last bit of detail work on Jodie and Ray."

Hawes rotated his chair. "How'd you set that up?"

"Third party, like Perry suggested."

"How—"

Holt pointed at his wireless earbud, then at the EMS live streams running on one of his monitors. "Heard the call come in. Hacked the neighbor's security doorbell footage. I considered the fight option, but given their injuries and gunshot trajectory, there had to be a third party."

"You wipe the security footage?" Hawes asked.

"Of course." Holt gave him a what-do-you-take-me-for look that made Hawes smile. "And the footage from the ATM across the street."

"Sloppy, Big H," Helena remarked.

She wasn't wrong. He expected more of himself. While he'd cleaned up the unexpected hiccup in the warehouse, he'd made a mess of things in the alley. It seemed everything had been off-kilter since Dante Perry's arrival.

"He checks out," Holt said, as if reading his mind.

The twin-speak and mind reading were about the only "twin" things Hawes and his brother shared. Where Hawes's light-brown hair was streaked with blond, Holt's dirty-blond was tinged with red. Hawes had the same cold blue eyes as Helena, miles away from Holt's warm brown. Hawes preferred suits, Holt flannel and jeans. And where most of Hawes's physical features were lean and overly sharp—nose, chin, elbows, knees, even the tops of his ears—Holt was a mountain of curved, sloping muscles. Big round shoulders, a wide barrel chest inked with tattoos, redwood trunks for legs, and a strong jaw that led to a round, dimpled chin, even though Holt covered it with a brownish-red beard cut to make his face look more square.

Their mother used to joke that Hawes was so much slighter and pointier than Holt because his brother had taken up most of the space in her womb. Which was also why, she claimed, Hawes was born first, making him the big brother, technically. Carrying that guilt, joke or not, Holt had been Hawes's vigilant protector when they were young, never letting anyone bully him for being smaller, or gay. But by the time Holt had left for army basic training, Hawes had grown to a lanky six-foot-plus and learned to protect himself using the weapons he did have—speed, agility, and the same sharp elbows that had helped save him tonight.

Those and Dante Perry.

"He give you that card you sent me a picture of?" Holt asked.

Hawes pulled out his phone and opened the card compartment. "He intentionally left a thumb and index print on each corner."

Holt tossed a remote to Helena on the way to his other desk. He fished a fingerprint kit out of the bottom drawer and cleared a desk corner with a swipe of his tattooed right arm, sending a stack of mail flying.

Amelia rolled her eyes. "Really, babe?"

"I'll get it later." Meaning he'd restack the mail until Lily eventually puked on it and made disposal necessary. He waved Hawes over, extracted the card with a pair of forceps, and got to work with the fingerprint dust.

Hawes left him to it and reclaimed his chair, rotating back to Amelia and Helena on the couch. "What do we know?"

Helena clicked a button on the remote, and pictures of Dante filled the screens—outside the restaurant, at the bar with Kane, inside the dining room, and on the porch in the alley, gun arm raised.

Helena hummed, same as she had outside, and Amelia laughed. "Down girl."

"The name and business check out," Holt said as he continued to work under an exam lamp. "Though he's only recently back in San Francisco."

"Where's he been?" Hawes asked.

Helena clicked the remote again, and a list of addresses appeared on one of the screens. "Bounced around a lot."

Seattle was Dante's last known address. Explained the rocker vibe. Grunge just wouldn't die, no matter how many curses Hawes laid at its flannel feet. "He licensed as a PI here?"

"BSIS issued his license a few months back." Helena changed to another screen. "And he's got a CCW permit."

Concealed carry, likewise issued a few months back. Not uncommon for PIs. Or cops. Mercs didn't bother. But first Hawes circled back to something else his brother had said, and something Dante had mentioned too.

"You said 'recently back.' He's from here?"

"Yearbook picture," Holt said, then to Helena, "Next."

Helena clicked…and recoiled, an arm thrown dramatically over her face. "Warn a girl, Little H."

"Hey now!" Hawes jostled his sister's bare foot, which was dangling over her knee. "We weren't all born beauty queens."

Staring at seventeen-year-old Dante Perry, Hawes felt more than a shred of sympathy for the awkward boy Dante had been. Features too big for his face, gangly limbs, an unruly cowlick. Hawes had been there. Had the bad school pictures to prove it too. His eyes flickered to the bottom of the page. Galileo High School. Before it became Galileo Academy, it would have been the closest public high school to the heavily Italian North Beach neighborhood. Dante had said he'd grown up in San Francisco. "Family still in North Beach?" Hawes ventured.

"Mom and a sister," Holt replied, back at his computers. He snapped a picture of the dusty card with his phone, tapped the screen a few times, then, after keying in commands on the computer, stepped back and wiped his hands off on his jeans. "Okay, that's done and analyzing."

"What else did Perry say to you?" Amelia asked.

"That someone in the organization wants to kill me."

Helena scoffed. "Tell us something we don't know."

Hawes curled his fingers in the fabric of the sling stretched over his chest. "That it's somehow connected to Isabelle Costa."

Indrawn breaths echoed all around. Holt wobbled where he sat on the couch arm next to his wife, and Helena took up tapping her nails against each other.

"Does Perry have any connection to her?" Amelia asked, the first to recover. Holt and Helena still looked off-balance.

Welcome to Hawes's world. "Not that I know of." He turned to his brother. "Dig deeper. See if their paths crossed. See if anyone is paying him. Is this business or personal?"

"Looked personal to me out there," Helena said with a nod toward the front of the house. "How are *you* gonna handle him? Something tells me you'll be seeing him again soon."

Hawes didn't disagree with her read, and that prospect—of seeing Dante again, sooner rather than later—both excited and troubled him. There was no denying the pull he'd felt, or that Dante had saved his life, but there was also no denying he was a threat to Hawes's family, given what he seemed to suspect about Isabelle's death. If Dante ever learned the truth, he'd be an enemy for sure. And there were more than enough of those these days. Except this one had already provided valuable information that had helped save Hawes. There could be more to learn.

"I'm going to work a potential source," Hawes said. "See what more he can tell us about Ray and Jodie and whose orders they were following. I'll use whomever I can to find out who's gunning for us."

"For *you*," Amelia said. "That's all we know so far."

"True, but all of you should be on guard. If this is the start of a coup…"

"Then they'll have to take us all down." Helena's voice had taken on that chilly edge again, her protective hackles rising once more.

"If Perry's got information, get it," Holt said. "I've got no flags and no unusual account activity on either Ray or Jodie." Everyone in the organization was monitored for irregular financial or travel activity, as well as potential points of leverage.

"They had to know and trust the person who hired them," Helena said.

"Because they believed the payout would be there," Amelia added, finishing the same train of thought that had occurred to Hawes earlier.

He nodded. "We need to find out who."

"How much did you tell Brax?" Helena asked.

"Nothing, but I did agree to give him a heads-up if things were going"—he cleared his throat and forced out the words—"tits-up."

Holt snickered. "Once more with feeling, Big H."

Hawes shifted and yanked at the sling, jiggling the ice pack on his back. "Do you want me to throw this bag of ice at you?"

"Brax is about to throw ice on both of you," Helena announced.

Sure enough, the chief, pissed-off scowl in place, was charging up the stairs to the front door. There was no time to stop him before he—

The doorbell chimed, and two seconds later Lily's muffled whimpers broke into a wail.

Holt bolted up, scooping his daughter out of the crib and into his arms.

"I'll go grab a bottle," Amelia said, likewise springing into parental action, their routine well practiced.

Holt installed himself in the rocker, the world forgotten as Lily, cradled like a football in his tattooed arm, became the center of his universe.

Hawes was more than fine with that. She was the reason they did any of this. They'd all give her the world if they could. Impossible, but what they could do was make it better and safer for her. Hawes leaned over and kissed the munchkin's fuzzy auburn head, then his brother's. "Get her settled. We'll handle Kane."

He waited for Helena to finish locking the computers, then followed her downstairs. She stopped abruptly on the second-floor landing, and if not for both their quick reflexes, Hawes would have run her over. "You need to change," she said, nodding to his old room, next to hers, where he still kept a closet full of clothes for when he crashed there, which happened frequently. "You've been home a while, remember?" She nudged the ice pack on his back. "And there's a wet spot here."

"You got Kane?"

"Yeah, I got him," she said with a wink.

He started toward his room, feeling more than a little sorry for the chief. He barely made it a step before Helena grasped his wrist and turned him back around. "Are you okay?"

Cattiness gone, she wore the same concerned expression she had when Hawes had uttered Isabelle's name. She'd been there that night. She'd had to drag him out of the shower when, no matter how hard he scrubbed, he couldn't seem to get the blood off his hands.

He couldn't lie to her now. "No, but I have to be."

FIVE

It was half past two by the time the Lyft pulled to the curb in front of Hawes's building. As predicted, Kane had read them the riot act, then questioned them in-depth about Jodie and Ray. Holt's cover story had held and was supported by the evidence called in. Relatively satisfied, or just dog-tired, Kane had given them a much sterner warning to keep him apprised of any situations, then cleared out. Hawes had done the same shortly thereafter, against Helena's wishes. She'd wanted him to stay at the house, but Hawes needed to decompress within the comfort of his own four walls.

Holt had swept the area around the four-story South Beach condo building and confirmed all was clear. Inside the unit was always a risk—Hawes refused interior cameras—but exterior footage from the past few hours showed only the usual residents entering the building. No one had approached his end-unit's door.

Apparently they hadn't looked hard enough, or more likely, the man leaning against the side of the building reading a paperback, knew exactly where to stand to avoid the cameras.

"Where's the bike?" Hawes asked. All the building's parking

areas were in view of Holt's or other surrounding cameras. They would have seen the Hog on the security footage.

"In a garage up the block," Dante answered as he tucked away the book, a popular fantasy series. "One that doesn't have wired cameras."

Caution dictated—more and more with each passing hour—that Hawes not let this man into his life, much less into his home. A well-founded warning. A perfectly timed kill. A work-around designed to thwart their security. Letting him in was a risk, but Hawes had committed to keeping this potential enemy close, to seeing what more he knew about the threat to his family, should he make another approach. And now here he was.

Those were the logical reasons to let Dante in. There was also the illogical. The part of Hawes that had been unsteady since the alley, that he'd kept hidden from his siblings, and that was already settling in Dante's presence. When Dante shoved off the wall and stepped directly into a camera's line of sight, it settled further.

"Could have given you a ride if you'd wanted." The smirk was for Hawes's benefit. The dark eyes flitting to the camera were for the benefit of whoever was watching. A white flag of sorts. He was exposing himself here as much as Hawes.

Good enough for Hawes, whose traitorous body led his mind astray, considering other things he'd like to ride. He pushed back one side of his leather jacket and dug his keys out of his jeans pocket, ignoring his vibrating phone in the other. "If I never ride on that bike again, it'll be too soon." He swiped his key fob over the building's lock and opened the front door for Dante to enter ahead of him. Less risk, relatively.

"You need to be more careful," Dante said, as if reading his mind.

"Right now, I trust about five people." Keeping Dante in front of him, Hawes motioned for the stairwell. "None of whom were in a position to drive me home. A Lyft tracks where I'm picked up, where I'm dropped off, and when my card is charged. Holt can track all that. And the person in my organization who wants to kill me isn't going to kill a civilian who's just trying to make a living."

Dante exited on the second floor without being told. Worry shifted forward in Hawes's mind—the PI knew exactly where he lived—until Dante's next words took the lead. "You sure about that?"

"I have to be," Hawes said, "if I'm going to sleep at night."

He wouldn't have another Isabelle Costa weighing on his conscience. Though maybe others didn't have the same moral hang-ups he did. Was that why someone was targeting him? Were their associates opposed to the new order? Five years in, it wasn't so new anymore, and no income had been lost, no innocents had been killed, and no one had gone to jail. Hawes counted those things as victories, but perhaps other operatives didn't. Operatives like Jodie and Ray who'd been frustrated with Hawes at different points tonight. Longer than that, apparently.

"Madigan?" Dante called from the far end of the hallway.

Hawes shook himself loose from where he'd halted midstep. At the door, he pressed his thumb to the scanner and entered his access code, the security significantly upgraded on his unit. "Sorry," he said to Dante. "Was just replaying the follow-up with Kane." A convenient enough excuse.

"He came by the house?"

"To discuss what looked like a third-party altercation." Inside, Hawes tapped the foyer light switch, and track lighting brightened the hallway leading into the condo's main living area. He toed off his shoes and shrugged out of his jacket, tossing both on the steps to the master bedroom loft. "Holt thanks you for that suggestion. Quicker backstory build."

A shadow streaked across the edge of the lighted area.

Dante drew his gun and lunged forward, a hand on Hawes's chest to hold him back. Considering for a split-second how much it would hurt his aching back and hands, Hawes acted anyway. Bandaged hands wrapped around Dante's wrist, he wrenched the hand away and crouched. He turned under Dante's outstretched arm and kicked, heel aimed at Dante's firing wrist. Direct hit. The gun clattered to the floor. With Dante's other wrist still in his hands, Hawes righted himself, spun behind Dante, yanked the man's arm up behind his back, and rammed him, chest first, into the wooden pillar by the stairs.

Dante struggled against the hold, but Hawes kept him pinned, arm twisted between them, leg thrust between Dante's thighs, his knee pressed to the pole.

"Why are you attacking me?" Dante gritted out, voice low.

Hawes, fearing no danger, didn't bother to moderate his volume. "Because I don't want you to shoot my cat."

The tense body under his relaxed and shook with laughter.

Hawes took a half step back, whipped Dante around to face him, and hand to his chest, shoved him back against the pole. "And because you need to know I can take care of myself. Don't ever do that again."

Dante lifted his hands, palms out. "Understood," he said with a smile. It faded, however, as he reached out and used his thumb to catch a bead of sweat trickling down the side of Hawes's face. "Fit guy like you breaks a sweat from a few self-defense moves?"

Hawes wanted to chase after the touch—rough and gentle, warm and dangerous—but he stepped away instead, using the opposite wall for support. "Ray brought his pistol down on my back before you got there."

"Must've been the shout I heard." Dante retrieved his gun, tucked it into his waistband, and crossed the hall in two strides. "And I saw what you did to your other associate. I know you can take care of yourself."

Hawes rested his head against the wall, trying to put space between them where there wasn't any. Dante had more muscle on his frame, but at about the same height, they were practically nose-to-nose. "Then what are you doing here?"

"You owe me a thank-you."

Laughter bubbled out of Hawes, unexpected and welcome,

even if it did set off another ripple of back spasms. He grasped Dante's biceps, rotated him toward the main area, and gave him a shove. "I wasn't sure if that rock-star strut was an act or if you were that damn arrogant."

Dante grinned over his shoulder. "I've been called worse."

"I'm sure."

At the end of the hall, Hawes hit the next set of switches, illuminating the open-plan kitchen, den, and dining areas. Track lighting hanging from the overhead beams reflected off polished hardwood floors, white cabinets and countertops, sterling-gray walls, and huge windows and glass balcony doors in the brick wall at the far end of the space.

Dante circled the den, laying his jacket and gun on the leather couch, while Hawes scratched behind the ears of his black Bombay cat, who'd taken up position on the dining table. She clawed at the bandages on his hand and hissed at the stranger in their domain. "Iris doesn't like you."

"Iris doesn't know me." Nevertheless, Dante wisely steered clear of her claws and came to a stop next to the rolling wooden ladder, which was locked in place on its short track. "Nice place, though I'm not sure about the ladder to nowhere." He snaked an arm through the rungs, showing off his broad chest and flexing biceps.

Hawes licked his lips. *Even better than the abs.*

"You want to show me?" Dante said.

"I hardly know you," he hedged. "You're lucky I let you in at all."

"Doesn't stop you from picking up guys in the clubs when you go out."

He'd been tracking him, then. Hawes tucked away that piece of information. "Those guys don't open by telling me someone wants to kill me."

"I may have gone about that wrong," Dante conceded.

"If you were trying to get into my pants, yes."

"Into your head?"

Mission accomplished there. Hawes ignored the phone buzzing in his pocket and rested a hip on the corner of the built-in desk behind the couch. As much distance as he could get from the too tempting man leaning against the ladder. "What do you want, Mr. Perry?"

"I want to stop the person trying to unseat you."

"My guardian angel sent from North Beach." Hawes folded his arms. "And why is that?"

Dante's posture remained casual, but his gaze sharpened, dark and ominous. "Because I think the same person is responsible for Isabelle Costa's death."

"Her death was ruled a domestic disturbance. Her boyfriend also died at the scene."

"We both know that's a load of horseshit."

Hawes remained motionless, even as bile stung the back of his throat. "Who was she to you?" he asked, trying to crack that door open wider.

"Someone who mattered."

She'd mattered to Hawes too. Not enough before her death, the world after.

He fled the scene of the crime a second time, avoiding Dante's gaze and ambling in the direction of the glass and brick wall. Ignoring the pair of tufted leather accent chairs, he draped his arms over the diagonal seismic strut, staring out the balcony windows and watching the fog creep into the moonlit courtyard. "I meant what I said at Danko. I always expect someone wants to kill me."

"Did you expect your lieutenants to make an actual attempt?"

No, the threats had never been so direct—so close. Two of his most loyal operatives turning on him right after they'd success-fully pulled off another job together. No flags, no warnings. If Dante hadn't been there, would Hawes have ducked in time to avoid Ray's shot? Would he be lying dead in that alley too? Would the rest of his family be far behind? Hawes closed his eyes and fought against the cold shiver that had slithered around his ankles all night, that snaked through him now like the fog outside.

Heat hit his back, and big, strong hands settled on his hips. "Let me help you."

Hawes leaned into the warmth, letting it chase away the chill, steadying him from the points of contact inward. "I hardly know you," he repeated, much less hedging, much more wanting. Need eclipsing caution.

Dante nuzzled behind his ear, nose and lips teasing the sensitive hollow there. "We could change that."

Hawes reveled in the offered heat and in the faint whiff of eucalyptus that wafted under his nose, the ends of Dante's hair tickling his shoulders. He opened his eyes, and their reflection in the window—broad, dark, and handsome framing his leaner, pale form—almost did Hawes in.

"Liked that suit tonight," Dante said. "Like this jeans-and-tank look better." He grasped the hem of Hawes's white tank and curled it in his fist, inching the fabric up and exposing skin.

Hawes watched, on the knife's edge of anticipation, gut clenched with desire, as Dante's other hand skated off his hip and slid toward his bared abs. He arched his back, wanting to feel Dante's touch on his skin, wanting to thrust his ass back to feel if other parts of Dante were as hard as his.

Reality had other ideas, and a spike of pain arced up Hawes's spine. "Fuck," he cursed, eyes scrunching closed as he leaned forward, fingers curling around the edge of the metal strut.

Dante's hand flattened over his back, gently rubbing. "You take anything for the pain?"

He shook his head. Amelia had offered, but he'd refused, wanting to stay clearheaded.

"You got ibuprofen around here?"

"Top drawer of the desk."

The heat at his back disappeared, and Hawes suppressed a whimper of disappointment. He slouched against another of the wooden support poles and tracked Dante around the condo, watching as the PI collected the bottle of pills and a glass of water. He brought them to Hawes, who tipped out two pills and tossed them back with a gulp of water. "Thanks."

"I saw what you did in that alley," Dante said as he took the glass and bottle from Hawes and set them aside. "Impressive."

"I have to be."

Dante braced his forearm on the pole over Hawes's head and crowded his side. "You don't have to do it alone."

He wasn't alone. He had his family and his trusted inner circle…as soon as he figured out who among them he could still trust. Beyond that? Maybe one day he'd have what Holt did with Amelia. What his parents and grandparents had enjoyed. A partner who got it, who understood and accepted what he did and stood by his side. Who'd help him protect his family and the empire they'd built. Fuck, he wanted that, but until then, he could only depend on himself and his family. Not on a stranger whose aims would ultimately be at cross-purposes with his. No matter how tempting the offered comfort was in the present moment.

His phone buzzed in his pocket again, right on cue. "That's my brother or sister," he said. "They saw us enter the building and condo together. If I don't answer soon, they're going to think you killed me."

Dante slipped a hand into Hawes's pocket, fingertips so close to where Hawes wanted them. The asshole grinned as he slowly removed the vibrating device and gently laid it in Hawes's bandaged palm. "Tell them you're set for a guard tonight." He loped over to the couch and picked up his coat, digging out his book. He tossed the coat onto the coffee table, shoved his gun under the couch pillow, and stretched out, one hand holding the book, the other tucked behind his head, those fucking biceps flexed to top temptation.

"How do I trust you won't kill me in my sleep?" Hawes sniped, more out of sexual frustration than any real fear. He felt more like himself than he had all night. Steady again.

"Same way I'm going to have to trust you not to kill me. You are the Prince of Killers, aren't you?"

Hawes bit his tongue, fighting the words that wanted to form. Twice in one night. Hawes's hate for the title crested once more. Hate that he was the prince when it was actually the three of them—him, Holt, and Helena—running the organization. Hate that he'd been forced into the role because he was the oldest, technically, and hate that when someone had to make the tough decisions, it was always him. He'd been the prince since he was sixteen and had given the doctors permission to turn off his parents' ventilators when neither his grandparents, who were absent at the time, nor his siblings could make the call.

Cold as ice, the stories went.

He hated the killer part just as much. It implied malice, evilness, and cruelty when Hawes had strived to take those variables out of the equation. He knew what he was, what his family did, but there was a place for them, a need for assassins in a world where people didn't play by the rules and legal justice missed its mark. He'd felt like a killer only twice in his life—that morning in the hospital when he'd become the prince, and that night three years ago when he'd spilled an innocent woman's blood. A day that had somehow brought into his life the man now stretched out on his couch. And Hawes needed him to think he was the Prince of Killers, for both their sakes.

For now.

So he held his words, bottled his hate, and exerted control over his body, his emotions, and the situation. He ignored the part of himself that desperately wanted to let go and accept Dante's offer to get to know him better. Ignored the twin flares of pain as he flexed his hands and straightened his spine. Ignored the bitterness in his mouth and in his soul as he declared, "I am," before retreating to his bedroom, alone.

SIX

Sprawled on his back, Hawes stared at the ceiling of his lofted bedroom, counting the rings around a knot in one of the wooden planks. From there he counted the planks and beams themselves, the track lighting fixtures, the sprinkler heads on the exposed pipes, and the cables that ran along the beam directly over his head and down the pillars on either side of the bed. The numbers hadn't changed since he'd counted an hour ago, when the gray light of morning had first trickled over the loft's half wall. Hadn't changed since yesterday morning, or since the morning after he'd bought the place once he'd turned thirty and could access his trust fund.

The counting usually helped after he woke from a nightmare, but only if it was light out. The predawn darkness was hell. Without light, all he could do was count the mistakes he'd made that night three years ago, replaying them over and over. Not fully vetting the tip. Giving chase without backup. Assuming the other passenger in the van was a traitor too, one who'd kill him or blow the van, exposing his family either way. Squeezing the trigger before he made a positive ID. Spending the first few hours of his thirtieth birthday scrubbing blood from his hands. There was more to the count, but those were the low points. They replayed in his head until it was light enough to count other things, to force himself back to sleep for a few hours. Today, however, those stolen hours of early morning sleep were out of reach, the smell of coffee and the sound of voices drifting up from the kitchen below.

His siblings had let themselves in fifteen minutes ago, set the coffee to brew, and Helena had commenced the grilling. "You don't have a bed of your own?" was her latest pointed inquiry. A little too pointed, the wrong direction, in Hawes's opinion.

"Hena!" he shouted, making his wakefulness known. "Leave him be."

"I have a sister," Dante called back. "I get it."

Hawes didn't think he did, unless Dante's sister was an attorney too. He needed to get down there. He tested his hands first—some lingering soreness, but under the bandages, his palms were back to normal. He threw off the quilted comforter and moved quickly but deliberately, careful not to antagonize his stiff back that wasn't as well recovered as his hands. He shooed Iris off last night's jeans, pulled them on with a clean T-shirt, and shoved his feet into a pair of flip-flops.

Helena, meanwhile, continued her cross-examination. "Where's your sister?"

"Here in the city," Dante answered.

"Your family?"

"Also here."

She was testing him and the answers she already had. "How long have you been a PI?"

"Going on ten years."

"Before that?"

Dante rattled off addresses and post-college odd jobs, all of which had been covered by Holt's background check. Relatively reassured himself, Hawes took the stairs down and ducked into the bathroom, brushed his teeth, popped a few ibuprofen, pitched the bandages, and washed up, then joined the others.

"Excuse her," he said. "She can't turn the lawyer off."

"Is that it?" Dante eyed the steak knife Helena was using to spread cream cheese on a toasted bagel.

"Just getting to know your new bodyguard," she quipped.

"Is that it?" Hawes parroted. He strolled past them and over to the couch where Holt sat, a laptop open on his knees, Lily in a polka-dot sling against his chest. Hawes brushed the baby's auburn fuzz, and his niece stared up at him with big brown eyes that were going to cause them all a truckload of grief one day. For now, she was quiet, content to be nestled against her father's chest. "Amelia on shift?"

"Seven to seven," Holt answered without missing a keystroke, his focus on whatever search he was running.

Hawes let him be and returned to the kitchen, claiming one of the metal barstools at the island. "Status?"

Helena handed him a coffee and cut her eyes to their visitor.

"He's not going anywhere. Not without answering some questions."

She gasped in mock offense. "You just told me to go easy."

"Not what I said." Hawes wrapped his hands around the mug, savoring its warmth, and took a long swallow. He curled forward, stretching out his back, then straightened slowly, flexing the other direction. The stiffness eased, and Hawes sighed in relief. He took another sip and returned his gaze to Helena. "You weren't asking the questions I want answers to." He shifted his attention to Dante. "What led you to the restaurant last night? To me?"

"Got a tip about a shift inside your organization. One that may not be to everyone's liking."

"From who?"

"Don't know."

Helena crunched through her bagel, loudly. Hawes would have laughed if not for his own mounting frustration. "That's not particularly helpful."

"You may have accelerated matters," Helena said around her bite.

Dante leaned against the stainless-steel fridge, mug in hand.

"Or flushed the traitors out into the open so you're aware of the problem and can deal with it."

"Speaking of…" Hawes rotated toward Holt. "Did you find anything else on Jodie and Ray?"

"As far as deposits, no."

Hawes didn't need twin-speak to discern the caveat in Holt's answer. "But withdrawals?"

"They made an unscheduled stop on the way back from Paso Robles last week."

"Shit," Dante murmured. "The hit on the winemaker was your group, and last night's warehouse fire was part two of the job. It wasn't the cartel doing cleanup. It was you."

"I remember Jodie and Ray being delayed," Helena said, skipping right over Dante's remark. It was one thing to acknowledge Dante's awareness of the organization. It was another to admit to the exact details of a hit. "They were a day late getting back. Said they were waylaid by car trouble so we didn't flag it."

"At a remote coastal inn?" Holt nodded at his computer screen.

Hawes stepped behind him and peered at the hotel website on-screen. He whistled low. "Were they taking the scenic route?"

"If they were, Avery and Lucas were taking it too, off-book." Holt popped up two more windows, each displaying credit card account registers with similar charges for the same night. "There weren't any other operatives there," he added, answering Hawes's next question. "Just these four."

At least there was that, but still, two more high-ranking, trusted associates were possibly involved. "It had to be someone Jodie and Ray trusted," he said, echoing their conclusion from last night.

"Avery and Lucas would fit," his sister replied.

"Shit!" He pushed off the back of the couch and locked his hands behind his head, ignoring the ache in his back as he paced in front of the windows. Avery and Lucas weren't just high-level turncoats. They were also the two people who'd accompanied

Helena to the scene of Isabelle's death. Who'd found Hawes on his knees on the rain-slicked asphalt, trying to staunch the flow of blood from a gunshot wound he'd delivered. He was starting to think Dante was right. Whatever was happening now was connected to what had happened then, on the night Isabelle Costa died.

That fact acknowledged—and the anxiety and unease that came with it internalized—a calm settled over Hawes. He counted the panes in the windows, waited for his breath and heartbeat to slow, then dropped his arms and turned back to his condo full of visitors. "I'll see what I can find out today at the pier."

"I've got a hearing at ten." Helena dumped her empty paper plate into the trash. "If I don't go by the station beforehand, I'll swing by there after. I can be at HQ by one."

"No," Hawes said. "Things need to appear as usual. I would normally be in this morning. You wouldn't."

"I'll go in with you," Holt said. He patted Lily's back through the sling. "She's having fun being out today."

Dante pushed off the fridge. "And I'll have their backs."

Helena blocked his forward momentum with her arm. "Look here, Mr. Hair—"

"Hena," Hawes chided, while Holt laughed.

Their sister, however, held the steak knife at-the-ready and had drawn nose-to-chest with Dante, though you wouldn't know it by her stance. For all she cared, she was taller than Dante, not a good foot shorter. "You've gotta give us more before I let you walk into this with my family."

"There's a flash drive in my coat pocket."

"I've got it," Hawes said, saving Holt the trouble of reaching around the baby and laptop. He retrieved the flash drive—generic, drugstore model—and held it out to Holt.

Holt's wary gaze split between him and Dante. "I'm not putting that in my computer without checking it for viruses."

"I wouldn't either," Dante said. "Which was why I checked it before I put it in mine. No viruses, I swear."

Holt still hesitated. Hawes slapped the drive into his hand with a firm, "Just do it." They didn't have time to argue.

Hawes moved behind Holt so he could view the screen as Holt disconnected from servers and wireless networks before inserting the flash drive. No blue screen of death appeared. Holt released a held breath, and Hawes put a hand on his shoulder, squeezing gently. Then harder, unintentionally, when Holt opened the first unnamed folder and the screen filled with surveillance photos—of Hawes. From various spots around town, from the pier, from outside the family fort in Pac Heights, and in front of his condo. Each had a bull's-eye drawn on his head.

Hawes rotated toward Dante, who perched on a barstool. "You could have taken these. Manipulated them."

"He didn't," Holt said before Dante could answer. "This footage was taken, edited, and loaded from an MCS computer." Hawes trusted his interpretation of the terminal window full of code gibberish.

"Can you find out who?" Helena asked.

"It'll take time, but yeah. Should be able to."

Was this someone making a grab for power or someone helping them stay in power? Hawes bet the former, given the bull's-eye, but why had they sent this to Dante? "Is this the tip you were talking about?"

"Open the other folder," he said, noticeably grimmer.

Holt double-clicked on the icon, and Hawes's nightmares sprang to life in pixelated form. Pictures of Isabelle's crime scene splashed across the screen.

"Your organization shifted that night," Dante said.

It had. No indiscriminate killing, no collateral damage, no unvetted targets. Hawes's rules—for himself and the organization. And he was working to get them out of the explosives business. The warehouse job was intended to be the last time they used them. All because of what happened that night three years ago.

Heavy footsteps to Hawes's right indicated Dante's approach.

Hawes shot him a pointed glare, and he halted next to the closest pillar, leaning a shoulder there. "I'm a PI," he said. "It's not hard to follow the breadcrumbs. Someone doesn't like the shift."

"And you care because?"

"Less death is a good thing."

Helena chuckled darkly. "You do realize who you're talking to, right?"

"Less innocent death." Dante straightened, long legs spread shoulder-width apart, bulging arms folded over his chest. He cut an imposing figure. "I want to know what happened to Isabelle that night. The truth, not the bullshit cover story. And I think this is the way in."

"You're using us," Hawes said.

"I am." There wasn't an ounce of shame in his admission. Cocky, arrogant, sexy. Honest. "It's in my interest to keep you all alive."

Until he got his answers. Once he learned the truth, where would his interests lie then? Hawes didn't think it would be with keeping them alive.

IN THE BACK SEAT OF HOLT'S SUV, HIS PINKY FINGER CLUTCHED IN his niece's tiny fist, Hawes watched as Dante, in front of him, struggled to take in all the new development around them. "You might be from San Francisco, but you haven't been down here in a while, have you?" Hawes said.

"I've driven by it on the freeway and seen it on sat-photos, but seeing it for real..." He dropped his book into his lap. "Christ, it's like a different place around here."

He wasn't wrong. The Central Waterfront/Dogpatch neighborhood, just south of the Giants ballpark, the UCSF Medical Center, and the Warriors arena, had been radically redeveloped over the past two decades. Around the shipyards and piers that used to dominate the area, office buildings, research labs, and apartments had sprung up, along with restaurants, coffee shops, and other retailers to support the neighborhood's new residents and visitors.

"Last time I was through here," Dante said, head swiveling, "it was parking lots for the ballpark and run-down piers."

Not surprising. Even if Dante hadn't been away until recently, in a place like San Francisco, one could go years without stepping foot in different parts of the city; its many neighborhoods separated as they were by topography, traffic, cultures, even the weather. Hell, it'd been more than a decade since Hawes had ventured into Golden Gate Park. He suspected the little girl holding his finger would change that soon enough.

Holt steered the SUV off Third, onto the road to the pier, and a couple of minutes later, eased the SUV to a stop in front of Madigan Cold Storage's retractable metal gate.

Hawes rolled down the rear window. "The piers and warehouses have come a long way too." He flipped open the nondescript box beside the intercom and thumbed the scanner. The touchpad turned green, and the gate began to swing open.

"High security," Dante said.

"Have you met my baby brother?"

Holt held up two fingers as he drove through. "By two minutes."

Hawes clapped his biceps. "And don't you forget it, Little H."

Two fingers became Holt's single middle one, and a sexy laugh rumbled out of Dante. The first of the day, and it made Hawes smile. Until he stepped out of the car and the easy mood evaporated. Suspecting your employees' occasional murderous intent and actually experiencing it were two very different things.

Holt nudged him out of the way and reached in to eject Lily's car seat.

Lily…here, where maybe there was someone trying to kill Hawes. Fuck, what were they thinking? "Holt, maybe you should—"

"No, we talked about this. We follow the regular routine." He handed Lily's carrier to Hawes, shouldered her diaper bag, and shut the door. "Besides, we have Mr. Hair for backup."

Dante rolled his eyes. "That nickname's gonna stick, isn't it?"

"They still call me Little H, and I'm bigger than both of them combined." Holt took Lily's car seat from Hawes and headed toward the main entrance. His gait defined military precision, even weighed down by the baby and her gear.

"You want to show me this fancy building of yours?" Dante said at Hawes's side.

Dante's easy manner, taken together with Holt's nonchalance, reminded Hawes that yes, while there were potential threats, they were more than equipped to handle them. Hawes ran a hand through his damp hair, fluffing the long top strands to cover his damnable cowlick, and buttoned the suit coat he'd changed into after a quick shower at the condo. "Yes, let me show you around." And let whoever might be targeting him see he wasn't afraid and that there was a new player on the board.

Rather than following Holt to the main entrance at the center of the three-story, U-shaped building, Hawes led Dante through the south wing first, where cold storage units stored products for fisheries and food service companies. Midmorning, this side of the building was mostly deserted, just a few employees double-checking freezer settings. By contrast, the north wing, where cold storage units were manufactured for use by MCS and for sale to customers, was noisy and bustling—engineers checking plans, factory technicians operating assembly lines, quality control professionals approving finished components.

"Quite the contrast," Dante said as Hawes led him toward the office portion in the middle of the building.

"Most suppliers and customers have come and gone already. Third-shift employees guide them through the early morning rush. Though at least half of the workers tend to linger in the main building after shift."

Today was no different. The ground-floor cafeteria and lounge areas were busy, third-shift employees grabbing food and waiting for the rush hour traffic to die down. The second floor looked and sounded like any other office—printers, copiers, keystrokes. All of MCS's admin for ordering, receiving, and processing happened here. It was also the company's gossip hub, which was working overtime today, the whispering growing louder as Hawes passed through with Dante.

"Guessing you're the topic of the day," Hawes said as he pressed a thumb to the stairwell keypad. The lock clicked, and Hawes pushed the door open.

Dante waited until he closed the door to run a hand down the sleeve of Hawes's navy suit coat. "This one's even nicer, and more fitted, than the gray one yesterday." He plucked at the cuff of the light-blue shirt sleeve peeking out from the jacket, then started up the steps. "You wear suits like this to work all the time?"

"I do," Hawes said, his gruff voice echoing in the stairwell.

Dante grinned back at him. "Those whispers aren't about me."

Hawes begged to differ, but the third-floor door swung open before he got the chance.

"Saw you coming." Holt stood in the doorway, his massive bulk blocking the entrance. His brown eyes glanced at Dante, then flitted over the PI's shoulder to lock with Hawes's.

Hawes knew what his brother was thinking, the silent question he was asking. How far do we let him in? Hawes had had the same argument with himself on the ride over. While they'd gotten a bit more out of the PI at the condo, Hawes still had a mountain of questions. At the same time, he sensed he was going to have to give some to get some. Dante had been clear; he was using them too. And what was Dante going to see here that others hadn't? MCS's company conference room and executive offices? Typically on the top floor. Holt's surveillance wall? Not that uncommon for a manufacturing operation like theirs. More importantly, if there were traitors still among their operatives, *this* was the floor they would be on. Hawes wanted the extra firepower at his family's back.

He gave Holt a nod, and his brother stepped aside, allowing

Dante entry. Hawes followed him onto the third floor and secured the door behind them. It wasn't nearly as loud or crowded up here.

Zoe smiled politely as they passed the conference room and main reception desk, which if anyone looked closely, was in fact a sophisticated surveillance setup. Zoe's primary objective was to warn them in the event of a breach. Her secondary objective was to hold off any intruders long enough for the floor to power down and assume the roles the rest of the company and world thought they played. Executives, support staff, and IT. Translation: Madigans, assassins, and hackers.

At the far end of the floor, overlooking the south inlet, Helena had one corner office, Hawes the other, and between them, Holt had knocked out a wall to make a single giant space for his setup, a mirror of the one at the house, except that the crib here was a pop-up version that slid under the desk when Lily wasn't with him.

Dante whistled low. "Between this"—he waved at the wall of electronics—"and the office, manufacturing, and storage functions downstairs, there's no way the original building supports the electrical load or the density of people and activity."

Hawes tossed his suit coat onto a chair. "Not in your research?"

"I can only dig so far," Dante replied. "The property is held in a family trust, so it's not regularly reassessed. There were permits pulled after Loma Prieta, and periodically since for routine upgrades and repairs, but without a change of ownership, you haven't been dinged enough for me to get a full picture."

"We saved and reinforced the foundations where we could. Along with other touches of the original structure." Hawes ran his fingers over the crenellations around the door. "Papa Cal has a thing for restoration."

"The house in Pac Heights?"

"He did all the preservation work on it." Hawes moved his hand from the fluted plaster to the steel bar that ran diagonally up to the roof. "Everything else here is seismically retrofitted and otherwise up to code, even if we don't have to be. Safer for everyone under our roof."

Dante cocked a brow.

Hawes raised one to match. "This *is* an actual business."

"With a personnel problem," Dante said.

And tour over. Back to reality, Hawes turned to Holt, who was at his keyboards. "Where are Avery and Lucas?"

A flurry of keystrokes, and then one of the monitors clicked over, showing the two operatives outside a south-wing loading dock. "Looks like they're helping with an off-load." Holt zoomed out. A cruiser was moored at the slip nearest the dock where Avery and Lucas were standing.

"We were just there," Dante said. "I didn't see them."

Neither had Hawes. "What the hell is off-loading this time of morning?"

Holt opened the day's manifests on another screen. "Nothing. Last transaction was scheduled for and clocked at seven."

"Looks to me like they're on-boarding," Dante said.

Hawes peered at the screen, and sure enough, Avery was carrying a box *from* the dock to Lucas, who ferried it onto the boat and below deck. "Keep it monitored," he said to Holt, then to Dante, "Ready to provide that backup you promised?"

Dark eyes glittered dangerously. "I'm all yours."

"Wait!" Holt said, and Hawes spun back around. "We've got bigger problems." His brother pointed at the top screen, which was feeding them visual from the security cameras at the entry gate.

Kane was leaning out the window of a nondescript sedan, requesting entry. Two police cars idled behind him. This could not be good.

SEVEN

The chief stepped out of the elevator, four officers behind him. Holt tensed in his chair on one side of Hawes, while Dante leaned against the conference room window behind them. He had their backs, but he was staying out of this. Hawes stood as Kane left his officers in the lobby and stalked across the reception area, unimpeded. Zoe was elsewhere on the floor, doing her job. Hawes was confident the three of them could deal with Kane quickly, before they lost Avery and Lucas to either their escape or law enforcement.

Kane pushed open the glass door, practically growling. "You didn't show up at the station this morning."

"Helena was supposed to stop by on her way to the courthouse."

"Your sister was not the one with Jodie and Ray before their deaths."

"*Hours* before," Hawes replied. "We went over all this last night."

Kane withdrew a folded piece of paper from inside his jacket pocket and slid it across the table. "In connection with the investigation of their murders, we have a warrant to search the premises."

"I thought that was a dispute between them and a third party," Hawes said. "What's it got to do with us?"

"They worked here, didn't they?" Kane gave a subtle nod to the warrant, and Holt reached for it. He unfolded the paper where Hawes could see, including the handwritten note from Helena inside.

Let them search. Limited parameters.

Kane was just doing his job, and Helena had already cleared it. The other clearance Hawes was waiting for appeared a moment later, Zoe back at the reception desk. "Go ahead," he said to Kane. "Zoe will show your officers to Jodie's and Ray's workspaces."

"They won't find anything," Holt said, once Kane stepped out. "This is why it pays to be paperless."

"Nothing's on paper?" Dante asked behind them.

"Not if we can help it," Hawes said.

Kane reentered the room, but before any of them could speak, a high-pitched wail erupted from the crib they'd rolled into the corner. Holt pushed up from the table. "It's like she knows you're here," he muttered.

Kane's foul mood broke on a genuine smile. "I can't help that she likes me."

"Oh, is that what you think it is?" Holt lifted the baby out of the crib, and Kane walked over close enough to coo without appearing too interested to anyone outside the conference room's glass walls.

As much as the sight warmed Hawes's heart, he needed to move this along. "Do you need me for anything else?" he asked Kane.

The chief shoved his hands in his pockets. "Any new developments?"

"We're looking into it."

"Dammit, Hawes."

"It's under control."

"I wouldn't count on it," Dante said, Holt's tablet in hand. "They're picking up the pace." He handed Hawes the tablet, open on the surveillance feed of the south-side loading bays. Avery and Lucas were hustling, as if they were using the police presence as a distraction. Or trying to move something out before the police found it.

"Do you need me for anything else?" Hawes repeated his question.

"Go handle it," Kane said. "We'll catch up later."

Hawes slipped out of the conference room, Dante on his heels. They took the stairwell to the ground floor and exited out the back of the building. At the south corner, Hawes halted, back against the wall. "With the cops on-site, let's get them on the boat."

"Close quarters," Dante said, "if a fight breaks out."

"I'm fine with that." The ibuprofen he'd taken that morning had done its work, dulling most of the lingering pain in his back and hands. "You?"

"Not a problem for me."

"Figured not."

Dante moved to draw his gun, and Hawes clasped his forearm. "Not unless you have to. We have an inkling they might not be loyal, but that suspicion hasn't been fully vetted. We need to question them first. Let's be sure, or as sure as we can be."

Something like surprise dashed across Dante's eyes. Surely he wasn't caught off-guard by Hawes's caution, not if he knew as much about the changes Hawes had made as he'd implied.

In any event, Dante got on board, leaving his gun in his waistband. "Who are you going to say I am, if they ask?"

"I'll tell them you're not a cop, *if* they ask. Otherwise, it's not their job to make personnel decisions or to question mine."

Dante's grin returned. "There he is."

Hawes agreed, the undertaking making him feel more like himself again. He rolled up his shirt sleeves. "Let's do this."

They rounded the corner, and Avery caught sight of them a few docks away. "Hey, boss," she said as they approached. Her dark eyes skittered past him to Dante, and Hawes took a step to block her view. Her attention snapped back to him, but her posture remained casual. Good call, as she couldn't be sure if Dante was friend or foe. Best not to lead on either way. "Something I can help you with? We're in a bit of a hurry here."

"Why's that?"

Her eyes flickered to Dante and back again. "Unexpected visitors."

"I'm not one," Dante said. "What are you hustling out of here?"

"Just some prototypes, to our facility in South San Francisco."

Hawes seethed. "Why the fuck are they here?"

Prototypes—a.k.a. explosives, when there were unreliable ears around—were expressly not permitted on these premises.

"Jodie and Ray delivered them yesterday," Avery said, dropping the casual act as she began to realize something was amiss. Genuine confusion colored her expression. Not fear at being caught, just fear of having pissed off the boss. "Lucas said we needed to move them ASAP."

That much was true. "Are they all loaded onto the boat?"

"Lucas is putting the last crate in the cabin now."

Hawes held an arm out toward the cruiser. "Time to go, then."

Avery boarded the stern deck first and adjusted the foldout seat into its upright position, no longer needing it as a makeshift conveyor. Hawes and Dante stepped onto the deck of the sleek cruiser, which looked like a hundred other yachts on the Bay. Fast and good cover, whether they were rescuing trafficking victims or moving illegal explosives.

"She doesn't know what's going on," Dante whispered.

Hawes agreed. "Lucas is the target."

No sooner had he said his name, than Lucas popped out from below deck, wiping his hands off on his jeans. "Avery, what's the holdup?" He straightened and locked eyes with Hawes. *Could go either way,* Hawes thought. Then Lucas caught sight of Dante, and his eyes widened with recognition. He must've gotten a report from his co-conspirators last night, before Hawes had dispatched them. His right arm went for the gun under his windbreaker.

Dante drew faster. "Wouldn't do that if I were you." He shifted to stand next to Hawes, blocking any hope Lucas had of escape.

"What the hell is going on?" Avery said from where she stood behind the steering column to Lucas's left.

His eyes flicked her direction.

Hostage.

Lucas registered the option a second later, his blue eyes flaring at the perceived advantage. He inhaled sharply, preparing to take it.

Stupid, stupid man.

Lucas dove for Avery, and Dante swung his gun, following the action. Hawes stepped in front of Dante with a sharp, "Hold!"

"Dammit, Madigan, move!"

One beat, two beats, then Hawes stepped aside…and barely held in a laugh at Dante's muttered, "Holy shit."

"She had it under control," Hawes said, eyeing Lucas's gun in Avery's hand. At her feet, Lucas lay unconscious, his arm clearly broken. If she hadn't just proven her loyalty without question, Hawes would be more than a little frightened.

"Does someone want to tell me what the fuck is going on?" she demanded.

"That's what I'm trying to figure out," Hawes said. "Steer us out of here, and you can help me."

"We're docked, boss," Avery shouted from above-deck.

"Good," Hawes called back. "Come on down."

They'd traveled a few miles south, to an abandoned pier in the old Hunter's Point Shipyard. Not the best neighborhood— arguably one of the worst in San Francisco—but they paid people here enough to look the other way where their activities were concerned.

Avery hopped off the last step, and Hawes slid to the left, making as much room as he could in the cramped cabin. Which wasn't a lot. To his left, Dante stood at the foot of the raised bed, and in front of Hawes, Lucas was passed out on the leather bench seat. He was slumped over facedown on the lacquered table, legs spread and ankles cuffed to metal posts underneath.

Not for long.

Rotating to the sink, Hawes filled a glass with water, turned back around, and chucked the cold liquid at Lucas's head.

Lucas came awake with a spluttering start, bolting upright and violently shaking his head to get rid of the water. On instinct, he tried to stand, failed, and howled when he attempted to move his broken arm in its makeshift sling.

"I'll make it hurt worse if you don't settle," Hawes said.

Lucas glared, nostrils flaring as he panted through the pain.

"You could have played dumb up there," Dante said. "Tried to cover."

"That would be an insult to them." Lucas jutted his chin at Hawes and Avery. "Kill me and get it over with. I knew the risk I was taking."

"Why'd you take it?" Hawes asked.

Lucas snapped his lips shut, determined resignation filling his eyes.

Hawes stepped forward and braced both hands on the table. It was a risk, looming over Lucas as he was, but with the operative's legs restrained, a broken arm, and all tactical weapons out of reach, there was minimal chance Lucas would reach him before Hawes could duck away.

"Who were you visiting in Big Sur last week?" he asked.

"I don't know what you're talking about."

Dante's scoff echoed Hawes's mental retort. *Now he wants to play dumb?*

Hawes said, "We have you and Avery at the same seaside inn as Jodie and Ray."

Avery gasped. "I wasn't in Big Sur last week."

"Your bank account says otherwise," Dante told her.

"Shit, I haven't checked it lately."

Even if she had, the charge might not have registered. Hawes kept his focus on Lucas. "Who was there with you using Avery's card?"

Lucas's face twisted into an unhinged grin. "Good luck figuring that one out."

Hawes cursed himself for not seeing this side of Lucas sooner. He was one of their most levelheaded operatives, a good balance to Avery's feistiness. Yes, he was an assassin, but he'd given no indication of malice or delight in the undertaking. Just cool, calm efficiency. Apparently Lucas had decided to let it all hang out, now that death was imminent.

"We can get video footage from the hotel," Dante said.

"Good luck with that too."

So they had a hacker on Team Betrayal. The same person who'd leaked the information about Papa Cal? Was that connected? A coordinated attack? Had the same hacker sent that flash drive to Dante? If so, why? For now, Hawes mentally pocketed the valuable yet disturbing nugget of information, ignored the questions it begged, and asked about another suspicion he liked even less. "You weren't going to the warehouse with the prototypes, were you?"

A single, insolent blink.

Answer enough.

Hawes pushed off the table and turned for the stairs. "Let's go."

Avery preceded him up, but Dante hung back. "That's all you're gonna ask him?"

"I got what I needed."

Dante had not. "Why'd you do it?" he asked Lucas. "Why'd you betray him?"

Hawes paused halfway up the stairs, listening for the answer.

"Because his pansy ass doesn't have the balls for this."

Ah, and there it was. Two for one, linking the organization's change of course to the fact Hawes was gay. While none of his operatives had ever expressed an issue with his sexual orientation, he'd be a fool to think there wasn't at least one homophobe among them. He'd hoped by now he'd proven his orientation didn't matter, that his ability to do the job had nothing to do with the fact that he was attracted to men, but he was a fool for hoping he'd convinced the bigots.

Hawes suspected not even Lucas getting his face bashed into the table would convince him, but Hawes appreciated Dante's gesture, the *thunk* and answering curse more than a little satisfying.

The satisfaction was short-lived. He cleared the door and came face-to-face with a pissed-off operative. Hands on her hips, Avery was livid, the halo of ringlet curls around her head only enhancing the angry-warrior effect. "Jodie and Ray weren't killed by a third-party rando, were they?"

Hawes had to proceed with caution. She'd been loyal thus far, but that was before she had the whole story, which she'd started putting together downstairs. "No, they weren't," he said.

"Did they try to kill you?"

"Yes."

"And Lucas was helping them." Not a question, a statement. "Someone used my card to make it look like I was too."

"We're going to find out who that was."

She stared him down for the few seconds it took Dante to climb the stairs and step behind him, close enough Hawes could feel his reassuring heat at his back. Two against one, though Avery's eyes never left Hawes. Dante didn't factor into the picture for her. She was judging Hawes's merit as a leader, making the decision based on what mattered here, regardless of how that played out for her life in the short term. Hawes also appreciated that.

She nodded. "I'll take care of Lucas and the prototypes. I'm here to help."

One more soldier he could count on. "Thank you." He navigated the narrow path off the boat and onto the dock. "Someone will meet you at the warehouse to help unload the prototypes."

"Sounds good," Avery said as she gathered her curls up in a bun and moved about on deck, returning to her usual self.

There was, however, a Dante-sized statue in her way. He stood, unmoving, right where Hawes had left him. Only his head rotated, looking back and forth between the cabin, Avery, and Hawes.

"We need to move," Hawes told him.

Dante hesitated another long moment before finally getting his ass in gear, clearing the stern as Avery revved the engines.

Assuming he'd follow, Hawes started down the dock for the shore. From there, it would be another ten-minute walk before they reached a street where a Lyft would actually pick them up.

He hadn't made it far when Dante's hand clasped his arm and spun him around. "You're just going to let them go?"

"Yes."

"She's gonna kill him."

At Hawes's silence, frustration flared in Dante's eyes, same as it had last night. Except Hawes was close enough to do something about it this time. He wrenched his arm free and hooked his right leg behind Dante's left. Surprise, and the threat of water on either side of them, gave Hawes the advantage. Enough that it outweighed the lingering stiffness in his back. He grabbed Dante's flailing arm and shifted them so Dante's back hit a pier pylon, catching them both. He pressed up against Dante, the precarious balance working in his favor. "Lucas betrayed me, and he betrayed Avery. She'll do her job." Dante cast his gaze aside, and Hawes grasped his chin, hauling it back. "Don't forget who I am, Mr. Perry."

"The Prince."

"Of Killers."

Still hated it. And still needed it, especially where this man was concerned, an unknown variable in a rising sea of unknowns. Hawes sensed this one was more dangerous than all the rest. A rip current of need was already tugging at him, threatening to drag him under, offering tempting relief. It was all he could do not to slide his fingers along Dante's stubbled jaw, not to shove his hand into all that hair, not to lean forward and claim his mouth. Not to rub against the hardness pressing into his thigh.

Hawes dropped his hand and rocked back a step. "I demand loyalty."

Dante pushed off the pole, erasing the distance between them. "I'm here to help." A mirror of Avery's earlier words, yet the layers beneath Dante's utterance were endless.

Hawes fought the pull, forced himself to turn, and started back down the pier. "Call us a Lyft," he tossed over his shoulder, not letting Dante witness the waves of contradictory emotions crashing over him. He felt more in control than he had the past twenty-four hours. He'd rooted out another traitor, extracted useful information, and secured the loyalty of one of his best soldiers. Yet another part of him, buried deep beneath the suits and locked-down demeanor, wanted to let go, wanted to go wild, for Dante.

EIGHT

They sat around a table in one of the hospice house parlors—Hawes shuffling a deck of cards, Helena and Holt tapping at their handheld devices, and Amelia breastfeeding Lily. Hawes riffled the cards once more, cut the deck, dealt them into four stacks, and distributed one to each player.

Helena picked up her cards. "It's consistent with what we know so far," she said, continuing the conversation from where Hawes had left off telling them about Lucas.

Amelia shifted Lily and picked up her stack. She fanned the cards with her nimble fingers, glanced over them once, then laid the spread stack back on the table, facedown. "Maybe I could have gotten more out of him."

"Doubt it," Helena said as she arranged her own cards. "No incentive if he knew he wasn't getting off that boat."

Holt didn't look up from his cards. "So it's an operative in my shop, given what Lucas implied about the wiped footage."

"Not necessarily." Hawes did the same card arrangement dance as his siblings. Papa Cal had taught them all to play Hearts, and in doing so, how to hold and play their cards, which made the pass fairly predictable.

Except for Amelia who, one-handed, chose her pass cards from where she'd last seen them and slid them to Holt. "It could be an outside hacker."

Holt shot her a glare, twice-over.

She smiled back at him in a way only she could get away with. "You are not the be-all-end-all of hackers, sweetheart."

"Local FBI's had two as good as you," Helena said.

"Who?" Holt scoffed. "Baller and Barbie?"

Helena muffled a laugh. "Never let her hear you call her that, or you won't have any balls left."

Amelia patted Holt's cheek. "She's right, and I love your balls, so don't."

Holt rolled his eyes, and Hawes laughed too, improbable as it was in this place, but so too was this discussion. That said, it was a distraction from the truth at the end of the hallway that none of them wanted to face. So, family hour at the hospice house had turned into a debrief.

"Besides, they're the good guys," Hawes said. "We know it's not them."

Helena threw down the two of clubs, starting the round. "And this looks more and more like an inside job."

"Start with your shop," Hawes said to Holt. "If you find nothing, branch out. It could be someone inside hiring out." They went for several tricks before Hawes spoke again. "Dante's right. We need to flush them out."

"We need to keep a low profile," Helena countered. "Brax is doing what he can, but there's only so far we can push. We got lucky this morning."

Because Lucas moved those explosives out at the last possible second.

"You sure the prototypes weren't there for SFPD's benefit?" Amelia asked. *And to our family's detriment*, she didn't need to say.

"They were definitely headed somewhere else," Hawes said.

While Lucas hadn't flat out said it, Hawes was confident Lucas had been equally motivated to get those explosives out before they were discovered.

"I'll check the dark web." Holt glumly collected another trick from the middle of the table. Despite being a genius at ones and zeroes, he was terrible at cards. He refused to count them, even though he could, and strategy was not his strong suit. "Let me see if anyone's put a call out."

Helena's phone vibrated on the table. She turned it over and glanced at the screen. "Speaking of putting a call out…" She slid the device to Hawes. "You may recall you assigned Jodie and Ray this one last month, after that shitshow of a trial."

The request had come in directly to Helena, Holt had vetted it, and Hawes had signed off on the job. That was before they were trying to keep a low profile. "Shit," Hawes cursed low. "He took the bait?"

"The meet is scheduled for three a.m.," Helena said.

Hawes threw down his last card and reclined in his chair, balancing on the two back legs, playing out the options in his head while the others finished the round. They could not afford extra attention right now, not when they were still reeling from last night. They also couldn't afford to pass up this opportunity. But who could he assign? No one else was up to speed on the contract or on the need for extra caution. The only people who had the full story, who could do this right, were him and the people at the table with him.

Holt cleared the last trick from the center of the table, and Hawes brought his chair back down. "We do it," he said, gesturing to the four of them. "We know all the variables in play."

"It's what Papa Cal would want," Helena said softly.

Hawes couldn't agree more. They owed their grandfather this much, for the legacy he was leaving them.

As if summoned by the mention of her husband, Rose appeared in the doorway. She looked like a shell of her normal polished self. Gray hair falling out of its French braid, her usually manicured nails chipped, weariness weighing down her shoulders. Hawes had seen her like this one other time. When she'd arrived home, weary from weeks on the run, to news that her son and daughter-in-law, Hawes's parents, were dead. It had been the final straw then, momentarily breaking her. Hawes feared they were fast approaching another such moment now. His fear and certainty ratcheted up when a somber doctor appeared behind her.

Hawes rose and moved to stand next to Helena. "What's going on?"

"Your grandfather has taken a turn for the worse," the doctor said.

Rose drove it the rest of the way home. "He's not asking for your parents anymore. He says Noah and Charlotte are there in the room, waiting for him."

Helena muffled a cry and reached for Hawes's hand. Across from them, Holt wrapped his wife and daughter in his arms, burying his face in Amelia's hair. Rose collapsed onto the arm of the nearest chair and covered her face with her hands, sobbing quietly.

Dread settled in Hawes's gut, on his aching back, and fuck if the crushing weight bearing down on him didn't feel like the heaviest straw known to man.

HAWES TURNED THE CORNER ONTO HIS STREET AND SPOTTED THE HOG parked out front, its polished chrome and pearlescent blue paint gleaming in the halo of the streetlight. And leaning against a nearby lamppost, reading a new book, was the bike's owner. Not hiding anymore.

"You making this a habit?" Hawes asked as he approached.

Dante pushed off the pole, tucked his book under his arm, and met Hawes in front of the building's steps. The PI had changed since that morning. Jeans and a tank again, this one gray, and his denim jacket had been traded for a battered leather duster. Hawes bet the soft-looking leather smelled amazing, years of life worn into its grain. One of a kind.

"When do you get your Benz back?" Dante asked.

Not one of a kind, aside from a few custom modifications. Generic, relatively. "When Kane decides to release it from the impound lot." If Hawes decided to reclaim it at all. He was leaning toward donating it to charity instead.

"Anything else from him today?" Dante asked as they made their way to the stairs.

"Nothing, though I haven't been back to the office since Holt and I left to visit Papa Cal midday."

"It's past ten. Where've you been?"

"Ballpark." He'd missed most of the game, arriving during the seventh-inning stretch, but after hours at the hospice house, with only Lily's whimpers to break the heavy silence that had settled over his family, Hawes had needed to zone out with baseball and a beer.

"Before that, Madigan."

"You don't know?" Hawes thumbed the sensor by his door, entered his code on the keypad, and once the door unlocked, pushed inside. "You seem to know everything. To be everywhere." The sudden spike of irritation surprised Hawes but didn't stop him from rounding on Dante with his own query. "Where have *you* been, if you weren't following me?"

Dante raised his hands, palms out. "Working on my end of this, then had dinner with my family." He stood outside the door, waiting for Hawes to invite him in.

Smart. And enough time for Hawes to consider and dismiss the usual concerns. Dante had already spent an evening at his place, had had his back today at the office and with Lucas, and when it boiled right down to it, Hawes didn't want to be alone tonight. He waved Dante inside.

"I didn't follow you because I'm not your keeper," Dante said as he closed the door. "You don't need one, as you keep demonstrating. You seem tense, is all, for having come from a game the Giants won."

Guess he hadn't zoned out as well as he'd hoped. A stiffer

drink, then. Hawes shrugged out of his suit coat, flung it toward the loft stairs, and made his way into the living room. Iris wove around his ankles, demanding attention, and he bent to give her a scratch. Once she moved on to Dante, Hawes righted himself and opened the built-in minibar in the cabinet next to the desk. He retrieved the squat bottle of Crown Royal Rye and two shot glasses.

"Would've figured you for a Macallan guy." Dante skirted behind him, his knuckles brushing the curve of Hawes's ass. "Something classier," Dante continued as he rounded the couch and collapsed onto the middle cushion.

Hawes stood frozen. Intentional or not, Dante's grazing touch had sent electricity crackling up his spine. If Dante had stopped behind him, if he'd rotated his hand the other way and cupped Hawes's ass, Hawes wouldn't have been able to stop himself from leaning into the promise of that touch.

Fuck, he was all over the place. Angry. Frightened. Impatient. Frustrated, in more than one respect. Not even the unusual steadying effect Dante had on him was working tonight.

Whisky and glasses in hand, Hawes closed the cabinet with his elbow. "One, this was world whisky of the year a few years back, and two, the expensive stuff is wasted on me." He sank onto the cushion next to Dante. "I don't drink enough to appreciate the difference. This or Jameson serves my purpose just fine."

Dante relieved him of the glasses. "To get drunk?"

"Basically." Hawes removed the decorative cork and poured them generous shots. He took his glass from Dante, threw back the shot, then poured another before setting the bottle on the coffee table. "Hospice visit took longer than anticipated."

"Complications with Papa Cal?"

"Obviously." Hawes winced at his snappish tone.

Dante didn't flinch, but his gaze was more assessing than usual. "I'm not the enemy here."

"How do I know that?"

The staredown that followed lasted a good half minute, until

Dante broke it to toss back his shot. His lips puckered, then parted as he let out a sharp gasp, a common response to the spicy rye. Hawes's nearly blinding need to throw a leg over Dante's lap and swallow that gasp with his own mouth was not so common. He wasn't sure he'd ever felt a spike of desire so strong.

Before Hawes could act on it, Dante removed the option by shifting forward to the edge of the couch. He set his empty glass on the table next to the bottle, then did the same with all his weapons, removing them one by one. Glock. Knife. Handcuffs. Tactical pen. Book, the next in the series. He took off his coat too and emptied his pockets. Keys, wallet, and phone.

"There," he said. "I'm unarmed now." He slid back, stretched an arm along the top of the couch, and crossed a long leg toward Hawes. "You and I both know you could take me either way, but for your peace of mind…"

Hawes chuckled bitterly. "I'm not sure even this"—he lifted his glass—"will give me peace of mind tonight." Slumping into the soft cushions, Hawes sipped his second shot more slowly, savoring the burn on his tongue and down his throat. He imagined it melting away the glaciers that had flowed near the center of his chest today. Impossible, of course, as the first of those ice blocks had been formed almost two decades ago.

He finished the whisky and rested his head on top of the cushion, staring at the ceiling. Counting planks and light fixtures brought him no peace either. "Right now, I'm pretty sure I couldn't take anyone."

"How bad is he?" Dante said, accurately reading his distress.

"He told Rose that my parents are there, waiting for him in the room." Hawes closed his eyes and recounted more of what the doctor had told them. "He's not eating anymore, after he choked multiple times over the weekend. His body can't even remember how to function properly."

Dante tugged Hawes's glass free from his hand and set it on the table. He scooted closer, judging by the fragrant waft of eucalyptus shampoo and the nearness of his lowered voice. "It's a terrible disease."

Hawes rotated his head and opened his eyes, meeting Dante's sympathetic brown ones only a few inches away. "You know someone?"

"Uncle. He was this big Italian guy with a huge personality to match. Best cook in the family, and we've got a lot of good ones." His unfocused eyes drifted over Hawes's shoulder. "Saw him tonight. He's lost half his weight, barely spoke to anyone, and struggled to remember the family lasagna recipe."

Hawes laid a hand on Dante's knee, briefly, before yanking it back, not trusting himself to resist the temptation to slide it higher. Not the time. He folded his hands in his lap. "No matter how much money we throw at it, Alzheimer's kills faster than we can keep up with it."

"You throw a lot at it, don't you? Annual donations the past three years to charities that support Alzheimer's research and to others that fund shelters for LGBTQ youth."

"I don't need all the money my trust provides. I used what I needed"—he gestured at their surroundings—"and found better uses for the rest."

Dante lifted a hand and brushed back the overlong top hairs that were tickling Hawes's forehead. "Careful, Madigan. Your soul is showing."

Hawes's eyes slipped shut as Dante's fingers lingered on his temple. Finally, the calm steadiness he'd missed washed over him. Be it from Dante's touch or the whisky, Hawes couldn't say, but he didn't pull away, unwilling to disturb the peace. "Some prince," he mumbled.

"King, before long."

And hello disturbance. A chasm opened beneath Hawes's feet, knocking him back off-balance. He stood and stepped away to avoid it. "What if I don't want to be?"

"A killer?"

"The king." Hawes locked his hands behind his head and

paced the area on the other side of the coffee table. "I don't want to be king. Not if I have to destroy my soul again to do it."

Dante uncrossed his legs and shifted forward, elbows on his knees. "Again?"

"I have the health care power of attorney. I ultimately have to make the decision if it comes to life support." Hawes braced himself against the side of the ladder. "Again." He closed his eyes against the flood of memories, and when that didn't work, buried his face in his arm.

Dante caught on a second later and was up and off the couch, his footsteps short and fast, drawing closer with speed instead of his usual casual lope. A hand landed on Hawes's hip, Dante's voice and heat close. "You made the decision about your parents too, didn't you?"

"My grandparents were out of town, laying low at one of the safe houses." He swallowed hard. "I was sixteen."

"Jesus, Hawes." Dante slid his arm the rest of the way around Hawes's waist in a loose sideways hug. He snuck his other hand under Hawes's chin, nudging until Hawes lifted his face enough to cup his cheek. "What do you need?"

"I don't want to be in control." No decisions to make, no kingdom to rule, no bad guys to sort from the good. Tonight, freedom was the most settling thought there was, especially if it involved the man whose body was pressed alongside his.

"Do you trust me?" Dante said.

Hawes half nodded, half nuzzled Dante's palm.

"Give it to me, then."

Hawes's eyes popped open, and an unexpected laugh bubbled out of him. "I'm not giving you control of my family's empire."

One corner of Dante's mouth turned up in a sexy smirk. "I don't want that either." With his arm around Hawes's waist, he shifted them so they were in front of the ladder, Hawes's back against the rungs, Dante's body blanketing his. The pressure, front and back, massaged away any lingering soreness from Ray's hit last night. Not that Hawes would care when Dante's long, strong fingers were skirting up the side of his face and into his hair, threading through the strands and cradling his scalp.

Hawes couldn't look away, couldn't stop his hands from curling into Dante's gray tank and hauling him closer. "Please."

"I want control of you." Dante's soft lips brushed the sharp right hinge of Hawes's jaw. "Let me help you." He moved to the other side. "Let me make you forget for a while." Then to the crease at the bottom of Hawes's chin. "Let go for me."

Yes.

Hawes lowered his face the half inch needed to bring their lips together. And let go. Of the last twenty-four hours. Of the control he'd exercised over family, company, and fate today. Of himself, where Dante was concerned.

He parted his lips on a groan, and Dante swept inside, grazing teeth and tongue, and Hawes relished the attention, the invasion. He parried, sucked, and opened wider, angling to give Dante better access. Ripe for plunder, Hawes wanted nothing more than to be laid bare. He'd gladly surrender to Dante's devouring mouth. To Dante's warm, hard body blanketing every inch of his cold, sharp one. To his hips rocking an impressive erection against the one straining behind Hawes's zipper.

Lost in the best kiss he'd had in years, Hawes didn't register Dante grasping his wrists and lifting his arms above his head, not until Dante broke the kiss and curled Hawes's fingers around the ladder rung. "Don't let go."

Hawes chased after Dante's mouth. "I thought that's what I was supposed to be doing."

"I want you to hang on," Dante whispered against his lips. "And let go for me."

Yes.

Hawes was glad for the handhold when Dante's lips skated off his mouth and traveled to his earlobe, nipping and tugging with his teeth. Knees weak, Hawes was half tempted to ditch standing altogether and hike his legs around Dante's waist. The better to grind his cock against those abs. The stray thought vanished as soon as Dante moved from nipping his earlobe to tracing the shell of his ear with his tongue, from the narrow top, down to the lobe again, and behind it. As if the tongue wasn't enough torture, the scruff of Dante's beard lit the surrounding area on fire.

"God, yes, more like that." Hawes rested his head on another rung, rolling it side to side so Dante could kiss and lick every inch of his throat. He didn't give a flying fuck if the occasional suck and nip left marks. And when Dante's tongue dipped into the crook of his neck, the groove made deeper by his pronounced clavicle, Hawes also didn't give a flying fuck if the neighbors heard him scream.

"Yes, fuck, yes!"

Dante grinned. "Sensitive spot?"

Hawes lowered a hand and tangled it in Dante's hair, the silky strands gliding through his fingers. He twisted them around his fist, holding Dante right where he wanted him. "Again," he tried to order, tried to voice his desire, but between his strangled voice and the desperate rutting of his cock against Dante's, the speed of which had increased with each kiss, his order came out closer to a plea.

Dante indulged him for one more dip of his tongue, one more nip of teeth, before he dropped a light kiss over the tortured skin. A shiver raced through Hawes. Dante chased it away with the molten look in his eyes and the gravel in his voice. "Who's in control here?"

Challenge flared deep inside Hawes. The instinct to fight back was there, where earlier it had wavered. Dante had stoked it back to life by taking the reins. Wanting that flame to burn brighter, Hawes untangled his hand and lifted it back to the rung. Holding on and letting go, letting someone else drive so he could just feel, ceding control so he could regain it.

Dante rewarded him for the power given, starting with the top button of Hawes's dress shirt and ending with the last. He kissed and licked every inch of exposed skin until he was on his knees, hands unfastening Hawes's pants while his tongue rimmed Hawes's belly button.

Like Hawes wanted him to rim a different hole. He closed his eyes, drowning in sensation. The pleasure intensified as Dante shoved down his pants and exposed his hip bones. Dante flared his fingers over them, tracing and teasing.

"Careful," Hawes said. "They cut."

"You are a pointy bastard." Yet Dante didn't seem remotely scared of Hawes's sharp edges, tongue following in the path of his hands, all the way down to the patch of light-brown hair at the end of the trail above Hawes's cock, which was woefully trapped beneath the waistband of his boxers.

Hand slipping off the rail again, Hawes pinched his puckered nipple, aiming to redirect his focus before he came in his shorts like a teenager.

Dante helped him out, yanking down the damnable boxers and finally freeing his cock. Hawes moaned in relief, then frustration, as Dante rose and stepped away, save for a single finger that traced the underside of Hawes's erection.

"Do you want me to leave you here like this, cock out, hard and aching?" Dante circled the head and pressed lightly at Hawes's slit, spreading the moisture there. "Dripping." Abruptly, Dante removed his hand and took another step back. He gripped himself through his jeans.

Hawes groaned at the length and girth on display, making his mouth water and his asshole clench. He wanted it in both. He squeezed his nipple, hard, one last time, then put his hand back where it belonged.

"Better." Dante closed the distance again, his smile predatory, and pressed his upturned lips to Hawes's, plunging into his mouth once more. Hand between them, he palmed the underside of Hawes's cock, moving it into position, and rutted his own against it, the denim friction sending Hawes's senses into overdrive.

"Oh God, too much," Hawes keened against his lips. "Too—"

Dante leaned far enough back to meet his eyes. Concern cooled the burning desire there. "Is it too much? I can stop."

Hawes shook his head. "No, good idea. Just intense."

"If it's ever not, if you need control back—"

"Sunshine." It had been his safe word whenever he'd played with past partners.

Dante smiled and rested their foreheads together. "Don't like the daylight?"

Hawes twisted enough to run his nose down Dante's cheek, inhaling his scent and reveling in the rough texture of his scruff. "Grew up in the fog."

Dante angled his face in turn, capturing Hawes's mouth for a kiss that stole his breath. That sent wispy tentacles of tangled emotions creeping through Hawes's veins, aimed for other more tender places. Hawes didn't bother to sort it out right then, not with Dante dropping again to his knees. He didn't waste time tracing the same path with his tongue that his finger had traveled earlier. He closed his mouth around Hawes's cock and swallowed him to the root.

Yes.

Hawes closed his eyes and held on tight. Letting go of everything and giving himself to Dante. Getting lost in the fog had never felt so good.

NINE

Hawes crept down the loft stairs in darkness, not needing light to take care of the basics—relieve his bladder, brush his teeth, pop a few ibuprofen, don a dark suit with multiple layers so he could change outfits if necessary, and arm himself. Not expecting a fight, he pocketed a garrote and strapped a single knife around his calf under his pant leg.

A text from Helena lit up his phone screen. **5 minutes**.

Hawes deleted the message, pocketed the phone along with his wallet and keys, and closed things up. He followed the faint trail of moonlight into the living area. Dante was stretched out on the couch, a book splayed facedown on his steadily moving chest, his light snores echoed by Iris's purrs. The traitor was curled up on his feet. She blinked once at Hawes, yellow eyes acknowledging his presence, then went back to ignoring him in favor of her new human pillow.

A pillow Hawes would've liked to curl up with too, if Dante would've let him. Instead, once Hawes had returned to earth after the best blowjob of his life, Dante had insisted he go to bed. Alone. Maybe it had something to do with Hawes dozing off against the ladder in his postorgasmic haze. He would have rallied for the chance to return the favor, but Dante had taken that possibility off the table. Hawes had been too tired to argue, and now time was too tight. He wanted to run his fingers through the long hair fanned out over the pillow, wanted to throw a leg around Dante's waist and stretch out over the length of him, wanted to steal a long, slow kiss. Wanted to taste all of him. Unfortunately, he couldn't do any of those things if he wanted to get out of there on time, and without waking Dante.

Leaving him there was a risk, but one Hawes was willing to take for the warmth that bloomed in his chest at the mere thought. He also liked the thought of Dante with him on the job. He could be an asset to them, but Hawes, clearheaded after a few hours of sleep, couldn't ignore the fact that he'd only known Dante a little over a day and that Holt hadn't finished vetting him. While those facts hadn't stopped Hawes from giving over his body last night, or from leaving Dante at his condo now, it did keep him from bringing Dante further into the fold.

Other than the kill he'd witnessed in the alley, Dante had no eyes-on proof of what Hawes and his family did for a second living. And as for the alley, they were even, Hawes having witnessed Dante's kill as well. Mutually assured destruction. But Dante hadn't seen the rest of Hawes's family in action, and Hawes wasn't about to risk them too.

His phone vibrated in his pocket. Time was up. Iris gave him another blink, and Hawes put a finger to his lips, shushing her. He scratched behind her ears and took one last lingering look at Dante. Not a bad sight before leaving for work.

Downstairs, a nondescript sedan waited at the curb, Helena behind the wheel, Amelia in the passenger seat. They didn't look like they'd gotten much sleep either.

"You good?" Amelia asked as he slid into the back seat.

He nodded and asked after Holt.

"Better," his brother answered out of the car speakers. "Now that Lily's finally down."

"You need more time?"

"Don't have more time," Helena cut in. "We're already late."

She was tense. Jobs like the one tonight tended to do that to her. As an attorney who specialized in freeing the wrongfully accused, Helena took the cases of the wrongfully acquitted personally. Which fit well with Hawes's realignment of the organization. He and Helena were on the same page regarding targets.

"Everything's in place," Amelia said as she handed him a tablet. "Jodie and Ray did a good job on the setup."

Hawes scrolled through the assembled case file on Walter Campbell III. Late-forties, white, rich, well-connected. Involved in local politics until he'd been accused of sexually abusing teen boys he'd met via a government-sponsored mentorship program. The charges hadn't stuck. That's what happened when traumatized teens overdosed on Gray Death, fentanyl-laced heroin popular on the streets; when witnesses changed their stories before they could testify; and when the abuser was fraternity brothers with the judge who tried his case. Not the same chapter, so supposedly there was no conflict of interest. Hawes called bullshit.

"Who does he think he's meeting tonight?"

"A fifteen-year-old kid he picked up online," Amelia answered.

Hawes read through the emails between Campbell and a person he thought was an underage boy. Ray had been working him for weeks, encouraging Campbell's promises of money and drugs. In reality, all Campbell ever left in his wake were bruises, addiction, and suicides. Hawes hoped there was an afterlife so this asshole could appreciate the irony of what was about to befall him.

"Jodie and Ray warned him?" Another of Hawes's new-order conditions.

"Three different times," Holt answered. "And I locked down his computer. Fucker hired one of *my kids* to go around it." Holt's "kids" were the homeless teens at the LGBTQ shelter Hawes regularly donated to and where Holt also volunteered his time teaching programming. The kids worshiped Holt, were loyal to him before anyone else, and Holt protected them like he'd protected Hawes growing up. This had to rankle.

"We're here," Helena said as she parked in the staff lot behind one of the Tendernob's trendy new hotels. Classy enough for Campbell's standards, not so classy as to draw attention, and close to his marks.

"Camera is going on loop in…" Holt's rapid-fire typing pinged through the speakers. "Three, two, one." The typing stopped. "You've got ten minutes."

Helena tugged on her gloves. "Plenty of time."

Words were at a minimum as they unfolded from the car and slipped through the hotel's open back door. Amelia shoved a wad of cash into the hand of the waiting night manager, who also confirmed all the rooms around Campbell's were empty. They took the service elevator up to the fifth floor, where Hawes and Helena waited, peeking around the corner as Amelia approached Campbell's door.

Her willowy figure was striking in a black trench, little black dress, and elbow-length gloves. Taken together with her alabaster skin, long dark hair, and bright green eyes, she made an effective Trojan horse on operations. She also wasn't in the public eye as much as Hawes or Helena, making it easier for her to take on personas and get a foot in the door. Assuming she could get the door open. After Campbell ignored her first few knocks, she slipped a folded note under the door. It opened a moment later.

"Good evening, Mr. Campbell."

He looked taken aback, surprised she'd used his real name. He'd used an alias in the emails Hawes had skimmed. Campbell glanced down at the note, then back up. "I'm sorry," he stuttered, "I was expecting… I didn't know he had a…"

"Pimp," Amelia said. "That's the word you're looking for. And you're a John."

"I'm not—"

She talked over his futile protest. "I meet all the new Johns first. Make sure everything is settled."

Campbell's wrinkled forehead smoothed out. "You're here to collect."

Blinded by her smile, Campbell held open the door and let her in. She kicked the rubber stopper into place, propping the door slightly ajar.

Hawes and Helena crept around the corner to either side of the door.

"I was worried for a moment," Campbell said. "I specified certain—"

"I know what you wanted."

"As do we." Helena stepped into the room ahead of Hawes, who closed the door behind them. "Even if the justice system doesn't believe it."

"But now," Hawes said, "everyone will know the truth by morning, after you confess your crimes and commit suicide."

Campbell made a break for the door. Stupid, as there were three people between him and it. Instincts were instincts, though, and Campbell was bigger than all three of them. He probably thought he could barrel right over them, but he was nowhere near as quick as he'd been in his college running back days. It took less than a minute to wrestle him into the desk chair and strap down his limbs.

"Who are you?" he croaked, voice trembling.

"Do you remember Adam Wilson?" Hawes said.

"Who?"

Helena, standing behind the chair, reached over his shoulder and opened his laptop. "Log in," she ordered.

"No, you can't make—"

"Oh yes, we can make you." Amelia's gloved hand hit a pressure point that made Campbell howl. She didn't stop until he logged in and the desktop appeared.

"There's a file waiting for you. *My Crimes.*" Hawes traded places with Helena and reached around Campbell. He clicked the mouse until Adam's picture appeared. "That's Adam Wilson."

"I don't remember him from the trial," Campbell said.

"Because he's dead," Helena said. "You plied a fifteen-year-old kid with Gray Death, got him hooked on you and the drug, and when you found a shinier toy, you left him high and dry. He overdosed on the parting gift you left him."

"That's not the name he gave me. I thought he was a professional!"

Hawes spun his chair around and braced his gloved hands on the armrests, getting in Campbell's face. "That doesn't make it okay, you sick fuck."

At Campbell's side, Amelia hit another pressure point, and tears sprang to his eyes. "I'm sorry. I didn't know who he was," he cried through the pain.

Hawes shoved back, and Helena stepped back in, her blue eyes burning with cold fury. "His father didn't want to tarnish his memory with that farce of a trial. You were never going to be convicted. Not when you're a former city supervisor and fraternity brothers with the judge. He should have recused himself, and you should be behind bars."

"I can pay you," Campbell tried to bargain. "Or swing a city favor your way."

"We don't need those things from you," Helena hissed and spun his chair back around. "No one needs you at all."

Standing at the side of the desk, Hawes rotated the laptop toward him, found the confession Holt had uploaded into the *My Crimes* folder, and opened up the electronic signature app. "Sign it."

He hesitated, and Hawes thought of Lucas. Campbell's incentive was withering by the second. He mentally reviewed Campbell's bio. No wife and kids, but… Hawes turned from the desk to Campbell's bag in the corner. It only took a few seconds to find what he was looking for. Fucking amateur. "You have a twelve-year-old nephew," he said, returning to face off against Campbell across the desk. He tossed the drug paraphernalia and baggie of Gray Death onto the middle of it. "Wonder what he'd do, if he found that just lying around?" Hawes would never do such a thing, but Campbell didn't know that.

The leverage worked. Campbell signed the confession, and Amelia snatched up the baggie and supplies. Elastic to tie off his arm, a syringe, a lighter, and a spoon.

"Oh God," Campbell whimpered as she expertly set up everything.

"Pretty sure God wants nothing to do with you either," Hawes said as Helena tied the tourniquet around his arm.

Amelia filled the syringe. "Were you really going to shoot a kid up with this stuff?"

"Wait, wait," Campbell hollered, still clutching at survival straws. "I have information."

"I doubt it's anything we don't already know," Hawes said.

"You're under investigation."

Hawes's blood ran cold. Jodie's and Ray's deaths had been kept out of the news. So how did Campbell know about it? Or was this about the winery or warehouse? Or a different investigation altogether? He held up a hand, and Amelia paused, the syringe an inch from Campbell's vein. "You have to give us more than that," Hawes said.

"There was a sealed document on the judge's desk last month. I saw your company's name."

Not Jodie and Ray, then. Nor the warehouse or winery. Something else. And there'd been something even more important in Campbell's words. Hawes sprang the trap. "What name was that?"

Campbell blanched and snapped shut his mouth, realizing his mistake too late.

"You know who we are."

Campbell remained mute, but his terrified eyes, and his earlier words, said it all. Still, Hawes had to be sure. He nodded at Amelia and Helena.

Amelia withdrew the syringe, and Helena pulled back Campbell's pinky finger far enough to cause pain but not a break. That wouldn't fit the picture they were creating. "Who are we?" his sister demanded.

"Madigan!" Campbell cried, his eyes never leaving Hawes. "Hawes Madigan."

"You should have kept that bit to yourself." Hawes circled the desk. "Now you're definitely not getting out of here alive. Not that there'd been a chance before." He held out a hand to Amelia, and she laid the syringe in his palm. "Do you know what they call me?"

Campbell shook his head, and the sweat from the ends of his hair joined the tears streaming down his face.

"The Prince of Killers." This was one of those rare times Hawes liked the moniker. Not just its usefulness as a deterrent, like at the warehouse, but for the terror it brought to the guilty eyes of those who'd put fear in the eyes of innocents. *This* was why he did what he did. When justice failed, Hawes and his family righted the balance. He was happy to rule this kingdom, as prince or king.

He found the protruding vein in Campbell's arm and pressed the tip of the syringe to it, breaking the skin.

"Wait, please!" Campbell cried.

"Justice has waited long enough." Hawes pressed the plunger.

TEN

Hawes took the stairs up to Holt's lair two at a time. It was still dark outside, and inside most of the house was too, except for the light filtering down from the brightly lit upper level. Holt had no doubt been running on all cylinders since they'd briefed him in the car about Campbell's nebulous warning.

"What do we know?" Hawes asked as he crested the top stair.

"That you've got a problem."

The answer, voiced by the last person Hawes expected, came from the far corner of the room. His grandmother sat in the rocker, a sleeping Lily in her arms, a cat on each foot, as if they'd conspired to never let her leave again. If that was the case… "Papa Cal?" Hawes asked, fearing the worst.

"Not yet." Rose closed her eyes and held Lily closer. "I needed to come home and check back in with reality." She reopened her eyes and pinned Hawes to the spot. "And what do I find? A mess."

She always could make Hawes feel like he was doing it all wrong. She didn't break out that imperious tone often, but when she did, nine times out of ten she was right. That was how Hawes had learned many of his most valuable lessons. He hated to think of her worried about the family and business now, when she was days from losing her husband. He unstuck himself and crossed the room. He bent to kiss Lily's head, then Rose's cheek. "We'll handle it. You don't need to worry—"

"Please," she said, patting his cheek. "Let me worry about something else for five minutes." She held his stare, and in her familiar blue gaze was the same determination Helena had had in her eyes earlier tonight.

"All right." He grasped her hand, squeezing it as he stepped to her side. "We've got a problem. The more brains the better, especially yours."

Holt spun from his bank of computers and turned his face up for Amelia's quick kiss. There were bags under his brown eyes, and his wide shoulders were slumped under the flannel. It looked like he'd slept less than Hawes lately. "I can't find any filed docs from a month ago regarding any investigation."

"Did you call Kane?" Hawes asked.

"Three times. He's not returning my calls."

"He's not our enemy here."

"That's impossible," Rose said. "He's the police. We run an illegal operation. Don't forget that."

Hawes didn't think Kane could ever truly be their enemy, but Rose was right. Their interests, for the most part, were at odds.

"I have court contacts I can work," Helena said. "I'll have better luck in the morning, in person."

"Do we have any idea what this is about?" Rose asked.

"He said the company was under investigation," Helena answered. "It could be law enforcement or the health department, for all we know."

"I'm running a comprehensive sweep," Holt said. "Filings, searches, flags, assignments. If it's on a government computer, I'll find it."

An investigation, on top of trying to find a traitor, the latter of which Hawes hadn't told Rose about yet. That was an additional stressor she didn't need. It didn't appear the two matters were connected, though Hawes couldn't dismiss the possibility. Pull one string, and who knew how many others would unravel. Would he have any clothes left when he took the throne? Which would be any day now, and his family was looking to him to make sure the kingdom prevailed.

"Okay, order of attack," he said. "Holt, stay on top of the searches. Amelia, make sure he sleeps some too."

She kissed her husband's head. "I'm on it."

"I'll work our health department contacts," Hawes continued. "Helena, you work the legal, and if you're near the station—"

"I'll make sure Brax gets a visit too," she said with a smile.

"Are we expecting any blowback from the job tonight?" Rose asked.

Hawes shook his head. "It'll get media attention, but all went according to plan. It'll look like suicide. Won't be tied to us."

"All right, just one more thing, then. What are we going to do about your new shadow?" She nodded at the surveillance feed of the hallway outside his condo.

All quiet, no sign of Dante.

"Has he left?" Hawes asked Holt.

"Negative." Holt flipped the footage over to the front of the building. Dante's bike was still parked under the streetlamp. "Unless he went out the balcony doors, but the security system reports no doors or windows opened since you left."

Hawes checked his watch. Almost two hours ago now. Almost a day and a half since Dante Perry had sauntered into his life. Was the PI pulling a string too? Or helping to hold the fabric together? Hawes had certainly felt unraveled last night. The good kind, though, that had helped him relax and sleep for a few hours before this morning's job. But one of Dante's motives couldn't be argued—he had admitted to using them. As such, Hawes felt no guilt using him too.

"Continue as if he's a potential threat," Hawes said to Holt. Caution was warranted. "Did you find any payments? Any connection to Isabelle? She meant something to him. Their paths had to have crossed."

"Not that I can find. And no one's paying him to be here or to investigate us. I tracked his recent deposits, and everything lines up with completed jobs."

"But something else doesn't," Helena said, her skepticism unwavering.

Hawes couldn't deny there were holes in Dante's story that required filling. "Keep digging," he said. "I'll proceed as if he's a source. See if he knows about the investigation Campbell mentioned." He gestured at the monitors. "Keep tabs on him after. I want to see if he takes the information and runs to someone." Authorities or traitors.

"Should we keep the meet today?" Holt asked. "If the buyer gets wind of anything amiss…"

"Canceling would be a bigger red flag." Except under one circumstance, which anyone, including their buyer, would understand. "Unless we need to cancel to be with you and Papa Cal," he said to Rose.

She shook her head. "You're right. You need to go ahead with the meet." Her approval quieted Hawes's doubts. "The last thing Callum would want is for the organization to stop running because of him."

It was also the last thing Hawes wanted. What they'd done that morning mattered; they needed to keep doing it. He might not have agreed with Papa Cal's reign of terror, or his parents' robotic efficiency, but with Holt and Helena by his side, and Amelia and Rose on board, he could shape the organization into something that worked for this generation and their legacy. Something for good.

HAWES EMERGED FROM THE ENTRY HALL AND STARED AT THE gorgeous, hilarious sight in front of him. "She's got you trained already."

Dante spread his arms where he sat at the dining table. He

looked hotter than he had any right to—olive skin glowing in the morning light, hair in a messy top knot, a book in one hand and a spoon in the other. That was the gorgeous part. The hilarious part was Iris's back paws on his denim-clad thighs, her front ones on the table, and her face in his cereal bowl. "She didn't give me a chance to finish." He tossed his book on the table. "Just jumped right up and claimed it for herself."

"That's my fault." Laughing, Hawes followed his nose to the pot of coffee in the kitchen. "I don't like cereal milk, so she always gets mine."

"You don't like cereal milk?" Dante gasped. "What kind of monster are you?"

"I don't know." He filled a mug with coffee, sipped the life-giving brew, and leaned a hip against the island. "You've had four hours here alone. You tell me. What monstrous things did you find?"

"Only one that was truly evil." He shooed Iris off his lap, stood, and pulled a cookbook out of the many on the buffet table. Hawes suspected he knew which one. Dante brought it over to the island and tossed it onto the granite countertop.

Suspicion confirmed. *Cooking Vegan.* A gag gift from Holt on their thirtieth birthday.

Hawes smiled into his mug. "Does that offend your Italian senses?"

"More than you will ever know."

"If it makes you feel better, I've never opened it."

"Marginally." Dante circled the island, coming to stand in front of Hawes. "You were gone early this morning."

"Duty called."

"You left me here." He stepped closer and slid a hand over Hawes's hip. "You trusted me enough to stay in your condo without you."

"Iris is a good watchdog."

"So's your brother. The security system was armed. He'd know if I left."

Hawes shrugged and set his mug aside. "He'd know, but you were free to leave."

"You assumed I'd search the place?"

"You're a PI, aren't you?"

Dante returned his shrug with a smirk, which Hawes promptly wiped off his face with a kiss. The one he'd wanted in the dark of morning, for his own reasons. Reasons that were still tugging at Hawes's gut and other places south. He dove deeper into Dante's mouth, indulging in the taste of sweet cereal mixed with Dante's rich, mysterious flavor.

Dante matched his fervor, sucking Hawes's tongue in farther and tugging his shirt loose from his pants, unraveling Hawes's control while conversely stitching him together into the prince, who had additional reasons, other than just his desire, to keep Dante close. His vibrating phone was a well-timed reminder. He slipped out of Dante's arms and started down the hall toward the bathroom, leaving a trail of clothes in his wake. "I need to shower."

As Hawes had intended, Dante followed. "Can I get in with you?"

"Not if I'm going to make my meeting in an hour." He tossed his phone on the vanity, opened the glass door over the spa tub, and turned on the shower.

Dante pressed against his back, making Hawes dizzy with want. "You sure about that?" His hands snuck under the waistband of Hawes's boxers and pushed them down. They fluttered to the floor, and Hawes's cock jutted the opposite direction, begging for attention. Dante gave it to his balls instead, tugging. Hawes groaned and dropped his head back onto Dante's shoulder. Dante ramped up the torture, dipping his tongue into the crook of Hawes's neck and driving him wild. "Maybe I'd let you return that favor from last night."

Hawes rocked his hips, ass rubbing against Dante's erection, even as he did the math in his head, counting minutes and drive time. As much as he wanted to accept Dante's offer, there was no way he could make it work. Dante circled the base of his cock, and Hawes jerked out of his hold before it was too late. "No," he said, spinning. "You stay right there"—he pointed at the half wall across from the shower—"and answer my questions."

Dante did not look pleased, but he complied, hopping up onto the wall. Hawes stepped into the shower and turned the water to cool, tamping down his erection. "Did you know Walter Campbell?"

"Fog City have you and your siblings to thank for that?"

Shampoo bottle in hand, Hawes stared at Dante blank-faced. "For what?"

"Walter Campbell committed suicide. It's all over the news."

"If the news said…"

Dante scoffed. "The court said he was innocent, which was also a lie."

"Well, then." Hawes closed his eyes and washed out his soapy hair under the showerhead. "It sounds like justice was served."

"Is that what you do now? Vigilante justice? The winery, the warehouse, Campbell."

Rather than answer and officially incriminate himself and his siblings, Hawes reverted to his original question. "Did you know him?"

"Other than from the trial coverage, no."

"What about anyone else in local politics or at the courthouse?"

"I have my contacts," Dante said. "Same as you all do, no doubt."

Hawes continued to wash while working his source for information. "You said someone is trying to unseat me. Are they trying to do that legally too?"

"What's this about, Madigan?"

"There's an investigation, under seal."

Dante hopped off the ledge. "That's not the tip I had."

"About that tip…"

"I showed you what I had."

Hawes washed off the last of the soap. "And yet I still don't know why you're here."

The shower door opened, and cool air rushed in. Hawes turned, meeting Dante's cold, hard eyes without the glass for a shield. "I told you why."

"Isabelle Costa." Hawes hoped his voice didn't tremble as much as his insides. "You said she mattered, but that's all I've gotten from you. Why have you inserted yourself into my life and family business, Mr. Perry?"

One of Dante's hands flattened on the glass, the other closed around the towel bar at the back of the shower, boxing Hawes in. Hawes expected his voice to be cold and hard, like his eyes, but it was soft and tender, guilty almost. "She helped me at a time when I wasn't in a good way. She didn't deserve to get gunned down in the street, by her boyfriend or otherwise."

"She didn't."

"She deserves justice too. That's why I'm here."

Hawes didn't disagree with Dante on either of those points. He shoved his hands and face under the shower spray, remembering that night again. The truth that varied from the official story. How the water had run red, then cold, his fingers raw and pruned by the time Helena had dragged him out. Three years later, Isabelle's blood was still on his hands.

"Hawes."

A different voice, a different time, and yet things felt all too familiar. Too connected. Except this time, he could do something about it.

He turned off the water and yanked a towel off the rack. "I need to get going."

"Can I go with you to this meet?"

Hawes shook his head and stepped out onto the bathmat. "A new face might spook the buyer."

"Buyer?"

"For the prototypes," he said.

"You're selling the explosives?"

"The prototypes." Hawes held his gaze, and his cover. "The prototypes business, actually."

Dante's eyes grew wide. "You don't think that's motive enough for a disgruntled operative?"

Fair point. He'd been thinking in terms of his new policies generally, not this one specifically. It was another stream of income, another line of attack, cut off to his operatives. The possibility had to be considered. "In the current context, yes." Someone like Lucas might read this change of course as another example of Hawes being a "pansy."

For Hawes, it was simply valuing life.

"You're still going through with it?" Dante asked.

"It's our empire now—mine, Holt's, and Helena's—and this is how we've decided to rule it. The prototypes are too much risk. Too high a cost." Too high a body count, collateral and otherwise. "We're getting out of that business."

The kiss Dante laid on him then was different than any other they'd shared. It was slow and deep, not riding the edge of blistering desire they'd been skating the past thirty-six hours. A deeper emotion rippled under the surface, something warm that Hawes wanted to settle into for hours.

Or yank himself back from a split-second later when Dante thrust a gun into his hand. He stared down at the awful weight, made heavier by the conversation they'd just had. "What the fuck?"

"If you're not going to let me go with you, then at least take protection, in case things go sideways."

"I'll have Holt with me."

Dante closed Hawes's fingers around the pistol. "You'll have this too."

Hawes wanted to vomit. "I can't use this." He shoved the gun back at Dante. At the man's frustrated look, Hawes bent, hiked up Dante's pant leg, and took his knife instead. "Satisfied?"

Dante tucked the pistol back into his waistband. "You don't like guns."

"They kill too fast, without thought. It's too easy to make the wrong call."

Confusing Hawes further, Dante hauled him in for another kiss. This one, however, was gentler than the last. Lazy, unguarded nips and licks of the sort Hawes dreamed of having the luxury to enjoy with a partner someday. And fuck if he didn't have somewhere else to be. He reluctantly broke the kiss and rested his forehead against Dante's. "I have to go."

"I'll talk with my contacts at the courthouse," Dante said after a couple of breaths. "Let me see what I can find out about this investigation."

"Thank you."

"That's two favors you'll owe me." Dante stole another kiss, then stepped out of the way, clearing Hawes's path to the vanity, save for a smack to his ass. "I do plan to collect."

Hawes grinned over his shoulder. "I hope so."

ELEVEN

Hawes swung Holt's SUV into the parking lot of the run-down buffet restaurant and parked among the cars scattered across the lot. Ride-share commuters, according to the realtor who had the property listing. The owner was still making money off the site, which had been sitting on the market for years. He was making more than usual today with the fee Hawes had paid to use it. Less than a mile from their South San Francisco warehouse, and only a few from SFO, where their buyer was flying in, the deserted restaurant site worked well for their purposes.

In the passenger seat, Holt was scrolling through news feeds on his tablet, reviewing the press coverage of Campbell's death. By the glimpses Hawes caught of the suicide headlines, they were still in the clear.

The glimpses of his brother were a different story. Holt's decline into zombie-dom continued—darker bags under his tired eyes, his auburn beard shaggier, and his washed-out skin contrasting starkly with his colorful tattoo sleeve. Tattoos that stood out more vividly when unobscured by a baby in his arm. Amelia had the day off and had taken Lily and Rose to visit Cal. Holt was jumpier without his daughter in sight, but it was safer this way. They weren't expecting danger, but it couldn't be ruled out. Helena was likewise absent, due in part to her job and in part to strategy. Whenever possible, they avoided putting all three of them in the crosshairs. One of them usually stayed back, as Holt had that morning and as Helena did now.

Hawes shifted, reaching into the back seat for the folder containing the sale documents and Holt's flannel. He dropped the shirt into his brother's lap. "Buyer's on time?"

"Landed twenty minutes ago." Holt tapped at his tablet screen. "And Lyft just ran his card. He should be here in ten."

Hawes snatched the realtor's keys out of the cup holder and spun them around his index finger. "Let's go on in." He rotated toward the door but was stopped halfway by Holt's hand around his arm.

"Wait!"

Hawes glanced over his shoulder. "There a problem?"

Holt's gaze darted all around, looking everywhere but at Hawes. "Are we sure we want to do this?"

"We?" Hawes twisted the rest of the way around to face his brother. "I'm sure. Helena's sure. Are you?"

"I don't want my hands in this any more than you and Hena do."

"Then why are you hesitating?"

Holt darkened his tablet, tossed it onto the dash, and slumped in his seat with a sigh. "The future."

"This is the future."

"There are so many unknowns, Hawes, and without this"—he nodded out the windshield in the general direction of their warehouse several blocks away—"it's another unknown. What if something happens to the cold storage business? Or to our other line of work?" He fisted his hands in his lap. "I still can't find the source of the leak about Papa Cal, who's dying. A PI shows up out of nowhere saying someone's out to kill you, and you can't keep your eyes off the guy. Brax has gone radio silent, and we're being investigated without knowing by whom or for what." His knuckles grew whiter and his breaths shorter, on the verge of hyperventilating.

"Hey, hey, hey." Hawes clasped Holt's arm, trying to shake him loose of the panic. "Breathe, little brother." And father… That had to be where this was coming from.

Holt confirmed as much when he relaxed his hands and lifted his fingers to his left pec, laying them over the water lily he'd had inked there after his daughter's birth.

"This is about Lily," Hawes said.

Holt leaned his head back and closed his eyes. "Mom and dad, our grandparents, they talked about legacy all the time, but I never truly understood until now."

"We all understand better with Lily in our lives. She's why we do any of this." To make a better, safer world for her, and to give her options, either in or out of the family business. But as much as she tugged on Hawes's mind and heart, he couldn't imagine the responsibility Holt felt. "That said, you're Lily's father. You and Amelia have the most at stake here. We all get that too. So if you want to call off this deal, we'll call it off. This only works if all of us are on board. That's how it's always been, and that's how it will always be."

"I'm sorry." Holt dropped his hand into his lap.

Hawes covered it with his own. "Don't be sorry. I'd rather you talk to me than bottle this up."

"It's been a lot."

"When's the last time you slept for more than three hours?"

Holt laughed, the sound exhausted and helpless, but thankfully without the earlier panic and doubt.

Hawes settled back into his seat. "What do you want to do here?"

"We go through with it," Holt answered without hesitation.

"Are you sure?"

"It's what's right." Holt straightened and reached for his tablet. "We have the trust fund for Lily."

"Mine too, if anything goes south."

Holt's gaze shot to him again; he looked stunned.

"Don't act surprised," Hawes said with a smile. "She's all our legacy. At least until she has to share it with more brothers and sisters. Or cousins," he added with a wink, then turned for the door. Holt didn't stop him this time.

Hawes stopped himself, however, when they were halfway across the parking lot, his mind snagging on something else Holt had said. "If you want me to tell Dante to get lost, I will."

Holt handed Hawes his tablet and shrugged into the flannel. "Not yet. He could be useful, and you like him."

"I do," Hawes admitted. "But our family means more to me. It always will." Any serious relationship Hawes had would only work if his partner understood and accepted all of him, family and businesses included, but that sort of full disclosure required trust. No guarantee. Not like the trust he had in his family.

Holt held out his hand for his tablet. "How is that fair to you?"

"It's not fair if I compromise any of you."

"Don't use us to push away every relationship." A flash of righteous indignation brought Holt's eyes to life. Hawes would take it, even at his own expense. "You have to trust someone."

"I trust you, Helena, and Amelia." Hawes grinned and clapped his shoulder. "We can't all be as lucky as you, Little H."

Holt covered his hand, holding it there. "If I could find a partner, if Mom and Dad did, if Papa Cal and Rose did too, then so can you and Helena." He squeezed Hawes's hand. "There's too much good in both of you not to share it with someone special."

P APERS WERE STREWN ACROSS THE LONE BUFFET TABLE REMAINING IN the cavernous shell of a restaurant. Disclosure packets, purchase agreement, grant deed, bill of sale, and the various other title and escrow documents required to transfer ownership of their warehouse. On paper, it would look like a simple real estate sale. In reality, what was inside the building on the property was far more valuable to Shawn Gillespie than the land or the building itself.

Gillespie and his two attorneys were flipping through the papers for a third time. Hawes didn't begrudge them their careful review, especially as the documents had not been emailed in advance. Too easy to disseminate and draw attention. And while the disclosure documents could have been sent electronically, the deed and tax documents had to be originals. Hawes would ferry the stack of signed documents to Helena, who'd file them at the end of the week, allowing Gillespie time to move out the inventory before the change of ownership triggered a building inspection and tax reassessment.

Hawes didn't mind the few days' delay. All he cared about was that the contents of the warehouse were no longer his inventory to move. They were officially getting out of the explosives business. No more using them and no more making them for anyone else either. Not when Hawes had no control over how they'd be used and who might get swept up in the collateral damage.

Like Isabelle Costa had been, albeit more directly.

Unbeknownst to anyone, Isabelle, a secretary at MCS, had been carrying on an affair with one of their operatives, Zander Rowe. According to an anonymous tip Hawes had received the night of Isabelle's death, Rowe, who was supposed to be transporting a truck full of explosives, was instead diverting it to the highest bidder, a domestic terror cell hell-bent on attacking City Hall. Hawes had raced out after Rowe, calling for backup but not waiting for it to arrive, too terrified for his city and his family's legacy. He'd caught up with the truck, and a gunfight had ensued between him and Rowe.

When a second person had climbed out of the truck's cab, pistol first, Hawes had fired on instinct, killing a woman whose only crime had been falling for the wrong man. A hostage who'd only been trying to protect herself. Hawes hadn't realized that until it was too late, when he'd knelt over her and seen her bruised face and mangled wrists. He'd failed to call out, so she wouldn't have known he'd won the shoot-out. She'd found Rowe's spare gun and was trying to escape. Hawes hadn't given her the chance.

Helena had eventually talked him down that night—one life lost to collateral damage versus the many more who likely would've died if that terrorist cell had gotten hold of the explosives, but that one life was too many for Hawes. The risk that a tragedy like that might happen again, that his own weapons could be used against his family or the city he loved, was unacceptable. He would've sold the explosives business the next day if he could have, but extracting themselves from existing agreements had been time-consuming, as had been vetting a buyer.

They'd found the right one, eventually. A real estate developer, Gillespie would be using the explosives for project demolition, not for criminal purposes. That said, he was getting a criminally good deal on materials and real estate, which made him willing to look the other way as to the explosives' origin. Except as Gillespie waved off his attorneys and began read-through number four, Hawes was beginning to wonder if his buyer was getting cold feet. This was not merely a careful review. If that were the case, Gillespie or one of his attorneys would have spent more time on the disclosures. Instead, Gillespie was hung up on the purchase agreement, staring at it with wide eyes and increasingly pale skin.

"Is there a problem?" Hawes asked from across the table.

Gillespie's eyes flickered up, then away, avoiding Hawes's gaze.

Tell one.

"No problem," Gillespie said. "Just making sure I understand everything."

Tell two.

Nothing in that standard form purchase agreement or the other escrow documents was out of the ordinary, especially for a developer who regularly conducted real estate transactions.

Hawes leaned back in his chair and crossed one leg over the other. "All the terms are consistent with our conversations."

"Yes, it's all here."

Beside Hawes, Holt held a pen out to Gillespie. "We'll sign after you."

Gillespie took the pen and spun it around his thumb. Once, twice, a third time.

Tell three.

The attorney closest to Gillespie cleared her throat. "If there's—"

"No, it's fine. I'll do it." Another pause, another spin of the pen, then Gillespie began flipping pages and signing. Quickly, almost as if he was forcing himself to do so.

I'll do it.

Tell four.

"What firm did you say you were with?" Hawes asked the attorney.

The other one, a man, rattled off a string of names Hawes recognized. A large West Coast firm with an office in downtown San Francisco.

"Your firm handled the China Basin redevelopment, right?" Hawes said.

"Yes," the woman attorney replied. "Years back now."

Tell five.

Hawes straightened in his chair. Next to him, Holt tapped at his tablet. "Amazing to see how much the area's changed," Holt said. "When I was a kid—"

"There." Gillespie threw the pen down. "Your turn."

"A moment, please." Hawes stood and picked up the signed documents. "We just need to clear signing authority with our attorney."

Holt was already up and headed for the far end of the room. He held out his tablet to Hawes, a text open from Helena.

Wrong firm, she'd replied in response to Holt's inquiry regarding the China Basin legal work.

"That's what I thought," Hawes said, voice low.

"Those attorneys are on the firm's website, but they could have hacked that, or asked the firm to change it for a day."

Hawes glanced back at an impossibly paler Gillespie. "Something's off for sure."

"'I'll do it' was a dead giveaway."

"Signaling us?"

"If those attorneys are actually law enforcement, and they told him who we were, who do you think he's more afraid of?"

Even if Gillespie didn't know they were assassins, he did know they had access to explosives enough to blow him and his buildings to bits. Leverage like that did tend to work in their favor, especially when law enforcement officers, by contrast, could leverage a target only so far, given the bounds of the law.

"They don't have probable cause to raid the warehouse," Hawes said, connecting the last of the dots. "They need him to purchase it to gain access."

Holt nodded at the papers in Hawes's hand. "And our signatures to prove we owned the building and trafficked the explosives inside it."

"Let's not do that." Hawes folded the papers in two. "We haven't done anything but discuss a sale of real estate so far. We can walk away."

"I think that would be wise." Holt darkened the screen of his tablet and tucked it under his arm. "Competing offer?"

"Works for me." Hawes led them back across the room. "I'm sorry, but we're going to have to cut this meeting short."

Gillespie shot to his feet. "All you have to do is sign."

"Your money will be wired immediately after," one of the "attorneys" added.

"There's another offer," Hawes said. "A better one."

"I'll match it!" Gillespie countered.

"That's good to know. We'll consider all our options and be in touch. Now, if you'd please." He held an arm out toward the restaurant door, beckoning them to leave. "The owner's realtor for this building will be here in five to collect the keys."

"Madigan, please. Let's make this deal."

"I'm sorry, Shawn," Hawes said, meaning it. He hated to think what the feds had on Gillespie to put that kind of desperation in the man's voice.

And what about what they had on him? Not enough to make a move, but enough to connect their activities to the warehouse. To the deal they'd brokered for its sale. Was this connected to the investigation Campbell had mentioned?

In any event, their investigation was stymied for now, or at least this play was. Recognizing defeat, Gillespie's escorts ushered him out, and Hawes closed the doors behind them.

"Find out what they have on him," he said to Holt, who was gathering the rest of the papers on the table. "Make it go away."

"He tried to set us up."

"You saw him. Did he look like a man with options?"

Holt grunted in acknowledgment and shoved the papers into their folder. He lifted his eyes, and they were more than a measure concerned. "It'll be viewed as weakness if word gets out that we let him do this to us without consequences."

"He didn't do anything. I think, in the long run, we'll get more out of saving him than damning him."

Holt didn't look convinced, but further argument was forestalled by Holt's ringing tablet, Amelia's face lighting up the screen.

"Hey, babe," Holt answered. "What's up?"

"You need to get to the hospice house," she said. "It's time."

Hawes jostled through the lingering lunch crew in the hospice house kitchen and bolted out the back door, desperate for space and air. He killed people for a living, but the last three hours, watching his grandfather die, had been utter hell. Counting the seconds between Papa Cal's last breaths, the tears running down Rose's face, the number of times Helena tapped her nails or how often Amelia and Holt handed off Lily, each of them needing the extra comfort in turn. Not to mention the twelve times Hawes had had to sign his name on the termination-of-life papers. How many more documents would he have to sign this afternoon? Funeral arrangements, corporate formalities for MCS, the list went on.

Hands laced behind his head, he stalked through the rows of the small backyard garden. His long legs ate up the distance in a few quick strides, but the high privacy walls hid what he didn't want the rest of the world to see. His own shortened breaths, his own tears, the number of times he drummed his fingers against his skull. He needed to get his shit together before he stepped out the front door a different man than when he'd entered.

Sweat dripped down his spine as he paced. The morning fog had burned off early, gracing San Francisco with a rare sunny summer day. Fitting for the last day of Cal's life, a man whose existence swung wildly from light to dark. Local businessman and beloved Pac Heights fixture during the day, the last man you ever wanted to see headed your way at night.

And fitting for the moment Hawes wasn't sure he was ready for.

A coronation by sun rather than his beloved fog.

The screen door squeaked open and banged shut behind him. The sound of footsteps didn't follow, but Hawes knew he wasn't alone. He lifted his right arm and waited for his sister to slide in under it.

Sure enough, a sniffling Helena snuggled up to his side and wrapped her arms around his middle. He hugged her close, and they stood like that for several long minutes, until Helena loosened her hold and walked over to the stone bench under the garden's sprawling plum tree.

"Thank you," she said as Hawes lowered himself next to her. "For always being able to do what none of us can."

Hawes curled his fingers around the front edge of the bench's carved seat. "What does that say about me?"

"That you're the strong one." She covered his hand between them. "You always have been."

"Don't discount yourself, Hena."

She cracked a wobbly smile. "You remember how Papa Cal used to practice saying my name with you? Mom and Dad loved to tell that story."

Hawes chuckled. "Every day until I got it." Cal would sit him down with a piece of paper—Helena's name written out phonetically on it—and use his heavy silver pen to tap out each syllable. Holt didn't need a lesson, he got it on the first try, but it had taken Hawes a year longer to work out that middle syllable. By then, the nickname had stuck.

"And the day you finally got it? Tell me the rest."

How could Hawes forget it? His grandfather had been so happy and proud. Not at all disappointed that it had taken Hawes so absurdly long in the first place. He'd called Noah and Charlotte back from the office, Rose down from the second floor with Holt, and Cal had repeated it over with Hawes, clapping and cheering when he got it right. "He went to Eastern in Chinatown and got a box full of those mooncakes I loved so much."

"Those things were the best. When was the last time you had one?"

Hawes racked his brain. "I can't remember."

"We should fix that." Helena bumped his shoulder. "Soon."

"I'd like that." Hawes lifted his arm and tucked his sister back against his side. "Maybe Rose would too, after a bit."

Helena ducked her chin, staring at her hands that had taken up their nail tapping again. "Can you imagine ever loving someone that hard?"

The image of Dante stretched out on his couch, book on his chest, Iris at his feet, jumped unbidden to Hawes's mind. He shook it off, unwilling to contemplate love in relation to a man he hardly knew. Attraction and lust were there for sure, as was that strange steadiness Dante provided, but love? Not quite so instantly. Not when loving and trusting the wrong person could spell disaster for Hawes and his family.

"Me neither," Helena mumbled, interpreting his silence as a no. Hawes didn't like the dejection in his sister's tone.

"Holt manages," he said.

"He's the brave one. You're the strong one."

"And you?"

"To be determined. I just can't imagine…" She cleared her throat. "To lose your other half like that, I'm not sure I could risk it. Maybe I'm the scared one."

"Maybe I am too," Hawes admitted.

Helena had it wrong. Their grandmother was the strong and brave one. She'd sat at Cal's side, crying but never letting go of his hand until Amelia had confirmed he'd taken his last breath. And even then…

"She wouldn't look at me," Hawes whispered.

"She wouldn't look at any of us."

"What if she doesn't forgive—"

"Don't go there." Helena wrapped both her hands around his arm. "She wanted you to hold the health care power of attorney because she too knows you're the strong one."

He sure as hell didn't feel like the strong one right then. Unsteady, uncertain, reluctant. All better adjectives for the jitteriness inside him. The fact that he knew exactly what—*who*—he needed to steady him, troubled Hawes all the more.

TWELVE

I went ahead and let him in.

The text from Holt pinged as Hawes reached the front steps of his building. Just in time to stave off the swell of disappointment at not finding Dante waiting out front for him.

Because he was waiting inside.

Hawes realized it wasn't wise to depend on this man he hardly knew, but after the day he'd had—from Campbell's ominous warning, to the explosives sale gone sideways, to his grandfather's death and the fifty-nine times Hawes had had to sign his name since—he needed someone else to be the steady one for a little while.

He needed to let go after white-knuckling the oh-shit handle all day long.

He'd had his moment of weakness in the garden with Helena, but then he'd pulled it together and been the strong one they'd needed, doing his job as eldest child and official head of the family businesses. Rose was settled back at the house with her cats and Lily, funeral arrangements were in motion, and Amelia, Holt, and Helena had been fully briefed on the day's events.

Hawes was dead on his feet and dead inside. Dark to dark, he'd gone with barely a breather, the only bright spot the brief exchange with Dante that morning. He'd kill for that shower together now…

But dinner, it seemed, was first on the agenda tonight. The rich aromas of sesame oil, soy sauce, and chilies wafted down the hall, reminding Hawes that in the chaos of his very long day, he'd forgotten to eat. And reminding him of his conversation with Helena. Of his grandfather, who was now gone.

The pink box of pastries on the coffee table brought the memories on stronger, a tsunami that forced Hawes to brace a hand on the nearest pillar. "Who told you?"

Dante looked up from where he stood behind the kitchen island, emptying takeout cartons onto plates. "Your sister." He blindly tossed a crispy shrimp to Iris, who was stalking the tops of the cabinets on the kitchen side of the loft wall. "Since I was in Chinatown, I swung by my favorite place for the rest. You hungry?"

Yes, said his brain, but he couldn't get the word out past the lump in his throat, drowning as he was in comparisons between this day and the day his parents died. He'd had to make the call that day too, and afterward, he'd brought Holt and Helena home from the hospital, cooked them breakfast, and tucked them into bed. Only once they were asleep had he retreated to his bedroom and screamed into the pillows. Alone. After he'd taken care of everyone else.

Unlike that day seventeen years ago, he wasn't alone tonight. Dante was in his kitchen, dishing out food and treating his cat. Taking care of him. It was domestic, it was different, it was welcome, it was everything Hawes wanted, and his gut clenched in hope and fear. Was this—*Dante*—his chance at what Holt and Amelia, his parents, and his grandparents had enjoyed? A partner who got it, who understood and accepted what he did, and stood by his side? Who'd help him protect his family and the empire they'd built? But only until Dante found out what happened to Isabelle. Then Hawes figured he'd be staring down the barrel of his gun instead. He might finally get what he wanted, only to lose it, because that's how his luck had been going lately. Hell, most of his life.

"Hey, Madigan, where'd you go?"

Hawes blinked, surprised to find Dante no longer in the kitchen but standing right in front of him. He stared into those bottomless brown eyes—wonder, hope, and dread a paralyzing cocktail.

Dante lifted a hand and coasted it over his jaw. "You with me?"

Hawes blinked again, shaking himself from the daze, and turned his face into the offered warmth, nuzzling Dante's palm. "Thank you."

"I'll take that as a yes to the hungry question."

"I'm sorry. I'm just—"

Dante cut off his words with a quick yet thorough kiss that left Hawes panting and pressed between the pole at his back and Dante's hard body against his front. "Don't apologize for anything tonight," Dante murmured. "Feel what you need to feel."

Hawes wanted to feel more of Dante—the bare biceps under his hands, the silky hair tickling his cheek, the hard thigh between his legs—but he also wanted to wash away the day and feel clean. And judging by the embarrassingly loud grumble of his stomach, he also wanted to feel full.

Dante chuckled, the sound rumbly and sexy, and Hawes was tempted to tell hygiene and his stomach to go to hell, but then Dante stepped back and turned him toward the bathroom. "Go rinse off, and I'll have everything ready when you get back."

Hawes couldn't argue with that plan. Ten minutes later, when he came back into the living room, the kitchen lights were low, the Giants game was on, plates of steaming food were spread out on the coffee table, and two place settings were set up in front of the couch, a bottle of beer next to each.

"This okay?" Dante asked from where he sat on the couch. "I

wanted to see the end of the game, but we can move to the dining—"

"This is good." Hawes fluffed the damp top strands of his hair, then bent a leg under himself and sank onto the cushions next to Dante. "Perfect, actually."

Dante handed him a beer and gestured at the food. "Pick your poison."

"Bit of everything would be great." Hawes took a swig from the bottle, the pilsner cold and refreshing. "I'm not too picky when it comes to food."

"Could tell that from the cookbooks. You've got everything from slow cooker favorites to fine dining."

Hawes shrugged. "The haute cuisine books are mostly there for the pictures, though I've tried a few of the simpler recipes. Sauces and the like." He wedged the beer bottle between his legs and took the plate and chopsticks Dante handed him. "You know as well as I do, growing up in a city like this, every food and cuisine is out there to try. Whenever I found one I loved, I wanted to make it myself. Cal gave me my first cookbook on my eighth birthday. He bought me the last two months ago, on my thirty-third. Or I suppose Rose did, but regardless, I have them all still."

"Did you ever want to be a chef?"

Hawes washed down his bite of Szechuan beef with a swallow of beer. "I flirted with the idea, but I also enjoyed afternoons at MCS with my parents. I wanted that too. I liked that our family had its own business."

"And the other business?"

"Honest to God, by the time Cal sat me down and explained it all, I was just happy to know that my parents, who'd been gone a month then, were coming home, and that they weren't dead or getting a divorce. I couldn't figure out why sometimes one was gone and not the other, or both of them together, for long stretches of time. Knowing the truth, a lot of things finally made sense."

"How old were you?"

"Twelve."

Dante's mouth opened—he wanted to say something, make some judgment—but he held his tongue, or rather occupied it with noodles instead and turned his attention back to the game. During the next commercial, he loaded up his plate with seconds. "Tell me about him, Papa Cal, and not the stories everybody knows."

Hawes lowered his chopsticks. "I don't want—"

"Trust me." Dante slid back into the cushions beside Hawes. "It'll make you feel better."

Hawes wasn't so sure about that, but the box of pastries on the corner of the table was an easy story he could share. Each story after that became easier, telling them between bites of fried shrimp, spicy beef, noodles, and then mooncakes. How Papa Cal had painstakingly restored every element of the Pac Heights house, and how Hawes's mother had spent hours with Cal, laying the entryway's mosaic tile, piece by piece, ultimately winning him over. How he'd regularly taken each of the grandkids to the office to see how the business was run. How, until the past few years, he'd taken Rose out to Tadich Grill every year on the anniversary of their first date. Then how Rose had brought the meal to him, once he'd been unable to go out anymore. How memory would flit through his eyes during those moments.

The stories went on, long past the food and the game, and what emerged was the picture of a patient, loving man when it came to his family, his friends, the waitstaff at restaurants, the neighbors up the street, the employees at his company. A counterweight to the quick, swift death he doled out in the shadows, that made him and the Madigan name feared in certain criminal circles. It was a balance, Hawes realized, one he was trying to recreate for himself and their family, albeit in a slightly different manner.

Dante reached out and brushed back the hair that had fallen over Hawes's forehead. "You know what you're going to say for the eulogy now?"

Hawes gaped at him. "How'd you know?"

"Who else would it be? You're the one who holds it together." His hand drifted down to cup Hawes's cheek. "I'm getting the sense you always have been."

"Doesn't feel like that." He closed his eyes and rested the weight of his head, his world, in the palm of Dante's hand. "Almost everything that could go wrong today did."

The statement begged the question, and Hawes expected the investigator to ask it. Instead, Dante curled his hand around Hawes's neck and drew him closer. "Well…then let's make something go right."

Right was Dante's mouth on his, deep and searching like their kiss that morning. Right was Dante gently pushing him back into the cushions so he could straddle Hawes's lap. Right was Hawes's hands touching every part of Dante he could reach. Over his hard chest and broad shoulders. Along his strong bearded jaw. Through the long strands of hair Hawes released from Dante's topknot, a curtain of brown waves falling around them.

Hawes could have stayed like that for hours, kissing and touching, except that their rolling hips reminded him of another something that would be oh-so-right. "I owe you a favor," he mumbled against Dante's lips. He slipped a hand between them and grasped Dante's erection through his jeans.

Dante grasped his wrist and pulled Hawes away from his prize, pinning his hand to the couch cushions instead. "This is about what you need tonight."

"I need this." Hawes thrust his hips up, his erection through his track pants nudging Dante's. He didn't care how needy he seemed, how desperate. If Dante was offering, Hawes wasn't holding back. He'd walked in here tonight feeling dead inside, but with Dante on his lap, kissing up and down his neck, he was burning up. Alive. He did not want that fire to go out. He clenched Dante's hand, drawing his smoldering gaze. "I need to taste you," Hawes said with another roll of his hips. "I want to return the favor."

One side of Dante's mouth ticked up. "All right, not gonna

argue that offer." He climbed off Hawes's lap, pushed the coffee table back with his bare foot, and stripped without preamble or modesty.

Dante standing naked before him gave *sexy* a whole new meaning.

Honest to God, Hawes didn't know where to look. The long legs and powerful thighs dusted with dark, wiry hair. The miles of ripped torso and fucking eight-pack abs. The light sprinkling of hair at the center of Dante's chest—even broader out of its tank— or the line of hair that ran from his indented belly button, down his pelvis between cut hip bones, to the dark patch of hair around his erect cock. A ruddier tone of olive, it was thick and long, with a vein running up one side and moisture pearling in the slit. Scratch that, Hawes did know where to look. The same place he wanted to taste. His mouth watered.

"Like what you see?" Dante rumbled above him.

Stripping off his tee, Hawes slid to the edge of the couch and spread his legs on either side of Dante's. Head tipped back, he shot Dante an incredulous look. "Has anyone ever said no to that question?"

"Not since high school."

Even then, Hawes doubted that once a person got a look at Dante's cock, they'd care overly much about his lanky limbs or then-unbalanced features. Teenage Hawes sure as fuck wouldn't have cared. As far as Adult Hawes was concerned, all those now-balanced, handsome features were window dressing compared to what he wanted right here, to the man Dante was proving to be. Except maybe the hair, which Hawes was rather attached to already.

And while he couldn't reach the long strands on Dante's head from where he sat, Hawes could treat his fingertips to the springy hair on his legs, to the muscles in his powerful quads, to his firm, round ass cheeks. He cupped Dante's generous backside, hauled him forward, and shoved his face into the crease between thigh and groin. Intoxicating, the powerful, musky scent tinged with a hint of eucalyptus body wash. Dante personified. The guy who rode a Harley, always had a book on him, looked and strutted like a rock star, and carried a pistol, knife, and cuffs. A mystery.

Hawes flicked out his tongue; the mystery tasted even better than he'd imagined. Fuck, he could live right there. Could forget everything and drown in Dante. In the smell, taste, and heat of his skin. In the blood thumping in Hawes's own ears, and in the two points of pleasure and pain dominating his present existence—Dante's cock brushing his cheek and his own achingly hard dick trapped in his pants.

Fingers wove softly through his hair. "You with me?" Dante asked again, voice both gentle and rough.

"Can I stay here?"

"Sure, but fair warning, you're gonna get come on your cheek in another minute or so."

That didn't sound so bad, though what a fucking waste. Hawes tilted his head back and raked his gaze up Dante's flushed torso. Power and desire surged through him at finding Dante's face equally heated. "Can't have that," Hawes said with a smirk.

Dante's answering laugh morphed into a moan as Hawes tongued the underside of his cock. He closed his lips around the head and sucked it into his mouth, the smell and taste of Dante kicked up a thousand. Wanting more, Hawes relaxed his throat and swallowed as much of Dante as he could before triggering his gag reflex. He fisted the base of Dante's cock to make up the difference and began working him over, savoring every ridge his tongue skirted over, every bead of tangy precome that tickled his taste buds, every one of Dante's moans that echoed in his ears. They grew louder, the thrust of Dante's hips more urgent as Hawes trailed a hand over Dante's ass, fingers sneaking into his crack to tease his hole. Hawes wanted to push inside, desperately, but the supplies he needed to make this good for both of them were in his room.

Not that this wasn't already amazing.

Dante gently squeezed his scalp, not directing but enough to get Hawes's attention. "You have boxers on under those track pants?"

"Nuh-uh," Hawes grunted around his cock.

"Pull it out. Jack yourself."

Best idea ever. Using his hand that was already slick with spit, Hawes shoved down the waistband of his pants and took hold of his cock, groaning in relief.

A shudder rippled through Dante, and his cock inside Hawes's mouth grew harder. "Get there, Madigan. Hurry." His hand slipped out of Hawes's hair and down his neck, lightly grasping his nape like a collar.

Hawes pressed into it, reveling in the added support and the rhythm Dante set for them. He sucked up and down, in time with his own fist, speed ratcheting up in intervals until he couldn't hold back his release any longer. Come spilled over his fingers, sticky and warm, and he groaned out his pleasure around Dante's cock.

"Ah, Christ," Dante cursed, body curling over Hawes's, both hands landing on his shoulders.

He needed Hawes to return the favor, to steady him, and it was enough for Hawes to stave off the oncoming postcoital fog. He just needed to push Dante the rest of the way over the edge, and then they could drift there together. He cupped Dante's balls with his come-covered hand and tugged. Dante thrust forward with a shout, coming over Hawes's tongue and down his throat. Salty, pungent, hot—all the flavors of Dante in one potent mixture. A mystery Hawes could happily spend years solving.

THIRTEEN

An increasingly familiar sight greeted Hawes the next morning. Holt and Helena were milling around his living area while Dante made himself at home in the kitchen. After getting a surprisingly good few hours of sleep, Hawes had left Dante snoring on his couch in the wee hours of the morning. Once awake, Hawes was doomed to tossing and turning, and he didn't want his insomnia to doom Dante too. Or his nightmare mumblings to unintentionally reveal the truth about Isabelle's death. He'd retreated to his bed to starfish on his own, until Holt had texted a half hour ago to say he and Helena were headed over. Hawes had gotten up to do his business. Dante too by the looks of it. Hair up in a loose bun, he was dressed and at work behind the stove.

"Is this also becoming a thing?" Hawes said from where he stood at the other end of the island, admiring.

Dante grinned back at him. "They're not trying to kill me this time."

"Not yet, Mr. Hair," Helena said as she claimed a barstool.

"Play nice," Hawes chided. He gave her a peck on the cheek, then made a beeline for the coffee maker.

Dante passed him in the narrow space, and Hawes instinctively lifted a hand, fingers itching to trail over Dante's back. But with his siblings in the room, he wasn't sure how they or Dante would react.

Dante answered the question for him, stealing a quick kiss on his way back to the stove, bag of shredded cheese in hand. "You'll need to make more coffee." He cut a look to the dining table, where Holt was typing furiously on his laptop. "Someone drank the first batch."

"Yes, please," Helena chirped from her stool, voice at odds with her narrowed, assessing eyes. She definitely hadn't missed the brief exchange.

Coffee before deadly sister. Hawes moved Dante's book clear of the machine, refilled it with water and fresh grounds, and pressed Brew.

"Rough night with Lily?" Hawes called to his brother.

"Rough night all around." Holt finished typing, then shifted to straddle the bench. "Got her down about an hour ago. Grandma's watching her. She seems to be one of the few things that brings Rose some comfort too."

"And Amelia?"

"Hospital. She thought it was more important to take time off for the funeral tomorrow and through the weekend."

For better or worse, Papa Cal's declining health meant funeral arrangements had been on standby. Hawes just had to sign the papers and give them the go-ahead yesterday. Everything had come together quickly.

The coffee maker beeped right as Dante flipped off the stove. "Mug's waiting for you on the table. Take that on over"—he nodded at the coffeepot—"and I'll be right behind you with the food."

Hawes peeked around him. "What did you make?"

"Egg scramble out of what you had in the fridge." He sprinkled the shredded cheese liberally on top. "Didn't have time to bake it into a frittata."

"This weekend?"

"That could be arranged. You'd owe me another favor."

"I'm good with that." Favors worked out well for both of them. Hawes grabbed the coffeepot with one hand and trailed the other over Dante's lower back as he'd wanted to do earlier.

Helena didn't miss that exchange either. She slid off her stool and matched Hawes's stride across the living room. "This is all very domestic." Assessing for sure, cautious too, which in a way, Hawes was glad to see after her defeated manner yesterday. This was the sister he knew.

"You told him about the mooncakes," Hawes said.

"You needed someone last night." Empathy eclipsed her vigilance, but only for a second. "Keep your guard up."

Definitely getting back to her usual self. And she was right. He couldn't let hope for a future he'd thought impossible make him complacent.

"You gonna stand there with the coffee all day or pour?" Holt said, holding out his mug for a refill.

"Are you sure you need one?" Hawes replied. "Or do you want to crash for an hour on the couch?"

"Nap sounds good, but we need to go through all this first." A mess of scattered folders and papers were spread between the four place settings.

This did not look paperless. "What is *all this*?"

Dante set the cast-iron skillet down on a trivet at the end of the table and began dishing out eggs. "While you all were dealing with matters yesterday, I did some digging."

"Why didn't you tell me about this last night?" Hawes asked.

"I mentioned that I was working on my end of things. But the details were not what you needed then."

The instinct was there to argue, which was good, but it was better that Dante had waited to tell him. Now he was clearheaded and ready to tackle whatever this was. "Did you find out anything about an investigation?"

"Nothing recent."

"What did you find?"

"Several avenues of investigation were opened five years ago."

Dante handed him three folders. "Health department, SFPD, and ATF." The usual suspects, given their various enterprises. "They went nowhere at that time. Ditto three years ago when investigations were reopened. The timing in both cases can't be discounted."

"When I stepped in for Cal," Hawes said.

"And after Isabelle's death," Dante added.

"They were looking for a way in," Helena said.

"Likely," Dante said. "If they'd found anything, they would have tried to use it against you. See if you'd bend or break."

Sausage, peppers, and eggs didn't taste so delicious anymore. Hawes forced down a bite with his coffee. "They wouldn't have gotten anywhere."

"I went back into the computer logs from then." Holt rotated his laptop so Hawes could see the screen. "Multiple pings and attacks. We shut it down—they didn't get through my firewalls—but someone was trying."

Hawes glanced at Dante. How much to disclose in his presence? The PI had been digging, he knew what they did, and he was still here, helping them. They'd be at cross-purposes soon, but at this juncture, they'd gain more by Dante being in on more of the story. Across the table, Holt seemed to reach the same conclusion, his eyes flickering to Dante, then to Hawes, followed by a nod.

"Okay, but all these investigations were in the past." Hawes nudged the folders with his mug. "Campbell said he saw a folder on the judge's desk *last month*. Why would the judge have any of these out?" He turned to Helena. "Did it sound to you like he was talking about an old case?"

"No," she answered. "I definitely got the impression it was current."

"Maybe one of the cases was reopened," Dante said. "Someone who thinks they can get to you another way, for a different reason."

"Cal's declining health."

"But you've been in control for five years."

"And all of a sudden I'm being challenged internally too."

Helena nudged the files back in his direction. "Maybe because an insider knows about these."

"The meet yesterday," Holt spoke up. "You said it yourself, Hawes. If we'd signed those documents and turned over the property…"

"And if Gillespie had given them access to it…" Hawes propped his elbows on the table and scrubbed his hands over his face. "Fuck, and I was trying to move the prototypes out of the organization."

Helena grasped his wrists and lowered his hands. "*We* were, and obviously, someone doesn't like that."

Didn't like how he was handling the organization at all. "Whoever it is, were they trying to eliminate me so the investigation didn't proceed? Or were they the tipster?"

"Doesn't matter," Helena said. "You're gone either way. Even if Madigan Cold Storage goes away, our other associates won't. They'll just reform under a new leader."

All because he wanted to do things right. "I'm trying to make things better. Cleaner. So there's less chance of collateral damage, less chance of an investigation. I'm trying to stop another—" Isabelle Costa. He cut himself off from saying her name aloud, not willing to go that far yet with Dante in the room.

"By eliminating the most lucrative part of the business," Holt said, wisely skipping over Hawes's near slip and reiterating his point from yesterday.

Hawes bolted up from the table, cursing.

Dante caught his wrist. "You're not gonna like what I say next."

"Seems to be a habit too."

"Not always," he said with a smirk. That crooked smile, together with the sure hold around his wrist, reined in Hawes's rising agitation. Until his next words. "I don't think you should go to your grandfather's funeral."

"But the eulogy. You helped—"

Dante squeezed his wrist. "I didn't have the whole story."

"Hawes—" Helena started.

Hawes brought his other palm down on the table, hard enough to rattle the dishes. "Absolutely not. The last thing I'm going to do is show weakness. And I won't disappoint Rose." He straightened, and Dante released his wrist. "Besides, didn't we begin this week with the idea of flushing out the traitors?"

Holt gulped. "At Papa Cal's funeral?"

"Hopefully not. Of course I don't want it disrupted, but either way, we're done with this bullshit," Hawes declared. "This organization is ours now. No one is going to take it from us."

"One of you has to stay behind," Dante said. "In case an attack does occur at the funeral."

Hawes and Helena spoke at the same time. "Holt."

"Why can't it be Amelia?" their brother protested.

"You need to be the one with Lily," Hawes said. "Out of all of us, your hands are the cleanest. You have the best chance of staying with her." Hawes walked around the table and held his brother's face in his hands. "You two are our legacy. I'm not letting anything happen to either of you."

FOURTEEN

Amelia turned from the front windows and straightened her black dress. "The cars are here."

Holt, dressed in jeans, tee, and a flannel, scooted to the edge of the chair where he sat with Lily. "Are you sure I can't go?"

Beside him, Hawes brushed his fingers over Lily's head. "You need to stay here, for her." He hated asking his brother to skip their grandfather's funeral. Papa Cal and Holt had been close. After their parents' deaths, Holt had floundered, and it had been Cal who'd suggested he enlist rather than go to college. It had been the right call. Holt had found his purpose, and the benefits were still paying off. Hawes could never thank Cal enough for that guidance. What he could do was protect Holt and his legacy. "We talked about this."

"I know. I just—"

Amelia laid a hand on Holt's shoulder. "I'll stay too."

She didn't look any happier at the prospect. Of all of them, she'd been closest to Cal. He'd recruited her ten years ago, a young nurse who hadn't blinked at his injuries when he'd turned up in her ER. She didn't blink either when he'd asked her not to call the cops. She'd been their on-call nurse from then on, and once Cal learned what she could do with pressure points—and with a troubled Holt when no one else could reach him after he'd returned home from the service—Amelia had been welcomed into the family. Then last year she'd given them the greatest gift of all: Lily.

Holt shook his head. "Grandma needs you."

Rose had seemed weaker since Cal's death, not unexpected when one lost their other half. Amelia had kept close watch, as she had over Cal.

"And with you there," Holt added, "I will be too." He dipped his face to kiss her knuckles.

The quiet comfort they shared made Hawes's chest ache. Ninety-nine percent of the time he was happy for his brother, but in that one remaining percent, jealousy always reared its head at the most inconvenient moments. He walked over to the window and braced his arm on the intricate casing. He wished the man out there, behind the wheel of Holt's SUV, was in here with him. He considered sending a text to ask for an update. Anything to reestablish the connection, to call up the steadiness that, over the past day of making plans for this one, had eroded. Had deteriorated further overnight as he'd stayed here with his family rather than with Dante.

Hawes reached for his phone but was diverted by the *tap-tap* of cat claws and the *click-clack* of high heels on the stairs. With the cats in the lead, Helena was on her way down with Rose on her arm. Hawes met them at the bottom of the stairs, and his grandmother, for the first time since the night before Papa Cal passed, lifted her face and met his eyes.

Her blue ones, the same icy shade as his, were weary yet determined. She'd done her grieving, and now she was ready to move forward. She'd been the same after Hawes's parents' deaths. Torn up privately, until it was time to present the public face of the family. She'd been Hawes's best teacher in that regard.

"You'll honor him today." Not a request—a demand.

"I'm ready." Because Dante had helped him get there.

"Good." She shifted from Helena's arm to his. "You'll do him proud."

Hawes's relief was palpable. Rose's approval mattered more to him than anyone's now. Cal's expanding ventures would have failed if not for her tireless efforts at making the social and political connections they needed to succeed, on both fronts. There'd be no legacy without her either, and while Hawes and his siblings were changing the way things were done, he didn't want her to think he was ruining or disrespecting everything she and Papa Cal had built.

On their way out, they stopped by a tormented Holt and snoozing Lily, Rose giving each a kiss on the cheek. Hawes did the same, kissing the tops of their heads, then escorted their grandmother outside, where July was back to normal in San Francisco. Cold and foggy. They took the stairs slowly, and at the curb, Rose insisted he ride in the town car with her, Avery at the wheel. Helena and Amelia would ride in the car ahead of them, Zoe driving. Hawes had figured Rose would want Amelia or Helena with her, but as long as he and Helena were in separate cars, they were keeping with the plan.

The plan that had Kane in an unmarked cruiser across the street, popping caramels and keeping an eye on Holt and Lily, and Dante in the SUV behind the two town cars. Hawes caught Dante's gaze in the rearview mirror. Brown eyes held his, and Hawes let the steadiness he'd missed wash over him. The next few hours didn't seem so daunting.

St. Patrick's had been packed for Papa Cal's funeral. It seemed all of Pac Heights had come down the hill to the giant red-brick cathedral where Hawes's grandfather had worshipped his entire life. Since safety concerns had forced them to forego the separate wake and graveside service, everyone who'd wanted to pay their respects had attended the service and waited in the receiving line after, their numbers spilling out into the church's courtyards. An hour after the service had ended, there were still people milling around his grandmother at the church's side doors. Off a bit from the crowd, Hawes rested against the metal rail at the bottom of the steps and surveyed the scene for anything amiss.

"So far so good," Helena said as she descended the steps. She leaned next to him and covered his hand. "The eulogy was beautiful."

"Thank you." Hawes ducked his chin, but only for a moment, before lifting his eyes and scanning their surroundings again. "I wanted to do him justice, as our grandfather. I wanted them to see who he was to us."

"Thank you for doing that and for handling everything. Like you always do." She patted his hand. "We ask a lot, and we forget to ask if you're okay."

"I'm okay, promise." He bumped her shoulder. "Just tired and ready for this to all be over."

"I'm glad nothing happened to disrupt the ceremony."

Hawes was too. He wanted to flush out the traitors, but he also wanted to honor his grandfather in peace. They'd gotten that much. Now he wanted to get his family home safely and move on to securing control, once and for all.

"Call up the cars," he said. "Let's wrap this up and get back to the fort."

She nodded and pulled out her phone, while Hawes corralled Rose and Amelia. "I'm sorry to interrupt," he said, smiling politely at the few lingering neighbors. "But the cars are on their way around. Time for us to go."

They said their goodbyes, Amelia confirmed next week's burial of the ashes with the priest, and Rose took Hawes's arm again as they descended the steps. "You could have done that thirty minutes ago."

"I was trying to be polite."

"I'm too tired for polite." She gave him more of her weight as they crossed the square to where the two town cars were parked at the curb. "I just want to get home, get out of these blasted heels, and see my great-grandbaby. You'll ride with me again."

"Yes, ma'am." It was more personality than she'd displayed in months, a glimpse of his spitfire grandmother from before Cal's condition had declined. Hawes was glad to see that life coming back to her, even if she did sound bone-tired. He opened the back door of the second car for her, watched as Amelia and Helena disappeared into the lead car, then waited until Dante swung the SUV around behind them before sliding into the back seat next to Rose. "To the house, please," he told Avery.

"Shouldn't take us more than twenty," Avery replied as they eased into the light traffic. "We're ahead of rush hour."

Five minutes later, just over Market, past the Theatre District curve, and waiting behind Amelia and Helena's car at an intersection, the hit Hawes expected finally came, but not from the direction he'd anticipated. He was discussing dinner plans with Rose when their car was rammed—from behind.

"What the hell?" He twisted in his seat, glaring through the back window at Dante, who slammed into the rear of their town car again.

"What the fuck's he doing?" Avery hollered over a crunch from the front end. "He's pushing us into them."

Hawes whipped back around, glancing out the front windshield. The force of Dante's repeated hits was plowing their car into the back end of his sister's ride.

"He's waving his phone," Rose said.

Hawes spun, looking again out of the back window. Face fraught with alarm, Dante was thrusting his phone toward the windshield and shouting words Hawes couldn't hear as he continued to ram their car, pushing them forward, into the intersection.

"Check your phone." That's what Dante was shouting.

Hawes dug his phone out of his pocket. The screen was lit with a group text from Holt. **Calls blocked. Car bomb incoming**.

Avery saw it the same instant Hawes did. A utility van shoving its way through cars, no regard for scraped paint or broken mirrors. Her foot moved from the brake to the gas. With traffic behind them, forward was the only direction they could go. Dante wasn't pushing them into the intersection. He was trying to push them through it. Before the van reached them.

"Go, go, go!" Hawes shouted, beating the back of the passenger seat.

In front of them, Zoe had gotten the same message and hit the gas, zooming the rest of the way through the intersection.

Behind them, Dante was pushing them out of the intersection and driving the SUV into the path of the oncoming van. Into the path of the bomb.

Oh God, no.

"We need to divert," Hawes yelled. "A different direction from Zoe. Get off the main streets." That was the best hope of drawing the van off Dante and minimizing collateral damage.

On the other side of the intersection, Avery broke left, and the van took the bait, swerving past Dante and onto a parallel side street, matching their direction and starting a game of block-by-block hopscotch. They stayed ahead of the van, just barely, thanks to Avery's driving skills, but they were going to run into traffic again soon.

Hawes's phone vibrated in his hand. **Bring him up Shannon. Trap**, read the message from Helena.

He gave the order, and Avery aimed them that direction, now herding the van. The van took the bait, thinking it was getting ahead. Avery gunned the engine, pushing them fast up Leavenworth, passing by the nose of the van at the intersection of Post and Jones. Then Avery hung a hard right onto Shannon, the back end of the car fishtailing.

The van's tires squealed behind them, but it righted at the last second, chasing them down the narrow alley. Hawes held his breath through the intersection at Geary, car horns blaring all around them. They made it through, the van still on their tail. As they cleared the first set of buildings, a flash of blonde appeared on the left. Helena, gun in hand, stood on the hood of the town car at the mouth of a parking lot. Then on the right, brown hair and denim, Dante taking a similar position in front of the SUV, in the lot on the other side of the street. Avery sped through the trap, and Hawes twisted in his seat, watching as the van did not, Helena getting its tires on one side, Dante the other. The van swerved and toppled over, glass shattering, metal scraping concrete, twisting and turning until Hawes could see the under-carriage.

And the timer and trigger attached to it.

0:05 in bright red digits.

Not enough time.

He banged the back of the passenger seat again. "Go!"

Hawes took one last look out the back window—watched his sister catwalk over the top of her car while Dante hauled ass the opposite direction, each of them taking cover in their respective parking lots—then dove forward, taking his grandmother down to the floorboard with him.

The blast behind them threw their car into the air, and gravity ceased to exist.

FIFTEEN

Sixty-two.

Hawes turned on his heel at the nurses' station and started back the other direction on lap sixty-three.

Helena stopped him halfway, nails digging into his biceps. "Enough, Big H. You're gonna wear a hole through this hideous floor."

"You think I'm the first person to pace this hallway?" He tried to wrench his arm free and failed. His sister's hold was expertly positioned to exert more pressure the harder he tried to escape. He shot her an annoyed glare and tapped his toe on the linoleum. "Floor's still here."

"Then take it easy on me. The circling is making me woozy."

He lowered his heel, and his ire, and studied his sister. She'd washed up after they'd arrived at the hospital, and with her makeup gone and damp hair in a bun, the week's strain showed on her pale, dainty face. Dark circles under her eyes, a deep groove between her brows, freckles that stood out more prominently across the bridge of her nose. He'd neglected to ask after her too. "Fuck, Hena, how hard have you been going this week?"

She let go of his arm and sank into the nearest bright-orange chair. "I've been working every contact I have on our shit, managing Brax, and also trying to move matters at work. I don't want to leave any clients in the lurch if we have to scramble."

Helena's legal work involved acquitting the wrongfully accused. If Helena ghosted on her clients, it could mean the difference between life and death. Hawes couldn't begrudge them or her that, otherwise all his efforts to minimize collateral damage were for naught. No innocent lives lost, period.

He lowered himself into the chair next to her and threw an arm around her shoulders. "I'm sorry. I should have asked sooner."

"You've been going hard too. All of us have."

"And yet you still saved my ass today." He kissed the top of her head. "Thanks for that."

"Thank Mr. Hair. He came up with that trap plan."

Hawes squeezed her tighter. "He wouldn't have had to if I'd listened to him in the first place."

Wouldn't have had to put himself in the path of the charging van or in the blast radius with the rest of them. Dante had been the first to reach them after too. He'd helped Avery out of their tipped car, and then the three of them had extracted an unconscious Rose and handed her over to Amelia to treat until the paramedics arrived. He and Dante had shared a single smoke-tinged kiss before fire trucks had come barreling down the alley. They'd only exchanged a few words and texts since, Dante staying on the scene while Hawes rode with Rose, Amelia, and Helena to the hospital. Where their grandmother now lay unconscious in a room across the hall.

"I made the wrong call and put all of us at risk. Maybe I shouldn't be in charge."

Helena drew back, litigator face on. "Don't be ridiculous."

But Hawes was on a roll, all the self-recriminations he'd banked tumbling out. "If I'd ceded power to you or Holt earlier, or hell, if I'd just stayed away today like Dante suggested, maybe there wouldn't have been an attack. Maybe our grandmother wouldn't be in there fighting for her life."

"Don't be so dramatic." Amelia stepped out of Rose's room and closed the door behind her. "She'll be fine."

"Is she awake yet?"

Amelia nodded, and Hawes shot out of the chair.

"Can I—"

At Amelia's quelling look, he shut up and sat back down.

"The doctor is checking her vitals. You can go in, one at a time, when he's done."

A baby's wail cut through the hospital noises, and Amelia was in motion before Holt and Lily even rounded the corner. They reached each other, and Holt wrapped Amelia in his arms, Lily between them.

Hawes forced down the wave of bile that stung his throat. "Fuck," he cursed low. "I could have taken her from them too."

"But you didn't," Helena said. "And you kept Holt and Lily out of the line of fire."

That didn't make Hawes feel much better. Neither did the dark look in Holt's eyes.

"Where's your guard?" Hawes asked before his brother could speak.

"At the crime scene doing his job." Holt handed Lily to Amelia. "He's on the warpath. Today could have been a lot worse."

Hawes expected no less from Kane. This was the very definition of tits-up. While they'd alerted him to a possible incident, the actual attack had been less contained and potentially more destructive than they'd anticipated. If that van had exploded near St. Patrick's or on a busier street, the body count would be much higher than just the driver. Hawes pinched the bridge of his nose, as if that would miraculously ease the headache pounding at the base of his skull.

"We need to talk." Holt's clipped voice was as dark as his eyes. "Someplace private."

"We can use an on-call room," Amelia said. She popped her head back into Rose's room, let the doctor know they'd return shortly, then led them into an unmarked room around the corner. It was a tight fit with the two sets of bunk beds and small vanity, but it worked for what it was lacking—no cameras and no listening devices.

Holt and Amelia settled on one of the beds, Helena on the other, and Hawes leaned against the door. "How did you know?" he asked Holt. "About the car bomb."

"We sent an operative to move the explosives out of the warehouse, like we talked about, while all eyes were on the funeral." Holt's face drained of color. "Except there weren't any explosives there to move."

"They're gone?" It only took a second for Hawes to jump to the next logical, horrible conclusion. "They were going to kill us with our own bombs?"

"Some of them. The rest... We don't know where those are."

Not an inconsequential amount of firepower out there in God only knew whose hands. Fuck, this was the last thing they needed right now. "How was the building accessed without us knowing?"

"Someone's in my system. Alarms were deactivated, and there are multiple surveillance-footage gaps. I should have caught it sooner." Holt hung his head, skimming both hands over it. "I don't think it's anyone in my shop. I've triple-checked, and there are zero red flags. It's someone outside, but fuck if I can figure out who."

"How'd you link it to the van?" Helena asked.

"I was monitoring your cars the entire trip. You hit Market, and the van darted out like a shot." Holt hugged Amelia close. "Saw that too many times in the desert not to recognize it for what it was."

Hawes crossed to Holt's other side and clasped his shoulder. "You did good today. Thank you."

"It'll take Brax a few days to ID the driver by dental records," Helena said. "Can we do it sooner? Traffic or ATM cams?"

"Analyzing," Holt said. "And I'm looking for ghosts of the

missing warehouse footage." He shifted his gaze to Hawes. "There's something else." That dark look had crept back into his eyes, and Hawes sensed he wasn't going to like what came next. "I'm not sure we can trust Dante."

Hawes stepped back and folded his arms. "Did you miss the part where he helped save our lives today?"

Amelia glared from her husband's side. "Hawes."

Holt, though, had enough anger for both of them. "No, I didn't miss that," he bit back. "Not a single damn second of it while Dante had me on the SUV's speaker as it was happening. He was the only one I could get through to."

Shit, Hawes hadn't known he'd been listening. He'd thought Holt had been in touch via the group chat only. He forced his hackles back down. "I'm sorry. It's just… He's done nothing to jeopardize us."

"That we know of," Helena said.

Holt continued before Hawes could reply. "I don't think he's working with the person trying to pull off this coup, but he still hasn't given us a good explanation for what he's doing here."

Hawes couldn't deny any of what Holt had said. He also couldn't deny he needed Dante. Needed his steady presence as everything else continued to unravel. Needed him most in moments when he didn't want to be the king. He couldn't do it twenty-four seven and keep his humanity. "Does it matter, if he's helping us flush out who that person is?"

"What if they're manipulating him too?" Helena said. "What if it's another way to weaken you?"

"You sent him to me the other night."

It wasn't a fair rejoinder. All bets had been off that night. She'd been trying to help him and had cautioned him again the next morning. He expected an icy response for his sharp retort, but she cast her gaze aside instead. Her shoulders slumped to match. "We all make mistakes."

"He *thinks* he's after what happened to Isabelle," Holt said, redirecting Hawes's attention from Helena's uncharacteristic concession. "That's his mission. It's stamped on his fucking card case."

"Wait. What?"

"I saw it in the restaurant footage from Sunday. 23:01 is stamped on one side of his leather card case. Isabelle's time of death."

"And you're just now telling me this?" Hawes nearly shouted.

Holt raised his hands, palms out. "Like I said, it's his mission. He's not hidden that from us, but I'm not sure who he's helping or who he's working for."

Hawes stiffened. "What else do you have?"

Holt withdrew his arm from around Amelia and stood. His massive form, unfolded, made the small room seem even smaller. "Brax ran the bullet from the alley Sunday night."

"Dante said it couldn't be traced."

"It was. To a federal evidence locker."

Hawes's heart skipped a beat. "Stolen?"

"Or accessed."

His heart skipped another beat, before his pulse kicked into overdrive. "You think he's a fed?" If Hawes had compromised them, he'd never forgive himself.

"There's no evidence of that, that I can find," Holt replied. "But how'd he get those bullets from a federal lockup? How did he get those investigation files? He's tied in."

"He's a PI, born and raised here," Hawes countered, grasping at straws. "He's bound to have connections."

"Or he's not who he says he is."

"What's that supposed to mean? He's not a PI? We have the licenses."

"I'm not sure if he's Dante Perry at all." Holt tapped at his phone a few times, then handed it to Hawes. It was the yearbook page they'd previously examined. "There's something wrong with that picture."

Hawes squinted and tried to see something other than the dark eyes, long nose, and angled jaw he'd come to know the past week. It was a younger version, but it was the same man. "That's definitely him. It's all the same features. He's not wearing any prosthetics to disguise them."

"I agree," Holt said. "But I could swear it's been altered. I'm having a hard copy of the yearbook sent to the house. I want to see it for myself."

Eyes closed, mind whirling, Hawes fell back against the door. He'd trusted Dante, more each day as this crazy week had gone on. Had he been wrong to do so? Was the future he'd begun to let himself hope for a figment of his imagination? Was Dante Perry?

DANTE WAS WAITING FOR HIM OUT FRONT WHEN HAWES RETURNED TO the condo. He pushed up from the step, tucked a folder under his arm, and fell into step beside Hawes. "What'd I do to piss off the gatekeeper?"

"Holt thinks you're a fed." No sense hiding the ball. Hawes had meant what he'd said earlier today. He was done with this shit, from all angles. "Or at the very least, that you're not who you claim to be."

Dante ran a hand through his hair and shook it out. Strategically so the thick fall of strands hid his face from the security cameras. No one, Holt included, could read his lips or hear him say, voice low, "And I think he's your traitor."

Hawes's bluster vanished, as did his breath. He would've missed the next step if Dante hadn't wound an arm around his waist.

"Let's get inside," Dante said, "and I'll explain."

But by the time they reached the second floor and Dante closed the condo door behind them, Hawes had wrangled his surprise and was flexing his anger. One safety net after another had been ripped out from under him, and now Dante wanted to rip away one of the few remaining, one of the most dependable.

He stalked into the living room and rounded on Dante. "Before you accuse my brother, explain yourself. Who are you?"

"Dante Perry. We've been through this. You've done the background checks. What did Holt find now to make you question me?" He tossed his folder on the dining table and straddled the bench.

Lower than Hawes and out of his direct path. De-escalation 101. Unfortunately, Hawes was way past de-escalation, too wound up from the day's events. "The bullet from the alley," he snapped. "You were wrong. It was traced to a federal evidence locker."

"According to Holt."

"According to Kane."

"Did you ask Kane?"

No, the chief had been too busy barking questions at him, but that wasn't the point here. Dante's deflection—his nonanswer— was. "Where'd the bullet come from?" he demanded.

"Pawn shop. Same place I got my gun. Guy threw the ammo in for free. Guess now I know why."

A plausible enough answer, but not the only thing that required an explanation. "Holt also thinks your yearbook picture is doctored."

Groaning, Dante covered his face with his hands. "Please tell me you did not unearth that thing."

Hawes stopped right in front of him. "Something you don't want me to find there?"

Dante dropped his hands, letting them dangle between his knees. A bright blush streaked over his cheekbones. "The worst years of my life, memorialized in print forever, and apparently now also digitized."

Hawes dug out his phone and opened the screenshot Holt had sent him. He shoved the device under Dante's nose. "That you?"

He took one look and glanced up at Hawes. "Of course it's me. Pinocchio nose and all. Right between the smoking-hot quarterback, Trey Palmer, and his girlfriend, head cheerleader Jenn

Petrie. Let me tell you how awkward that was, passing their love notes back and forth in homeroom, sucking him off in the locker room after fifth period, then taking her to prom."

Hawes flipped the phone in his grip and slid the line of pictures left so he could read the names. He spread his fingers on the screen to zoom in. Richard Palmer III. Dante Perry. Jennifer Petrie. The names weren't visible before; Dante hadn't seen them. Hell, he'd barely even looked at the screen. Relief unknotted Hawes's shoulders, and irony sent a brow climbing. "Jocks and cheerleaders?"

Dante shrugged and gave him a half smile. "I was seventeen. They were hot." He lifted an arm, curled a hand over Hawes's hip, and tugged him between his spread knees. "Your brother is seeing ghosts. Or he's trying to put doubts in your mind to distract you."

The relief dissipated. "From what?"

Dante put his other hand on Hawes's opposite hip. "From the fact that he wasn't there today. That the explosives went missing on his watch."

Unsteady, Hawes clasped one of Dante's forearms. "He warned us."

Dante drew him closer. "Scared you too, didn't it? Maybe into thinking you should step down?"

Hawes closed his eyes, recalling his conversation with Helena. That's exactly what he'd been thinking.

Dante gave him a gentle shake. "Look back at the past week. The botched deal with the explosives."

Holt had hesitated before the meeting, concerned about the hit to the family's income.

"The theft of the explosives by operatives Holt can't track."

The first time Hawes had ever known his brother to be stumped.

"Wiped electronic records, missing surveillance footage from the warehouse and the hotel in Big Sur, leaks about your grandfather's health, and the flash drive sent to me. There was never an inside or outside hacker, Hawes. It was the best hacker you already have. Holt Madigan."

The tip to Hawes the night of Isabelle's death.

"No!" Hawes protested, as much to himself as to Dante. "He's my twin. I know him better than anyone. I know how he thinks."

"Do you? Are you married, with a kid? Always the second? Never the prince, never the king?"

"Don't call me that."

"Your grandfather is dead. You are the king."

Hawes whirled away and laced his hands behind his head, pacing, as Dante carried on with the truth he didn't want to hear. Holt couldn't strategize how to win a card game. How the fuck could he do this?

"Did you think this was going to go easy? Power transfers rarely do."

Hawes dropped his arms and slumped against the nearest pillar, caught between wanting to run from these terrible ideas and wanting to curl up in a ball on the floor. Except Holt had always been his protector when he'd succumbed to the latter, all the way back to the playground. His fiercest ally. "He's never said anything…" Yes, he'd been worn down lately, maybe retreating a little, but Hawes had thought that was due to the very things Dante had mentioned. Lily. Amelia. Focusing on surveillance and digital assassination. "He's supposed to be the one who stays off the criminal grid. Clean. So he can always be there for Lily." The family's escape route, God forbid they ever needed it.

Dante stood, and approached slowly. "Did anyone ask Holt if that's what he wanted?"

No, but… "You've seen how he looks at Lily."

Eyes swirling with an emotion Hawes couldn't place, Dante lifted a hand and cupped his cheek. "He looks at her like he wants to give her the world. Like any father would. Do you know how he does that?"

Hawes turned his face into Dante's palm, hiding from the truth.

Didn't stop Dante from voicing it. "By being in control, and you've made sure he isn't a target for the cops. Not that he ever would be."

"Never," Hawes whispered. Not as long as Braxton Kane was the chief of police.

"There's more."

Hawes opened his eyes and winced at Dante's exponentially grimmer face. Like he'd been holding back the worst part. Hawes's stomach sank, but he had to know. He curled his fingers around Dante's wrist and drew his hand down. "Tell me."

Using the hand in his, Dante led him back to the table. He reached out and drew the folder to them, flipping it open.

Account records from an offshore bank Hawes recognized. Their family regularly did business there. "How did you get these?"

"Friend of a friend did a little hacking for me." He spread out the first three sheets. "Jodie, Ray, and Lucas did get paid."

Significant amounts, according to the highlighted records.

"By?" Given Dante's theory, Hawes knew the answer but needed to see the evidence for himself.

It was more painful than he'd imagined.

Dante pushed the fourth sheet in front of him. "All the deposits came from this account." Multiple entries were highlighted on the ledger. Dante drew his attention to the account holder's box. "You recognize the name?"

Tears pricked the backs of Hawes's eyes, and words fought to get out past the lump in his throat. "Holt's military call sign, and our mother's maiden name."

Dante curled a hand over his thigh. "There were two more payments of interest." He pointed to the most recent at the top of the page. "This one is to a trust fund for the benefit of Max Bailey's family. Do you know who he was?"

"The name sounds familiar." But Hawes couldn't place him.

"He was a platoon mate of your brother's. He's been in and out of mental health facilities since retiring from the army. PTSD."

That triggered the memory. "Holt was his peer support contact when Bailey returned home. What does he have to do with this?"

"Max Bailey rented a cargo van last night." Dante withdrew a photo from the folder. It was the same van that had been rigged to blow them up today.

"Oh God." Hawes pitched sideways, burying his face in Dante's chest. He didn't want to believe this. Didn't want to believe that his calm, quiet, devoted brother had manipulated a friend, someone who'd needed his help, into sacrificing himself. Didn't want to believe that he would sacrifice his family, his own wife, for control of the family empire.

"There's one more thing you need to see."

Hawes shook his head. He'd seen enough. He was coming apart at the seams—his empire, his family, his world disintegrating around him. There were no nets, just an endless free fall. He wanted it to stop.

Dante had other ideas. Hand around his neck, he drew Hawes upright, then turned over the highlighted bank account record. One line was highlighted on the back, an older transaction. "A payment was made to Zander Rowe, the day of—"

"Isabelle Costa's murder." Hawes recognized the date. It cut worse than the account holder's name on the front. "But all that was before Lily."

"And Holt's cleaning up the mess now, because of Lily. Securing the world, the empire, for her."

Hawes covered his face with his hands. Was it really possible? Had his own brother engineered the worst moment of his life? Put him in a situation where he'd made an impossible choice and an innocent woman had lost her life? Soaked Hawes's hands in blood? "He wouldn't do that to me."

Dante's hand landed on the knot between his shoulders. "We all have a blind spot where family is concerned."

"No!" Hawes rocketed to his feet and shot out an arm, swiping the table clean. This wasn't a blind spot. This was his brother, his twin. He ran from the truth, nearly falling over the bench in his hurry to escape. He caught his balance on a tumbling lunge and stumbled into the nearest pillar.

Dante was at his side the next instant, looping an arm around his front and clasping his neck. Hawes wanted none of the steadiness he offered. Spinning meant maybe he could grab on to another explanation. Anything but the truth staring him in the face. Steadiness meant standing still and accepting that the person he thought he knew best in the world was the one he knew least.

He fought out of Dante's hold and circled the living room. "What the fuck am I supposed to do? I can't ki—" He cut off the heinous thought. "He's my brother."

"You bring him back in line."

"And my sister?" Helena had looked so stretched thin lately. Had she been helping Holt? "And Amelia? Whose side are they on?"

"We can't be sure."

Was that car bomb today only meant for him? Had he risked Rose's life by riding in the same car with her? She was awake when they'd left the hospital, would go home tomorrow if she remained stable overnight, but she would've never been there if not for Hawes, either because he was the target or because he made the wrong call. His fault, either way.

"I should have listened to you and not gone to the funeral. I keep making the wrong decisions. Maybe I shouldn't be in charge."

Dante stepped in front of him, blocking his path. "That's what he wants you to think. You are exactly the Madigan that needs to be in charge." Dante cradled his face with both hands. "You are the one that changed the organization for the better."

"*We* did it," Hawes said, staring at Dante through the tears pooling in his eyes, willing the other man to understand. "Me, Holt, and Helena. Who am I supposed to trust now? I can't do this alone."

"You don't have to." Dante brushed his thumbs over his

cheeks, wiping away the wetness there. "Trust me. I'm on your side."

Would he stay that way once he learned the truth about Isabelle's death? Hawes doubted it, and then he'd be well and truly alone. Without Dante and without his family. He closed his eyes and leaned his weight against Dante while he still could. "I don't know how to do this."

Hand under his chin, Dante forced his gaze back up. The desperate flailing in Dante's eyes caught Hawes by surprise, but as quick as the turmoil appeared, it was gone, resolve hardening the swirling brown. "We'll figure this out, the two of us." Dante leaned their foreheads together. "But you have to trust me."

Hawes had to trust *someone*. Dante had his own agenda that would eventually make them enemies, but for now, he'd proved himself to be on Hawes's side. Maybe the only one left there.

"I trust you." He tunneled his fingers into Dante's hair and pulled him back, just enough to lock eyes. "Please don't make me regret it."

Dante kissed him, and regret was the furthest thing from Hawes's mind. As steadiness rushed back in, Hawes realized what he had to do.

SIXTEEN

Hawes felt more than a little guilty for tossing the past three hours of planning out the window. Guiltier still about the sedative he'd slipped into Dante's drink. Guiltiest of all about stealing his bike. But there was no way Dante would've let him do what he needed to otherwise, and without his bike when he came to, Dante would be further delayed. Hawes had bought himself an extra fifteen minutes, if not more. The hair-raising ride over was worth it.

"Where's Perry?" Helena asked from her usual perch above the drive, her blonde hair and Ka-Bar glowing in the lights from the house.

Hawes finished steadying the bike, then started up the stairs, taking his chances with the truth. "My condo. Passed out on the dining table."

Standing over Dante, chest tight, Hawes had gently pushed back the long strands of his hair and admired his handsome face, peaceful in sleep. Hawes did trust him, even if they'd only known each other a week. His heart was getting on board too, which was a dangerous first. Someone else he had to protect. But Hawes's heart and mind also trusted his brother, no matter the abundance of evidence to the contrary. Hawes understood why Dante believed it—the bank records and other connections to Holt were damn convincing. But not enough to turn Hawes against his twin. There had to be an explanation, and here was the best place to get one.

"He's still at your place after what Holt showed you?" Helena spun the knife in her grip. Hawes suspected it was as much a nervous tic by now as it was keeping her weapon at the ready.

Hawes sat on the ledge and lifted her bare feet into his lap. "He convinced me otherwise."

"What else has he convinced you of?"

"That someone is trying to tear apart our family."

The knife stilled in her hand. "Could it be him?"

"I don't think so. This started long before he came into the picture."

"But it escalated when he showed up."

"Or when it became clear Papa Cal was near death."

She cast her gaze aside, and in the quiet night, her gulp was loud.

"Chicken-egg problem, Hena."

"I don't trust him."

"You don't have to." He squeezed her ankle and waited for her eyes. "You just have to trust me."

"Do you still trust us?" She tightened her grip on the knife, as if bracing for pain yet also ready to dole it out, if that's what she had to do. She called him the strong one, but she was the glue that held them together, the one who asked the hard questions, and their family's best defender.

She didn't need to brace or defend in this instance. Never against him. "Always," he answered.

Her grip on the knife relaxed, as did the tension in her back, braced against the column. "Good." She lifted her feet out of his lap and swung them around to the tiled landing. "There's something you need to see."

He followed her inside and upstairs to Holt's lair. As he crested the top step, he faltered. One sweeping look and he wished he could unsee it all. From his crying brother in the corner rocker, Lily clutched in his arms, to the wreckage of computer equipment strewn across the floor, to the wall of monitors displaying the truth that had been hiding in all their blind spots.

He carefully stepped around the mess on the floor and inched closer to the monitors, struggling to believe, to understand, what he was seeing. Every image, every detail, struck like a bullet, tearing his battered insides to shreds.

Amelia entering the offshore bank, the logo over the door matching the logo on the account records Dante had shown him.

Amelia in the arms of a frayed-looking man dressed in army fatigues, the patch on his camo jacket reading: BAILEY.

Amelia meeting Jodie, Ray, and Lucas outside the hotel in Big Sur.

Amelia and Bailey at the warehouse earlier in the week, the timestamp matching a gap in the surveillance footage.

It wasn't Holt trying to pull off a coup. It was Holt's wife.

Amelia, who'd been recruited by Papa Cal, who had an eye into everything, and who could play cards with one look at her hand because she had an eidetic memory. Who was always looking over Holt's shoulder. The person in the best position to make it look like he was the guilty party.

"We found her print on one of the car-bomb components." Stepping out of the front alcove, blanket in hand, Kane moved behind a shivering Holt and tucked the knitted wool around his shoulders. "We don't know why she did it."

"Lily," Hawes said as he regarded his slumbering niece in her wrecked father's arms.

Dante had the motivation right, just the culprit wrong. The traitor in their midst was the other person who would do anything to secure Lily's future, including framing her own husband and stealing the throne.

Hawes turned away from the monitors and crossed the room to kneel in front of Holt. He brushed the fuzz on Lily's head and looked up at his brother. "She's safe, Holt. That's all that matters."

Tortured brown eyes lifted to his. "I'm sorry, Hawes. I should have—"

"This is not your fault." He lifted his hand from Lily's head to Holt's arm, clasping it tightly. "She fooled all of us."

"What's she after?" Kane asked. "What's her mission?"

"A seat at the table, officially. At the head of it."

"If anyone should have seen it, it was me." Helena tapped her nails, trying and failing to fight her own tremors. "She was so quick to come back to work, and when we'd talk, she was obsessed with the family holding power."

Power. To hold for Lily.

"That's what she cares about," Helena said, reaching the same conclusion Hawes had. She aimed a pointed look at Kane. "Not alliances." At Hawes. "Not any sort of code." And finally her gaze landed on a heartbroken Holt, sympathy in her eyes. "Not even love."

Twin tears raced down Holt's cheeks as he held Lily closer. Kane readjusted the blanket around them and left his hands on the top of the chair, standing guard. Holt huddled with his daughter in the blanket, hiding from this awful new reality.

Hawes couldn't hide. This was his kingdom to protect now. He rose and turned to Helena, who was standing by the monitors. "Where is she?"

"Approaching your condo." She gestured at the surveillance feed showing the hallway outside Hawes's front door.

Hawes's earlier guilt came crashing back, a tidal wave compared to the earlier breakers. On the other side of that door was Dante, drugged and defenseless. Because Hawes had left him that way.

⎯⎯⎯ ╦╦╦ ⎯⎯⎯

"FASTER!" HAWES HELD ON TIGHT AS HELENA PUSHED THE HARLEY harder, flying around turns and sailing over hills. For once, he didn't care about his own potential death-by-motorcycle. He was more concerned with Dante's potential death-by-sister-in-law.

They skidded to a stop around the corner from Hawes's building, out of sight and hearing range. Helena killed the engine, and Hawes toggled on the comm device over his ear.

"Kane, update."

While Holt recovered, the chief had taken over comms. *"I've got this,"* he'd said before they left. *"I'll monitor things until I have to call in the cavalry."*

Holt had spoken up then, misery in every syllable. *"Don't hurt her, please."* Gaze fixed on Lily, his Adam's apple bobbed as he fought to get the words out. *"She's her mother."*

"Give us a twenty-minute head start," Hawes had told Kane, then after a parting kiss to Holt's and Lily's heads, had raced out with Helena.

That had been fifteen minutes ago. This time of night, the streets were mostly deserted, making their ride through downtown fast.

"No movement outside the building," Kane reported. "Or outside your door."

But he couldn't speak to inside, which Amelia had entered with her thumbprint and code, one of the few other people who had full access. Hawes cursed his no-cameras-inside rule. His privacy was a small price to pay for lo—

Helena saved him from having to cut off his own dangerous thought. "How are we getting in?" she asked. "We can't just go up and knock."

Hawes had an idea, but it required Holt's assistance. "I need my brother," he told the chief.

"Hold on a second."

Muffled voices preceded a disgruntled wail from Lily. She quieted a moment later as Kane took up a horribly off-key lullaby. Hawes couldn't help but smile, circumstances be damned.

"I'm here," Holt said, and the flurry of keystrokes told Hawes he was in front of his computers.

Exactly where Hawes needed him. "We need your help."

"Let me guess. You need to break into your own panic room." Holt's voice cracked, evidence of his earlier tears, but his deadpan sarcasm was back where it belonged.

Hawes smiled wider. "Twin powers activated."

"Knew there was a reason we bought that upstairs unit."

Technically owned by MCS, the condo above Hawes's was a blank box they rented out to artists as studio space and sometimes also used for shelter activities. Unbeknownst to renters, the locked "owner's closet" was actually a panic room for Hawes's condo below.

Holt had them inside it in less than two minutes.

"How do you want to do this?" Helena asked as she yanked off her boots. "Where do you think she is in the unit?"

"I'd guess either end of the main space so she can see the entire length of it, plus more weapons in the kitchen, but I can't see or detect anything through these walls. It's a panic room for a reason."

"Don't need it," Holt said. "I can use the Wi-Fi signals from your network and Amelia's phone to get her location."

"That sounds an awful lot like cameras, even if there are no pictures."

Holt talked over impossibly fast keystrokes. "I might have loaded some beta software on your router and in your smart-home-system app. I swear I haven't tapped it until now."

Hawes didn't totally believe him, but again, small price to pay in the current situation. And he'd latched on to a different, more important tactical advantage in something Holt had said. "Can you create a distraction using the app?"

Helena nodded, following his train of thought. "Kill the lights and blast the music when we drop through. I like it." She made a slicing motion with her hand by her ear—their signal for cut it—and flipped off her comm. Once Hawes did the same, she asked, "Can we do that and get her out alive? We promised him."

"That's my plan."

"Will Dante be on board with that plan?"

"Are you?"

Banked anger flashed in her eyes, but she shut it down just as quickly. "For Holt and Lily, yes," she said, resolved. She checked to make sure her gun and knife were secure. "But if I bloody her nose, can't be helped."

"No one will blame you." Hawes reactivated his comm and checked his knife and garrote were in easy reach. "Where is she, Holt?"

"Kitchen, according to the Wi-Fi."

"I go low, you go high," Hawes said to Helena. That had always worked well for them when dropping into blind situations.

She grinned and bounced on her bare toes. "Ready."

Hawes put his hand on the button next to the panic room door. "Cue the music."

"On my count," Holt replied. "Three, two, one."

Helena's "Go!" was the last thing Hawes heard before he slammed his palm against the button and the Ramones' "Blitzkrieg Bop" rent the air.

SEVENTEEN

The retractable door in the ceiling slid open, and Hawes dropped through, riding the soles of his Oxfords down the ladder rails into his living room.

He hit the floor, curled into a crouch, and Helena leaped over him. In the moonlight, she was a flash of black leather and blonde hair, practically walking on air as she took off from the middle rung, used him as a vault, and grabbed hold of the exposed overhead piping. She swung to the coffee table, landed graceful as a cat, then launched herself onto the couch, scampering up the cushions to the back frame.

Glass shattered from the direction of the kitchen. "Here!" Dante shouted over the music, confirming his position. "She's got a—"

Gunfire cut short the warning.

Hawes flipped up the coffee table, sending remotes, cookbooks, and Dante's paperbacks flying. Using the tabletop as a shield, he advanced, staying low, and Helena kept to higher ground, springing from couch arm, to barstool, to the kitchen island.

"Lights!" Hawes shouted to Holt at the controls.

The overhead track lighting blazed on, and the music dropped out. Hawes, at the end of the couch, dropped the table and grasped his knife. Helena stood on the island, knife in one hand, the other holding a gun trained on Amelia.

Their sister-in-law stood in the back corner of the kitchen, a swaying Dante in front of her, a gun pressed to his temple. "Sis," Amelia hissed, her green-eyed gaze locked on Helena.

While they squared off, Hawes took stock of Dante. Glassy-eyed, unsteady, hands tied in front of him. Even with her torture skills, Amelia was hauling him around more easily than should have been possible, given their height and weight differences. Noticing his attention, Amelia used her free hand to grab something off the counter. She tossed it at Hawes's feet. "You really shouldn't leave your pets home alone."

A syringe. She'd drugged Dante, on top of the sedative Hawes had given him.

Shit!

He glanced again at Dante, whose gaze kept wandering off him and toward the couch. Hawes thought it involuntary until Dante's left hand also twitched. Was he pointing at the couch?

"You gonna shoot me, sis?" Amelia said to Helena, her focus redirected.

Hawes used the distraction to sneak a look to the right and spied the butt of Dante's pistol peeking out from behind a pillow.

"You'd make an orphan of your niece?" Amelia taunted.

"She has a father."

Amelia pitched a flash drive onto the island, the plastic clattering on the granite. "All his crimes and yours." She cut her glare to Hawes. "All three of you. I send that to the FBI, and Lily won't have a father—or aunt and uncle—much longer."

"Why?" Hawes couldn't stop from asking. It had to be about more than securing Lily's legacy, if Amelia was willing to send Holt away too.

"Because we could be so much more, if you'd just take the fucking gloves off."

"I have no desire to start a war in my city."

"Our city. That's what it could be, Hawes. Who the fuck's going to beat the Madigans? Get your shit together, and the four of us can take what your grandfather built and make it even more powerful."

Power.

Helena had been right. This was what power looked like when it corrupted, when the desire for it went too far. He fucking hated that it had to be his sister-in-law who taught them this lesson.

"It's not about who we can beat," Hawes said as he inched closer to Dante's gun. He loathed the thought of using it, even for distraction. He hated the thought of turning it on Amelia even more. He'd promised Holt he wouldn't, but if it came down to her or the other two people in this room, Hawes would do what he had to. The kill, God help him, was vetted, but he had to try and bring her around first.

"It's about who we are, Amelia. Why we do what we do. For justice, not for money. *That* will make us more powerful," he said, appealing to her driving motivation. And to the other one too. "*That's* the legacy we want to leave Lily. Empires built on fear never last, nor do empires that kill the innocent, blindly or collaterally. That's not the empire or the legacy we want to leave Lily."

Amelia sneered. "Ever since that night—"

A flurry of movement erupted—Dante flinched, Amelia jerked him to the side, Helena stepped to the edge of the island—and for a split-second Hawes thought he was going to lose it all. "Wait!" he shouted, and everyone froze.

"Weapons down!" Amelia demanded.

Hawes dropped his knife and garrote at once. "Hena, stand down." He waited for his sister to lay down the gun and knife, to straighten with her arms and legs loose, ready to spring, before addressing Amelia again. "That night did change us," he said. "For the better."

"Gonna have to disagree with you." Amelia shoved the muzzle of her gun against Dante's temple, hard enough to make him wince. "You didn't handle it then, and now look what it's brought to our doorstep."

Dante clenched his tied hands. "Now, Hawes!"

Hawes lunged for the gun, ignored the bile rushing up his throat, and fired at the cabinet above Amelia's head, distracting her. Dante twisted away, wobbling precariously until he got his feet under him and swung his clenched fist up. He connected with Amelia's firing arm with enough force to knock her gun loose. He kicked it clear and shoved Amelia into Helena's waiting choke-hold. Amelia went limp in seconds, her unconscious body hitting the floor a second after that.

That fast, it was over. That fast, Hawes realized it could have all been over for him and his family instead. As Helena brought the butt of her gun down on the flash drive, shattering it in defense of their family, Hawes dropped Dante's pistol, a wave of unsteadiness taking out his knees. Dante was there, as he had been all week, albeit a bit wobbly himself. He looped his bound hands over Hawes's head and drew him into his arms, the two of them leaning on each other. "I've got you."

IF THERE WERE EARTHLY PORTALS TO HELL, HAWES WAS CERTAIN THE SFPD headquarters was one of them. Not that there was anything particularly hellish about the place itself. The shiny new building was spacious and modern, quite nice compared to other station houses in the city. Not nice were the looks Hawes was catching, especially from old-timers. Thinly veiled fear, outright loathing, and wary caution from the officers and detectives who'd come up during Papa Cal's heyday. They no doubt wondered how the Prince of Killers's reign would compare, given its bang-up start.

Curiosity was likewise a popular look among the younger set, officers who cut Hawes a quick glance as they passed by, or who openly stared at him from their bullpen desks. Hawes counted and tagged each one and mentally shuffled them into one of three buckets—too new to know better, still trying to make sense of the rumors, or on board with the Madigans' recent vigilante streak. He'd relay his observations to Holt next time they reviewed the SFPD's roster. Reactions and perceptions could be useful in the future, but given the option, Hawes would've skipped this visit altogether.

That, however, was not an option. Not while Kane interrogated Amelia in the room across the hall. True to his word, the chief had given them a head start, which put the cavalry on scene shortly after they'd subdued Amelia. She'd come to in the back seat of a police cruiser, and other than to confirm her identity and to answer yes to the Miranda warning, hadn't spoken. Hawes doubted she'd say anything more to Kane, but he had to wait to find out. Had to make sure his family was safe, even the one who'd betrayed them. He had to see this mess through to the end.

Helena appeared from around the corner with two coffees in hand. Hawes gladly accepted a cup, anything to battle back the cold chill and weariness creeping into his bones, a week's worth of sleep deprivation catching up to him.

"Heebie-jeebies, Big H?" Helena leaned against the wall beside him, as comfortable as she could be. Why wouldn't she be? Her day job required her to visit this and other station houses multiple times a week.

Hawes shivered at the thought and gulped more coffee. "I don't know how you spend so much time here."

"Not every accused criminal is guilty. Present case excluded" —she tipped her cup toward the interrogation room—"I like to think I'm better equipped than most to judge."

"Balancing out your karma?"

"You have your code, I have mine."

Hawes's chuckle was cut short by Kane emerging from the interrogation room. Through the open door, Hawes caught sight of Amelia, handcuffed to the metal table. Stone-faced and dead-eyed, she looked like a shell of her usual fiery self, even as she stared straight at him.

Kane closed the door, cutting off Hawes's view. "She's not talking."

At least there was that. He couldn't discount the risk of Amelia turning state's evidence—it would be another way to take him down—but she couldn't do that without taking the entire organization down, which had never been her goal. She'd wanted more power, but that was out of reach now. If she cared for her daughter, which Hawes truly believed she did, she'd want Holt free and clear to raise Lily with the family resources behind them.

Kane's hazel eyes landed on Helena. "She did ask for an attorney."

"Nope." Helena shook her head sharply. "Conflict of interest and she doesn't meet my criteria."

Hawes did laugh then, as did Kane, though the chief's amusement quickly turned grim. "Probably a wise decision. With her actions today and tonight, together with the evidence Holt and Dante collected and Amelia's prints on the explosives, we've got her for conspiracy to commit murder, attempted murder, kidnapping, and numerous financial and firearms charges. I don't see a convincing legal defense."

"Get her someone good," Hawes said to Helena, trusting she had the contacts to make it happen. "It's what Holt would want." It was what Lily deserved. Amelia was still her mother.

"You heard from him?" Kane said.

Helena laid a hand on his forearm. "He's fine. Lily was fussy for a bit, but he got her down. He seemed pretty distracted when I talked to him last, like he was on the trail of something else."

There was no shortage of disturbingly open threads: the whereabouts of the rest of the explosives, whether Amelia had more allies, how far back her treachery stretched, Dante.

"Where's Perry?" Kane asked, as if hearing Hawes's thoughts.

"Here." Dante rounded the corner. "Was getting my vitals checked and an IV push to flush the sedatives."

Something was off about him; Hawes noticed it immediately. The sedative was out of his system, but Dante's shoulders were stiff and his gait was more rigid than his usual casual lope. Then again, it had been an off night for all of them, and Dante had taken the brunt of the hits.

"Everything okay?" Hawes asked.

"Fine." Dante slid a hand over his lower back, and a measure of the steadiness Hawes had missed returned. "Except that part where I got drugged. *Twice.*"

Hawes cringed. He'd apologized on the ride over, but he understood if Dante was still angry, probably more so after giving his statement. "I'm sorry," he tried again, and got a stern, dark-eyed look for his efforts.

"We'll be discussing that later," Dante said, voice lowered.

Necessary, as their growing number was attracting attention. Noticing the same, Kane ushered them into his office and closed the door. "I need a straight answer this time," he said to Hawes. "Is this some sort of turf war that's going to bleed into my streets?"

Hawes wanted to tell him no, but he also didn't want to lie to Kane. That wouldn't be fair after all the chief had done to help them. "Apparently my way of doing things, *my alliances,* are not universally accepted."

Behind his desk, Kane ran a hand over his head. "Are you questioning those alliances?"

"Don't be obtuse, Brax," Helena said.

"Are you?" Kane pressed.

"You know where I stand," Hawes replied. "I'm taking my family's work in a different direction. There are bound to be detractors."

"You think it runs deeper than Amelia?"

"She recruited Jodie, Ray, and Lucas to her side. Tricked Bailey into helping her. I can't say for certain there aren't others. I assume that's what Holt is working on now. Assessing her reach."

Dante leaned a hip against the side of Kane's desk and filched a caramel candy out of the corner bowl. "What'll you do to the traitors?"

"Has anyone heard from Lucas lately?"

"Fucking hell, Hawes," Kane muttered. "I didn't hear that."

Hawes crossed his arms. "Hear what?"

Kane cursed and shooed them toward the door. "There's nothing more to do here tonight. Go home before you make a bigger scene of my station."

Dante pushed off the desk. "Keep us posted."

"And you do the same if things—"

"Go tits-up. Got it." Hawes waved a hand in the air as they filed out. "We're in the shit now, Chief."

Hawes shut the door on Kane's half groan, half laugh. In the hallway, Helena hung back by his side. "Give us a minute," she said to Dante.

Dante clicked the candy against his teeth. "I'll be outside."

Watching him go, Hawes worried again over his stiffer than usual gait. Was he hurt or just tired? Or angrier than he was letting on about Hawes drugging him? About going rogue? Hawes put money on the latter.

"Don't think I have to ask where you're staying tonight," Helena said as they followed slowly after him toward the exit. "So tell me, is it a ten?"

"More like a twelve."

"I hate you," she hissed, but her small grin said *good for you.*

"I'll be by the house in the morning."

Hand on his arm, she stopped them by the stairs. Her grin vanished, all her typical catty bravado gone, weariness and concern dampening her eyes. "Please be careful. I can't lose any more family this week."

Hawes wrapped her in a crushing hug. "You're not gonna lose me, Hena. Not as long as you've got my back. Thank you for that tonight."

"Holt's gonna need us to have his too. Now more than ever."

"And we'll be there, for him and Lily."

"Good." She squeezed him tight, then drew back with a sly

smile. "Enjoy your night with Mr. Hair and be home in time for breakfast." She kissed his cheek. "I'll put a pillow on your chair."

He rolled his eyes and started down the stairs, Helena's laughter echoing after him. He couldn't deny that the laughter and relatively normal, teasing exchange felt good.

Also welcome and good was the sight of Dante astride his Harley, waiting at the curb for him. "Your steed awaits."

"Thanks for not killing me for stealing it."

"We'll talk about that too."

Hawes had no doubt they would; he only hoped for other nontalking activities first. He climbed on behind Dante and wound his arms around his middle, reveling in his solid presence. In the steadiness Dante provided. Hawes wanted more of that, wanted it all night long. "Take me to the castle."

EIGHTEEN

Hawes got as far as flipping on the hallway lights before Dante spun him by the arm and trapped him between the foyer pillar and his big body. Hand palming one side of his jaw, Dante dragged his tongue up the other, on his way to nipping Hawes's earlobe. Hawes failed to see the problem with being stuck between a rock and a hard place. Not a damn thing wrong with this. He tunneled his fingers through Dante's hair and encouraged him to keep going.

Taking cues like a pro, Dante swirled his tongue in the divot behind Hawes's ear. "You hurt anywhere?"

Hawes rolled his hips, dragging his aching cock, trapped behind layers of material, alongside Dante's, similarly straining his zipper. "Only one thing hurts right now." Fuck, he'd been hard the entire ride here. Cock pressed against Dante's backside, Hawes had been too distracted to worry about death-by-bike. Distracted by the abs he'd traced under Dante's tank, by the strands of windswept hair that had tickled his face, by the vibration of the bike between his legs, all of it stoking his desire. Seemed Dante's desire had been stoked too. Time to do something about that.

Hawes slid his hands under the collar of Dante's jacket and pushed it off his shoulders. "How are *you* feeling?"

Well enough to spin Hawes again, shove him face-first against the wooden pole, and jerk his suit jacket off over his arms. A protest was on the tip of Hawes's tongue, but it died with the thrust of Dante's cock against his ass. Turned into a needy moan when Dante yanked aside his shirt collar and sucked at the sensitive crook of his neck.

"Yes." Hand on the pole, Hawes canted his hips, and Dante's dick nestled against his crack. Exactly where Hawes wanted him. He wrapped his other hand around Dante's nape, keeping his face buried in his neck. The two points of contact were driving Hawes wild.

Then Dante added a third. Sneaking a hand around, he grasped Hawes's erection, taking layers of material with him as he slid his fist from tip to root. Hawes's braced arm gave way, and he collapsed onto his elbow.

Dante lifted his head in time to avoid a collision, but his hand around Hawes kept up the torture. "I'll feel better once I fuck you."

Now Hawes saw the problem. "Bed," he gasped out.

"Can fuck you just fine here." Proving his argument, Dante deftly unbuckled Hawes's belt, lowered his zipper, and slipped a hand inside his boxers. Another few seconds and he'd have Hawes's dick out and his ass bared, at which point Hawes would be a goner.

Summoning his last ounce of restraint, Hawes pushed off the pole and sent both of them stumbling backward. He rotated and clutched Dante's shirt, counterbalancing to keep them upright, and also keeping Dante an arm's length away. Steadier, he sucked in breaths while promising his dick and Dante, "Two minutes. I need to feed Iris and make sure everything out there"—he nodded toward the living area—"is secure. And since I'm going to pass out right after you fuck me, I'd rather it be in my bed than against the foyer pole."

Dante chuckled. "Fair enough." A flicker of some emotion streaked across Dante's face, killing the humor and dampening the heat.

"Hey, you okay?" Hawes moved to close the distance between them, but Dante sidestepped his approach, heading toward the living area instead.

"You're asking me that?"

"You were held hostage tonight, after being drugged twice."

Dante deflected again, looking around the living room, whistling low. "It's like it never happened."

"Madigan Cold Storage—both enterprises—cleans up after itself." Hawes skated his fingers over Dante's abs as he passed in front of him. At the *snick* of the cat-food lid, Iris bounded down from the loft. Hawes set her bowl on the floor and scratched behind her ears. She gave him a tail shake, then ignored his existence in favor of food. Straightening, he continued with his security checks. Balcony doors, check. Doors, check. Panic room, check.

"So the ladder to nowhere does go somewhere," Dante said.

"It does," Hawes said as he climbed down the ladder. "And you still haven't answered my question."

Dante stepped forward and caged him in, a knee between Hawes's legs, hands on the ladder rails on either side of his head. "I let myself be held hostage until you got here."

"You were drugged, for which I am sorry."

"I know you are," he said, voice softening. "And I know why you did it. Can't fault you for putting your family first. Just don't do it again."

Hawes nodded. "Thank you."

"As for being held hostage, I could've made a break for it."

"Why didn't you?"

Dante's gaze slid sideways, toward the kitchen, where chaos had erupted earlier. He opened his mouth like he was going to speak but shut it before words escaped. He refocused on Hawes and restarted. "It was your decision how to handle Amelia. You're the king now."

Hawes didn't think that was what Dante was going to say at first. He probably would have liked those words better. "Don't call me that."

"It's true."

"Tonight, I'm just the man who lost a dearly loved family member. The brother and uncle who is going to have to pick up the pieces." He grasped Dante's chin and drew him closer. "The lover who almost lost someone he cares about. A future he didn't think possible." Dante's eyes flared, and Hawes kissed him, quick and hard. "I'm just a man who could have lost everything."

Dante lifted a hand off the rail and cradled Hawes's face, thumb tracing the sharp hinge of his jaw. "You are not just a man."

"And neither are you." Hawes covered Dante's hand with his and coiled a leg around Dante's, trapping him close. "Don't ever sacrifice your safety for me like that again."

"I won't make that promise."

Hawes started to object, and Dante returned the earlier swift kiss. "Trust me in those situations to make the right call. I've earned that much."

Hawes's mind whirled as Dante captured his lips. He still had questions—Holt's and Helena's lingering concerns about Dante couldn't be disregarded—but no doubt, Hawes trusted Dante to handle himself when the shit hit the fan. He could use an ally, a partner, like that. And Hawes trusted Dante to handle him, especially tonight when other needs were so much closer to the surface.

Relaxing against the ladder, he opened wider for Dante's kiss, inviting his tongue to tangle with his as it swept inside Hawes's mouth. Dante tasted sweet, like the caramel candy he'd taken off Kane's desk, on top of the Dante flavor Hawes had come to enjoy so much this week—dark, mysterious, dependable. A favorite cocktail that filled Hawes's insides with steady warmth. That both ensnared and freed him. Dante's thigh between his legs, the rhythmic rocking of hips, his hard chest beneath Hawes's palms. The long, silky hair Hawes could wrap around his fist and hold on to. Or use to pull Dante back when it became clear, once shirts were shed and pants undone, that they were gonna fuck right there against the ladder if Hawes didn't move them elsewhere. Granted, the blowjob Dante had given him there ranked among Hawes's hottest sexual encounters, but it wasn't what he wanted tonight. "I'm not sure this is better than the foyer pole."

Dante fought his hold. "Picky, picky."

Tugging Dante's head back farther, Hawes licked a stripe from his throat to his ear. "Fuck me in my bed," he whispered hotly, then released Dante's hair and trailed his hands over his shoulders to his biceps. "And let me fall asleep in your arms after."

Dante righted his head, wretched confusion swirling in his eyes, same as it had in the foyer. Hawes recognized the emotion now. He opened his mouth to ask about it, but Dante blinked it away the next instant. Desire returned, his dark eyes molten with hunger, and the instant after that, Dante shucked his pants and boxers. He pushed down Hawes's too, and as he stood he curled his hands under Hawes's thighs and boosted him into his arms. "Let's go, then."

Hawes flailed an embarrassing half second, unused to being so effortlessly manhandled, but then chagrin gave way to turned-the-fuck-on. He wrapped his legs around Dante's waist, cock delightfully nestled against warm skin and hard muscle, and looped his arms around Dante's neck. He drove his hands back into his long hair and attacked his mouth, trusting Dante to navigate to the bedroom despite Hawes's greedy kisses. His trust wasn't misplaced, his back hitting the bed in no time.

Dante came down on top of him. "Is this what you want?"

"Getting there." He kicked out a leg, taking Dante's knee with it, and braced a hand in the mattress, pushing up. Hawes rolled them so he was on top, but he was only there a second before Dante wrenched them the opposite direction. As they continued to wrestle, their slick cocks bumped and slid, limbs tangled, teeth nipped, and tongues licked, and the smell of sweat and precome filled the room. Hawes had never before grappled with a bedmate of equal strength and skill, and it was fucking exhilarating. By the time he finally got Dante onto his back, Hawes's knees on either side of his hips, his hands pinning Dante's to the mattress, Hawes was panting. His nipples scraped against Dante's chest with each breath, only making him more desperate to be fucked.

He glared down at Dante, daring him to make another move. "If I reach over to the table to get a condom and lube, are you gonna stay?"

Dante grinned and rolled his hips. "Risk you're gonna have to take."

Worth it, as were the consequences Dante delivered. Hawes had barely wrapped his fingers around the foil packet and bottle when Dante grabbed an ankle and flipped him onto his stomach.

"Tell me you want this," Dante said as he sat astride Hawes's thighs.

Hawes grasped the headboard rails and lifted his ass. "Yes."

Dante dribbled lube between his cheeks, and Hawes hissed at the cold. Dante chased it away with kisses dotted across his shoulders and fingers spreading the lubricant down his crack and around his rim. He pressed a thumb against Hawes's hole. "And this?"

"Fuck yes."

Dante's thumb pressed in, and Hawes saw the sun behind his closed eyelids. A bright burst of pain, then as his muscles gave way and sucked Dante in, a whole sky of stars came out to play. Endless and beautiful, made more so by Dante's fingertips teasing his taint.

A warm weight covered Hawes's back, Dante stretched over him. Hawes opened his eyes, and a curtain of brown waves fell around his face. "Christ, you're tight," Dante murmured behind his ear. "How long's it been, Madigan?"

"Too long." Fingers tightening around the rails, Hawes struggled between riding Dante's hand and humping the mattress for friction. "Need more, please."

Giving it to him, Dante worked him open until he was begging for his cock, wanting Dante inside him before he exploded. The rip of foil and snap of latex had never sounded sweeter. Even sweeter was the sound and sight—because Hawes had to look back—of Dante lubing up his cock, fist shuttling up and down his hard length. It was the most erotic thing Hawes had ever seen.

And the next second it was the scariest sight of Hawes's life. Stars became black holes, and Hawes came untethered, free falling with nothing but the bed rails and sheets to grab hold of. It had been too long. Years since he'd opened himself up like this—to the possibility of more than just sex, to a potential partnership, to making love with another man in his bed. With all that riding on the here and now, he needed more control.

"Sun—"

He didn't even finish the safe word before Dante shifted off and flipped him back over.

"Hey, hey, hey," Dante cooed, voice gentling. "I got you."

Hawes gasped out a giant breath, then sucked in a bigger one. "I'm okay, just need a sec, but stay with me, please."

"Not going anywhere." Dante straddled his hips, but not so tight or close as to be confining. Comforting instead. Same with his forearms on either side of Hawes's head, his fingers gently brushing back Hawes's hair while his own hair created a cocoon around them. Dante waited for his breathing to calm, then asked, "You still want this?"

"Yes. Want you inside me, together."

Dante lifted Hawes's hands and put them on his shoulders. "Hold on to me, then," he said, eyes burning with desire and understanding. "Hold on to me and let go, but only as much as you want to."

It was exactly what Hawes needed to hear, exactly the power he needed back, and with it came a swell of emotion that Hawes poured into the kiss they shared. Everything he'd never dared hope for, everything he never thought he could have. Until now. He dug his fingers into Dante's shoulders and held on tight, riding that hope as Dante slid into him.

Riding it higher with each thrust and roll of their hips, with each kiss stolen between quickened breaths, with each stroke of Dante's hand around his cock, until Dante snapped his hips hard one last time, their gazes locked, and Hawes exploded with him, as high on hope as he'd ever been.

NINETEEN

Light bloomed behind Hawes's eyelids, a sudden burst that pushed him from dozing to awake. For the sun to have broken through the fog, to be shining so bright that it poured through the windows and over the loft wall, it had to be midday. Fuck, when was the last time he'd slept so late? Probably the last time he'd been laid so well. Which was an understatement. Fucked into oblivion was more like it. Dante had been powerful, wild, and caring, totally in tune with him. Hawes had barely spoken his safe word, and Dante had adjusted. He'd given Hawes exactly what he'd needed.

And fuck, it had been good.

So good that Hawes woke relaxed and rested, eager for the day ahead for the first time in a week. There were loose ends to deal with still—pending investigations, missing explosives, imploding family—but today Hawes felt more like a king than he'd ever felt like a prince. Like he could walk out the front door and onto his city's streets with the same easy confidence Dante carried himself.

Or better yet, he could get fucked again first.

Eyes closed, he scratched his bare chest and stretched from the toes up, pausing when his ass gave a twinge of protest. He carefully bowed his back off the mattress, counting each vertebra as it bent. No pain there. He could make this work. He just needed to convince Dante. Hawes didn't think it would be too hard. Right arm above his head, he inched his left over the sheets, searching for the other warm body in his bed.

And came up empty.

Cool sheets. No Dante.

Maybe he was scrunched on the far edge of the king-size bed. Hawes did have a tendency to starfish when he slept. He moved to stretch farther and was yanked back—by cold metal around his right wrist.

He instinctively yanked at his arm, hard, nearly jerking his shoulder out of its socket. Eyes popping open, he arched his neck and spied one end of Dante's handcuffs around his wrist, the other around a headboard rail. The one Hawes had had his fingers curled around last night as Dante had…

Ah, seemed his lover had in mind the same start to the day as Hawes. Still in tune with him and what he needed.

A sly smile spread across Hawes's face, and his morning wood, already stiffening further at the memory of last night, plumped to full attention. He lowered his back and shoulders to the mattress and listened. Sounds drifted up from the bathroom. There was his lover.

"You know," Hawes called, raising his voice. "It defeats the purpose to cuff me to the bed, naked, and then leave. You're missing the good stuff."

The toilet flushed and steps thudded up the stairs, as if Dante had his boots on. Had he gone out somewhere? Hawes inhaled deep. He didn't smell coffee or food, just the leftover musk of their lovemaking.

Before Hawes could enjoy another flash of memory, Dante appeared at the top of the stairs and robbed Hawes of thought. And all his breath.

Fully clothed, gun in hand, this Dante was not the same man Hawes had spent last night with, much less the past week. The top half of his hair was tied back in a ponytail, a holster was clipped to his hip, and his posture was rigid, as if those blips Hawes had noticed yesterday had taken root and grown into towering redwoods overnight. Worst of all were his eyes. They were all wrong. Not the molten brown Hawes had stared into as they'd come together. The fire in them was gone, snuffed out and replaced by cold, hard detachment.

Dante's voice was dead to match. "This exactly serves my purpose."

Dread settled like a boulder on Hawes's chest.

In his mind, Hawes replayed last night through a different lens. Was it possible he'd misread Dante's hunger, their flirtatious grappling, the passionate fight for and exchange of power? By the look of the stranger at the foot of his bed, the answer to that question was highly likely.

Shit.

Hawes tensed, preparing to reach across his body to the bedside drawer.

Dante, who'd become well acquainted with his reflexes— because fuck if Hawes hadn't goaded him into multiple displays of them—raised his pistol. "Nuh-uh-uh, I already removed the knife and panic button."

Hawes seethed. "I trusted you."

"You should have trusted your siblings."

Shit!

Holt hadn't been the only one suffering a blind spot. Hawes had been so eager for the steadiness Dante offered, for an ally and partner, for a life he'd written off as impossible, that he'd forgotten it was impossible for a reason.

Someone was always gunning for the king.

Silencing his naive hopes for more than thrones and empires, Hawes ignored his grieving heart and wrenched his mind into operative mode, evaluating exit strategies as he kept Dante talking. "Were you working with her?" he asked.

"With whom?"

"Amelia."

Dante laughed. It didn't sound amused at all. He stepped around to Hawes's side of the bed and stared down at him. Hawes yanked again at the cuff, testing the rail, and no longer comfortable under Dante's intense gaze, even if fire did momentarily flicker in those dark depths. "No, I wasn't working with her," Dante answered. "But she did tell me some interesting things before you and Helena showed up."

"Such as?"

"She was working for someone. Your throne's not safe. And my mission's not complete."

Hawes paused in his assessment of escape routes to unpack those three deceptively simple sentences. There were obviously more loose ends than he'd accounted for, but what struck Hawes most was Dante's use of the word *mission*. Tactical, in the same way his ex-army brother and Chief Kane often used it. Committed, in a way that spoke to abject devotion, above all else. Above any feelings Dante might have developed for Hawes.

"Your mission?" Hawes asked, every hair on his body standing on end.

"To bring Isabelle's killer to justice."

Hawes forced himself not to laugh. Not to cry. Isabelle's killer was right here, handcuffed to the fucking bed. Did Dante know that? Was that one of the interesting things Amelia had told him? Or did Dante remain in the dark about that most essential fact? Like Hawes had been in the dark about the most essential question Dante had dodged all week.

"Who was she to you?" Hawes asked again, sensing he'd finally get the answer and that he wouldn't like it one damn bit.

He was right.

Dante reached into his back pocket, withdrew a black leather billfold, and tossed it onto Hawes's chest. It landed open—to a gold-and-blue badge with a distinctive eagle on top. Hawes picked it up with his shaking left hand and confirmed his hairs had stood on end for a reason. "You're ATF?"

"Special Agent Christopher Perri."

Hawes flipped to the other half of the billfold, to the stranger's credentials, and read the truth for himself. Holt had been right. The digital copy of the yearbook had been altered. The picture was the same man, and he'd be in the same alphabetical position in the class roster, only a letter's difference between his real last name and the one he'd used for his cover, but the first name… "Christopher?"

"My partner used to call me Dante. She thought it was funny, given my nose and the fact that I always had it in a book."

Hawes's gut clenched. "Your partner?"

"Isabelle Costa."

Don't stop now!
Continue reading Hawes & Dante's story in *King Slayer*!

KING SLAYER

FOG CITY, BOOK TWO

ABOUT THIS BOOK

It wasn't all a lie.

Christopher "Dante" Perri had one goal: vengeance for his
murdered partner.
But truth is rarely so black and white.
And assassin kings are rarely so addictive.
He can't get enough of Hawes Madigan.

But now that Hawes knows he's a fed, the new king wants
nothing to do with him.

Chris aches to be near him, to help secure his throne and keep him
safe.
Hard doing when Hawes is determined to put a bull's-eye on his
back.
His bravery is as attractive as it is infuriating.

When Chris's desperation boils over, Hawes finally lets down his
guard.
But behind his walls lies a terrible secret.

Once learned, Chris will stop at nothing to destroy the king who stole his heart and more.

Twists and turns—and cliffhangers—continue in book two of Hawes and Chris's M/M romantic suspense trilogy. Read at your own risk!

ONE

Never fall for a mark.

Undercover 101. Hell, avid reader 101. As many assignments as Chris had worked, as many books as he'd read, he fucking knew better. He should've recognized the signs and thrown up a wall sooner.

Would it have mattered?

Looking down at Hawes Madigan, naked and handcuffed to the headboard—his trim, hard body coiled for a fight, his blue eyes liquid fire, his cock still half-hard, and his sharp mind no doubt working overtime—Chris figured probably not. No amount of training, no amount of reading, no amount of proper carriage, hair ties, or weaponry would change the fact that the place he most wanted to be right then was in that bed—with the enemy.

With the Prince of Killers.

No, the king.

Fuck.

Chris blinked away the frustrating hunger, blanked his face, and banked his futile desire. It didn't matter what he wanted. What mattered was the badge lying open on Hawes's chest and Chris's mission. The mission he'd spent three years preparing for and that had led him here.

His last mission.

The one that had come to a head yesterday and now required him to blow his own cover before someone else did.

"Your partner?" Hawes said, his voice a disbelieving whisper.

"Special Agent Isabella Constantine."

"Isabella. Constantine." Hawes repeated Izzy's first and last name slowly, as if wrapping his brain around the differences between fiction and reality. They were subtle—the first names so close, like Perri and Perry; Izzy's last name an Americanized version of her family's Greek one.

She had taught Chris that lesson early on in his ATF career. Construct a cover close to reality—name, occupation, history. Less likely to make an undercover slip, more likely to fool a doubting target. She had been a good agent. The best mentor and partner Chris could have asked for. Bringing her killer to justice was no less than the person who'd saved his life deserved. And the key to doing just that was currently at Chris's mercy. He'd never get a better shot, a more captive audience.

"You're going to help me find her killer," Chris said as he stepped toward the bed.

Hawes's gaze shot to his, clashing and sparking with incredulity. He laughed out loud—the same harsh, bitter sound that had scraped over Chris's bones the night they'd first met. "Are you insane? You're a fucking fed."

"Since when do you have a problem working with a badge? Braxton Kane is the chief of police."

Hawes's chilly laughter waned, as did the color in his hollow cheeks. "Did he know who you really were?"

"No."

Hawes held his gaze, judging the truth of Chris's answer. "I trust Brax," he said after a long moment. "I don't trust you." Emphasizing the point, he yanked again at the cuff around his wrist, the other metal end battering the rail where Chris had attached it.

Chris wrapped his free hand over Hawes's cuffed one and

waited for Hawes to still. "You trusted me up until five minutes ago."

"Five minutes ago, I thought I knew who you were." Hawes arched and twisted his torso, casting the badge off his body and onto the opposite side of the bed from Chris. "Lies, all of it."

Gun trained on Hawes's lower half, deterring any kicks or sudden movements, Chris released Hawes's wrist and stretched over him to retrieve his badge. He pocketed it but remained leaning over Hawes, nose to nose. "Not everything."

Facts that were close to the truth, as Izzy had taught him, and emotional truths too, no matter how much Chris wished otherwise. Lies would make his job a hell of a lot easier, would make being done with this a whole lot less complicated.

Heat, doubt, and hope flared in Hawes's eyes, and the tension drained out of him—chin lowering, chest collapsing, spine hitting the mattress. An opening Chris's heart rate ratcheted up to accept. Only to have the door slammed in his face. Elbow locked, wrist flexed, Hawes swung his left arm up and aimed the jutting heel of his hand directly at Chris's temple.

Concussion incoming.

Chris batted down the attack and reared back, out of Hawes's reach, fighting the magnetic pull that had sprung up so quickly between them.

Hawes was clearly doing a better job of resisting the pull than he was. Tender emotions wiped from his eyes, they burned with anger, hate, and betrayal. "I'm not fucking helping you."

Well, if that's how he wanted to play things… Chris straightened, squared his shoulders, and kept his pistol at the ready, not trusting the assassin. "I have you on murder."

"I have the same on you."

"Self-defense in the act of an investigation."

"And mine wasn't?"

Chris couldn't argue that. Jodie would have killed Hawes. He'd acted to defend himself, more so than Chris had in killing Ray. But Jodie wasn't Hawes's only kill. "Lucas."

Hawes smirked. "Lucas disappeared."

It was Chris's turn to laugh. "Into the Bay, on your orders."

"I gave no such order. You were there."

"Explosives trafficking," Chris countered.

"You know I'm trying to get out of that business."

"But you're not out yet, are you? You manufactured and, until yesterday, were in possession of illegal explosives, which you'd planned to smuggle to a new owner under the guise of a real estate sale. Did I get that right?"

Hawes bit his bottom lip, as if struggling to hold in a string of fiery curses. The dam didn't hold long. "Fine, haul me in," he exploded. "I'm still not fucking helping you. I've done enough damage already. I'm not going to make it worse. Fuck, I'll be lucky if Holt and Helena ever forgive me as it is."

Chris lowered the hammer. "Funny you should mention them. You know what'll make things worse? The backup of Amelia's flash drive. She told me where it was before you and Helena stormed in. I get a hold of that, and I'll have everything I need to arrest you and your siblings."

As expected, Hawes froze, his struggle with the handcuff forgotten, Chris's threat to the people who mattered most to him capturing all his attention.

"You might not care about yourself, Madigan, but I know your weakness. That soul you can't hide. The one that'll do anything to protect your family, even if they aren't exactly innocent either."

Hawes gulped and slowly cast his gaze down, eyeing Chris's gun. Chris could swear he heard the brush of long lashes against pale cheeks. And again on the way back up.

But that was impossible... *Fuck!*

Realizing his mistake too late—that the faint, wispy sound had come from behind him—Chris shifted to defend himself. And in the next instant he was defenseless, the gun knocked from his grasp by a bare foot.

"And we'll do anything to protect him," Helena declared.

Chris spun her direction with a, "How the fuck—" but was cut off by Hawes's, "Low, Hena!"

She instantly dropped into a crouch. Metal clanked against wood behind Chris, and he whipped back around. Too late. Abs curled, Hawes was levering onto his shoulders and scissor-kicking his legs into the air. Not at Chris. At the exposed pipe hanging from the ceiling above the bed. Lofted as the bedroom was, Hawes had no problem reaching the pipe with his long legs, locking his heels around it, and—

Fuck!

Chris caught a face full of water, the dislodged pipe acting as a high-pressure hose. Spluttering, he raised a hand to protect his eyes and sidestepped the geyser. The crack of splintering wood had Chris dropping his hand and flinging off water, desperate to get clear eyes on the situation. Too late again. Hawes flung away the broken headboard rail dangling from the handcuff and vaulted onto his knees, while Chris fell to his, kicked from behind by Helena. He couldn't catch his breath, much less make a move to get ahead of them, their coordination practiced and deadly.

Helena cinched his wrists behind his back with a zip tie, then shoved him facedown onto the mattress. She scaled his back, light as a feather, lethal as a viper, then planted one foot on the mattress and the other on his nape. "Tell me right now why I shouldn't break your neck."

Chris ignored the instinct to fight and forced himself to still. Grappling with Hawes was a well-matched challenge. Add Helena to the mix, take away Chris's weapon, and it was a no-win situation, no matter how good he was at hand-to-hand combat. He had to be smart, had to use what he'd learned about the Madigans, and offer them something they couldn't refuse.

"I wasn't lying about the flash drive," he said.

"We'll find it," Helena replied, then told someone on the other end of a comm unit, "Kill the water." Holt, Chris assumed, had to be somewhere in the building in order to manually shut off the pipes.

"Maybe you'll find it," Chris said, once the geyser quieted. His next words were aimed at Hawes, wherever he'd slid off the bed to. "And killing me is against your rules."

Helena pressed harder on his neck. "You're a threat."

"Who is after the same thing you are."

"Let him go, Hena."

She backed off with a gasp. "Hawes!"

Righting himself, Chris glanced across the room in the direction of Hawes's voice, and immediately understood Helena's change of tone. Hawes stood in the far corner, sheet wrapped around his waist, Chris's gun in his hand.

Chris stayed on his knees, intentionally at a disadvantage. Not a threat. "You won't use that."

Hawes lifted his arm and aimed the gun at Chris's head. No tremble, no hesitation. "Right now, you don't know what I'll do."

"Big H…"

The quiver in Helena's voice, together with Hawes's dark words and steady grip, were indication enough that Hawes was close to stepping over his self-imposed redline. One Chris respected. Pulling that trigger was the last thing Chris wanted to goad Hawes into doing.

"I'll go." Chris rested back on his heels, eyes downcast, chin lowered. He'd put his hands up too, if he could. "But my offer—"

"Didn't sound like an offer to me."

Lifting his head, Chris locked eyes with Hawes. "You need to know who is trying to unseat you. I need to know who killed my partner. We've worked well together the past week. We can solve this too."

"Get out, Agent Perri." Flat. Cold. Deadly. Not a trace of warmth or any other emotion.

Chris rose to his feet, and Helena perp-walked him down the stairs to the door, where she cut the zip tie with her knife. Chris held out a hand to Hawes, who stood behind her. "My gun?"

"No," Hawes said. "I think I'll keep it. Might come in handy."

Chris hoped like hell it didn't, almost as much as he hoped

like hell Hawes stuck to his rules. Otherwise, there'd be no way out of this for any of them.

CHRIS SWUNG INTO THE SOUTH PARK LOOP AND FOUND A SPOT IN THE line of cars parked along the curb, backing the Hog in behind a hideously flashy Maserati. He killed the engine, dismounted, and rifled through the books and detritus in his saddlebag for his earbuds. South Park was only two blocks from Hawes's condo; he couldn't have missed much.

Earbuds in, he opened the surveillance app on his phone and waited for the signal to connect. He kept his gait casual as he strode toward one of the perimeter benches in the bustling neighborhood park. As many times as he'd parked here the past week, the residents probably thought he was a new employee at one of the start-ups that rented space around the oval. Just another tech bro on his phone, nothing to see here, even if he did look half-drowned.

The static in his ears resolved, and Chris lowered himself onto the nearest bench, listening intently.

"Condo is clean," Holt said, confirming Chris's suspicion that Hawes's twin had been on-site. Not directly in the line of fire—all three Madigan siblings rarely were, especially if Holt had his daughter with him—but nearby to help control variables and get there quickly for the debrief. "No devices I can find."

Chris smiled. His supposedly undetectable tech was so far undetectable. Good. That said, given the bug's location, the volume of the voices inside the condo fluctuated depending on its carrier's proximity to the speaker. For now, it remained close enough to clearly transmit their conversation.

"I told—" Helena started.

"Don't need to hear it," Hawes said. "Already thought it myself. What led you here?"

A *thump* echoed through the comm, something solid landing

on a table or the kitchen island. Chris had to kick up the volume on his device, the voices farther from his bug, the carrier likely scared off by the noise.

"You got the yearbook," Hawes said.

"And a lead on who was paying him." Holt paused to shush Lily, who, judging by her cries, also hadn't liked the sudden noise. Couch cushions groaned, and then a flurry of keystrokes followed. "When I couldn't find Perry with a *Y*, I searched variations."

"And found Perri with an *I*," Helena said. "The hard copy of the yearbook confirmed it."

"And his bank accounts are at a federal credit union," Holt said.

Chris pictured the giant man sitting on the couch, daughter strapped in the sling against his chest, laptop open on his knees, reaching around Lily to point to evidence on-screen that would confirm what Chris had told Hawes.

"Because he's ATF," Hawes said. "Saw the badge myself."

"We figured he was a fed. Guessed ATF, but we weren't sure."

"Regardless," Helena said, "I got here as fast as I could."

"Thank you for the save," Hawes replied.

"You would have rescued yourself, eventually." The smirk in her voice didn't last long. "Given our businesses and past investigations, ATF made the most sense."

"Wait, rewind," Holt interrupted. "How does *Christopher* translate to *Dante*? There are no references in the yearbook to him as Dante, even as a nickname. Was it just a cover?"

"No way," Helena said. "He responded to it naturally, and it's pressed on his card case."

Chris patted his coat pocket, panicked for a second that the leather bifold had fallen out when Helena had thrown his coat out after him. He released his breath when he found it secure in the inner pocket where he always kept it. Izzy had given it to him as a graduation gift when he'd completed Special Agent Basic Training. She'd had *Dante* pressed into one side. After her murder, he'd had her time of death pressed into the other. A reminder of his mission.

"Not just a cover," Hawes said, filling his siblings in on the same. "His work partner gave him the nickname."

"Partner?" Helena said. "At the ATF? Who's he work with?"

"Work*ed* with, past tense. His partner was Special Agent Isabella Constantine." As before, Hawes emphasized the last *A* of Izzy's first name and every syllable of her surname. "Or as we knew her, Isabelle Costa."

Holt and Helena inhaled sharply, and Lily wailed an angry punctuation.

"She called him Dante," Hawes explained, "because his nose was always stuck in a book."

While Helena muttered an impressive string of curses, Holt resumed his furious typing. With new search parameters, he'd find where Chris's and Izzy's paths had crossed in no time.

Unlike his siblings, Hawes was silent. No words, no pacing footsteps, no whisky bottles clinking against each other. Where was he? Leaning against the kitchen island or one of the condo's wooden pillars? Or was he standing in front of the balcony windows, arms draped over the metal seismic strut? Like he had been that first night Chris had sweet-talked his way inside the condo. Chris had tried to sweet-talk Hawes into more than just an invitation to enter. He hadn't set out to seduce the prince that night, but when the opportunity had presented itself, he'd considered it an inroad to the information he needed.

What Chris hadn't needed were the sparks that had flown between him and Hawes, the heat that had drawn him like a missile to his mark. He'd nuzzled behind Hawes's ear, inhaled the subtle scent of expensive aftershave mixed with dangerous man, and he'd been the one seduced. Add to that Hawes's humor and honesty, the curious glimpses of vulnerability, and the barest hint of submission, and Chris had actually wanted to help him, which was the last thing he'd needed.

This was supposed to be his final mission, and not because

he'd gotten fired for falling for the mark, at least not yet. He couldn't let that happen, couldn't let that be the way this all ended. Get vengeance for his partner, then get out. That was the plan. He was shit at the ATF political game—that had been Izzy's thing, not his—and there was nowhere left for him to go in the agency that was as good a fit as undercover work. Except he was tired of being other people. After ten years of UC work, he needed to figure out who he was and where home was, for real. But, fuck if 'Dante' and Hawes's condo hadn't felt awfully close to real the past week, which only made the light at the end of his escape tunnel harder to see, diffuse and refracted like the fog Hawes loved so much.

"How's Rose today?" Hawes's question about his grandmother brought Chris out of his head and back to the present.

"Improving," Holt answered. "She'll be discharged tomorrow."

"You're not actually considering working with the fed, are you?" Helena persisted. "The risks if he finds out—"

"I know," Hawes snapped. "He can't."

Can't find out what?

Chris had no delusions about being fully read in. He'd known the Madigans were keeping secrets from him. They were too smart to tell him—a relative stranger—everything. He was outside their inner circle, even further now. And further still from whatever this thing was that affected him and the organization. It had to be about Isabella. Or the explosives. Or both. Chris was almost certain the two were tied together. What was it about that night that had pushed Hawes to make such radical changes in the organization? What exactly did Hawes know?

"We can't trust him," Helena said. "If that's not clear after today…"

"No argument here," Hawes replied. "But do we need him? I started the week getting close to a source, working him for information on who was moving against us. Can we still use him as such?"

Acid churned in Chris's gut. While neither of them had hidden the fact that they were using the other, hearing point-blank he'd gotten played was a kick in the balls. Was that all Hawes had been doing? Playing him? Had it all been a lie on his end, no matter how real it had felt to Chris? He didn't think so, given the betrayal in Hawes's eyes this morning and the heat in them last night, but Chris couldn't be sure, and he couldn't hang his hat on the 'started the week' qualifier in Hawes's statement. Not that Hawes's intentions, then or now, fucking mattered.

All that mattered was the mission.

Hawes again seemed to get that better than Chris, asking, "Can we use him and his resources to find out who is behind the coup against us?" When met with silence, Hawes barked, "Holt!"

"Huh?" Holt said, likely lost in computer code. "Sorry."

"I said, do we need Agent Perri's resources?"

"Let me see what I can do first."

"When's the last time you slept?"

Or the hacker had dozed off before and he didn't like being called out on it. "Broken record much?"

Hawes ignored the retort and shifted the conversation. "We need to find out where that flash drive backup is and get to it before Perri, if, in fact, he knows where it is."

"You think he's bluffing?" Helena asked.

"Yes." Good call. Apparently, Chris had shown Hawes more than a few of his moves too. "Have you been back to see Amelia?"

"Not yet," Helena said. "Holt?"

"I can't. And now with this…" His pained voice, brought on by the mention of his wife, made Chris wince. "Did Brax know who he was? Who he worked for?"

"Dante—" Hawes paused, cleared his throat, then corrected. "Chris said he didn't."

"I don't think Brax would betray us," Helena said.

"I don't either," Hawes concurred, "but the only people we can completely trust now are in this room."

They could trust Kane, and Chris needed the chief to trust him too. As tightly allied as he was with the Madigans, Kane was the best positioned to serve as an intermediary. And Chris needed one because Hawes was right. They could still use each other—Hawes to find out who was behind the coup, Chris to find out who killed Isabella. Each had information the other needed, and Kane could broker that exchange. But if Chris had a shot in hell of getting Kane on board, of securing the flow of information, he had to be the one to tell Kane the truth before anyone else did.

And time was tight. Chris's boss had filled his voice mail overnight with warnings of her imminent arrival. He needed to beat her there. He pushed off the bench and hustled back to the Hog. Next stop, SFPD headquarters.

TWO

Chris was halfway across the bullpen floor before he considered that Kane might not be here today after their long night that had bled into morning. Chris dismissed the absurd thought as quickly as it had formed. Kane was up to his eyeballs in this shit, same as him. Given all that had transpired, Chris would lay odds on Kane being in one of three places—here at the station, at the Madigan family fort in Pacific Heights, or at the waterfront headquarters of Madigan Cold Storage. Since Chris would likely get shot if he visited either of the latter two, he prayed Kane was here instead.

Half the staff was out for lunch, but the remaining officers, each a pair of trained eyes, tracked Chris as he wove through the rows of desks. Maybe he was just as likely to get shot here. Had news of his blown cover leaked already? Had the Madigans alerted other allies on the force? Chris was sure Kane wasn't the only SFPD officer in their pocket. Or had someone on the force— Kane, perhaps—pieced together why he'd been lurking the past week, asking questions about a three-year-old investigation?

Or none of the above.

He turned the corner and a familiar voice echoed from inside Kane's office. "You should have called this in earlier, regardless of Agent Perri's actions. Given the explosives involved and previous investigations, this matter is squarely within the ATF's jurisdiction. It's our case now. Officially."

Fuck.

So much for telling Kane the truth first and salvaging some sort of working relationship. Vivienne Tran had beaten him here, and by the sound of it, she was approaching things in her usual incendiary manner. He sucked in a deep breath, readying to enter, then paused to do a quick pat down. Hair pulled back, shoulders squared, gun holst—

Fuck!

Tran would spot the empty holster, and when he'd have to confess it was in the hands of their target—an assassin—the dressing-down would be epic. Maybe epic enough to yank him from the case altogether, which he couldn't let happen. He unclipped the holster and searched for a place to stash it, trying the conference room door across the hall.

Locked.

Fuck, fuck, fuck!

"You need some help?"

Chris spun toward the voice and had to stop himself from laughing. The rubber-ducky-printed tie around the person's neck was the first welcome bit of hilarity today. The humorous tie was in direct contrast to the pressed khakis and starched dress shirt but made a certain amount of sense with the platinum Mohawk and gumball ear gauges. The person's dangling ID badge read: *Jax Dillon, SFPD IT*, and handwritten in marker in one corner: *They/Them.*

Chris hadn't seen them around the station before, but the laptop they carried had an SFPD sticker and barcode on it. Part-time intern, perhaps, or an employee just back from vacation. In any event, they didn't seem to know who he was. Good. Chris could use that.

"I do, actually." He held out the empty holster. "Can you hold this for me?"

Jax glanced at the leather case, then back to him, brow cocked above a skeptical green eye. "Why?"

"'Cause I asked nicely."

"I don't even know who you are."

Chris dug out his badge and flashed it open. "Special Agent Christopher Perri. ATF."

They thrust out a hip and shrugged, unimpressed.

Chris failed to hold in his laughter this time. All right, bribery it was, then. "You know Angelica's Bakery in North Beach?"

"Everyone knows AB's."

Local, if they knew to call it by the neighborhood shorthand. "You hold this for me"—he extended the holster again—"and I'll get you a box of mistletoe cannoli."

"But it's July."

And AB's mistletoe cannoli were only available one week a year, between Christmas and New Year's. Unless you were family. "Angelica's my cousin. I'll get—"

Jax snatched the holster out of his hand. "I'm in IT. Other side of the floor." They tucked the holster between the computer and their chest, turned on their heel, and strode toward the stairwell.

Chris was still smiling as he rapped his knuckles on Kane's door.

"Come in!" the chief shouted. Chris pushed open the door, and hard hazel eyes shot to his, killing Chris's lingering grin. "*Agent* Perri, I understand."

"Perri," Tran said, and Chris swung his gaze to the woman seated in the guest chair. One suited leg crossed over the other, dark hair in a tight bun, face calm, and black eyes flat, she was the picture of serenity. No hint that she had been flexing her jurisdictional muscle and vocal cords a second ago. "Was there a reason you didn't identify yourself to the chief of police in the jurisdiction where you were conducting an operation?"

Kane appeared equal parts furious and fearful. The former on behalf of those he considered family, the latter over whether that fact would be exposed. Brax knew exactly why Chris hadn't identified himself to him.

Time to tap-dance and win back some of that trust he needed. "Given the irregularities of the prior investigations," Chris said, "I thought it best to maintain full cover."

"Chief Kane wasn't involved in those prior investigations. He was only recently appointed chief."

"Ma'am—"

"You didn't think local law enforcement needed to know the ATF was pursuing an explosives trafficking lead in their backyard?"

"Explosives trafficking?" Still standing, Kane braced his hands on the desk, knuckles white where they curled around the edge. "I thought you were helping—" A sharp shake of Chris's head, and Kane adjusted. "I thought you were helping out on a missing person's case, *as a private investigator.*"

"The private investigator part was his cover," Tran said to Kane before redirecting her attention to Chris. "The other part was not your assignment. Is that why you haven't logged status reports in over a month?"

"Deep cover."

"Oh, cut the crap, Perri." She pushed to her feet. "You've gone rogue—*again*—after being repeatedly told to drop this."

"Drop what?" Kane asked.

"The investigation into Special Agent Isabella Constantine's death."

Kane's eyes widened, round as saucers. "As in Isabelle Costa?"

"Constantine," Chris corrected.

"Isabelle was ATF?"

"Isabell*a* was my partner. She was murdered, and she deserves justice."

Blanching, Kane bowed his back and hung his head between his outstretched arms. Before Chris could say more, Tran stepped between them. At five foot nine, closer to six feet in heels, she commanded his attention. "Agent Constantine's murderer was killed at the scene. That case was closed."

Chris scoffed. "Without a thorough investigation."

"Because doing so would have compromised the agency's mission, *her* mission, which you are here to complete. That's your assignment, Agent Perri. To get a lock on the explosives, secure them before they fall into even worse hands, and shut down the Madigans. Not go dark—off mission—like your partner also did."

Silence hung heavy in the office until it was cut by the groan of abused chair springs as Kane lowered himself into the leather swivel behind his desk.

"Status report, Agent Perri," Tran demanded.

"The person who last moved the explosives is behind bars." He flicked a hand in the air. "In this building still, I think."

"She is," Kane confirmed.

Not good enough for Tran. "And where are the explosives?"

Silence blanketed them once more. Chris didn't have an answer.

Tran glanced over her shoulder at Kane. He didn't have one either. But she had one for them. "Agent Wheeler will be here on Monday."

Chris bit back a groan, sure it would be louder than the chair springs if it escaped. Scotty Wheeler was a fucking by-the-book menace. Tran's pet UC wrangler. No undercover agent wanted to hear his name near their case. It was as good as getting a case ripped away.

"Respectfully, ma'am, I don't need a babysitter. And my cover—"

"Is shot to hell, judging by the events of the past twenty-four hours and by this bullshit exchange the past five minutes. You went rogue, it backfired, and now you're scrambling."

And that right there was how Vivienne Tran had climbed the ATF political ladder. She'd spot your weakness, what you were trying to hide, and use it to her advantage. A scorched-earth approach, and she was the last one standing with the blowtorch. Chris bet her favorite movie was *Aliens*.

"Your case is imploding, Agent Perri. The window for success is closing fast. You need help if the agency is going to secure the explosives and arrest the targets before they flee."

Kane flinched. Because Tran had referred to the Madigans —*plural*—as targets? Or at the notion they might flee? Chris wasn't sure how to read Kane, but he was sure about the Madigans, at least in one respect. "They won't flee," he told Tran. "Not with their power threatened, and not with—"

"Holt Madigan's wife, the mother of his child, in custody," Kane said, completing Chris's thought. "Holt won't leave."

"And Hawes and Helena won't leave without him," Chris added.

Tran stepped back and split her glare between them. "Good, but I'm still sending Wheeler in." She'd never intended otherwise. She grabbed her bag off the floor and headed for the door. "Get the explosives, Agent Perri. Shut down the Madigans. Do your job while you still have one."

THE DOOR SLAMMED SHUT BEHIND TRAN, AND CHRIS RELAXED HIS shoulders, the tension draining from his posture. After a week of being Dante, he wasn't used to standing at attention, as one did when facing the agency firing squad, but he'd survived. He'd have an obnoxious, Scotty Wheeler-sized Band-Aid to show for it come Monday, but at least Tran hadn't pulled him off the investigation. Now he just had to survive the other firing squad. He turned to face Kane, who'd risen as Tran had left. Chris lifted both hands, placatingly. "Brax, listen—"

"Don't." Fear gone, the chief's fury rumbled in his deep voice. Drawing himself up to his full height, Braxton Kane was an imposing figure. Granted, he was built more like a spindly pine than a redwood, but that flexible strength was probably what had helped him weather countless storms—army, Madigan, and otherwise. "You lied to all of us."

Chris sank into the chair Tran had vacated. He needed to refocus this conversation. Get back to his original purpose for coming here—to bring Kane around to his side, or, at a minimum, around to working with him. "You're law enforcement," he said. "You know how undercover works."

"I do." Kane crossed his arms, fingers digging into the wiry muscles of his sleeved biceps. "You're supposed to liaise with the local authorities."

"Except when those authorities are compromised." Chris had a guess as to what—or rather *who*—was Kane's Achilles' heel, but he didn't need to strike at that weak spot. Yet. "What would you have done if I'd told you who I really was? I didn't put you in that position because you're more valuable to me, and to them, if we're working together."

"Cruz vouched for you," Kane said.

"Because she knows the real reason I'm here."

"The explosives."

"Isabella."

Sighing, Kane released the death grip on his biceps and ambled over to the window. He skirted a hand over his short hair, then rested his forearm against the window frame, back to Chris. "Zander Rowe killed Isabelle Costa." Not an attestation, more like a weary chorus. Same as the man himself.

"If you're half the cop I think you are, you know that's just as much a cover as my partner's name was."

Kane rotated and rested back against the window. "So Tran was right? You went rogue? Isabelle too?"

"Not rogue. Neither of us." Chris filched two candies out of the bowl on Kane's desk and tossed one to the chief. "Izzy went off the map a few days before her death. I still don't know why, but I think it has to do with those explosives and why she was killed. Which is my number one priority here."

"But not the ATF's."

"My priorities aren't ranked the same as the agency's."

"Oh, is that it?"

"I also knew there was a threat to Hawes."

Kane pitched the foil wrapper in the trash can and popped the candy into his mouth. "You used that to get close to him."

"Yes, until I realized what Hawes was trying to do." He clicked the hard candy against his teeth, recalling that morning in Hawes's bathroom. A double-edged sword—doubt and respect— had pierced his chest at learning Hawes was maneuvering the Madigans out of the explosives business. And then that blade had melted under the heat of something more when Hawes had turned down Chris's offered gun. He'd poured his conflicting emotions into the kisses he'd given Hawes that morning. All of it real in that moment. Same as Hawes's intentions for his family's empire. "They're not the same Madigans anymore, are they?"

Kane didn't reply. Smart, better not to let on how much he did or didn't know.

"They're moving away from high-risk, disreputable ventures," Chris continued. "And someone doesn't like that. Doesn't like Hawes."

"Amelia."

"Was working for someone else. The threat is still out there." He cast out a baited line, fishing. "To all of them."

Kane pushed off the window and returned to his desk. "So what do we do?"

And fish caught.

Chris pointed at himself. "*I* keep hunting Izzy's killer." Then gestured between them. "*We* work the explosives angle, which is connected to the attempted coup. The faction Amelia was working with and that wants to overthrow Hawes, stole those explosives. Finding the person behind the theft and the coup is in all our interests." He shifted forward and braced his elbows on his knees. "I need a meet before Wheeler arrives."

Kane spread his hands, palms up. "What makes you think they'll talk to me now?"

The defeat in Kane's voice sent a pang of regret rippling through Chris. He didn't like putting the chief in this position either. "I told Hawes you had nothing to do with it. That you didn't know who I was."

"But they know we'll be coordinating now."

"Then convince them we're still on their side." They'd believe Kane before they'd ever believed him.

"How do I know you are?"

"I could have turned them in at any point this week. I didn't."

"And why is that?"

"It's not in my interest to do so." Not when Hawes and his siblings could lead him to Isabella's killer. And not when his interest in Hawes had drifted beyond mark—beyond target—to something else, whether Chris had wanted it to or not.

"The bust you could make…"

"I don't care," Chris said. "I'm out after this case."

Kane's brows climbed to his hairline.

"I want Izzy's killer brought to justice, then I want to get on with living *my* life, or whatever's left of it."

"You want to come home."

"I do." He ignored the image that flashed behind his eyes—of Hawes in his bathroom—and stood, hand outstretched toward Kane. "Will you help me?"

The chief considered too long a moment, long enough to make Chris wonder whether he'd miscalculated in his approach, before he finally stood and shook Chris's hand. "This is my home too. I'm sworn to protect it." *And them*, he didn't have to say. "That's what I'll do."

THREE

Phone in hand, Chris glared at the dark screen. Over twenty-four hours and no word about a meet. He'd spent the day following leads on Amelia's flash drive. He'd bluffed about knowing its location. No luck finding it, at least in the places he could search. So he'd come here instead, to his mom's house, seeking distraction.

Which arrived right on cue. "Christopher?" His mother's voice echoed up from the downstairs garage. "Are you here?"

Chris dropped his phone back into his apron pocket and shouted over the footsteps trudging up the steps. "That's my bike down there, isn't it?" He'd left the door at the top of the stairs open, anticipating their arrival home from evening mass.

"Dad's bike," his sister said, appearing first through the door. "And it's missing an exhaust bolt."

Even with a living room and kitchen island between them, Celia's weary bitterness slammed into Chris. Three family dinners since he'd been back in town, and she'd been this way at each of them. He'd chalked it up to a mood the first time, had accepted her work excuse the second, but now a third time, and he figured he knew what was really up. But she'd bite his head off if he said a bad word about *him* in front of the kids, so he stuck to the topic at hand instead.

"Not the first time one of those has rattled off."

"And the helmet?"

"Left it in a hotel room somewhere."

"Uncle Dante!" Marco, his nephew, skirted around his mom. He half swaggered, half jogged across the living room, trying to play it cool but was hopelessly earnest. He held out a fist for a bump. "What's up?"

Chris formed a fist to bump back. "Lookin' sharp, Plato."

The nicknames had stuck since he'd first brought Izzy to one of their family dinners. Marco, then just a kid, had wanted one too, so Izzy had reached back into her heritage and picked a famous Greek philosopher.

With his other arm, Chris caught Marco in a playful chokehold and knuckled his head, messing up the dark curls he'd gelled into submission for Saturday mass. "Fuck, I'm too old for this shit," Marco protested.

"Language!" Celia chided as she hefted a tote bag onto the island. Her cuticles were wrecked, not just from caked on shop grease, and the bags under her eyes were more pronounced than last week.

Laughing to cover his scrutiny, Chris released his nephew and batted down his flailing right hook. "Maybe one day you'll land it."

Marco flipped him off, then snuck behind him to peer into the pot on the stove. "Butter chicken, yes!"

"Mia will be disappointed she missed it." Gloria, Chris's mother, joined Celia beside the island and added a bottle of wine to the bounty.

"Where is she?" Chris asked after his niece.

"Dinner with her boyfriend's family," Celia answered.

Marco rolled his eyes, hard, and Chris stifled another laugh as he unloaded the bag. "All I needed was cilantro," he said, ten other items later.

"And all I needed was cacciatore for dinner tomorrow night," Gloria quipped.

Chris chuckled. "Fair enough." He finally found the cilantro and set about picking off the leaves while his mother put the rest of her groceries away. "I'll call the shop tomorrow," he told his sister. "Set up a time to get the bike fixed." They, and before them, their father, had put in too much work to keep the classic Hog running. Chris wouldn't slack off now.

Celia jutted her chin at the stove. "How much time we got left?"

"Ten minutes or so. Just waiting on the rice."

"No need to call the shop. I have tools and bolts in my truck."

Before he could object, Celia was backtracking toward the garage, pulling up her cascade of dark curls as she went. She fumbled with the rubber band around her wrist once, twice, then let the hair fall back down, giving up the effort. More signs of her exhaustion, but gone were the days when they could talk about it, about anything really. Their relationship had changed, irrevocably, a decade ago. Not his choice then, but he hadn't pushed to repair it over the years and he'd all but abandoned it the past three. Had he missed his chance?

For now, he'd settle for providing the help she'd accept. He grabbed Marco by the shirt as he tried to sneak out of the kitchen. "Go help your ma."

He grumbled about being told what to do, not about the task itself. Like his mom and grandpa, Marco rarely passed up the chance to get his hands greasy. He wasn't legally old enough to work in the shop yet, but he was there every chance he got. Stripping down to his undershirt, he tossed his tie and dress shirt on the couch before disappearing down the stairs.

"You didn't want to come with us to mass?" Gloria asked.

He bent and kissed her cheek. "Wouldn't have made it in time."

"But you made it here in time to get dinner started?"

"Priorities," he confessed with a cheeky grin.

She swatted his shoulder, then dug the bottle opener out of a drawer. "Shut your mouth before St. Peter hears you."

"Pretty sure I'm already on the Do Not Admit list."

"Nonsense," his mother said. "You're a good boy." Chris laughed out loud, and she giggled along with him. She'd picked him up from detention enough times to know better. She spritzed the naan with water and tossed it into the preheated oven. "Now that brother-in-law of yours, he's not getting anywhere near the pearly gates."

Just as Chris had suspected. "Dex is gone again?"

"Hopefully for good."

Chris agreed, but they'd said the same thing the countless other times his sister's sorry excuse for a husband had decided family life wasn't a good fit for him. "What's the likelihood of that?"

"About as likely as you ever settling down."

"Ma…"

"I know." She picked up her glass and took a swallow of her favorite rosé. "With everything you've lost, it's easier to keep moving. I can't fault you for that." Disappointment tangled with compassion in her voice, and Chris ducked his chin to force down the lump in his throat.

UC work had kept him away except for random fly-bys, and even those had dwindled since Izzy's death. He missed his family —the humor, the food, the love—but being around them reminded Chris of the other things he missed—the life and future he'd lost. It was easier to ignore the painful losses when he was someplace else, someone else. Izzy had recognized that and steered him onto a new path, one where he could lose himself for weeks, months, on end. He'd be forever in her debt for that blessed courtesy.

But he couldn't run forever. Like Celia, he was exhausted, tired of running from his demons. And he wanted to be here for his family. But had he been gone too long to reclaim his spot? Was there a place for him here, for the person he was now? Or would be, when he figured out who the hell that was? He'd cooked and laughed with his family the last few weeks, but it wasn't the same. They thought he had one foot out the door, as usual. Truth be told, he hadn't fully committed to stepping over that threshold the other way either.

Gloria threw an arm around his waist. "I'm glad to have you back in town, for however long you can be here."

"Thanks, Ma." He kissed the top of her salt-and-pepper head. Then took a first step. "I'm hoping it'll be longer this time."

"How much longer?"

Chris looked from his mother toward the voice, and his gaze clashed with Celia's dark, haunted one. She stood next to the couch, clutching Marco's dress shirt.

He took another step, most of the way over that threshold. "For good, I hope."

Gloria gasped, then clapped, while Celia white-knuckled her son's shirt. "You hope," his sister scoffed. She looked almost frightened yet sounded pissed he'd added the 'I hope' caveat. Did she want him back or not?

"Cee," Chris entreated, confused as fuck.

"*Your* bike is fixed." She spun on her heel and headed back toward the garage. "We're going to the store to grab soda." The garage door slammed shut behind her, cutting off any reply.

Gloria rested her weight against Chris's side. "It's been a rough week."

Chris laughed, both bitter and sympathetic.

The same dark eyes as his and Celia's stared up at him. "You too?" his mother asked.

"Oh yeah, me too."

"Butter chicken will fix that." She lifted her glass and swirled the pink contents. "So will wine."

"Pour me a big one, then."

Snickering, she poured him a tankard's worth, far more than was decent in any wine glass. "Are you really coming home?"

"Can I?"

"Always, Christopher." She handed him the glass and clinked the rim of her glass against his. "Well, not to this house, because I've earned my peace and quiet, and you have your own home, but you will always have a place in this family."

"Thanks, Ma." He gave her another peck on the head and smiled, covering the worry that still swirled over Celia's reaction, over what was going on in his sister's life. Worry that continued to mount as he put the final touches on dinner. Two sets of footsteps were on their way up the stairs, and Chris had just set the steaming plates of rice and butter chicken on the table, when the phone in his apron pocket vibrated. He pulled it out and read the text from Kane.

Gary Danko. Tomorrow night. 8:30.

Finally.

Except now that was another worry added to the mountain.

Chris drained what was left of his wine and helped himself to another too full glass, muffling his worry and the dangerous hope of home—not just with his family—that threatened to eclipse it.

CHRIS FLIPPED THE CARD CASE IN HIS HAND, END OVER END, IN TIME with his bouncing thoughts and measured steps, back and forth across his study, working off dinner and working through ideas. He had a meet with Hawes tomorrow. Progress. He wanted more.

But two hours later, the temporary high of forward momentum had withered and died, leaving behind his old friend frustration. His constant companion the past three years.

Start from the top.

Izzy's voice rang in his head—consonants sharp, vowels long, all of it nasal. Her New York accent—Astoria, Queens—had been like nails on a chalkboard at first, grating and obnoxious. Now it was a comfort, if only in his imagination.

"Hawes Madigan," he said, speaking to a ghost. "King, head of the empire." Chris rested on the corner of his paper-strewn desk, which he'd crammed into the bay window nook in the front room of his condo. He glanced at the long wall to his right. It was covered with photos and colorful strings, arranged in a pyramid of sorts. He'd used his and Izzy's case notes, and the notes from the previous investigations, to construct a hierarchy of the Madigan organization.

The illegal one.

Helena and Holt were on either side of Hawes on the top line of the chart. Hawes didn't make an impact decision without discussing it with his siblings. He was the king as far as the outside world was concerned, but Chris knew his secret, confessed on a night when the crown had been too heavy to bear. Hawes didn't want to be king, not if he had to destroy his soul again to do it. It had been a devastating blow when sixteen-year-old Hawes had had to make the call to take his parents off life support. Then last week, he'd had to guide the family through his grandfather's passing. Hawes needed his siblings to step up and into equal roles in the organization's leadership apparatus if he was going to survive, regardless of who else was gunning for them.

On either side of the triumvirate—not a row down, but not quite on the same line—Chris had put the rest of the nuclear family: their grandmother, Rose; Holt's wife, Amelia; and Kane. Not related by blood or marriage, as far as the chief went, but he was family to them and vice versa. The next line down listed the organization's lieutenants: Jodie, Ray, Lucas, Avery, Zoe, and Rowe. All of them, except Avery and Zoe, had red string X's over their pictures—deceased. Below them, captains Chris had heard mention of but hadn't laid eyes on. And below the captains were soldiers, some of whom Chris had seen at MCS. All in all, not an uncommon structure for a criminal enterprise. More complicated than the mafia but not unlike the cartel Chris had infiltrated in Florida or the gun-running motorcycle club he'd busted in Seattle.

Where does the next hit come from? Izzy prompted.

Chris ruled out Hawes's siblings. He'd mistakenly gone down

that path before, wrongfully accusing Holt, and he had the mess on his hands now to show for it. He'd come around to Hawes's conviction: Holt and Helena wouldn't turn on their brother. Same as Chris would never turn on Celia. Nor on his mother. He ruled out Rose accordingly, and besides, she'd been in the car with Hawes when they'd been targeted after Papa Cal's funeral. Taking out the matriarch would have been another powerful blow to the family, possibly too devastating to come back from after just losing Cal.

Kane was a nonstarter. The chief had nothing to gain and everything to lose from a coup that would overthrow and threaten the trio. Avery had proved her loyalty. Zoe too. Which left…

"The captains."

Unless…

"An uprising among the soldiers."

But Chris doubted a lowly soldier was pulling Amelia's strings. She was too much of a force in her own right, too focused on power for herself and for Lily's legacy, albeit a different one than Holt and his siblings wanted for the munchkin. No, someone else with more juice had manipulated Amelia. They'd moved her around the board like they'd done with Jodie, Ray, and Lucas.

"An outsider," Chris reasoned. "Someone who'd promised Amelia the head of the table when this was all over. Someone who wanted an ally there and was willing to use those explosives to do it. Maybe for something else too." He picked up his tacks and string and put a red X out to the right side of the org chart.

Good, Dante. Now, when did the outsider enter the picture?

He rotated and examined the opposite wall.

Crime scene photos and reports from the night of Izzy's death were assembled in a collage with three years' worth of case notes. It had been the first thing Chris had arranged in his home office when he'd returned to San Francisco for this operation. He didn't care about the holes in the walls; they needed a fresh coat of paint anyway. He'd do that once he completed this mission, once he was done and had time to transform this place back into a home.

He reached out and grabbed the top folder off the stack on his desk. Withdrawing the offshore bank account ledger he'd shown to Hawes, he flipped it over to the oldest highlighted transaction on the back. He grabbed another tack and added this latest piece of evidence to the collection. Three years ago, Amelia had paid Zander Rowe from that account. Two years after Hawes had assumed the throne, operationally if not officially.

Their mysterious outsider was playing the long game. They'd decided fairly quickly that they didn't want Hawes in charge. Had made an attempt using Rowe somehow, and it had backfired. After Izzy's death, Hawes had solidified the organization's new direction. Gone even further toward caution and vigilantism versus straight-up fear and power. So the objectors, led by this outsider, had waited until Papa Cal's death—the official transfer of power—to strike.

Why, Dante?

"Because transfers of power are hectic. A good time to strike."

But that couldn't be all. He glanced out the bay windows on the other side of his desk. He couldn't see the Bay from here, but it was out there. And so too was Lucas, somewhere at the bottom of its inky depths. He remembered what the traitor had said on the boat that day Hawes had all but ordered him killed. Remembered what Amelia had said in her final stand at the condo. "Because someone thought Hawes was weak."

Hawes, however, had embraced the perceived weakness—in his person and his motives—and had made it his strength. And now he wasn't just a prince but a king. A threat of the highest order.

To whom?

"Competitors, former allies, former clients."

And who can lead you to those?

"Amelia Madigan."

Chris had been focused on digging into Hawes's connections,

then into Holt's. Time to shift gears. Amelia was his way in. Who had she crossed paths with? Where did her loyalties truly lie? Were the answers on the flash drive backup? Where the fuck was it? He needed to find it before the Madigans did. And he needed to find the outsider before Hawes did, because, while it was in the ATF's and Chris's interests to catch that person and put them on trial, to get justice for Izzy's death, among other crimes, Hawes, Chris expected, had a very different endgame in mind. The only one that would secure his family's future and protect those he held dear.

You can't let that happen.

"I know."

Even if a not small part of Chris didn't object to Hawes's brand of justice.

FOUR

The light on the flash drive plugged into Chris's computer blinked orange, signaling the file transfer was in progress, just as the *click* of electronic door locks sounded from his desk speakers. He'd powered them on and synced them with his phone as soon as he'd returned home. Someone else had finally returned home too.

"Hey, girl," Hawes said. "Sorry I was gone all day." His voice was gentle and quiet—and tired, his exhale breathy, his syllables long. People claimed there wasn't a California accent, and Chris generally agreed, except there was a distinctive cadence, which was more noticeable when it was off, like it was in Hawes's voice now.

Iris let out a warbling *meow*, sounding both angry and confused. She made the noise again, then screeched a protest *yowl*. Hawes's words were amplified when he spoke next. "Just me, you little traitor."

Chris smiled at the memory of being stretched out on Hawes's couch, pretending to be asleep with Iris on his feet while Hawes prepared for a job, and at the irony of Hawes's words, more true than he knew. Chris had tucked his bug into the narrow folds of

Iris's collar, which was transmitting loud and clear with the cat in Hawes's arms.

"I still love you anyway," Hawes cooed. "Let's get you some food." His voice faded as he put Iris down, the cat no doubt scampering off to her bowl in the kitchen.

Chris turned the speaker volume down and tried not to listen too closely as Hawes moved about his condo. If Hawes contacted his siblings or another organization associate, Chris would detect the change in tone and tune back in. Until then, he didn't want to completely trample Hawes's expectation of privacy. The condo —*his home*—was a safe haven, from work, the organization, and his family, when he needed a break. As it was, it had been violated by the chaos Amelia had wrought. Chris didn't want to compound any insecurity Hawes already felt inside the space... which consideration for his mark was fucking ridiculous. Chris should be doing everything he could to throw Hawes Madigan off-balance, to make him feel unsafe and on-guard. He'd be more likely to make a mistake then, and Chris had an inside track. He knew better than most which buttons to push to multiply the mistakes. He'd made a physical and emotional connection with the cold, untouchable, beautiful, and efficient killer Izzy had described in her files. Chris didn't disagree with the latter two, but the first two couldn't be further from the truth. Everything about Hawes was hot, and every inch of him was eminently touchable. The waves of light brown hair, the smooth pale skin dotted with freckles, all those sharp angles. Chris had convinced himself that he'd been the one taking Hawes apart that night in the condo against the ladder, finding a way into the assassin's mind and body, but Hawes had snuck under Chris's skin too. Further even, if the ache in his chest and groin were any indication.

Not good, Izzy chided.

"No shit, Sherlock."

He propped his elbows on the desk and scrubbed his hands over his face. Fingers tunneling into his hair, he loosened the tie around his topknot and massaged his scalp as the long strands fell free. This couldn't be about what he wanted. None of that mattered until he was done, *after* he found Izzy's killer and closed the ATF's investigation into the explosives. Chris had a better chance of succeeding on both fronts by working with the Madigans against whoever it was working against them. That was the real enemy here—the party who wanted to turn the organization back into the indiscriminate killing machine of Papa Cal's reign. The party who would use the stolen explosives to make their objective a reality. It was all twisted and tied together. Chris couldn't solve one without the other.

Which was what he needed to focus on. Not the *clink* of whisky bottles, not the *splash* of water in Hawes's shower, not the snippets of the Giants game on replay, and not Hawes's light snores. Not how rumpled and enticing Hawes must look lying on his couch. Like he'd looked Friday morning before Chris had woken him—wavy top strands sticking out in every direction, lean, corded muscles relaxed in sleep, a layer of darker scruff shadowing his angular jaw.

He wanted him still, maybe even more so than when he'd last seen Hawes. But what would be left of what he wanted when he was done with what he had to do? Was there a shot in hell Hawes would ever forgive him? That he'd ever touch—

Stop it!

His voice, not Izzy's. He shut down the thoughts making his jeans uncomfortable and got back to work. He took another spin through his and Izzy's files, recasting contacts and events around Amelia, searching for her connections and hiding places. An hour later, he was scrolling through search results—pre-Madigan-Amelia's last known addresses and places of employment cross-referenced against all persons flagged in the previous Madigan investigations—when Hawes's voice trickled out of the speakers again. Chris turned up the volume so he could hear it more clearly.

"No, no, no," Hawes mumbled. "Get off me! I can't just leave!"

Chris shot to his feet and snatched his keys off the desk. Someone was in Hawes's condo trying to force him to leave. Granted, Hawes could take care of himself, but if the intruder had surprised Hawes in his sleep, like Chris had done yesterday, then Hawes could be at their mercy. *Fuck*, Chris needed to get there. But he couldn't get there quickly enough from his place in Mission Dolores. He should alert Kane, get an officer on Hawes. Or better yet…

Chris grabbed his phone and scrolled to Holt's contact info. But then he stalled, thumb over the Call button, as his mind pushed through the panic to comprehend what he was hearing.

"No, no, no," Hawes repeated. "Get off me! I can't just leave!"

If an assailant was in the condo, if an actual fight was imminent, Iris would have bolted, not gotten closer, as indicated by Hawes's louder mumbles. Add to that her frantic purring, so loud it sounded like the hum of Chris's Harley, and he deduced the cat was trying to wake her owner from a nightmare.

Finally, she *meowed*, so plaintive and piercing that Chris winced.

And Hawes fell silent. Until the counting began. Same as it had the first night Chris had slept there, then again the night after Papa Cal died. Those times Chris had been in Hawes's condo. He could have gone to him if necessary. But Hawes had shaken himself out of it after a few repetitions, the arrival of his siblings hastening the process. Tonight, however, Hawes was alone, the counting continued, and Chris was halfway across town, feeling untethered, like Hawes had described feeling earlier in the week.

Chris tapped back to his contacts list, thumb hovering over Hawes's name. Would he even take Chris's call? In the unlikely event he did, what the fuck would Chris say? He had zero reason for calling at one in the morning. It wouldn't be case related. They already had a meet scheduled for that. No, this was dick related at best, heart related at worst.

"Fuck!"

Chris bolted out of the study and charged into the kitchen,

nearly ripping the fridge door off in his haste to get a beer. He tossed the phone onto the island, dug out a bottle opener, and popped the cap, which bounced off the tiles and rolled across the hardwood floor toward the study. Tempting him to follow it back in there. To listen. He rounded the kitchen island and leaned back against it, pretending not to see the cap there, not to hear the only other sound in his too quiet condo.

Hawes's counting.

Through half the bottle of beer, then the rest of it.

Chris snatched up the phone and hit the Call button.

Iris hissed, knocked something over as she skittered across the metal coffee table, and Chris realized he only had a couple of seconds to move—the time it would take Hawes to reach for his phone—or else Hawes would hear the echo from Chris's speakers.

He hustled the length of the open kitchen, past the dining table, and down the long hallway bisecting his unit, to the seating area at the back of his narrow, second-floor condo. This area was intended as a mudroom entry from the stairs leading down to the backyard, but Chris rarely ventured out there. Instead, he'd made this room his reading nook—a leaning bookcase brimming over with paperbacks on one short wall, a coffee table and low-slung chaise on the long wall, and across from the chaise, big casement windows through which he had a decent view of the city. South, toward the condo and the man in it, who answered his call with, "It's late."

Better than the "fuck off" Chris had expected. He moved a stack of books from the chaise to the bookshelf, then lowered himself into the lounge's soft padded corner. "You're awake."

"So are you," Hawes said, rough and rumbly. "At one in the morning. Why's that?"

"Was reviewing Izzy's case files."

"Izzy." The background noise of the TV quieted. Still in the den, and by the lack of footsteps anywhere, still on the couch. "Your partner."

How much to disclose? Chris wanted to keep Hawes talking,

keep him engaged, and this particular cat was out of the bag already. A little truth could go a long way. "I considered her that, as much as two undercover agents could be. She recruited and trained me at a time when I needed a new direction. One of us would be in the field, undercover, while the other was operational backup. Then, about four years ago, we were assigned separately. I was sent to Florida on a cartel sting."

Hawes was silent, long enough that Chris checked to make sure the call hadn't dropped. "Hawes, you there?"

"And she was sent to infiltrate my organization." His dark tone set off a ripple of goose bumps that lifted the hairs on Chris's arms.

"That's right."

"And three years later, here you are." Hawes hummed, contemplative. "Patience."

"Something like that."

Pensive gave way to indignant. "You waited until I was weakest."

"No." Chris shifted forward on the chaise, as if to emphasize his point to an imaginary Hawes leaning against the windows. "I waited until I got that flash drive and it became apparent someone else was making a move."

"So that wasn't bullshit?"

"I told you it wasn't all a lie."

"It's hard to sort out what was and wasn't."

"Ask me." The truth had kept Hawes talking so far. Chris could offer him more, anything, to reestablish this connection. For the sake of the case, of course, nothing to do with what he wanted.

"Are you really from here?" Hawes asked.

Chris bit back his sigh of relief and settled in for the conversation he'd wanted all day. Lifting and bending one leg, he rested it on the cushions and slung an arm along the back of the chaise. "Yes, born and raised in North Beach."

"Is your family still here?"

"They are."

Hawes huffed in disbelief. "Why would you tell me that? You're putting them at risk."

"I'm not." Of that, Chris was sure, more so with Hawes's organization than with any other he'd investigated. "Hurting them would be against your rules."

"My rules…" Hawes's words died on a bitter chuckle.

It scraped over Chris's bones, same as it had earlier. He hated it, hated the doubt he'd added to that mix. "Your rules are a good thing, Madigan."

"Should have recognized that for what it was. *Cop.*"

"Why didn't you?"

"I considered it when you walked into Danko." The leather of the couch creaked and fabric shifted, Hawes relaxing more on his end too. "But then Brax didn't know you, and…"

"And what?"

"That hair."

Chris's cheeks heated, recalling how often Hawes's gaze had strayed to the long strands, how his hands had tunneled through it, how he'd curled a hank around his fist and tugged. Chris had nearly come on the spot. "You like the hair."

"Too fucking much." Judging by the gravel in Hawes's voice, his mind had gone to the same place. "That, plus your *Madigans.* Sexy."

Chris dropped his arm off the back of the chaise, hand landing on his thigh. "Street ran both ways, with your *Mr. Perrys.*"

"So the formalities wouldn't have done me any favors, *Mr. Perry?*"

"Christ." Chris scooted down and spread his legs, trying to make more room for his thickening cock. "No, *Madigan,* they would not."

This was not the conversation Chris had anticipated tonight. He'd needed to get closer again, for the case, but this… This was the closer he wanted but didn't need. And he was powerless to stop it. Just like he was powerless to stop from sliding his hand toward his erection, which was pressing against the back of his zipper, demanding attention. He gripped himself through the denim, intending to stave off the building desire. He stroked down his length instead. "Probably would have fucked you sooner," he gritted out. "Taken you on that deserted dock if you hadn't stormed off."

Hawes had been glorious. Fitted, navy suit pants that showed off his high and tight ass, light-brown hair fog kissed and windswept from the ride on the yacht, blue eyes that burned bright with power and lust. Chris bet those eyes were burning bright again now.

Another stroke and Chris bit his lip to hold in the groan.

"I would have let you," Hawes replied raggedly. "Was already hard."

"Like you are now?"

"Fuck, Dante."

Chris bobbled the phone and had to interrupt another stroke to save the device from crashing to the floor. Recovered, he put the phone on speaker and set it on the arm of the chaise. He needed both hands to get his fly open and his dick out as fast as he could. "I remember how you tasted later that night," he said. "Like the fog." He swiped his fingers over the slit, collecting moisture, and spread it down his cock, slicking his grip. He closed his eyes and dropped his head back onto the chaise's arm. "Light and dark," he said, remembering the moment. "Hidden and open." Reliving it. "Suffocating, then freed."

"I can't," Hawes gasped.

Chris paused his strokes and rolled his face toward the phone. "Say the word, and I'll hang up."

"Too late."

Yes, it was, on so many levels. And on this one, Chris wasn't going to pump the brakes any more than Hawes was. "Get your dick out of those track pants," he said, figuring that's what Hawes had changed into after his shower. Commando, as he was prone to do. "And pull your shirt up." He closed his eyes again, imagining the sight. Hawes laid out on his couch, track pants bunched around his thighs, ribbed tank rucked under his chin, bared torso clenched with tension, the pale skin blotched red with rising heat as Hawes's hand shuttled up and down his cock.

Chris pushed his own jeans down farther, stripped off his shirt, and stroked himself faster. "Let me help you," he urged. "Let go for me."

"Look where that got me. You lied. You betrayed me. I should fucking hate you." The smart, rational part of Hawes's brain was fighting him, even as precome made his strokes audible, even as his breaths between words grew short and choppy.

"You liked being under me."

"Fuck, too much." Hawes groaned, wanton and needy, and Chris had to squeeze his balls to stave off his charging orgasm.

"I liked it too. All that straining muscle, all that strength matching my own. Your hands digging into my biceps. Holding on for dear life."

"Oh God." Hawes panted, breaths uneven, his words stuttered. "Too good. Too close."

"No such thing," Chris said, right there with him. He wished like hell he could see Hawes, wished he was there with him. But they could get somewhere else together. "Get there, Madigan."

Hawes's groan was long and broken, and on it, a wrecked, "Dante."

Chris tumbled over the edge with him, streaks of come splattering his torso as pleasure, desire, and desperation erupted in a blinding orgasm.

They caught their breaths in rhythm, together still, and Chris was the first to speak. "Wish that had been my mouth on you again."

"That jock and cheerleader really didn't appreciate what they had."

"You've seen the yearbook now. No better in print and no better in real life then either."

Chris's chuckle was met with dead silence on the other end of the line. A beat later, Chris realized the mistake his lust-fogged brain—and mouth—had made.

"How'd you know that?" Hawes asked, his voice a dangerous whip. Fully alert, all trace of their shared pleasure gone.

"I assumed," Chris tried to cover. "Holt said he was retrieving it."

"Or my condo is bugged."

"I assume you swept for bugs."

"You assume." Hawes's quick, determined tread echoed over the line. He was on his feet, moving around the condo. "Your assumptions and your plans, Mr. Perri. I can't trust any of them. Lesson learned." Ice cold, not the least bit of heat.

Chris fucking hated the freeze-out, especially after they'd just burned so hot together. After he'd managed to get close again. Dammit! He had to get back there, or at least try to. Trust—that was the key. That was where they kept getting tripped up.

He wiped off his torso with his shirt and stood, hiking up his pants. He hustled to the study and turned the speakers up, listening. "Give Iris a scratch for me," he said. "She's in your closet."

Hawes ended the call, and a moment later snuffed out the bug, a blast of static giving way to silence.

"It wasn't all a lie," Chris said to no one.

FIVE

Chris pushed open the restaurant's heavy glass door, and the wave of déjà vu almost made him stagger. The same hostess stood at her stand, Kane sat on a stool at the bar, and Hawes occupied the corner booth on the far side of the dining room. But that's where the similarities to last Sunday ended. No lively music played, no enticing aromas wafted from the kitchen, and no other diners filled the rest of the tables. The only patrons tonight were the king and two of his most loyal, most deadly allies, Helena and Avery.

The hostess stepped out from behind her stand and extended an arm toward Hawes's table. "Your party is waiting, Mr. Perri." Coat draped over her other arm, she sidestepped Chris and placed a set of keys on the bar next to Kane. "Anything else, Chief?"

Kane drew the keys toward him. "We're good, Ashleigh." Chris couldn't see Kane's face, but his bedraggled voice said plenty about the weekend he'd had. Worse than even Chris's. "Thank you."

"Just drop the keys in my mail slot before dawn." She squeezed his shoulder, flashed a smile at Hawes's table, then slipped out the front door, ignoring Chris completely.

He waited for the door to thunder shut behind her before sliding into the space next to Kane. "They bought the place out?"

"They don't trust you anymore." The chief rolled a cut-crystal tumbler between his palms, sloshing the two fingers of amber liquid inside the glass. Scotch, judging by the color and peaty smell tickling Chris's nose. "Don't trust me much either."

"And yet we're both here, and they haven't shot us."

Kane side-eyed him. "Yet."

Chris didn't doubt that Helena and Avery had their weapons within reach, if not drawn and trained on him beneath the table.

"Thanks for setting this up."

"You're lucky they answered my call." Kane drained his scotch and reached over the bar to place the glass in the sink. "And don't thank me yet." He straightened, wiped his hands, and slid off his stool. "Let's see how this goes first."

Kane led the way across the dining room rather than standing guard at the bar. He was joining them this time. As a mediator? Chris didn't dwell on the thought too long, his attention seized instead by the man seated at the middle of the table—the man whose lips were pressed into a thin line, whose posture was on guard, and whose blue eyes tracked his every step. Chris tried to take each step more like Dante, less like Special Agent Perri. Dante was the name Hawes had moaned last night when he'd come, the man he'd let in again. The man Chris had wanted to be more than anyone else for those too brief minutes, maybe who he wanted to be now more than a little—a lot after this was done. More than who he wanted to be, Dante was who Chris needed to be for this meet to pay off.

A meet he was lucky to have. After disclosing the location of the bug to Hawes, Chris had waited all day for the cancellation call to come. He'd taken a gamble, which could have gone either way. A final destruction of trust or an ounce of it earned. The phone never rang. Either he'd won back enough trust for Hawes to keep this meet, or this was a trap and he'd walked right into it.

Hawes's frigid "Mr. Perri" made Chris think the latter. No sexy rumble, no trace of warmth, no hint of a *Y* instead of an *I*. This was the cold, untouchable Hawes Madigan from Izzy's files. The only sign of emotion was the quiet, restrained anger that practically vibrated off him, as though his dark, fitted suit was the only thing keeping him contained. "I don't know what more we have to say to one another, but you requested this meeting"—he spread his hands—"so we're here."

Chris lowered himself into the chair next to Kane and nodded a greeting to Helena and Avery. Helena appeared aloof, while betrayal burned in Avery's dark eyes. Still loyal to her employers. Good. And of their missing party… "How's Holt?" Chris didn't expect him to be here if Hawes and Helena both were, but he probably wasn't far away.

Hawes's gaze flickered to Kane, a look passing between them. "Fine." Holt was anything but fine, if Chris had to guess from that terse response.

But before he could question further, Helena turned her I'm-barely-tolerating-your-presence glare on him. "Get on with it, Mr. Hair."

Chris chuckled, the tension-filled air around them lightening a smidgen. "We're sticking with that, then?"

"What else am I supposed to call you? Dantopher?"

And lightening a bit more. He held up his hands, palms out. "Things got out of hand Friday."

Stony silence. So much for the reprieve.

"We can still work together," he ventured.

"I don't see how that's possible." Hawes pointed a finger at him. "Fed." Then at himself. "Target of a federal investigation."

Chris jutted a thumb at Kane. "LEO. You work with him."

"Because we've known Brax for over a decade," Helena said. "He's proved he can be trusted." She tilted her head, long blonde hair cascading over her leather-clad shoulder. "You, not so much."

"Let me see if I can change that." He pulled back one side of his denim jacket, moving deliberately and obviously, and reached inside the inner pocket. He bypassed his leather card case and withdrew the flash drive he'd prepared last night. He pushed it across the table. "That's a copy of the file from the judge's desk." Not wanting to implicate them in front of Kane, Chris didn't mention Campbell by name, the target who'd given Hawes the tip on the current investigation right before Hawes and company had murdered him and set it up to look like a suicide.

Eyes flaring, Hawes accurately read between the lines. "So it was the ATF?"

Chris nodded. "Higher-ups got wind you were moving the explosives. Reopened the prior investigation."

"They thought they'd get us on the sale?"

Chris nodded again. "I convinced them I could infiltrate quickest."

Hawes traced his index finger around the rim of his glass. Chris thought he detected a tremble. "Because you thought you could seduce me." Or, given the barely contained fury in Hawes's voice, the assassin was readying to pick up the heavy cut crystal and throw it at him.

Chris backpedaled, fast. "Not part of my original plan."

Hawes rolled his eyes. "And we've come full circle, back to your *plans*."

Chris ignored the jab and made his case before objects started flying. "I had Isabella's files and knew them better than anyone. *That's* why I thought I could infiltrate fastest. Other than Izzy, no one else at the ATF knew you or the organization better." He leaned forward, rested his forearms on the table, and clasped his hands. "What I quickly realized, however, between recon and working with you, was that yours isn't the same organization Isabella, and those before her, had investigated. And you're getting out of the explosives business. I have no interest in stopping or arresting you."

"That's not what you said yesterday morning."

"You weren't listening."

He clasped the glass, knuckles white. "I was handcuffed to the fucking bed."

"You're not now," Chris said, fighting to keep this conversation focused, fighting not to get sidetracked by the image that flashed behind his eyes—Hawes naked and writhing and seething mad. So mad then, and now, that he still wasn't listening. "I need you to hear me, Hawes. *My* mission remains the same."

Hawes stifled a noise and averted his gaze, dropping his hand from the glass.

Helena took up the conversation. "To find Isabella's killer."

"Yes," Chris answered. "And also less death, which means stopping whoever is trying to overthrow you and your brothers. Our interests are aligned. We track the explosives and determine who is behind their theft and the attempted coup, and we stop them."

"We," Hawes scoffed. A flicker of something softer, sadder, passed across his eyes, before a sheet of ice slammed down over it. "I don't trust you."

"Then trust me," Kane spoke up. "I've got all sides of this covered."

Brows scrunched, lips pressed together again, Hawes did not look convinced by Kane's assertion, but the chief pressed on, and Chris kept his trap shut. He was getting nowhere, maybe Kane could.

"I do not want a bloodbath on my streets," Brax said. "Be it a war within your organization, an explosives sale to the wrong party, or a war between you and the ATF. I've got too much at stake here." More than just his job, given the strain in his body and the plea in his voice. "I'm trying to protect all of us. Trust me to do that and to keep my promise. Ten years and I haven't wavered. I won't now."

Hawes kept his gaze locked on Kane—calculating, assessing—for an interminable five seconds, before it flickered to Chris, then to the flash drive. He drew the device toward himself and pocketed it. "We'll consider it." He stood, Helena and Avery rising beside him.

Chris stood as well. "Thank you."

Helena gave him a departing, "Mr. Hair," Avery another stony glare, and for his part, Hawes paused at the door and leveled him with fiery blue eyes and a "Mr. Perri" that was a few octaves closer to last night's version. Chris counted it a win.

SIX

Monday morning arrived with no follow-up messages. Chris's phone was obnoxiously silent again, no matter how many times he'd checked it. Nothing from Hawes, nothing from Kane, not even an intrusion alert to indicate Holt was poking around in his system. Granted, there was a better than average chance Holt had circumvented his enhanced firewalls, but Chris fully expected the hacker to leave him a middle finger start-up greeting to let him know exactly where he'd been. But his computer, like his phone, transmitted no messages this morning.

Standing outside the 16th Street BART station, he glanced once more at his phone. Still nothing. An answer on how they were going to play this would be helpful sooner rather than later, given his babysitter's imminent arrival. He shoved the phone back into his pocket, rearranged his saddlebag so the strap crossed his body, then entered the teeming mass of commuters descending the stairs to the trains.

Taking BART one stop over to UN Plaza and the Federal Building was easier than finding parking for the Hog downtown. Also quicker this time of morning, even with the broken escalators that plagued the stations. On second thought, maybe he should have taken the bike. He could have wasted time finding a parking spot and delayed facing the terror that was Scotty Wheeler.

By all accounts, Wheeler was a good agent, but he was not a UC agent. Need a tome-sized file built out for a case? Wheeler was the guy. Need to find a needle in a haystack? Wheeler was the guy. Need to delicately infiltrate a tight-knit family of assassins? Wheeler was so not the guy. He was about as subtle as a bag of hammers when it came to conducting investigations. And hammers were the last thing Chris needed when he was already skating on thin ice.

Once on the train, Chris shoved around the files in his bag and dug out his book. He hoped the starter files he'd spent all day yesterday preparing—on Amelia Madigan and the organization's soldiers—would keep Wheeler busy. Let Scotty dig for that particular needle while Chris went about his work, in his own way, relatively unimpeded.

He read a few pages before the doors slid open at the next stop. He exited the train onto the platform and into the sea of people, the tide moving slowly toward the stairs, as the escalator was broken at this station too. Packed in as they were, Chris didn't realize the person directly behind him was an enemy until they pressed the muzzle of a gun against Chris's lower back.

"No sudden movements, Agent Perri," the woman said.

A man appeared on Chris's other side, a half step back like the woman, but close enough to prick Chris's right flank with a knife, behind his bag and just above the waistband of his jeans. "Keep walking," the man said.

Chris did as told but slowed his pace, enough that his would-be captors were forced by the crowd to pull even with Chris, giving him a better look. He recognized them from the pictures on his home office walls. Tamela with the gun to his left and Devon with the knife on his right. Madigan soldiers. Was this Hawes's answer? Or were Tamela and Devon working against their boss?

"Did Hawes send you?"

No comment, not that Chris had expected a reply. Soldiers

knew better. But they did falter at the base of the stairs as the crowd in front of them undulated backward in response to a commotion on the level above.

An opening.

Chris heaved his paperback at the ceiling, scattering the rafter pigeons and jostling the platform crowd around them. Avoiding a knife to his kidneys, Chris slung his bag around to cover his lower back, spun toward Tamela, and grabbed her pistol by the barrel. It was a risk. She could pull the trigger and kill him, setting off a mass panic down here, but he was no good to them dead. She wouldn't fire.

It was the right call. Chris wrenched the gun from her grip and let momentum carry his right elbow back into Devon's face. Chris counterbalanced with a kick to the left, planting a boot in Tamela's stomach. Not enough to take her down, but enough to get the crowd really scattering.

Several of the closest bystanders screamed—"Fight!" "Move!" "Gun!"—having spotted the weapon in Chris's hand and Devon's combat knife clattering to the cement floor.

Chris had no choice. "ATF! Clear the area!" he shouted, sealing the deal on chaos. Better for the public to know law enforcement was on the scene and better to announce himself to any converging BART Police. He'd reach for his badge if he could, but Devon, behind him, was trying to strangle him with the strap of his bag. Chris wedged his free hand under the strap, curled his fingers around it, and shoved outward, extending his arm. Victim to momentum again, Devon rammed into his back. Chris reached back his other arm, curled it around Devon's neck, and bending forward, hauled Devon over his back. The soldier hit the ground hard enough to knock the wind out of him, mouth opening and closing as he struggled for breath.

Chris was having trouble catching a breath—or break—of his own. Back on her feet, Tamela was preparing to attack. She shook out her limbs and eyed the gun Chris had trained on Devon.

Escalating shouts from the crowd drew Tamela's gaze off Chris long enough for him to tuck the gun into his waistband. He couldn't risk using it down here, even if most of the commuters had heeded the warnings and cleared out. With Tamela still distracted, Chris shrugged off his bag, wound the strap around his fist, and cocked it for a throw. Full of files, there was enough heft in the bag for a good hit.

The maneuver proved unnecessary.

A flash of gray silk, starched white cotton, and ice-blue eyes streaked in front of Chris, kicking back down a resurging Devon and sending Tamela to the ground beside him, the crack of bones unmistakable. She tilted forward, trying to curl over her awkwardly hanging arm, but the wire around her neck hauled her back upright.

"Not yours?" Chris said to the man holding either end of the garrote.

"Not anymore." Hawes leaned down and spoke right next to Tamela's ear. "Tell me why I shouldn't kill you, traitor."

Tamela didn't struggle or appear surprised. On the contrary, she looked satisfied. Downright smug.

The pieces snapped together in Chris's head. "Madigan, stop! It's what they want."

Hawes tightened the wire. "They're vetted."

"Why are you here?" Chris asked, snatching up Devon's knife.

"Got a tip."

"Exactly." He pointed at the black-domed cameras all along the platform and at the foot of the stairs. "There are cameras everywhere."

Hawes's smile was wicked. And beautiful. "Not anymore."

Chris tamped down the near overwhelming desire to kiss that deadly, gorgeous smile right off his face. He'd come for him. No, fuck, someone had sent him. "They may have information we can use."

Shouts echoed on the level above.

"ATF!"

"Police!"

"Move, move, move!"

"Guessing they got a tip too," Chris said to Hawes. "This is a setup, Madigan. Don't play into it."

"I knew what it was the second I got the tip, but I wanted to know who the rest of the traitors were. Now I know two more." He backed off and waited for Chris to secure Devon and Tamela. "And I had to be sure you—"

Inconveniently, the urge to kiss him crested again. "I can take care of myself too," Chris said instead. Not that he wouldn't have done the same thing, had he gotten a tip that Hawes was in mortal danger. Which was the very definition of going rogue, and Chris, recognizing that fact, still wouldn't do anything differently. He'd still race to save Hawes, for reasons beyond his value to the mission. Reasons that Chris needed to sort out, but not with the cavalry bearing down on them.

He shoved the gun and knife into his bag, not wanting either to trace back to the organization. From his experience with Amelia, he knew the soldiers wouldn't talk. The weapons were the only evidence. He thrust the bag at Hawes. "But thank you for the assist. Now get the fuck out of here."

He expected Hawes to take the bag and run. He did not expect Hawes to step closer, to shove a hand in his hair and wind it around his fist, to yank back Chris's head. "I still don't trust you." He crushed his mouth down onto Chris's, acting on the same adrenaline-fueled desire that had been riding Chris. A slide of lips, a swipe of tongue, a nip of teeth, a groan from each of them. The kiss was brief, stunning, breathtaking in its force and surprise, and Chris would have happily stayed right there in Hawes's arms if not for the official-sounding shouts a level above getting louder, closer.

Chris drew back and whispered, "Go," against Hawes's lips, then the king was gone, bag in hand, disappearing into the morning fog snaking through the train tunnels.

SEVEN

A fuming Scotty Wheeler was waiting for Chris in the field office lobby. "You let him get away."

"Let who get away?" Chris said, then flashed a smile at the receptionist, who tossed his access badge onto the counter. While the ATF's local division office was in Dublin, the smaller SF Metro office was Chris's home base when he was between assignments. Which was seldom enough that he didn't bother to keep—and lose—his access badge. Better to leave it here and claim it when needed.

Unneeded: Wheeler's welcome party. "Don't fucking play dumb with me, Perri." Wheeler turned on his heel and marched across the bullpen, the end of his tie flying over his suited shoulder. Always the properly dressed agent. Professional attire, clean-shaven, not a blond hair out of place. A far cry from Chris's beard, jeans, and tees, though he'd upgraded to a Henley today, owing to the office visit. He didn't even own a suit anymore. He'd tossed his only one the day after Izzy's funeral. The same day he'd tossed his hair clippers.

Wheeler spun in the conference room doorway, blocking Chris's entrance. He was shorter than Chris by a good half foot but packed into that compact body were muscles that spoke of daily hours spent in the gym. Not someone you wanted to tangle with. "Witness statements indicate a man matching Hawes Madigan's description was at the scene."

"But you've got no positive identification?"

"Don't I?" Wheeler stared up at him with big brown eyes that, on any other man, Chris would have considered attractive. Not, however, on the man who was about to make his life a living hell.

"Hawes Madigan was not at the scene." A phantom tingle ghosted over Chris's lips, reminding him that Hawes had most definitely been there.

Wheeler's ears and cheeks reddened with anger, the same frustration glittering in his dark eyes. He wanted to argue, but after a beat and a huffed breath, he thought better of it and retreated into the conference room. Chris bit back a victorious smile. Had he let it loose, it would have been short-lived, dying as soon as he entered the room and glimpsed Wheeler's work to date. File folders were scattered the length of the conference table, a flip board near the door was covered with pictures from both crime scenes last week, and the two wall-mounted whiteboards at the far end of the room were full of scribbled notes, including a Madigan org chart similar to the one Chris had constructed in his home office. Wheeler's chart had each party's official and unofficial capacity listed beneath their name, and off to the side, under the heading *Wildcard,* was written *Braxton Kane.*

Fuck.

Tran had lied. Wheeler hadn't just been put on this case. This level of detail required weeks, months, years of work. Had Tran been running parallel investigations? And from the setup here, when had Wheeler actually arrived in town? Definitely before this weekend.

"You took those two operatives down by yourself?" Wheeler asked.

"I did."

"We'll see what they say when we question them."

Devon and Tamela had received medical attention at the scene and were now in the FBI's holding cells downstairs, neither cognizant enough yet for admissible interrogation. The SAC would let Chris and Wheeler know when they were ready. Not that Chris expected the soldiers to say much. If this went the way questioning Lucas and Amelia had, they'd stay mum. The opposing faction wanted to bring Hawes down and wrest control of the organization, not destroy it completely.

Chris strolled to the coffee maker at the other end of the room, checked it for water and fresh-enough grounds, then set it to brew. He rotated and rested back against the counter, gaze drifting again to Wheeler's case notes. "There's a flaw in your workup."

Wheeler turned halfway around to the board. "What's that?"

"The explosion after Cal's funeral was an attack on the Madigans, not one engineered by them."

"Amelia Madigan was behind it."

"Yes, but—"

"Let's get something straight, Perri." He shifted back around to face Chris. "Neither I nor the ATF care about whatever feud is going on in the Madigan organization. We're bringing it all down, starting at the top." He pointed at the picture of Hawes, sitting alone at the top of the pyramid. Another flaw in the workup, but Chris didn't clue Wheeler in on that one. If Wheeler wanted to focus his attention on Hawes, let him. Hawes could handle Scotty. There'd be less attention on Chris as he worked with Holt, Helena, and Kane on the thing that was supposed to matter to the ATF.

"According to Tran," Chris said, "the explosives are our primary objective."

"Which are where?"

Chris poured a mug of coffee and sipped in silence, not admitting to the unknown that was more dangerous than any of the Madigans.

"Exactly," Wheeler said, correctly reading his nonanswer. "You don't know where they are. Explosives made by professional assassins, which could land in the hands of even worse killers. I want to eliminate the organization that made them thereby stopping them from making more and eliminating those who could put the explosives to use."

That was one way to look at the situation. A bit Rambo-esque in its idealism, because fuck knew they couldn't eliminate all the targets.

"And you're going to help me," Wheeler added.

"What do you think I've been doing here? The past week with the Madigans, the past month of getting everything into place, the past three years following Izzy's leads? I'm trying to find a way in so we can identify the real killers and find the explosives."

"Well, you failed, King Slayer."

Chris gritted his teeth.

"Isn't that what they call you?"

There was a reason he understood Hawes's loathing of his Prince of Killers moniker. A reason Chris knew exactly when to needle him with it and when to let it go. Because after taking down more than a few heads of criminal empires, Chris had earned his own moniker. One he liked about as much as Hawes liked his. Unfortunately, every time he slayed a king, collateral damage was unavoidable. Innocents wrapped up in the organization. Partners, kids, organization members who were just trying to do right by their families. Another reason why Hawes's new order had resonated with Chris, why he wanted to help him, not slay him. But Chris couldn't tell Wheeler any of that. "Yes, that's what they call me," he said instead.

Wheeler grinned, victorious. "Then let's slay the fucking king already."

IF CHRIS HAD THOUGHT ALL EYES WERE ON HIM FRIDAY AT SFPD headquarters, it was nothing compared to Monday afternoon. Badge around his neck, backup weapon holstered on his hip, he was no longer hiding his identity, and the curious looks were coming from all directions. He'd have to address the rumor mill at tomorrow's interagency task force meeting, but first he had a meeting with Kane—without Wheeler.

Maybe also with a certain Madigan.

Chris had mentally replayed that morning's altercation in the BART station too many times, like the best broken record ever. Hawes's too brief kiss, a phantom tingle on his lips that had lingered delightfully, torturously. His speed and skill in taking down Devon, the same agility and grace he'd displayed in dispatching Jodie. That wicked smile after. Chris couldn't get the scene—or the man—out of his head.

Trained in combat as he was, Chris found something undeniably sexy about a person whose skills rivaled his own, a person who exercised that much confidence and control over their faculties and surroundings. Even sexier had been Hawes ceding all that confidence and control to Chris in their moments alone last week. He'd done so because he'd trusted Chris, and Chris had betrayed that trust, though not to the extent Hawes believed. Chris had a way to go toward winning back that trust, but last night's meet and this morning's kiss were good starts. Granted, the brief lip-lock was ninety-nine percent fueled by adrenaline, but Chris could work with the one percent.

"You gonna stand out there all day?"

Kane's voice startled Chris back to the present. The chief was leaning his head and shoulders out his office door as if hiding something—*someone*—inside.

Chris's hope bloomed cautiously. "Sorry," he said. "Was going over some details from this morning in my head."

"We've got some other details to discuss." Kane inched the door open far enough for Chris to slip inside, then closed it behind him.

One look across the room and Chris's hope died, nipped in the bud by a wisp of disappointment and then a flood of concern. A folding table had been positioned in front of the shuttered bullpen window and the visitor chairs moved behind it. In one sat Jax, typing away on their laptop, and in the other sat Holt, with Lily strapped to his chest in a polka-dot sling.

He looked like utter hell.

The last time Chris had seen Hawes's fraternal twin was Thursday, before Papa Cal's funeral. Holt had looked rough then. Four days and a mountain of shit later, the former soldier looked four-months-in-the-desert rough. Auburn beard untrimmed, freckled skin blotchy, brown eyes bloodshot and underlined by dark bags. Even his tattoo sleeve, peeking out from under the rolled right cuff of his flannel shirt, appeared dull. But as tired as he looked, his typing was no less sonic, the one-handed speed mind-boggling. He cradled Lily with his other arm, as if he were afraid to let his daughter go. She was out like a light, stealing the hours of sleep her father had clearly missed out on.

Kane collapsed into his protesting desk chair, which had been rolled to the short end of the folding table, closest to Holt. "He came in to meet with Amelia and her attorney."

Chris leaned a hip against Kane's desk and snagged a candy. "How'd that go?"

Holt lifted his fingers off the keyboard, then lifted his eyes, glaring daggers at Chris. "How do you think it went?"

Chris diverted to a safer topic. "How's Lily?"

"Misses her mom."

Or not so safe. The big man's tension only eased when Kane reached out and brushed his fingers over Lily's head.

Jax watched the quiet, familial moment fondly, unsurprised. In fact, the IT specialist didn't appear surprised about any of what was going on here. "You're helping out on this case?" Chris asked them.

They jutted an orange nail at Holt. "I'm one of his kids."

Chris raised a brow. "One of his—"

"Jax was Holt's star mentee at the LGBTQ shelter," Kane supplied.

"Got my GED, then my BS, and started here last year."

How convenient. Another member of Team Madigan here at the SFPD. A hacker. Any other time, Chris would worry about conflicts of interest, but more allies—and less traitors—were a good thing right now.

Kane reached behind Holt and picked up something off the floor. "I believe this is yours." He heaved Chris's saddlebag onto the table.

"You go through what was inside?"

"Of course," Holt answered. "Most of it was on the flash drive you gave us, though some of the additional...casework...was..." Holt swallowed hard and averted his gaze—to Kane, to Lily, to his laptop. All the new materials had been about Amelia. More shit for Holt to bear while processing a broken heart. No wonder he looked like shit.

"Busy work for Wheeler," Chris said as he rifled through the folders and gave Holt time to gather himself. Everything except the weapons was still in the bag, including a new copy of the book he'd sacrificed to the pigeons. Ducking his chin, Chris hid his grin and lowered the bag to the floor. "Scotty's gonna be a problem," he said. "He's not just after the prototypes." Chris used the Madigans' code for the explosives, unsure how deeply Jax had been read in. "He's out to take your family down."

Holt's narrowed eyes darted up. "Scott Wheeler?" His fingers flew across the keyboard, and then he rotated the laptop toward Chris. "This guy?"

On-screen was Wheeler's profile page from the ATF's supposedly unhackable intranet. "That's him."

Holt cursed and snapped the laptop lid shut. "He was one of the feds posing as attorneys for the last buyer."

"At the meet last Tuesday?" Chris recalled Hawes's haste that morning. He'd turned down an offer of shower fun because he couldn't be late to that meeting. "For the sale of the prototypes?"

Holt nodded. "Hawes and I ran every feature we could remember through recognition databases until we got an ID. We weren't one hundred percent sure, but—"

"That's him, for sure. He's a good agent, but very by the book." Chris turned to Kane. "He's clearly been on this case longer than Tran led us to believe."

Kane rose, snagged a candy, and unwrapped it as he paced the threadbare carpet behind his desk. "She also led us to believe she'd call off the investigation if we secured the weapons. That's the ATF's jurisdiction."

Chris had thought so too, but he wasn't sure now. "Except jurisdiction gets murkier depending on who we find the proto-types with, how they came to be there, and if they can be traced back to the manufacturer."

"We're in the clear," Holt said. "They won't trace back to us."

"Someone could testify against you or manufacture evidence."

"Sure." Holt shrugged. "And I can manufacture evidence otherwise."

Kane tossed the balled-up candy wrapper at Holt and covered his ears with both hands. "Christ, Private."

One corner of Holt's mouth quirked up. Just the teensiest bit. Chris would have to buy Kane more candies.

"Any luck finding Amelia's missing flash drive?"

"So you admit you don't know where it is?" Holt countered.

Chris tilted his head. "In the new spirit of honesty."

Holt chuffed. Another good sign. "Fuck your honesty, but no."

Jax didn't hide their amusement, chuckling out loud before getting back to business. "What I do have is a new lead on the explosives." Read all the way in, then. They held out a tablet to Chris. Paperless—definitely one of Holt's kids. "This was posted on the dark web."

Chris took the tablet and read the solicitation on-screen. It was for bidders for a private auction of demolition prototypes happening tomorrow evening. The location would be provided to "pre-qualified bidders."

"You think this is your stockpile of explosives?"

"Pretty sure," Holt said. "We know from our last buyer that there was no one else in the market offering this much firepower."

"But why?" Chris asked. "If Amelia and her faction are after power, why are they selling off their most powerful weapons?"

"It's just a portion," Holt said.

"Funding the operation?" Kane ventured.

"Could be," Chris said. "Or it could be another trap like the one they tried to spring on Hawes this morning." He shifted his attention to Kane. "We'll have to prep the bust with multiple scenarios in play."

"We want to be there," Holt interjected.

"Did you fucking miss what I just said?"

"*We* have as much interest as *you* in finding out who's behind this."

Chris's frustration—and volume—rose to match. "Ask your fucking wife. She's not talking to any of the rest of us."

"You think I haven't tried!"

Lily's wail ended the argument as quickly as it had escalated. Chris backed off while Holt fussed over his agitated daughter.

"Madigans get eyes on," Kane offered as a compromise, his hand lightly clasping Holt's shoulder. "Jax, can you set up a closed channel?" They nodded, and then Kane said to Chris, "I'll give my team the order to capture, not kill. Will your team agree to the same?"

"I'll make it happen."

"I don't know if I can," Holt said to Kane. "I have to talk to—"

"Clear it with them." Kane squeezed his shoulder. "We'll get answers, but let us lock down the explosives first. It'll buy us all some breathing room."

"I'll see what I can do," Holt said with a nod.

Forward momentum. Chris wanted to cheer. At the same time, he worried his window for getting answers on Isabella's death was closing. Tran and Wheeler didn't care—their top priorities were the explosives and the Madigans, order debatable. While the night of Isabella's death marked a turning point for the Madigan organization, Hawes and his siblings' top priority now was holding on to control so they could keep the family and organization on the path they'd chosen. Chris was the only one putting Isabella first, and he couldn't let her down.

EIGHT

"Start with Devon," Chris told Wheeler, splitting his attention between his babysitter and the retreating backside of the FBI Special Agent in Charge who'd showed him to the interrogation rooms. Chris had heard stories—Irish accent, tailored three-piece suits, shiny cuff links, and a great ass—all true, except the SAC's rumored blond hair was in reality a far more attractive shade of red.

"He's been awake longer. He'll be more alert," Wheeler countered as he gathered his files off the table in the observation room. "We might get more out of the woman."

"We won't." If Chris had learned anything about Hawes's organization, it was that the women were the toughest. Given a choice between the three siblings at the top, Helena was the one he least wanted to meet in a dark alley.

Chris tucked his two file folders under his arm and stepped fully into the observation room, viewing Devon through the one-way glass. Cuffed to the table, the ex-Madigan soldier was in better shape than his partner. Chris had broken Tamela's fingers when he'd snatched her gun away, and Hawes had broken her forearm when he'd interceded. Each of them had left shoe-size bruises on her torso, not to mention the "interesting" bruising around her neck. Chris had slipped the medic a Benjamin to sell that bullshit vagueness to Wheeler. By contrast, Devon had a few scrapes and bruises. He probably also ached from Chris's flip and Hawes's kick, but Devon hid those tells, sitting at attention in his chair.

"We don't have them on anything but assault," Chris said.

"You were a federal officer doing your job. Class D felony."

Chris leaned a shoulder against the wall next to the glass. "I was on my way to work. Not in the middle of an active operation."

"You sure they didn't have any weapons? Some of the witnesses—"

"Are mistaken. They were panicked by the altercation." He held one of his folders out to Wheeler. "Even if Devon did have a gun, he's got a permit for it, and it's clean. No criminal history on it."

Wheeler flipped through the papers, then snapped the file shut. His gaze flickered to the mirror and back. "He doesn't know that."

Chris bet Devon did, but Wheeler was done arguing. He shoved the folder against Chris's chest, grabbed his own off the table, then stepped past him. He held the interrogation room door open for Chris, and the two of them entered, claiming the chairs across the table from Devon.

"Mr. Henderson," Wheeler said.

"Devon," the soldier corrected.

Wheeler pushed a piece of paper across the table. "This is your signed Miranda waiver. You can change—"

"Unnecessary," Devon said. "No attorney needed." He was as calm and confidently resigned as Lucas had been on Hawes's yacht. This was fucking useless.

"You work for Madigan Cold Storage?" Wheeler said.

"Worked. Recently quit."

As in this morning. Chris stifled his scoff.

Wheeler thankfully didn't notice. "Why was that?"

"Didn't like the direction the company was headed."

"What direction was that?"

Devon's gaze drifted to Chris, even as he answered Wheeler. "Management got more selective of their clientele. Didn't seem like the best business decision for growing the company."

"What exactly did you do for Madigan Cold Storage?" Wheeler's restraint impressed Chris. He was drilling down on Devon's cover instead of going straight for reality.

"Marketing," Devon answered.

"Why does a marketing professional need a forty-five and a concealed carry permit?"

"Personal reasons."

"Like the fact that you're an assassin for the Madigans."

"I closed deals for my former employer." No widening eyes, no twitching lips, no reaction whatsoever.

Chris didn't expect any less. He did, however, expect Wheeler to follow the line of questioning about the history of the gun.

The other agent swerved instead. "Why did you attack Agent Perri at the BART station this morning?"

"My associate and I only wanted to have a conversation with him. He"—Devon tilted his head toward Chris—"escalated the situation."

Bullshit, but Chris couldn't say that without disclosing the weapons he'd denied the presence of to Wheeler. Avoiding that possible question, Chris asked a different one. "What did you want to discuss with me?"

"The weather."

No holding in that scoff.

"Who took you down?" Wheeler asked. "At the station."

"Agent Perri."

"Alone?"

"Not my finest moment."

Wheeler did not let up. "Was Hawes Madigan at the scene?"

"I don't know where Mr. Madigan was this morning. I'm no longer his employee."

Wheeler was missing the point, lost in details that didn't matter. Chris focused on the forest instead. "Whose employee are you, Devon?" He leaned forward, resting his forearms on the table. "You're someone's. I know that much, and it's not Hawes Madigan's. Nor is your boss Amelia Madigan. She hasn't spoken to anyone but her counsel since her arrest."

The assassin clammed up. Not so chatty anymore.

"What was the plan?" Chris pressed. "Kill me? Lure Hawes to the rescue so you could frame him?" Chris chose his next words carefully. "Clear the way for your boss to take over the company?"

More silence.

Chris opened his other file folder, took out the single sheet of paper inside it, and slid it across the table. He'd wheedled the printout from Kane, over Holt's strenuous objections, and only after Jax had assured their mentor they'd isolated the printer and data from SFPD's network. "Is your boss the one engineering this auction?"

Devon's eyes widened a fraction, and his breath stuttered once. An average observer wouldn't notice the reaction, but Chris caught it. The flash of surprise that law enforcement was onto them. Seeing it too, Wheeler leaned forward to peer at the paper. Chris held his breath until Wheeler sat back in his chair, trap still thankfully shut.

Chris continued with his line of questioning. "Why?" he asked, trusting Devon would understand the question.

"Same answer, Agent Perri. I don't agree with the current direction of the company. If MCS wants to stay at the top of the market, maybe it's time for some new blood."

Threats and judgments wrapped in slick marketing lingo. Devon played his cover well, except for the clue he'd dropped.

Chris reached for the printout and tucked it back into its folder. "I'm good here." He stood. "Thank you, Mr. Henderson. We'll be keeping you in custody until we have a chance to question your associate."

Devon smiled. "I'll take that lawyer now."

Chris bet he would. Now the traitor was in a hurry, no doubt eager to avoid a night in jail and to relay to his boss that law enforcement was onto their plan.

"We'll get right on that," Chris lied.

Wheeler followed him back into the observation room. "What was that printout about? An auction?"

Chris shoved the folder at him. "Read up. And make sure no one gets in there with him. I don't want word to get back to his boss, whoever that is, that we know about this."

"We should question—"

"She'll tell you less, trust me."

Wheeler backed down, the second time in the last few minutes. Good. They needed to be on the same page in their approach to this case. And Chris could use Wheeler's help. He needed the agent who could find the needle. "Briefing's in an hour. We've got work to do."

⸺⸻⸻

NIGHT HAD FALLEN AND THE FOG HAD ROLLED BACK IN BY THE TIME Chris emerged from the BART station and walked the several blocks west toward Mission Dolores. The city park and mix of residential and commercial buildings gave his neighborhood a bustling vibe, no matter the hour, but the cool summer night had driven some folks inside, the foot traffic on his street lighter than usual.

The person sitting halfway up his porch steps, however, didn't seem the least bit fazed by the cold. Bundled in a puffy teal vest, his niece sat with a pink pastry box on her knees and an e-reader in her hands, index finger swiping pages. Her nose was rarely out of a book, electronic or otherwise. She'd come by that honestly.

Chris rounded the front of the cement stairs and propped a boot on the bottom step. Mia glanced up but only for a second before she went back to reading. "Got those mistletoe cannoli for you."

"You've also got keys to the place. Why didn't you let yourself in?"

She shrugged one shoulder. "After that heatwave last week, I'm savoring the cold."

"It was one day." Tuesday. When Hawes's grandfather had died. There'd been a few hours of sun on Friday too, but it had disappeared as quickly as it had come, just like his cover had gone poof that day.

"One too many," Mia said, bringing him back to this week. She tucked her e-reader into her vest pocket and stood. "I had to take my breaks in the pastry freezer."

Chuckling, Chris climbed the rest of the way up the stairs and opened the front door. His niece breezed inside, flipping on lights as she strolled down the hallway toward the kitchen, more at home here than he was. When she'd turned thirteen, he'd started paying her twenty bucks a month to check on the place when he was gone. Other than annually upping her rate, she'd never once complained, happy to have her own private sanctuary. He blocked out the thoughts of what else his teenage niece might have used his place for. And the worry that she resented him for returning and taking away her refuge. He'd like to avoid a pissed-off teenager; they were scary, or at least he had been when he was a teen, before things had changed.

Mia dropped the pastry box on the island. "So, who you bribing with these?"

"A tech at SFPD. They did me a favor." He peeked under the lid, mouth watering. "Thanks for bringing them over. You didn't have to. I was gonna pick them up this weekend."

"Was in the neighborhood."

Chris lifted a brow. Mission Dolores wasn't completely on the other side of town from North Beach, but it also wasn't on Mia's way home from AB's, where she was working for the summer.

"Ethan lives a couple blocks over," she added.

"The boyfriend?"

She cocked a hip and put both hands on her waist. At the same time, her face took on a wistful expression. "He's more than just a boyfriend."

Ah, young love. Chris would rather deal with the pissed-off-teenager version of his niece. "You being safe?" That ought to do it.

Sure enough, Mia's dreamy expression vanished with an annoyed eye roll and dramatic, put-upon sigh.

Chris laughed. No sense getting angry back; that wouldn't get him the answer he needed. He circled the island, opened the fridge, and pulled out two pints of Blue Bottle NOLA iced coffee. He bumped the door shut with his elbow and set the cartons on the island.

"Ooh…" Mia's dark eyes lit up. "One of those for me?"

Chris kept a hand on both. "When you answer the question."

Another eye roll, but this time accompanied by a huff of laughter. "Yes, Davos, we're being safe."

He scoffed, over-the-top and gasping for effect. "I'm not that old!" He slid a carton across the counter, then held up both his hands, wiggling his fingers. "And I have all of these."

Mia cut her eyes to the pastry box as she worked open the coffee. "And yet you're smuggling out-of-season cannoli as bribes."

"Touché. In that case…" He flipped open the box lid and snagged a cannoli, setting it on a paper towel he'd ripped from the roll. "Smuggler's tax."

Before he could take a bite, Mia shoved a hand under his nose, palm up. "Call me Salladhor, then."

Chris couldn't help but smile. She was whip-smart, having outpaced him in reading their favorite series, and witty, having outpaced him in this conversation. Sassy, just like her mother… used to be.

He handed her one of the white chocolate, pistachio, and cranberry confections, a cannoli version of the white chocolate-dipped pistachio and cranberry biscotti Grandma Perri used to make for Christmas. At first bite, they both hummed in delight, then enjoyed a few minutes of companionable silence as they ate.

But Chris hadn't forgotten where his thoughts had left off. "How's your mom?"

"Fine." Too fast, too short. And too obvious in her effort to look anywhere but at him. She polished off her coffee and wandered over to the dining table, shuffling through the books there. She stopped when her hand landed on the hardback at the bottom of the stack, fingers tracing the faded gold seal on the cover. "This was her favorite. She used to read it to me whenever I came over here to play. Mom wouldn't let me have it."

"You remember that? You were only five."

She smiled fondly, genuinely, a rare sight on her fifteen-year-old face, and lowered herself into the closest chair. "Of course I remember. She was my best friend. I worshipped her."

Chris tossed their empty cartons, then claimed the seat next to her. "She used to read it to me too, every night before bed. I lost count how many times we went through it. She'd read, I'd make the character noises. It never seemed to scare her."

"Scared the shit out of me, but it was worth it. Because she loved it so much." Mia turned glassy eyes toward him, her tears held hostage by sheer will. Not so much in her voice, though, as she croaked out, "I miss her."

Chris threw an arm around his niece and hugged her close. "So do I. Every day." He swallowed hard, fighting back his own tears. This was the hardest part of being back here. What he'd avoided for the past ten years. Picking up the pieces of a life lost and trying to put it back together. Unlike Hawes and the Madigans, he'd taken the easy route and run from his pain, from his demons, when he should have held close the family he had left. How much damage had he done—to all of them—by leaving things a scattered mess? Was it too late to fix this? Could he really come home again, like his mom had said?

And what of Hawes? Was he part of the picture of home? Did

he belong in the puzzle? And if he did, where did he fit when both of them kept bending the edges and changing the shape of the piece?

As if reading the direction of his thoughts, Mia asked through her sniffles, "Are you back? Nonna said…"

"I'm thinking about it."

That got her attention. She drew back and looked up at him with a raised brow. "For real?" she asked, a bit of fire back in her voice.

"For real." He reached behind him for the roll of paper towels, tore one off, and handed it to her. "But I didn't want to get your hopes up until I was more sure."

She blew her nose, graceless and uninhibited, and Chris's heart swelled, loving her all the more for it. But then his heart broke at her next words. "We need some hope, Uncle Chris." She sounded like her mother, far too weary, more so than any fifteen-year-old kid should ever be.

The investigator reared his head, but he gentled his voice. This was his family. He needed to be Uncle Chris here, not Agent Perri. "You want to tell me what's going on?"

"Adults don't think kids notice." She punched her nails through the paper towel, ripping it apart. "They think we don't know what's going on."

But certain lessons from his professional life were applicable here. "You know," he said, "if I'm at a crime scene and there's a kid among the bystanders, or God forbid directly involved, they're the first person I go to. They see more than anyone." He reached out and closed a hand over Mia's. "Tell me what you see, Mia."

"Mom's so unhappy, and Dad…"

She stiffened, a slight shiver she covered with a shake of her dark hair, and both the investigator and the uncle saw red. Only his ten years of undercover work kept Chris calm—because that's what Mia needed—but his anger was barely contained. "Has he hurt you?"

She shook her head again. "No, but I worry about Mom and about Marco. The example he's setting. It's toxic."

"Marco's a good kid."

"He's twelve and impressionable. Just last week he decided yellow was his favorite color because the cute camp counselor likes yellow. In the spring it was purple because that was the favorite color of the kid he liked in class." The ramble and accompanying eye roll were enough to temper Chris's fury. "You'd make a better impression," she said. "We need you." Her plea shifted him fully back into uncle mode.

He circled her shoulders again and squeezed. "I'm always here for you, Mia."

"Here"—she jostled against his side—"and on the phone aren't the same thing."

No, they weren't. They were further apart than Chris had realized. And the urgency to close that distance ratcheted up another notch on his priority ladder.

NINE

Chris hadn't expected the explosives to be at the auction. Strategically and tactically, it made no sense. Too big a stockpile to transport and too big a risk to take until a deal was made. Close by, though, was a reasonable assumption. That had been his and Wheeler's assertion to the joint task force yesterday. So when word had come down an hour ago—Holt via Kane—that the auction would take place this evening in one of Potrero Hill's new mixed-use buildings, Chris had savored a small victory.

Potrero was in the target vicinity if the explosives were at one of the old Hunter's Point piers on the other side of Highway 101 or in a warehouse just down the peninsula in South City, near where the Madigans had originally stored them. Chris had already sent agents out to both areas, but nothing so far. He radioed for them to step up their searches. Better shot of victory there than at the auction site itself.

Right on the neighborhood's main drag, the building was six stories high with commercial space on the ground floor and residential units on the five floors above. None of the units had balconies, the windows were irregularly shaped and spaced, and all of the building's glass was that godforsaken green-tinted shit that was all over the city now.

A bitch to adequately surveil, compounded by the weekday rush hour. Impossible to evacuate or cordon off without alerting the auction organizer. Challenging to identify whether people entering the building were residents, customers, or targets. It was a tactical nightmare and cleverly chosen for precisely that reason.

And because the top floor units were vacant.

There'd been a delay obtaining the materials for the penthouses' luxury interior finishes. While most of the rest of the building was open and operating, the top floor wasn't ready for renters yet. Chris was sure the auction organizer knew that too.

"Got one!" Jax called, voice raised over the traffic in the room.

Chris turned from the window he'd been staring out. They were two buildings over from their target, and all they could initially see from here—their makeshift joint task force command in a vacant commercial space—was the sidewalk leading to the target building. Jax, however, had secured them a better view via the camera in the nonoperational sidewalk ATM. It was supposed to go live next week, when the lobby-level bank it was attached to officially opened. Two calls—one to the local FBI, then another to the local US attorney—and Chris had a court order for the bank to partially power on the ATM. To passersby, it looked dead—no lit screens, no cash to dispense—but Jax had accessed the machine's camera, giving them a view of who was coming and going.

"Who is it?" Wheeler said as he crossed from the far corner where he'd been standing with the tactical team.

One of the monitors on the table they'd set up as Jax's workstation flickered to life and displayed the face captured from the ATM.

"I'll take human trafficker for five hundred, Alex," Jax quipped. Another burst of keystrokes, and a picture of the cartel captain appeared on-screen, together with his mile-long rap sheet.

Glee flashed across Wheeler's face, swift and ruthless, before he remembered to conceal it. Composed once more, he peppered the tactical team with follow-up questions. A bigger opportunity had presented itself, and Wheeler would pluck all the tail feathers he could.

By contrast, Chris was desperately trying to staunch the wave of bile climbing his throat. Hawes would be devastated if his family's explosives fell into the cartel's hands. He was taking the organization in the opposite direction. Hell, he'd been systematically cutting down the cartel over the past few months, not aiding them.

Chris remembered his wall art at home—the "outsider" he'd marked with an X on the right side of the org chart. Was the cartel the outsider player here? Were they trying to remove the threat against them by engineering a coup against Hawes? It made tactical and logical sense, but Chris had a hard time believing Amelia would ally herself with an organization that traded in drugs and flesh. She had her faults, had fallen prey to the temptation of power, but everyone had a redline, and Chris didn't think she'd cross this one.

"Got another!" called Lance, the ATF agent running the station next to Jax.

Behind them, Wheeler paled and moved a hand toward his sidearm as if on instinct. A face flashed up on the screen next to Lance, and Chris almost lost his battle against the bile. He understood Wheeler's reaction, understood why every LEO in the room had gone on high alert. Chris didn't need to see the rap sheet. They all knew this asshole. A white supremacist with a rabid online following, who was connected to half a dozen domestic terrorism incidents, who always managed to slip free of charges, and who was suspected of making threats against immigration offices in sanctuary cities, including San Francisco. And here he was in Chris's city, bidding on weapons to do just that. Again. Same as he'd tried to do the night Izzy had died. It had been the last report she'd logged before her murder. Was this—*today*—connected to that night three years ago? Was this more than just an attempted coup?

Chris's stomach roiled, forcing him to turn away and catch his breath. Splaying a hand on the window, he waited for the cool glass to temper his boiling insides. Slow going, but better than punching a hole through the wall, or worse, outwardly railing while Wheeler was on the horn with Homeland Security.

"This isn't what they wanted," Kane said, joining him at the window.

"I know." If the explosives landing with the cartel captain would devastate Hawes, that much firepower falling into the hands of a dangerous bigot—one who'd use it against their city— would be more than Hawes's soul could handle. "He's just trying to protect them," Chris said as he looked down at the packed side- walk. "All these people going about their rush-hour business. Oblivious to the threat walking among them. Unaware that if those explosives fall into the wrong hands, they could be dead tomorrow."

"All this just to fund the takeover."

Chris glanced over at Kane. "That what this feels like to you?"

The chief didn't reply.

"Me neither," Chris said. "Something's off."

"Target Alpha sighted," Lance said, and Chris whirled around, not believing his fucking ears.

No denying his eyes, though. The screen grab from the ATM didn't lie. Dark, fitted suit, dark dress shirt, blue eyes bright, and light-brown hair ruffling in the breeze. Hawes Madigan. Chin held high, beautiful sharp angles on display, he walked right into the last place on earth he was supposed to be. Imperious, confi- dent, like he owned the place.

"Can you zoom out?" Chris said to Jax.

A few keystrokes later, they had a wider view of Hawes and his surroundings. And of the absence of other operatives. He was alone.

"Fuck!" Chris cursed.

Jax shot him a worried look, while Wheeler shouted new orders to the tactical teams. "Madigan is on-site. Move him to priority one!"

"The explosives are priority one!" Chris insisted. "The stockpile and the seller are our primary targets."

"And I'm not convinced Hawes Madigan isn't our seller," Wheeler countered. "If it turns out you're right and he's not, then so be it. But he's still an agency target. I can get him, the weapons, the seller, plus two other criminals." That same glee streaked across his face again, too overpowering to contain. "It's going to be a good day."

Or one of the worst days of Chris's life.

"HEAT SIGNATURES INDICATE BIDDERS ARE GOING TO SEPARATE UNITS on the top floor. Three total." Jax didn't have to raise their voice now that only a handful of people remained. The tactical teams, comprised of ATF agents and SFPD officers, had left command thirty minutes ago, moving into position at or near the auction site. Dressed in plain clothes over fitted tactical gear, they entered the building as if they were residents or shoppers. They'd hold there until Wheeler ordered them to the next position.

"Any indication of who and where the seller is?" Wheeler asked.

"Don't know who," Jax said, "but maybe this room here." The building was U-shaped, and the penthouse Jax indicated was at the top end of the southeast wing, as far as possible from the other occupied units, which were on the west and north sides of the building.

"The bend to the southeast wing would be guarded against anyone who started up the hall to the isolated unit," Chris said.

Jax nodded. "And just across the hall is a service elevator. Separate access versus the common area elevator the buyers traveled up." They pointed to the main bank of elevators at the center of the building, the bottom of the *U*.

"Anything else?" Kane asked.

"Two other people headed up the north stairwell, but they turned back and exited on five."

"Probably just residents that were talking and went too far," Wheeler said. "What about on the top floor? Any other movement?"

"Someone is going back and forth from the isolated room to the other units."

"Ferrying bids," Chris surmised.

Wheeler gestured to the heat signature of the person who remained in the presumed seller's room while the runner went back and forth between it and the others. "That still figure must be Madigan."

Here we go again.

"Not him," Chris said. "He's not the seller."

"If he's not the seller, then what the fuck is he doing there?"

Chris jabbed a finger toward the seller's room. "Trying to figure out who that is, just like us." Then he gestured at the other rooms. "And trying to figure out if any of them are in on it. He doesn't do business with people like these anymore."

"Or he's the third buyer," Wheeler said, pointing at the three buyer-occupied rooms. "There to buy back the explosives. I've got him, Perri, one way or the other."

"For fuck's sake, Scotty, he's trying to keep them away from the others."

Kane stepped between them, voice calm and level. "The explosives aren't here. We've gone over this."

"But someone in that building *will* take us to the explosives." Wheeler turned away and raised the comm to his mouth. "Teams, move into second positions."

Chris cursed again and retreated to the opposite corner. "What the hell are they doing?" he asked when Kane joined him. "This is not *eyes only.*"

Kane held his phone so Chris could see the log of unanswered calls to Holt. "He's not answering me or Jax."

That niggle of doubt in the back of Chris's mind blew loud as an air horn. Louder still as Wheeler radioed the teams to converge on the fifth floor, one below the penthouses. "If this auction isn't about funding the coup, then what's it about?" Chris said.

"Power," Kane replied. "That's what it's always been about. Hawes and his siblings have it. The opposition wants it so they can take the organization in a different direction. Backward."

Chris picked up the thread. "So assume this auction is about power too. The seller arranged the buyers like that on purpose. Into separate rooms and only communicating through a runner."

"The seller is keeping each buyer on a string, controlling them," Kane said. "They can keep the auction going or shut it down."

Control. Shut it down.

The words, the niggle, resolved into a single sound, a single thought. This auction wasn't about alliances with outsiders or only wiping Hawes off the map. It was about consolidating power, period. "Fuck! It's a trap." As Chris had thought it might be, but not for the reason and person he thought. "Not just for Hawes."

"They want to take out the buyers," Kane followed.

Chris nodded. "And with all those agents and officers in there too. "Fuck!" Chris moved to go, but Kane grasped his forearm.

"You stay, I'll go."

"Brax."

Hard hazel eyes clashed with his. "I made a promise."

"To Hawes?"

"As good as." He shifted his gaze to Wheeler. "And you need to stay here to convince him to evac. He won't listen to me, but he might listen to you. You have to get him to pull back."

Kane didn't give Chris a chance to argue. He released his arm and sprinted toward the exit. Chris didn't waste time either, charging toward Wheeler. "Pull back! It's a trap!"

Jax spun in their chair. "What?"

"They're going to blow the place."

"Hawes?" Wheeler said. "The Madigans?"

"No!" Chris shouted. "The person who wants him dead." He gestured emphatically at the buyer-occupied rooms. Rooms with major underworld players waiting in them like sitting ducks. "And them too. Everyone who might challenge their power."

Wheeler hesitated. Good. "Do you know that for sure? The bust we could make—"

"Isn't worth our agents' or innocent lives."

"We don't know—"

"Agent Wheeler," Jax called. "Seller and runner are on the move."

He and Chris both whipped around. "Which direction?"

"Down the service elevator."

"They're leaving the scene," Chris said. "Before they put some of those explosives to use."

A radio crackled and a broken voice came through, resolving after a moment. "Beta team to command." Wheeler radioed back confirmation, and the team leader continued. "We've got a device in the north stairwell."

Wheeler's eyes grew wide. "What kind of device?"

"Receiver for a remote detonator."

"Can you disarm it?"

The service elevator opened on the bottom floor. They had seconds before the seller and runner left the building. And blew it. "There's no time," Chris said.

Wheeler didn't hesitate. "Abort! Pull the alarms, clear the lower floors. Emergency evacuation protocols." Wheeler shoved a radio into Chris's hand. "Help me coordinate."

Sirens rent the air, and residents—and LEOs—began pouring out of the building. All Chris wanted to do was run in there and make sure Hawes got out alive too, but Kane was already on it. Chris had to prioritize getting the residents, agents, and officers out.

"Jax," he said. "Keep an eye on that service exit. Tap and record nearby footage." Chris waited for their nod, then returned his attention to where it was needed. He raised the radio to his mouth and worked in tandem with Wheeler to expedite the evac.

Wheeler was doing a sit-rep with his teams when Jax interrupted. "Agent Perri, something you need to see." He expected footage around the service door, a possible ID on the seller. Instead, they pulled up the heat signatures on the top floor again and rewound the past two minutes. While agents and officers had been busy clearing the lower floors, and the seller and runner had been on their way down the service elevator, the buyers in their rooms had done...nothing. They were perfectly still.

Too still.

"What the fuck?" Chris was still trying to put it together when, behind them, Wheeler confirmed, "Lower floors are clear."

"What about Kane?" Jax asked. "Where's the chief?"

Wheeler radioed, to no response. Chris tried as well, to no better.

"Is he up on the top floor?" Wheeler asked. "What's going on there?"

"Buyers are still in their rooms," Jax answered vaguely with a flick of their eyes to Chris.

"Can we move on—"

Whatever Wheeler was going to say, the answer was no they couldn't. Windows shattered, a boom echoed, and one half of the top floor erupted into flames.

With Hawes and Kane still in there.

Chris's heart stopped, then fell to his feet along with his acid-filled stomach. He grabbed hold of Jax's chair, struggling to keep the rest of his weight from collapsing at the loss.

He didn't want to believe it. He closed his eyes, blocking out the smoke and fire and praying that this awful reality was like Izzy's voice in his head, a figment of his imagination. That any sign of an explosion would be gone when he opened them again.

No such luck. In reality, the smoke billowed darker and the flames burned brighter.

Two good men. Gone. A friend and competent law-enforcement officer in Kane. Something infinitely more intriguing, more promising, in Hawes. The chance at something real together was slim—a lawman and a man constantly hunted by the law, that only happened in the books he read—but fuck if that slim possibility hadn't infiltrated his mind as deeply as he'd infiltrated Hawes's organization.

And now that puzzle piece was gone. Not just the corners bent and ragged from the past week of shifting truths. Gone, and in that second, Chris tossed out the question of whether Hawes had been a piece of that home puzzle for him. The picture of home—at least the one in Chris's head—would be incomplete without him. He'd be a third missing piece, like the one lost a decade ago and the Izzy-shaped one three years gone now.

And fuck, if the gaping emptiness in Chris's chest was enough to steal his breath, he hated to think how Helena and Holt would react when word reached them. After losing Papa Cal to death, then Amelia to prison, could the family come back from a double hit like this?

Chris's feet—his soul—itched with the need to run. Dive back into his case, into oblivion. But how, when his best leads on Izzy's killer were gone? Working with Hawes, with the Madigans, with Kane, had been his best shot at the truth. No one else would avenge his partner. Tran had made that clear. Chris had been closer than anyone else, closer than he'd ever managed from afar. And now all that was gone too.

Mission fail.

While Chris fought to keep himself upright, Wheeler paced on the other side of the table, raking a hand through his hair. Not so perfectly coiffed anymore. "Can you get any readings?"

"Fire's too hot on the top floor," Jax replied. "Checking the lower... Wait... I've got four bodies coming down the service stairwell."

"Alpha team, converge on the service stairwell exit," Wheeler ordered. "Possible targets—"

The service door, in sight of the ATM camera and over half a dozen tactical helmet cams, banged open. Out of the billowing smoke walked two men, each with a child in his arms. Two men Chris had never been so happy to see in his life.

"Stand down!" he forced out around his hammering heart, which had rocketed from his feet up into his throat. "Stand down!"

Wheeler gasped. "That's Madigan."

"And Kane," Chris shot back. "Carrying two kids rescued from a burning building, so for once in your goddamn life, stand the fuck down!"

Quelled, Wheeler raised one hand and lifted the radio in his other, relaying the order to stand down. "I just want to talk to Madigan," he said, once temperatures in the room had cooled.

"So do I, but he's not going anywhere." Chris nodded at the surveillance feeds, which showed Hawes and Kane across the street from the building now, being mobbed by relieved parents and residents, while EMS and law-enforcement officers waited at the edge of the crowd. They were hemmed in. And if that weren't enough, at either end of the block were press vans. "You'll get your chance. But Hawes Madigan just saved two kids, and together with Kane, who knows how many other agents, officers, and residents."

Wheeler jabbed an accusing finger at the other monitor, at the top floor of the building that continued to blaze. "While he let the buyers burn."

TEN

As bad as it initially looked, the explosion had been relatively contained. Newly constructed, the building was equipped with all the latest fire-suppression equipment, and SFFD had been close by and on alert for operation support. Only the top-floor penthouses occupied by the buyers had been materially damaged.

Just enough to cover the evidence. Exactly as the clever auction organizer had intended. With a few hours' distance from the event now, Chris had worked out the math. Adding together the too still buyers he'd glimpsed on-screen just before the explosion, plus the charred remains of the bodies they'd found in the penthouses, plus what he'd learned of the way this new generation of Madigans viewed their role in dispensing justice, the sum of the equation was obvious.

It had been a fucking job. Either orchestrated by the Madigans, or neatly taken advantage of when the opportunity had presented itself. Regardless, Chris was fucking pissed. He'd been left out of the fucking loop, his and Kane's people had been recklessly endangered, and worst of all, he'd had to watch Hawes walk into a trap, think him caught, and for two harrowing minutes, believe him dead. He'd made Chris doubt his mission, his purpose, his burgeoning plan to stay here and make a home. Made him forget about being the uncle Mia and Marco needed, the brother Celia could rely on, and the son Gloria deserved. Hawes had sent his insides on a roller coaster and almost made him run.

And for what? A goddamn power trip. A war that, while seemingly connected to Izzy's death, wasn't going to stop if Chris solved the latter. A battle Hawes and his siblings clearly intended to fight on their own. Granted, Chris being on the outside looking in was in no small part due to his own betrayal, but this was about more than just him. Holt had sat there in Kane's office, looked them in the eye, and given no indication that this was anything but the op they were planning. And that order had no doubt come from Hawes, who'd risked more than just his own life.

But Chris couldn't be angry with him, literally. The target of his rage had dodged him in the hours since the blast, all while being treated like a fucking hero. Local news channels ran a loop of the footage of Hawes and Kane emerging from the building with those kids, and even the agents and officers were handling Hawes with kid gloves.

Everyone except Wheeler, who didn't buy that Hawes just happened to be in the building this evening to view one of the penthouse units. Didn't buy that Hawes hadn't reached his destination before the explosion. The property's sales manager had vouched for Hawes, of course. Had that been the person who'd stayed in the "seller's room" while Hawes ran back and forth to the buyers? Chris wondered how much Hawes had paid the guy to risk his life and jail time.

Wheeler didn't believe Hawes or the property manager, but he'd let it go, temporarily. He'd been too busy cleaning up the almost mess he'd made sending agents into a hot zone. Kane had likewise been busy dealing with SFPD's role in the situation, while also fielding media requests and stifling his own boiling anger. Chris wasn't sure which of them was more irate. Kane had also been left out of the loop, inadvertently endangered his officers, and run into a wired-to-blow building to "save" a friend's life. Chris was sure Hawes and company would hear about it from the chief, if they survived Chris's wrath first. As angry as he was, he might earn that King Slayer title Wheeler was so damn eager to pin on him. The risks Hawes had taken today, if Chris was right, were too fucking high.

He was so mad, so distracted running scenarios in his head of what he'd do to Hawes Madigan if he could only fucking find him, that Chris almost fell on his ass when he walked into his condo and found his target standing next to the kitchen island, drinking a beer. Free of soot and suit, dressed in jeans and a Giants pullover, Hawes looked like he'd just returned from the ballpark, not like he'd barely escaped an explosion.

"Mr. Perri."

Standing in the foyer, Chris was battered by the emotional dissonance. Relief, surprise, desire, and the heated anger that had simmered all evening, rising to a rolling boil and burning away the other emotions. But he'd be damned if he let Hawes see that. Not until he got his fucking answers.

Chris shrugged off his coat and hung it on the rack by the door. Small, everyday motions to keep the rage banked. Innocent, conversational questions to lead into the big ones. "You adding breaking and entering to your rap sheet?"

"Wouldn't be the first time."

Chris measured his steps down the hallway, forcing his gait to remain casual as he passed Hawes on the way to his bedroom. "You found where I lived," Chris said as he moved around the room. He opened his closet and secured his sidearm in the safe with the other empty holster.

Hawes rattled around in the kitchen. "Once I had the name right, it wasn't too hard."

Chris checked to make sure the locked door to the room between his bedroom and the study was secure and untampered with, then headed back out to deal with his intruder. "I'm sure it wasn't hard for Holt," he said, coming to stand beside Hawes at the kitchen island.

Hawes handed him an open bottle, then took a long drag from the fresh one he'd helped himself to. "He's good at what he does."

"Which I'm guessing isn't being a messenger."

"Oh, he's good at that too. 'Eyes only.' I heard you. I just didn't listen."

"Or you set it up to start with."

Hawes grinned around the mouth of his bottle, and it took every bit of restraint Chris had to wait until Hawes lowered the bottle from his lips before snatching it out of his hand and slamming it on the tiled countertop.

So much for playing it cool. At least he hadn't broken the bottle. "What the fuck were you thinking?"

Hawes, by contrast, was the epitome of cool. Of controlled. Hip to the island, he rotated to face Chris. "Why should I tell you anything? I don't trust you."

"Then why are you here?"

"You think I want to be?"

Chris scoffed. "Please, you wouldn't be here if you didn't want to be."

"I *shouldn't* be here." A flash of fire in those eyes, a crack in the ice of that cool exterior. "I don't trust you. But after today, you're the only one who—" He cut himself off and turned his face away, made to move away too, but Chris grabbed his wrist and held his hand to the bar.

A sharp inhale. More cracks.

Chris wanted the rest of that sentence. Wanted to swallow that inhale. Desperately, on both counts. But he still needed fucking answers. Needed to make clear that today couldn't happen again, for everyone's sakes.

"You left me and Kane out of the loop." A little of his previous anger crept back in, and he forced it down, leveling his voice, same as he'd done with Mia last night. He wanted to drive home his point, not drive Hawes away. "You put my people and Kane's in danger today. You put Kane in danger. Because you didn't tell us the whole story. I want it now. I might not deserve your trust, but I deserve that much."

Hawes inhaled deeply, as if centering himself, then effortlessly freed his hand. Chris's control had been sheer illusion in that regard. But Hawes didn't move away. "You're a fed."

"Whatever you say stays between us. I'm not gonna turn you in."

Hawes held his gaze an agonizingly long minute, assessing, before he reclaimed his beer and took a long swig. "I was thinking I was tired of playing defense," he said as he lowered the bottle. "That I wanted to go on offense."

"You were trying to lure them out?" Like Hawes had done with Papa Cal's funeral last week. He'd been tired of waiting then too.

"*Trying* being the operative word. I also needed to test the outside influencer theory."

"The other buyers." Chris had wondered the same thing. "And?"

"Those three weren't involved, which gives me some comfort."

"I saw two enter—cartel and neo-Nazi. Who was the third?"

"Arms dealer who had a unit in the building."

"So you killed the three of them?"

Hawes shrugged. "That gives me comfort too."

"Jesus, Madigan." Chris held his own beer to his forehead, praying for patience and futilely hoping the cold bottle would stem the cresting wave of anger.

"I had contracts on them too."

"Isn't that convenient?"

Hawes cocked a brow. "Are you actually arguing on behalf of a human trafficker, a white supremacist, and an arms dealer, all of whom have threatened our city and escaped justice multiple times?"

Chris drank from his bottle.

One corner of Hawes's sinful mouth quirked up. "Didn't think so." He set his bottle aside, pried Chris's free from his clenched fingers, then stepped closer, only a few inches between them. "I needed to show whoever is behind this grab for power that I know the game they're playing, that I can play it too, and that I'm not afraid to do what it takes to win. That I'll fight for what's mine and for the way I do things." Gone was the ice. His eyes were energized, brimming over with a king's confidence. And heated, the look in them a magnified version of the fire Chris had seen in them yesterday at the BART station. Right after the takedown, right before the too brief kiss.

Chris lifted a hand, wanting desperately to touch, to wallow for a spell in the desire that was pushing away his anger and in the relief that Hawes was safe. And here with him. But what right did he have? Yes, Hawes had initiated the kiss yesterday, but after all that had transpired between them, after Chris's betrayal, he didn't have a right to anything more from Hawes than what he'd given him already. Especially when more was the last thing Chris should be doing.

Hawes didn't give him a choice. He captured Chris's flailing hand and placed it on his waist, encouraging the touch, reestablishing the connection. "I wanted to know who was selling the explosives," he said. "This was the quickest way to getting a shot at that info."

Gliding his hand under the pullover's hem, Chris curled his fingers into warm skin and rubbed his thumb over the jut of Hawes's hip. "You said you weren't using the explosives anymore."

"I didn't."

Chris dropped his hand, forgetting all about Hawes's sharp angles. "Come again?"

"I didn't set those explosives." Righteous indignation flashed across Hawes's face. "I wouldn't risk all those innocent residents, or the property manager in the control room, or you, or Brax, or your people. You were wrong about that part." Umbrage gave way to a sly, satisfied smile. "But my plan worked."

"Because the real seller had been there to set those explosives."

Nodding, Hawes erased the inches between them and ran a hand up Chris's chest. "We can figure out the timeline. Maybe their identity. You do your work, and we'll do ours."

"Why'd you tell us about the auction but not the whole story?"

"I took a risk that I could get in and out in time. If the seller had been there when I was, then I would have delivered them to you. I needed law enforcement on-site for that, and in case anything went sideways."

"Did you factor in that they—or we—could've turned the trap on you?"

"I did. Remember that 'I don't trust you' bit..." Hawes cast his gaze aside and stepped back. The magnetic pull between them tugged at Chris's insides, making the absence painful after being close again. Even more so when Hawes turned on his heel and ambled toward the reading nook. He braced an arm over his head, propped against the window casing. "That's why it was only me there."

Chris feared that was the answer, recalling the surveillance footage of Hawes approaching the building alone. Holt had surely been in his ear, but he'd had no on-site backup.

"You would have sacrificed yourself," Chris said as he stopped next to the end of the chaise.

"You wouldn't make that promise, to not sacrifice yourself. And I won't either. If that's what it takes to keep my family and city—you—safe."

"How the fuck am I supposed to argue that, Madigan?"

Hawes rotated and rested against the window. He raised his chin and his eyes, both defiant. "Don't."

Too much confidence and too dark a death wish. Then and now.

Chris closed the distance between them and braced his hands on either side of the window, caging Hawes in. Keeping him close, avoiding the loss that had almost struck today. "Don't keep me in the dark. And don't make me watch you almost die."

Hawes pushed off the window and brought their bodies flush, their lips a breath apart. "I'm just a mark."

"Don't fucking lie either."

Chris made sure he didn't tell any more fibs, crushing their mouths together in a kiss that made words, thoughts, breath impossible. Every bit of desire, relief, frustration, and fear that he'd banked the past four hours, the past four days, was unleashed, driving him to press Hawes back against the window, to run his hands over every sharp angle, to plunge his tongue between Hawes's lips and into his mouth, tasting all that confidence. Tasting the submission when Hawes lifted his arms above his head and clutched either side of the window frame. Open and spread out like he'd been on his condo ladder last week. Hawes needed relief too—from the tightly wound control he'd so expertly wielded today—and Chris wanted to give it to him, wanted that trust back, maybe more than he'd ever wanted anything.

But Chris hesitated, their earlier exchange drifting back into his mind, a tendril of remorse coiling like Hawes's beloved fog through his veins. Guilt over the lies he'd told. He curled his fingers around Hawes's wrists in a loose grip and leaned their foreheads together. Before he could say anything, though, Hawes rolled his hips and pressed his hard cock against Chris's groin. Chris failed to bite back a groan, and Hawes blinked up at him with lust-darkened eyes.

Eyes that wanted to surrender, but did Hawes understand to whom? Reminded again of his remorse, his guilt, the trust he needed to win back, Chris dragged his hips away and released one of Hawes's wrists. He lowered his hand and cupped Hawes's cheek. Hawes nuzzled his palm, and Chris nearly lost his resolve for good. All that softness under all those sharp angles was like a lasso around every tender part of Chris, hopelessly ensnaring him.

The satisfying snap of a puzzle piece into place.

He rubbed his thumb over Hawes's lovely, sharp jawline,

waiting for Hawes to lift his eyes again. "Are you sure about this?" He squeezed Hawes's wrist still in his hand against the glass. There was no mistaking his question. "Before, you gave this to someone I wasn't, and I'm sorry for that."

Hawes snaked his free hand around Chris's neck and into the hair at his nape. Fingers splayed, he combed outward and forced the tie out of Chris's hair, freeing his topknot. "You said I could trust you." He raked his fingers through the long strands, making Chris shiver. "It wasn't all a lie, was it?"

"You can, and it wasn't." Chris sighed softly, helplessly. "Fuck, Hawes, most of it was true, but I'm sorry, so very sorry, for the parts that weren't."

Conflicting emotions, too many to dissect, raced across Hawes's face, flowed out to his fingers that clenched in Chris's hair, then combusted. Hawes melted under him, and Chris held him up with his body, pressed between him and the glass again. "I'm sorry too," Hawes whispered hoarsely. "For not telling you the truth."

"You had your reasons."

He cleared his throat. "I knew the risks today, owned them, did what I had to do for my family, my city." He untangled his fingers from Chris's hair and lifted his arm back into position, mirroring the other. "Now I need to let go, *for me*. That's why I'm here. I want to do that *with you*. I need to."

Leaving Hawes's arms raised, Chris ran his hands down their toned length, across Hawes's broad chest that led to a tapered waist, then under his pullover and thin T-shirt. He splayed his hands across Hawes's cool skin and ribbed abs, then skirted them over his hips and down inside the waistband of his jeans. His ass cheeks were cool from the window and gloriously firm and round, filling Chris's hands. He hauled Hawes forward with a grunt and ground their cocks together. "How the fuck am I supposed to argue that?" Argue any of it.

White-knuckling the window frame, Hawes used his abs, like he did when he'd lifted his lower body off the bed on Friday, to do that again now, circling Chris's waist with his legs, capturing him, locking them together. "Same answer. Don't."

Chris conceded and stole back into Hawes's mouth, until other needs became pressing. As much as he loved the lithe, powerful body trapped between him and the window, loved Hawes's cock rutting against his abs, loved every nook and cranny of Hawes's mouth he reacquainted himself with, he loved the thought of a naked Hawes more. And this position was not conducive to making his thoughts a reality.

Hands around Hawes's wrists, Chris brought their arms down behind Hawes's back. Following the cue, Hawes bowed his back and thrust his chest forward, more of his weight onto Chris. "On three."

Chris skipped one and two. "Three," he said, and hauled them off the window. Spinning, he took two steps and put a knee to the chaise. He laid Hawes against the corner, spreading his arms across the top of the chaise and his legs half on and half off the seat cushions, wide enough for Chris to crawl between them.

Hawes nestled into the cushions and smiled. "Definitely softer than the window."

"Wanna know what's not soft?" Chris palmed his cock through his jeans, stretching denim across his thickening length.

Hawes's smile morphed into a wanton growl. "Bring it to me."

Chris nearly caved at Hawes's desperation-soaked command. Could see himself feeding Hawes his cock, could imagine how good the rumble of his groan would feel around the tip. But not yet. "We'll get there," he promised, getting back to the task of undressing.

He ran his hands under Hawes's pullover and shirt and slowly worked them up his torso, torturing with tongue and teeth every inch of skin he exposed. "When we're done here," he said between licks and kisses, "I want you to stay."

"I can't." Hawes gasped as Chris barely breathed on a nipple. "I need to—"

"Fall asleep in my bed tonight." Chris wanted it as much as he wanted to get his mouth around Hawes's cock. "Fall asleep in my arms again, here in my home, with me." Maybe even more, after the events of today. "I need that after almost losing you." He took a nipple between his teeth, and Hawes arched his back. "After almost losing this."

Hawes kept his arms spread across the top of the chaise, fingers digging into the cushions as his body writhed for contact. "Yes. I'll stay."

Chris's chest clenched as he was reminded of the hole there that had been filled again. He amped up the torture as a thank-you, as a promise. He held his body above Hawes's and focused all his efforts on a single point of contact, his tongue swirling around one, then the other of Hawes's nipples. They puckered and strained like the rest of Hawes's body. Like Chris's to match.

Unable to resist Hawes's "Need to feel you" pleas any longer, he made quick work of getting their shirts off. He lowered himself on top of Hawes—chest to chest, skin to skin, mouth to mouth— and lost himself in kisses, in touches, in softness. Except their cocks, which grew harder as they rutted together with increasing urgency.

Chris braced one foot on the floor and bent his other leg between Hawes's spread legs, knee on the cushion. "The other night on the phone, I was here on this chaise." He unbuttoned Hawes's jeans and tugged them down with his boxers, enough to set his cock bobbing free. Chris stretched back out over Hawes, whispering hotly into his ear, "Your voice..." He wrapped a fist around Hawes's hard length and stroked slowly. "Made me so hard, like you are now."

"Dante..."

"Thought about you spread out just like this." Another stroke. "Wanted to taste you again." A swipe of his fingers over the leaking head. "Suck you down until you let go."

Hawes keened for more, his arms slipping off the back of the chaise. Chris released his cock and grabbed each wrist, spreading them back across the cushion tops. "Keep 'em there, and hold on tight while I take you apart."

He slid to his knees beside the chaise and yanked Hawes's jeans and boxers the rest of the way off. Chris bent over his lap and licked a stripe up the crease of Hawes's balls. As intended, Hawes lifted his ass off the chaise, chasing the touch, and Chris gave it to him. He shoved a hand back to tease Hawes's taint and hole, while the other fisted the base of Hawes's cock. His mouth swallowed him down, teasing and tasting. Sharp, irresistible, like the rest of Hawes.

"Fucking hell," Hawes cursed. "I'm not gonna last if you keep that up."

"And I'm not gonna last when I get my cock in your mouth." Chris kissed down Hawes's length as he spoke. "Gotta make sure you're ready to go with me." Then took him back into his mouth.

Lost in the perfect, aching hardness, in his mouth and in his own jeans, it wasn't until Hawes shouted, "Christopher!" that Chris came back to himself. And to Hawes staring down at him with eyes that were nearly black, the blue reduced to a thin ring of icy fire. "Get your cock in me now, one way or the other."

Chris almost came at the delicious snap of command in Hawes's voice. Driven wild, he had to act before it was too late. He stood, stepped back, and shed his jeans and boxers. He took another step back, and Hawes opened his mouth to object, but Chris circled the chaise, stopping behind the corner were Hawes's head was, and Hawes caught on to his fantasy.

His objection died on a groan. "Oh fuck yes."

Chris ran a hand through Hawes's silky top strands, tipping his head back. With his other hand, he moved one of Hawes's off the back of the chaise to the patch of hair just above Hawes's cock, urging him to take himself in hand. "Together," he said.

Hawes grinned and slid his hand down, circling his cock. "Don't think that's gonna be a problem."

Neither did Chris as he fisted the base of his own cock and fed it between Hawes's parted lips. Deciding where to look became almost as hard as his cock—Hawes's fist shuttling up and down that lovely, slick cock, or his lips stretching around Chris's length, his cheeks hollowing out with suction.

"Christ." Chris curled forward, tangling the fingers of his free hand with Hawes's on top of the cushions. Hawes clutched back, hard. This wasn't going to last long for either of them.

Hawes took him deeper each time Chris thrust forward, throat tightening around the tip as he swallowed, tongue twirling around the length and head as Chris drew back. "Oh fuck, that's it. That's perfect." It was the hottest fuck Chris had ever had, and if the orgasm barreling his way was any indication, it was going to be the hardest he'd ever come too. "Hawes…" He started to pull out, but the fingers around his clenched to almost breaking.

Commanding him to stay. With him.

Chris knew exactly where to look. Knew exactly whose order to follow.

His king's.

He thrust back into Hawes's mouth, ecstasy trilling up his spine with Hawes's deep, satisfied groan as they came, together.

ELEVEN

Chris followed the scent of coffee out from his bedroom, the condo still in shadows, the dark of night outside just starting to give way to morning. Inside, the under-cabinet lights cast a soft glow in the kitchen, and across from the island, another low light emanated from the study.

While they'd fallen asleep in the same bed, Hawes wrapped in his arms, as negotiated, Hawes had beaten him awake and was snooping around the locked study he'd picked his way into, judging by the bent wire on the kitchen island. Not that there was anything in the room that wasn't on the flash drive Chris had already given him.

He leaned a shoulder against the doorjamb and admired the graceful, efficient motions of his lover. Dressed in his jeans and one of Chris's tanks, Hawes looked at home here, with his feet bare, his hair tumbled, and a mug of coffee in hand. He was the first person since Izzy to invade his space—his life—so effortlessly, so comfortably. It should worry him that it was Hawes Madigan, of all people, but it was the first time in years he didn't feel alone in his own home. And that's what it felt like for the first time in years too—a home. The pieces all fit, even if they shouldn't.

"You didn't look around last night?" he asked after another minute of creeping on the handsome, dangerous man.

Hawes didn't startle, no doubt aware that Chris had been standing there, staring. "Needed the beer, and the sex." He grinned over his shoulder, but then the smile fell as he considered the photos of Isabella's crime scene. "Was still shook up from the almost dying."

"You hid it well."

"Not the first time." He swung his gaze back to Chris. "We're professionals."

"We are."

Hawes got that about him and vice versa. Maybe that's why Hawes didn't feel like a stranger in his home. Chris pushed off the jamb, ambled over to him, and slid an arm around his waist. "Doesn't make it any easier, does it? Risking your life on a daily basis is still risking your life."

Hawes set his mug on the desk, then turned into Chris, warm hand on his bare chest. The other curled around the waistband of his athletic shorts and tugged Chris closer. "You do, though. You steady things. I don't know why…"

"You do too, for me." Chris didn't know why either, only knew that he needed to kiss Hawes, needed to taste him this morning, unlike the last morning they'd woken up in the same place yet on opposite sides. Chris mapped every sweet, delicious corner of his mouth while Hawes mapped every inch of Chris's back and torso, sending ripples of heat coursing under his skin, through his veins, aimed straight for the center of his chest. When air became necessary again, Hawes rested against his chest, and Chris combed fingers through his wild morning hair. "Find anything interesting?"

"You have a lovely home."

Chris chuckled. "For an ATF agent."

Hawes leaned back in his arms. "I didn't say that."

"Didn't have to." Chris dropped a quick kiss on his lips, then stepped out of Hawes's arms. He grabbed Hawes's empty mug and headed for the kitchen to refill it for him and grab his own. "It needs some updates," he said as he ran a hand over the counter-tops. Chipped in places, grout an indescribable color, the tiles themselves a nineties off-white that never looked clean even if he scrubbed them to gleaming. "But I'm not a fool. I know the gold-mine I'm sitting on. Bought it fifteen years ago before prices went crazy. It's almost doubled in value since."

"You thinking about selling it? If you're not here much…"

"I primarily work UC. I'm gone a lot." He pulled down another mug. "But I'm not planning to sell anytime soon. It's not exactly lived in, not like it used to be, but I like having a place of my own when I am here. My four walls, not my mom's or my sister's."

"I understand that." Hawes circled the adjacent dining table, eyeing the books scattered haphazardly across it. "And you have to have somewhere to keep all these."

"I like to read."

Hawes stepped away from the dining table and laid a hand on the hallway wall between Chris's bedroom and the study. "That a hidden library in here? Or a panic room? There's no door here or on the study side."

"You didn't try to open the door in the bedroom?"

"It seemed private." Chris rolled his eyes, hard, and Hawes dropped his hand, chuckling. "More private than the other areas."

Chris smiled as he filled their mugs. "It's nothing quite so fancy." He handed Hawes a refreshed cup. "It's storage now, but it was a nursery."

Hawes bobbled the mug, and Chris, hand still close by, expecting the reaction, helped him steady it. "A what?" Hawes said.

Chris hadn't planned on telling Hawes this truth quite yet, but after yesterday, Hawes needed to know the truth, all of it, so he could understand where Chris was coming from, why he'd made the decisions he had, why losing Hawes wasn't an option, and why solving Isabella's death was at the top of his priority ladder.

Chris grabbed his own mug, took Hawes's hand with the other, and led him back to the reading area. He beckoned Hawes to sit on the chaise, handed him his coffee, and turned to the bookcase. He pulled the single hardcover book—*Where the Wild Things Are*—off the top shelf, where he'd put it back after his conversation with Mia, and carefully flipped the pages until he reached the photo tucked inside. He withdrew it and held it out to Hawes.

Perched on the end of the chaise, Hawes set the mugs on the floor and took the offered photo. He ran his finger over the kindergartner's face and smiled, much like he did anytime he looked at Lily. He'd make an incredible father someday. "Is this your niece? She looks like you. Same dark eyes and dark hair." He ran his thumb over the nose and laughed. "Even the nose. Did she stay with you?"

"That's not my niece. Mia is incapable of smiling at a camera. That"—he nodded at the picture—"was my daughter, Rochelle."

Hawes gasped. "Daughter? You have—Wait, *was*?"

Chris lowered himself next to Hawes and slipped the picture from his trembling fingers. "Ro would have been seventeen this coming December." He smiled at the photo of his beaming daughter on school picture day.

"You had her in high school?"

"Well, I didn't have her, technically." His smile dimmed, remembering her first cry, imagining her last. "Don't have her anymore either."

Hawes gently squeezed his knee. "Dante..." Then squeezed tighter. "Shit, Chris, I'm sorry. That's..."

Chris laid a hand over his, drawing Hawes's gaze. "I like when you call me Dante." He placed the picture of Ro on the side table, then retrieved their mugs off the floor. He handed one to Hawes, then scooted behind him into the corner of the chaise, a leg on either side of Hawes, who took the hint and repositioned himself, back to Chris's chest.

"You remember Jennifer Petrie?" Chris asked once they were settled.

"The cheerleader from the yearbook?"

"That's the one. Knocked her up the night of senior prom."

"And she had Rochelle."

Chris took a long sip of the perfectly brewed coffee and remembered those wild months of his eighteen-year-old life, wishing he'd had an IV drip of caffeine then. Jenn's panic when she came to him with the news, his mother's glee and support, his own fear, and then something so much more the day his daughter was born. "The reason I was so sure Holt was the traitor was because I know how he feels. To have your whole world suddenly realign and revolve around this new life. One you'd do anything to protect. That was Ro for me."

"And Jennifer?"

"Wanted to do right by Ro, but we weren't in love, and she had no interest in being a mom yet. She had a scholarship to Florida and a shitty family at home. She needed to get out, for her own safety and future."

"Whereas you had your mom, dad, and sister."

"I had the support network to make it work, like Holt has all of you. And I had a job working on bikes with my dad at the family shop and a spot at San Francisco State. I was in a better position to care for Ro." He cleared his throat, and when that didn't dislodge the knot there, gulped back more coffee. "She was my whole world the second she first wailed."

Hawes twisted in his arms to look up at him. "You don't have to…"

Chris leaned forward and nuzzled the hollow of his cheek. "You need this piece of the story." Hawes nodded, and Chris settled back into the corner, Hawes against his chest again. "I graduated with a degree in criminal justice and became a private investigator."

"So you really were a PI?"

He draped an arm around Hawes's chest and squeezed. "Told you it wasn't all a lie." Hawes chuffed and dipped his chin to nip at Chris's forearm. Improbably laughing, Chris left his arm there, lightly holding Hawes, enjoying the feel of him in his embrace and steeling himself for the hardest part of the story. "PI work paid well, and with some help from my parents, I bought this place. The job gave me more flexibility to be at home here, with my kid."

"Sounds ideal."

"It was a good setup, and the PI gig was how I met Isabella." Hawes tensed in his arms, then relaxed when Chris tightened his hold, comforting them both. "I was running down a lead on a firearm when I first crossed paths with her. We worked well together—both of us getting what we needed for our respective cases—and then we went our separate ways."

"Until something happened to Ro? You said Isabella helped you at a time when you weren't in a good way."

The mug began to shake in Chris's hand, and he leaned down to set it on the floor. Righting himself, Chris found his hand captured in Hawes's, their fingers lacing together, giving him the strength he needed to go on. "My sister had picked her daughter and Ro up from school. Drunk driver ran a red light less than a block from the house. He died, and so did..." Chris lost his words, and Hawes raised their joined hands, kissing across the knuckles until Chris could speak again. "The rest of my family was okay, but Ro didn't make it."

Hawes rotated so his side rested against the length of Chris's torso, his breath gentle where it coasted over Chris's skin. "Take your time."

There'd never be enough time to digest that loss, all the feelings wrapped up in it. Chris carded his fingers through Hawes's hair instead, taking comfort where he could, short-lived as it was. "You need to go," he said after another minute. "Before it gets light out."

"It's fine," Hawes replied. "Tell me the rest."

The whip of an order underlying the gentle tone was enough of a distraction from the sorrow. Chris smiled as he cleared his throat. "I barely made it too. My whole world was gone. I was ready to join her. I used one of my connections to get hold of a gun."

"You didn't have one?"

"I did, but I wanted it clean. Untraceable so no one would be implicated but me. That's what I told myself, and it was stupid. Years of therapy later, I understand what I wanted was to be stopped."

"And that's where Isabella came in."

"The gun I'd bought wasn't clean. She had it tagged for a case. I was five minutes from pulling the trigger when she walked in." He remembered that day, would never forget it. At the end of a dark tunnel, literally and figuratively as he sat in the dark in this very room, when the tall, bossy lady with a mane of black curls and a thick New York accent came looking for him. "More like strutted in, to this very house, and rather than trying to coax or offer sympathy, she dropped a file on the floor in front of me. For a seven-year-old girl being held captive by a cult."

"Smart," Hawes said. "You couldn't save Ro, but you could save the other girl."

"Izzy was recruiting me. She gave me a purpose." He gently pushed Hawes up, wanting to see his face for this part, or rather, wanting Hawes to see his. This was too important. "Which is why I can't let her killer go. I couldn't avenge Ro's death, but I can avenge Izzy's. I have to."

Hawes stiffened in his arms one second and vaulted out of them the next, rocketing off the chaise like he'd been burned. Chris caught his wrist before he could shut down and put Chris out of reach again. "Hey, what's wrong?"

"Nothing." Hawes cast his gaze down, then at the bookcase, then out the window. Anywhere but at Chris.

Not nothing. Chris ran a thumb over the inside of Hawes's wrist, the racing pulse point there thrumming under his fingertip. "You've known all along that finding Izzy's killer is my primary mission. The ATF has me on the explosives, but I won't drop this until I find out what really happened to my partner. I wanted you to understand why it matters."

"I did. I do." Hawes swallowed hard but still wouldn't look at him. "It matters to me too," he said, barely a whisper.

Chris believed him. The changes Hawes had made in the organization since the night of Izzy's death were proof. So why wasn't he proud of them? Why did he always tense when Chris brought up finding her killer? Unless he knew more than he was letting on, in which case... "Who are you protect—"

Noise from outside cut off Chris's words. Louder than the usual critters, but not so loud that it would wake the neighbors. If both he and Hawes weren't trained as they were, they may not have heard it either. But they were, and they did.

Chris cursed. "My gun's in the safe." He started to let go of Hawes's hand, to head for his bedroom safe, or if there wasn't enough time, to the kitchen knives, but Hawes reversed their grip, grasping his wrist and halting him mid-stride.

"Hold a second," he whispered, on alert but not tensed to battle-ready. Before Chris could ask what he was on about, a set of knocks rapped below the window. Hawes's form relaxed, and he dropped Chris's hand. "I invited them." He crossed to the back door as footsteps started up the stairs. He opened the door, and Holt and Helena entered, Lily in her aunt's arms for a change.

Chris thought to object—they all knew where he lived now—but Holt had figured that much out already and given Hawes the address. At least Hawes had invited them, unlike at Hawes's condo, where they barged in unannounced on the regular. A heads-up would have been nice, but Chris hadn't given Hawes a chance, having jumped right into the history lesson.

On cue, the baby in Helena's arms wailed her disapproval of the rising sun, and Chris couldn't help but smile. "You got a microwave in this place?" Helena asked. "Bottle time."

Chris held an arm out toward the kitchen, and the troop of Madigans made themselves at home. Holt set up at the bar, computer open, Hawes got another pot of coffee brewing, and

Helena dug a bottle out of the baby bag and stuck the bottle in the microwave.

That done, she rotated and leaned back against the counter, surveying the space. "Nice place, Mr. Hair."

"Glad it meets your approval." He circled the end of the island, opened the junk drawer, and fished out a folded Post-it. He slid it across the bar to Holt. "In case you need the wireless password."

Holt's tired, dark eyes flicked from the faded neon slip of paper, to the drawer Chris had pulled it from, to Chris. He looked more like himself again, albeit still weary. "I wouldn't connect to your system." He withdrew a hot spot from the baby bag and plugged it into the laptop. "I'm not an idiot."

The snarky judgment made Chris laugh. "Of course not." Ice broken, he lowered his voice and said to Holt, "You didn't tell him about Ro." He was sure Holt must have turned up that info in his revised search.

Holt's eyes tracked to his daughter, to Chris, then back to the screen. "Not my story to tell."

"Thank you." Smiling, Chris moved the rest of the way around the island to the fridge and pulled out the creamer, readying it for when Hawes passed out steaming mugs of coffee.

Holt gulped back half of his, then spun his laptop around so they could all see the screen. "This was the tip we received this morning."

Chris scalded his throat in his haste to swallow. "What tip?"

Hawes gestured at the screen. "This is why I invited them here."

Chris leaned forward and read the email. "The seller made contact…" He looked over his shoulder at Helena. "With you?"

"With me." Her expression was deadly serious, even as she fed Lily her bottle and patted her bottom. "They're offering me a chance to buy back the explosives."

Chris shifted his gaze to Hawes. "Why are you bringing this to me now?"

"We kept you on the sidelines yesterday," Hawes said. "That was a mistake, and it almost didn't work out. We need to coordinate. I won't have those explosives loose in my city."

"So your play worked," Chris said, satisfied that their interests were aligned. "They're on the defensive and trying to pick off the pass."

Hawes sipped from his mug. "Likely."

"Could this be Amelia?"

"Possibly," Holt answered. "She knows how to disguise the IP address. But we told Brax not to give her access to a computer."

"I called him," Helena told them. "Confirmed it. No access to any mobile devices either."

"So she told someone how to do this, then," Chris said. "Or they have another hacker, and this plan was on her flash drive. Any luck there yet?"

Holt shook his head.

"But she can vet the tip," Hawes said. "She can tell us if this was part of the plan, fallback or otherwise."

Or lead Hawes right where her faction wanted him. "It's a trap," Chris said.

"That's what I told him," Helena said, and Holt nodded too.

Hawes finished his mug and set it in the sink. "We all agree on that point. Now, how do we turn the trap back around on them? Because I am done with this shit."

Chris tilted his head toward the study, and the lot of them followed him in. Helena whistled low and handed Lily off to Holt, who grumbled under his breath about "too much fucking paper." Chris chuckled as he walked over to the org chart. "They've wiped out your lieutenants, and two of your soldiers are in custody."

"They?" Hawes said, hip against the desk, arms folded over his chest.

"One of them." Chris pointed at the layer of captains.

Hawes shook his head. "We don't think so. Alibis check out. Half aren't even here. They're out on contracts."

Chris rested a hand next to the X adjacent to the chart. "Then someone out here."

"The competition," Helena said. "We were thinking that already."

The reason they'd set up the trap at the building yesterday.

"Three of which are gone," Holt added.

"I have my ideas," Hawes said, then glanced at Helena. "We need to talk to Rose. There could be older players we're not familiar with who are looking to exploit the perceived power vacuum."

"Get a list from her, and then I can see if they crossed paths with…" Holt's words drifted off, and he stared out the front window, holding Lily closer.

It had been a nice reprieve—the siblings firing on all cylinders, a sight and process that fascinated Chris—until reality reentered the picture. Hawes moved to his brother's side and squeezed his arm.

"Be sure you look back three years," Chris said, keeping them focused. "To the night—"

Hawes's gaze shot to him, but it was Helena who spoke. "To the night your partner died."

"Was murdered." Three pale faces stared back at him as he rapped his knuckles against the wall between the X and the org chart. "I'd bet my badge that this person, whoever they are, was responsible for Izzy's death."

"And what are you going to do to them?" Hawes said.

"Find out who they are, and then we spring the trap."

An awkward few seconds of silence followed before Lily broke it with a wail. "We need to get her home for a nap," Holt said.

Helena kicked into action, moving back into the kitchen to pack up their bags, Holt on her heels. Hawes, however, stood frozen, gaze whipping back and forth between the wall of crime scene photos and his siblings. Was he imagining them there? Or himself? They'd all been in the line of fire this past week, intentionally and not.

"Hey," Chris said softly, stepping close and cupping Hawes's cheek. He waited for blue eyes to meet his, then rested their foreheads together. "We won't let anything happen to them. And I won't let anything happen to you."

"Thank you." He leaned forward and captured Chris's mouth, stealing his breath and heart in a stunning kiss, one that said more than their words or previous kisses ever had, including a confounding trace of *goodbye*.

TWELVE

Up early owing to his overnight and morning visitors, Chris beat most of the agents and staff into the office. All but one. Light shined from under the partially closed war-room door, and strains of The Grateful Dead floated out into the otherwise quiet space. Of course Wheeler had pulled an all-nighter. Chris didn't expect anything less from him.

He didn't, however, expect the decent choice in music from someone so uptight. Nor did he expect to push the door the rest of the way open and find the other agent facedown on his files, asleep. Coat, tie, and vest folded neatly over one of the other chairs, Wheeler had his wrinkled dress sleeves rolled up and his head pillowed on his folded arms. He continued to snore lightly, undisturbed by Chris's entrance. For Wheeler to be that dead to the world, he'd probably only recently fallen asleep. Chris surveyed the rest of the room, confirming his suspicion. Wheeler had been at this all night from the impressive look of it. The whiteboard of notes behind him was impossibly more packed with sharp, slanted scribble, and at the other end of the room, the flip board was now covered in photos, plans, and notes from yesterday's scene.

Chris skirted behind Wheeler, turning down the music and

flicking the coffee maker on as he walked to the other end of the room. He stood before the board, arms crossed, examining what Wheeler had pieced together. Building schematics. Before and after shots of the buyer rooms and the destroyed ventilation unit on the roof above them, where the explosion had originated. Charred remains of the three buyers. The trigger device in the stairwell. The heat signatures showing the path Hawes had run, room to room, killing his targets. Ferrying bids, as far as Wheeler knew. Surveillance photos from the hour time window before and after the explosion, a red circle drawn on two of them—by Wheeler, Chris presumed—around the head of a man Chris didn't recognize. Hawes with his head held high as he entered the building, then with his face covered in soot and a child in his arms as he later emerged next to Kane.

A chill snaked up Chris's spine, as he was reminded again of how close he'd come to losing everything he'd worked on for the past three years and everything he'd found the past week.

As the scent of stale coffee began to waft around him, Chris rested back against the table, examining the evidence from a thirty-five-thousand-foot level. Trying to assess how and when the seller had infiltrated and set the explosives. On the schematics, another red circle was drawn over a set of sub-sidewalk basement doors and a red line led from there to a utility closet inside the building. Right next to the north stairwell. Could that be the access route they were looking for? Was the man in the photos the person who traveled the path?

Per the debrief yesterday, Jax was gathering surveillance from the time period between when the Madigans had posted the auction ad to the time of the blast. The ATM had only been clicked on that afternoon, but there were traffic cams and other sources they could maybe pull useful footage from. Get a lock on who had come and gone from the building. Had the stranger been there another time? Chris withdrew his phone, snapped pictures of the photos and the schematics, and shot them off with a text to Kane and Jax, suggesting they refocus their surveillance backtrack to the indicated location with an eye for this person.

"I'm sorry about yesterday."

Chris dropped his phone into his pocket and rotated toward the voice.

Upright, Wheeler scrubbed both hands over his face and into his hair, doing a terrible job of taming it. "You were right. We could have lost agents, but I was too busy trying to get the bust to end all busts." He slumped back in the chair and dropped his hands into his lap. "I wasn't going about it the right way."

Add another check in the impressed column. An agent who could admit when he was wrong, who could adjust and learn, was a valuable asset. Chris mentally added two checks, since Wheeler was also taking on more of the blame than he deserved in this case. But he couldn't tell him that.

"It happens," he said instead. "And we didn't lose any agents."

"We're still waiting on an ID on the third body."

Chris couldn't tell him who that was either, not without letting on the full truth of yesterday's incident. "But all our agents and all of Kane's officers are accounted for, yes?"

"Yes, thankfully. We assume it was another buyer, given the location. We'll see who else turns up in the surveillance. Match it against dental, if we can salvage that much."

"ME say how long?"

"Couple days, if there are dental records."

Not likely. He needed to get that ID to Wheeler some other way before it served as another point of distraction. Or led Wheeler somewhere Chris didn't want him to go. "Pull the resident records," Chris said. "Let's see if there was anyone already in the building who could be a buyer."

"We already did that," Wheeler said. "Before the bust."

"Check it against aliases." He tapped the photos of the stranger. "And against this guy you circled. Do we know who he is?"

Wheeler shook his head. "No, but other than general databases, I didn't have much to go on other than my gut, which tells me he might be one of the heat signatures in the north stairwell just before the explosion."

"You might be right. Let's see if he's a resident or connected to one."

Wheeler held his gaze, searching, and Chris worried he'd given away too much, but then Wheeler leaned forward and opened his laptop, shooting off an email. While he did that, Chris filled a mug, set the coffee next to Wheeler, then rounded the table to sit across from him.

"Thank you," Wheeler said before taking a sip and grimacing. "I thought y'all were supposed to have good coffee in this town."

It was the first slip of Southern accent Chris had detected from the Georgia-born agent, and the twangy word, along with the observation, made him chuckle. "Have you been in many ATF offices that have good coffee?"

"Touché."

"You want good coffee, raid the FBI's stash. The SAC is a coffee snob."

"Good to know." He took another long swallow, face pinching slightly less this time, then lowered the mug, hands still wrapped around it. His gaze drifted to the Madigan org chart. "You know these people better than anyone. I should have listened to you." Then drifted back to Chris. "The explosives are our objective."

Assured of Wheeler's redirected focus, Chris withdrew the piece of paper from his inner coat pocket and slid it across the table. "You'll have another chance. Friday."

Wheeler's eyes grew wide as he read the email to Helena. "How did you get this?"

"Doesn't matter."

Skeptical brown eyes shot to his. "Perri…"

"Do you want to secure the explosives?"

Their stare-down lasted a good ten seconds before Wheeler

finally nodded. Chris slowly let his held breath out through his nose.

"Good," he said. "You're going to spec out this strike. We don't know where yet, rolling location, so it's going to be complicated. We need to consider all possible locations and have contingencies ready. I'll coordinate with the Madigans." His eyes flickered to the picture of Hawes and back. Wheeler nodded again. "And I'll add what I know to the mission planning, after I vet the tip."

"Vet it with whom?" Wheeler asked.

"Amelia Madigan."

BY THE TIME CHRIS MADE IT TO SFPD HEADQUARTERS, KANE WAS well on his way to pacing a hole through the floor outside the interrogation rooms. Tie askew, top button of his dress shirt undone, bags under his eyes, and deep creases at the corners of his drawn mouth, the chief looked to be living the longest twenty-four hours—longest two weeks—of his life. Chris was sure it was nothing compared to Kane's time in the military, but family had a way of complicating matters.

"The arraignment?" Chris asked, worried something else had gone off the rails. Seemed to be their luck lately.

Kane paused in his circuit and ran a hand over his head. "As well as it could go. Bail denied. Flight risk."

"I'm sure all those pictures of her at the offshore bank helped."

"That and a slush fund north of ten million that Holt found last night."

That explained why Hawes's brother had seemed both more engaged and more worn down this morning. He'd had a successful hack and found the last thing he'd wanted.

"Any luck tracing the funds?"

Kane resumed his pacing. "He's working on it."

Chris leaned against the wall, out of his way. "Amelia still tight-lipped?"

"Relatively."

"Probably gonna make this harder."

"Tell me what's going on before we walk in there," Kane said. "No more of this getting blindsided shit."

"Someone reached out to Helena offering to broker a sale."

Kane's steps faltered, and his eyes grew wide. "For when?"

"Friday. But I need Amelia to vet it."

"Are we sure this tip is—Wait, that's why Helena called to confirm Amelia hadn't accessed any devices?"

Chris nodded. "Which makes me fairly certain that, yes, this is a legit tip," he said, reading where Kane's previous question had been going. This wasn't a Madigan-engineered setup like yesterday. "We need Amelia to confirm it's from the right outside party. Not from someone else trying to insert themselves into the feud for their own gain."

"Might not be as hard as you think," Kane said. "Holt and Lily were in the courtroom today." He stopped and stared at the interrogation room door, empathy swirling in his hazel eyes. "She misses her daughter, and I think she even regrets betraying Holt. But the judge didn't give her a chance to say that or visit with them. Just ordered her back to solitary lock-up as soon as we're done here, until the present threat has passed."

As a parent, Chris had an inkling of what Amelia must feel. Knew well that tug of the heart demanding you do anything to get back to your kid. He felt that everyday about Ro, still, but there was no getting back to her. She was gone. But Lily wasn't, and neither was Amelia, and if there was one thing Chris didn't doubt, it was that Amelia loved her daughter. She might have lost sight of that temporarily, or interpreted her actions as being taken out of love, but as a new mother, this had to be killing her.

Which gave them leverage. "If we can change that…"

"Exactly," Kane said. "Give her the thing she wants most."

Chris didn't think it was power anymore. He hoped it wasn't, or this strategy—the only one they had—would backfire.

He entered the interrogation room and slid into the chair beside Kane, across from Amelia and her counsel. One look at Nurse Madigan, and Chris upgraded their chances. Kane was right. Her posture and manner were stoic, but her eyes and nose were red, her dress hung loose on her willowy frame, and she kept her hands clasped in a fist in front of her, as if trying to hold in the trembles that rippled out over the rest of her body.

"Did you always know who I was?" Chris asked. That question had been gnawing at him since the weekend. How much of a pawn had he been? "Or did you just figure it out last week?"

Amelia's green eyes flickered to Kane, then back.

"Cat's out of the bag," Chris said, answering her silent question.

Her clasped hands relaxed a measure. "Guess that explains why you weren't at the arraignment."

"And who exactly are you?" her lawyer asked.

Oakland Ashe, or "Oak" as Kane had greeted him, was a handsome man by any objective standard—dark hair, gray eyes, trim, fit body for a man in his mid-forties—and all of him was expensive. From his three-figure haircut to his tailored suit, to his shiny shoes, to the diamond-encrusted wedding band on his ring finger and the matching gold-and-diamond Rolex on his wrist. The Madigans had spared no expense getting Amelia the best. And he was earning his paycheck.

Chris dug his badge out of his back pocket and tossed it onto the table. "Special Agent Christopher Perri. ATF."

Oak picked up the badge and examined his credentials. "You're the agent from the incident at Hawes's loft?" At Chris's nod, Oak closed the billfold and sent it skidding back across the table to him. "My client doesn't have to answer that question if it will incriminate her."

"More than she already is?"

Oak opened his mouth to object, but Chris cut him off. "She's got enough charges to deal with. I'm not looking to add more. I'm just looking for some backstory." He turned his attention to Amelia. "My goal is not to get you more time in jail, but less."

Amelia couldn't hide her full-body tremor. "Less?" Or the lilt of hope in her voice.

Kane was right. They could use this.

"Ms. Madigan, you—"

Amelia waved Oak off. "Yes, I knew who you were before you showed up last week."

"Because your boss told you?"

"They did."

The gender-neutral pronoun gave nothing away. Her caginess, however, did. "Amelia, if you're protecting someone…"

"I'm protecting my family."

"By setting them up to take this hit?"

"Not all of them."

Just Hawes. Consistent with her actions and those of her faction last week. They didn't want to take the whole empire down. Only remove the king. "Is that why someone reached out to Helena?" He withdrew the copy of the email and pushed it across the table. "Is she your boss's backup plan or the ultimate goal?"

Surprise flashed across her face for the second time in as many minutes. "Helena almost shot me. You saw that with your own eyes."

"Oh, I don't think she's your ally," Chris said, convinced now that the siblings wouldn't turn on each other. No, this was someone else's doing. "But your boss is moving all of us around on the board, and it looks like they cut you loose in favor of the other sister. The real one."

It was a low blow, but had the intended effect. Amelia's shoulders slumped, and her gulp was audible.

"Amelia," Kane said, voice gentler, playing the good cop. They'd been friends once, and he was the known quantity here. "We're trying to protect them too."

She turned soft, too seeing eyes on Kane. "I know you are, Brax. But you're both so far out of your league."

"Are we at least on the same field with this?" Chris nudged the sheet of paper. "Is it from your boss? Was this the plan?"

Her eyes glided back to him, less soft, more amused and calculating. "Who's left, if not Helena?"

"I need more to vet this."

"Vet," she scoffed, her demeanor changing again on a dime. "You sound like him already. Everything has to be *vetted*. You're adjusting your frame of reference the wrong direction. We're all here because of the one night it all changed, the one night he didn't vet something."

The one night it all changed.

Chris was right. This was all connected to that night three years ago. "The organization didn't vet who Isabella really was," he said, tying it together. "Did you know that too? Is that why she was murdered?"

"Ms. Madigan—"

"Don't worry, Oak," Amelia replied, even though her eyes stayed locked on Chris. "I know better than to answer that one."

"Anything you can do to help us will factor into sentencing," Kane redirected, getting them back on track. "We don't want to take you away from Lily. She needs her mother."

As fast as the fight had resurged in Amelia, she deflated, reminded of what was really at stake here. Her shoulders curled forward, her chin dipped, and tears pooled in her eyes.

"Please, Amelia," Kane urged.

"Yes," she said quietly. "We always intended to recruit Helena."

"But earlier when we showed you the email," Chris said, "you were surprised."

"That they're doing it so soon."

"Did you actually think it would work? That she'd betray her brothers?"

"Me, no," Amelia said. "But they're running out of time."

Because Hawes's plan had worked. "They're spooked."

"It would appear so," Amelia said. "Maybe we misjudged you. And him."

Same as Chris had done. "Lot of that going around."

THIRTEEN

From the outside, across the intersection at Hyde and Beach, it looked like any other Wednesday night at the Buena Vista. Red neon sign lit out front, yellow globe lights casting the interior of the old haunt in a warm, soft glow, a smattering of patrons on stools at the ornate wooden bar and at the low, round tables, most of them sipping the Irish coffees the establishment was famous for. Appearances, however, Chris realized as he crossed the intersection and entered the bar, could be deceiving.

The female couple at one of the low bar tables: Avery and Zoe.

The bartender in his white jacket and thin tie: a Madigan captain.

Two more Madigan captains posing as patrons at the bar.

And around the table in the small dining area at the far end of the space, past the bar, up two steps, and out of view of the big plate-glass windows: Hawes, Holt, and the last person Chris expected to see there, Rose.

The Madigan matriarch looked like the million-plus bucks she was worth, not like she'd been discharged from the hospital earlier this week. She cut a stack of cards with her nimble, ringed fingers and riffled them in a bridge. She glanced up, spotted him, then began doling the cards out into four stacks. The shift in her methodical shuffling drew the twins' attention. Holt gave him a cursory glance, then went about rearranging Lily in her sling. Hawes, unlike his grandmother and brother, tracked Chris's every step as he approached, fiery eyes searing him like they'd done last night. Chris tucked away that memory as fast as it had come, before he embarrassed himself in front of all these people, especially Rose. He figured he was already at the top of her shit list.

Confirmed as she skipped right over his inquiry as to how she was doing, and asked, "Why should I trust you with my family?"

"Because I could have arrested any one of you over the past ten days, and yet, you're sitting here, dealing cards."

Eyes the same blue shade as Hawes's—except as far away from icy hot as humanly possible—pinned him to the spot. "I could also be dead."

"But you're not, because I pushed your car out of the way and put myself in the path of that van."

Risky move, going head to head with her, but Chris didn't think Rose was the type to tolerate, much less appreciate, bullshit. Direct seemed more her style.

She pushed a stack of cards in front of the empty chair to her left. "Sit."

He'd judged correctly, then. "What game are we playing?"

"Hearts," Hawes said from across the table, one corner of his mouth hitched up.

"How's Amelia?" Holt asked as they each passed three cards to the right. "We didn't get to talk to her at the arraignment."

"She's tired, missing you both, and cooperative as a result."

"Did she say who she's working for?" Hawes asked.

Chris shook his head, eyes still on Holt and Lily. "She says she's protecting her family."

"Someone's threatened them," Rose said.

"Maybe someone's threatened all of you."

Holt laid his cards on the table, facedown, and gathered Lily closer to his chest, holding her tight. Hawes grasped his shoulder, squeezing. "We won't let anything happen to Amelia, or to you two."

Rose tossed the two of clubs into the center of the table. "I made a list."

"Can I see it?"

"No." She cut him a withering side-eye. "I wouldn't put it past a few of the names on it to make such threats."

Chris withdrew two sheets of paper from his coat pocket. "Can you tell me if any of these names"—he pushed the residents list to her first, then the photo—"or this man are on it?"

Her eyes flickered to the photo first. "I don't know him." Then she scanned down the residents list, front and back. "None of them either, but Holt, run them against aliases."

"We did that," Chris said. "Came up blank, except for the victim we already knew about."

Holt half coughed, half laughed, while Rose kept her cool tone. "Our resources are more extensive than yours."

Hawes cleared his throat. "We're also seeing if any names crossed paths with Amelia, like we talked about."

Chris was doing the same with the picture and residents list, but if they were going to keep some secrets, so was he.

"Did she confirm the email?" Holt asked.

Chris nodded. "Recruiting Helena was part of the plan, but this is sooner than expected."

"Check the list against Hena too," Hawes said to his brother. "She's impressed someone."

"Not hard to do," Chris said. "She's the scariest of the lot of you."

"And the unlikeliest to turn on her family," Rose said.

She spoke it like it was a given fact, and Chris was surprised neither Hawes nor Holt reacted to or protested the statement. After a moment's consideration, though, Chris had to agree. As far as he knew, as far as his, Izzy's, and Wheeler's research went,

Helena didn't have outside influences diverting her loyalty. No children, no partner, no lover. She had her job, but she didn't need it for the money. It was a labor of love, and as long as her clients were taken care of, she could split. Had already been preparing to do so the past week. And while she and Hawes were generally on the same wavelength regarding the organization's targets and direction, Chris imagined Helena's redline was much further out, and a good bit blurrier, than Hawes's. Ruthless, smart, and loyal. Impressive.

"She should remain the point for us," Rose said, drawing Chris back out of his head. "Confirm the meet, but no one is going in alone this time."

Hawes had the good sense to appear chastened. Chris had the good sense to keep the conversation moving while it was going his way. "We're working through the mission parameters on our end. I should have a full workup to share by tomorrow."

"Is Wheeler going to play ball?" Hawes asked.

"He's focused on the explosives now, not on you," Chris told him. "We're all trying to stop the same thing here. The same person. We have been for three years, albeit separately. We can do this together. We're close."

Rose tossed her cards onto the table, ending the half-finished round, and Chris thought he'd lost the hand, lost even more. But then she drained her coffee, stood, and said, "We'll be expecting your call, Agent Perri."

Meeting over, Holt rose beside her, handed Lily to her, and shouldered the diaper bag. They headed out of the restaurant, Avery and Zoe on their heels, while Hawes hung back.

"You handled her well," he said.

Chris met him midway around the table, near the back corner of the room and out of sight of the windows. "She's intimidating as fuck."

Hawes smiled, a bit wistful, a lot somber. "Everyone thought Papa Cal was the scary one."

"She doing okay with that?"

"She did her grieving. She's over it." But Hawes wasn't, judging by the way he averted his gaze. "She was the same way when Mom and Dad died. A wreck for a few days, then completely put back together and in charge."

Stepping closer, Chris lifted a hand and cupped his cheek. "And you? It's only been a week since you lost him too. I'm sorry. I should've asked…"

"When?" Hawes said with a weak laugh. "We haven't had a minute."

That wasn't totally true. "You listened to me as I unloaded this morning about Ro and Izzy. I should have—"

Hawes cut him off with a hand around his wrist. "You needed to tell me that, and I needed to hear it." He turned his face into Chris's palm, nuzzling. Jawbone sharp, stubble prickly, and lips soft as they caressed Chris's skin. "Thank you for trusting me."

Two steps forward and Chris crowded him back against the corner. "I should be thanking you." He pointed at himself. "I'm the fed who lied."

"Good movie title." Hawes loosened his grip and trailed his hand down Chris's forearm, goose bumps lifting in his wake. "And you're not like any fed I've ever known."

"Known a few, have you?"

He shrugged one shoulder, and the opposite corner of his mouth hitched up, the hint of a smirk chasing away the melancholy. The next instant, Chris was wrenched forward by the arm, spun, and shoved front first into the corner. Hawes's heat slammed into his back and wafted over his ear, lips and breath tickling there. "You're my favorite."

Chris's stomach flipped, and his dick hardened. "Good to know, and fuck them."

Hawes laughed and nipped his nape. "Tomorrow, Agent Perri."

"Tomorrow," Chris repeated to Hawes's backside as the king, head held high, strode out of the restaurant and into the night.

CHRIS WAITED LONG ENOUGH FOR HIS ERECTION TO SUBSIDE, THEN paid the table's bill, crossed the street, and turned down the alley where he'd parked the Hog. And found he wasn't alone. Hawes stood leaning against the wall across from the bike, knee bent, one foot propped on the cinder blocks. Fog crept around the ankle of his other leg, around the slits of his suit coat, and overhead in the faint halo of light cast by the street lamps at either end of the alley.

In the blue eyes that swiveled Chris's direction.

Chris took a mental picture, the essence of Hawes Madigan captured in a single shot. Like the fog he loved so much, Hawes was a creature of shadow and light, playing in the corners, at the edges, until the wispy, indefinable mist slunk in all around and was too overpowering to see your way out of. You could fear it, fear the uncertainty, or let go and accept it. In this city, there was no escaping it. So you grew to love it. Like Hawes had the fog, like Chris had the man.

Fuck, he'd totally fallen for the mark.

Priorities shifted with each step Chris took toward Hawes. Keeping this man alive rocketed even higher up the ladder. Finding Isabella's killer was paramount. Securing the explosives and Hawes's empire likewise near the top. But it wasn't only because Chris agreed that less death was a good thing or because he was on board with the way Hawes ran things. Chris wanted—needed— Hawes to be alive at the end of all this. Hawes could take care of himself, he'd proven that time and again, but after almost watching him die yesterday, feeling like the bottom had dropped out of his world for a third time, he couldn't handle that reality coming to pass.

Not when an alternate reality was making itself known. His head wasn't totally on board yet, unsure how to make their differing approaches to justice work, but his heart had tasted home again and was loath to part with it. Or with the man who'd stoked that feeling to life.

"Are you on board with this plan?" Chris said as he approached.

"Did you hear me object?"

"I didn't hear you say much of anything." Chris rested carefully back against the bike. An exercise in balance, and in restraint, every muscle in his body screaming to press along Hawes's, to claim another taste of home, but he needed to make his point. Needed to be sure. "I need to know you're on the same page. That we're in this together."

Hawes leaned his head back and stared at the sky. "It would be a tactical error, keeping you out of the loop again."

"Fuck the tactical reasons." The frustrated bark in Chris's voice jerked Hawes's gaze back to him. "I'm talking about keeping you alive. Because yesterday can't happen again."

"You know what I am. I know what you are. Let's not be naive. Death is always a risk."

Chris hung his head, curled one hand around a handlebar, and the other around the leather seat, and inhaled deeply.

"I don't want to lose you either," Hawes whispered from across the alley, voice as tortured as Chris's insides. Full of the same storm of emotions Chris was fighting, brought on by realities that couldn't be denied. Acknowledged, then, but so too had been what was at stake for both of them.

Fuck restraint. Chris pushed off the bike and closed the distance between them. He bent his head and swirled his tongue in the deep groove between Hawes's neck and shoulder. "Did those other feds know how you like to be kissed, right here?"

Hawes whimpered and threaded a hand through Chris's hair, holding him there. Chris enjoyed the tugging hold while he nipped at Hawes's collarbone, then soothed the freckled skin with his tongue. But as he trailed a line of kisses to Hawes's ear, he grasped Hawes's wrist, withdrew his hand from his hair, and pinned his arm to the wall. "Did they know how you like to let go?" He rolled his hips, and Hawes rocked back.

"They didn't know me like this. No one has." He leaned in for a kiss, and Chris dodged. "Dante, please."

Chris pressed against him, a rolling wave of need cresting from thighs, to groin, to chest, to the breath across Hawes's cheek and the hand tangled with his. And at each point of contact, Hawes rolled back with the same need. "Did they know what it's like to have all this writhing under them?" He kissed down Hawes's cheekbone and snaked a hand between them to cup Hawes through his slacks. "What a fucking gift all this is?"

A tremble wracked Hawes's body, and he froze. Chris leaned back far enough to see his face, afraid he'd said or done something wrong. But it wasn't anger or confusion staring back at him. Instead, Hawes's eyes were wide and full of chilly sorrow. "I'm no one's gift. A curse maybe…"

"Wrong." Chris kissed him hard, blasting heat to chip away at that damnable ice. "And even if you were a curse, I'd have no interest in breaking it."

"You're just going to break me."

"Good, then we'll be even."

Hawes laughed, deep and rumbly, breaking the tension, and breaking any hope Chris had of holding back. He crushed his mouth against Hawes's, and from there it was a race to see who could break the other faster. Pants ripped open, hands dove into boxers, fists wrapped around cocks, stroking each other in the darkness, the cool fog curling around them, hiding them in their own little world of heat and desperation.

It was reckless, sharing this here in a public alley, doing this at all, for both of them, but putting on the brakes was no longer an option. And when Hawes took both of them in hand, exerting control, Chris scrabbled at the wall on either side of Hawes's head, struggling to hold himself up against the onslaught of pleasure. Gasping between frantic, hungry kisses, he thrust into Hawes's fist, against his long, hard cock, foot on the gas, speeding them toward orgasm.

When they came together, Chris's hand covering Hawes's, clasped around their cocks, the both of them rutting and spilling over their tangled fingers, "Even" was on Hawes's lips, and a prayer was on Chris's, a fervent wish that this spell never be broken.

FOURTEEN

Chris's head was still spinning the next morning from the surreal meeting with the Madigans—and the surreal after-encounter with Hawes in the alley. So much so that he would've fucked up Mia's omelet if not for Marco snatching the bag of chopped ham out of his hand.

"She's a vegetarian this week, remember?" his nephew said.

"Good catch, kid." He reclaimed the bag and dumped the remaining meat in the other skillet, making Marco a double-stuffed Denver.

Marco laughed. "Thinking you need coffee as much as I do." He reached for the pot, and Gloria swooped in, batting his hand down.

"The answer is no," she said.

"Ang is just going to stop and get us venti iced lattes on the way to Marco's day camp," Mia said from the table, where she sat with an e-reader propped in front of her. "Her favorite coffee shop is in that neighborhood."

"But I didn't serve it to you," Gloria said. "Your mom's rules."

Marco made a Vanna White worthy sweep of the room with his eyes and arms. "I don't see Mom, do you?"

Chris bumped his hip. "Go sit down, Plato. Not the time to argue."

Mia rolled her eyes. "He has so lived up to that nickname."

Laughter broke the tension, but not Chris's concern, which had been piqued by Marco's throwaway comment. Where was Celia?

He slid each omelet out of its skillet and onto a plate and carried them over to the table, where he slipped a ten to each of the kids. Marco gave him a fist bump, Mia a smile. He'd take that and the way they happily dug into their food.

He returned to the cutting boards and utensils in the sink and his mother's knowing grin. "I saw that."

"Like Mia said, they're gonna get it anyway. Angelica shouldn't have to foot the bill. And she made me a box of mistletoe cannoli."

"And the truth comes out." Gloria drained her first cup, then refilled it and one for him too. He finished filling the sink with soap and water, then wiped his hands off and accepted the offered brew. She added, "Thanks for helping out this morning."

He lowered his voice so the kids wouldn't hear him. "You said your gout was acting up, but you're moving around just fine, so why am I really here?" She glanced over her shoulder at the kids, confirming Chris's suspicion. "Where's Celia?"

Before she could answer, a car horn blew outside, and his niblings clicked into fast-forward, shoving last bites into their mouths and stuffing their scattered daily detritus into bookbags.

"Dishes in the sink," Gloria said, and they scurried over to drop their plates in the soapy water.

Marco gave them both a hug. Mia gave Gloria's cheek a kiss and Chris a wave of her e-reader, and then they were gone, the slam of doors and the squeal of Angelica's tires outside making Chris laugh. Of all the Perris, his cousin had the heaviest foot and the speeding tickets to prove it.

Chris returned to the sink and dipped his hands beneath the suds. "You didn't answer my question," he said to his mom as he scrubbed dishes. "Where's Celia?"

"Right here. And I'm fine."

He turned his head the opposite direction, toward his sister's voice, and thanked the saints that his hands—no, his fists—were hidden under the water. His sister was clearly not fine. Her slight frame drowned in the folds of their dad's old flannel robe, but Chris supposed it gave her some comfort. Some protection against the reality of her black eye, busted lip, and hobbled gait as she slowly crossed the living room toward them.

Mia's worry from the other night had come to pass.

"I'm gonna fucking kill him." So much for keeping his anger in check.

"Don't," she said, gingerly lowering herself into the chair Mia had vacated. "He's not worth it. I'd rather you help me get a restraining order."

About fucking time. "Done." He grabbed the last dish, rinsed it off, and set it in the rack to drip dry. "I know a lawyer. It's not what she does, but she knows everyone. She'll make it happen." He figured this was right up Helena's alley, in more ways than one. And Kane would be more than happy to enforce said order. "He won't come near you again, Cee."

Gloria set a steaming mug in front of her, then claimed the chair beside her. "And you won't go back to him either."

Celia looked away from them, swallowing hard. With a clear view of her blackened eye, of the finger bruises on her neck that her hair had hidden, Chris had to wrap a towel around his fists to keep from punching through the wall. "Where is he? So we'll know where to serve him."

Celia laughed, tired and bitter. "So you can go beat him up? No, not that I have any idea where he went...after..." She gestured at her face, then cinched the robe tighter around herself.

Fuck, the last thing she needed right now was him in rage mode too. He unwound the cloth, took a deep breath, and sat in the chair across from them. "I know this is tough—"

"What do you know about this?" Celia snapped. Her dark

eyes sparked to match, but not with anger, with hurt and regret. "You're never here."

Chris raised his hands, palms out. "You're right. I have been gone too much, but I'm hoping to change that." Aside from the momentary panic when he'd thought Hawes was dead, his hope and commitment to stay had only solidified over the past week and a half. He wanted—needed—to stay. For whatever this thing was with Hawes and for his family.

But his sister didn't look happy about that declaration. She cast her gaze aside again and swallowed hard.

"You don't want me here?" Chris said.

"Of course I want you here."

"Then what is it?"

She righted her gaze, and there were tears in her dark eyes, one escaping and racing down her bruised cheek. "She looked so much like you." Her voice wobbled—"It's my fault"—and broke, Celia with it, as she covered her face and cried into her hands.

Chris's heart broke too, for all that they'd lost, and for the weight of it that Celia had been carrying, because he'd run from it, hadn't been around to help her shoulder the load, to tell her she didn't need to shoulder it at all. This was the damage he'd done.

He rose, circled the table, and knelt by his sister's side. "Fuck, Cee, I'm sorry," he said, and when she wouldn't give him her eyes, he lightly grasped her chin and rotated her gaze to him. "You are the last person I blame for what happened to Ro. If you hadn't been driving, we would have lost you and Mia too." He cupped her unbruised cheek. "Please stop blaming yourself."

She hid her face in his hand. "I keep replaying that day. If I'd done something different, if I'd not taken that shortcut…"

"Stop." He rose and gently pulled her into a hug. "It's been ten years, Cee. Stop punishing yourself. Stop letting him punish you." Because that's what she'd been doing. Taking the hits because she thought she deserved them. He held her as tightly as her injuries would allow. "Your whole life has been stuck there, honey. Ro wouldn't want that."

The damn broke, her sobs coming loud and ragged, and the tension finally, finally, flowed from her body. Chris held his sister like he should have more often the past decade, not the awkward hugs of strangers, but of two people who'd been best friends growing up, who'd always had each other's backs.

Gloria scooted closer, rubbing her daughter's back. "Everything changed that day. We lost Ro, but we also lost you."

Celia drew back, wiping the tears from under her eyes and the wetness from under Chris's eyes as well. "We lost you too that day," she said to him. "Ro wouldn't want that either."

Everything had changed ten years ago. He'd lost the center of his world, been set adrift, and almost turned the lights out on himself. But Izzy had found him and changed the course of his life. And he'd been punishing himself ever since. Jumping from one undercover assignment to another, pretending to be someone he wasn't, so he could block out all he'd lost. It had worked when he'd needed it to, but now? Being back here with his family, being with Hawes, a little of the old Christopher and a little of the new Dante were blending together—someone who was the same but not, the reality of himself now, and he was looking for a port to come home to, but the fog made it hard to navigate. Fog from all the years spent thinking himself weak in that moment of darkness, from the mistakes he'd made. Because he also felt responsible for not being there then, and now. And the past three years, he'd thrown himself into the hunt for Izzy's killer. Another distraction, another act of retribution and self-blame.

Retribution. Self-blame.

Chris froze, the words echoing in his head, shifting his frame of reference as puzzle pieces of a different sort fell into place.

Everything changed that night.

The night of Isabella's death.

Because Hawes felt responsible.

Or because he was responsible?

Chris was glad he'd taken the Hog to his mom's place. It had made navigating back home easier. Faster. Less time for him to jump to conclusions without first reexamining the evidence from the night of Izzy's death. Reconsidering that night that had changed everything from a different perspective. Not from his own, as an outside investigator. Not from his partner's, as the victim. From Hawes's. As the what?

Just like Chris's life had changed the day Ro had died, Hawes's life, and the trajectory of his organization, had changed the night Isabella died. Chris had witnessed those changes in action, had counted on them in revealing certain information to Hawes, and was working with Hawes to protect them from those who wanted to go back to the old ways.

Under Hawes's regime, targets had to be vetted and collateral damage eliminated. Lofty morals for an assassin descended from parents who, by all accounts, were efficient killing machines, much like Helena. From a grandmother who wielded words like Holt did his keystrokes. And a grandfather who'd built an empire on fear, much like the Prince of Killers moniker Hawes hated but stoked when needed.

A new regime that had come into being after Izzy's death.

Why? Izzy asked in Chris's head. *What changed for him that night?*

Why did Hawes, like Celia, feel responsible? He wasn't exactly punishing himself like Chris's sister, but he'd changed his whole life as a result of that night.

Chris paced the study as he talked it out with his partner. "Because his family was threatened. Infiltrated by the ATF. He didn't want it to happen again."

Except that wasn't right. Genuine surprise and betrayal had flashed across Hawes's face when Chris had revealed his and Izzy's true identities. He hadn't known last week, much less three years ago, that his organization had been so deeply infiltrated by the ATF. That wasn't the reason.

What's the other side of that coin?

"He thought you were an innocent." He turned on his heel to face the collage of crime scene photos and notes. Izzy's and Zander Rowe's sheet-covered bodies on the rain-slicked street. The reflection of blue and red lights, evidence markers, and two pistols. "One of his employees, a secretary, who was trying to defend herself, killed by one of his lieutenants." Hawes cared about the legit organization as much as the illegal one. He'd take it personally, bear the brunt of the responsibility, if one of those employees was unwittingly caught in the crossfire.

What crossfire?

It sure as fuck hadn't been a domestic disturbance. While evidence at the scene pointed to that easily enough—Izzy's mangled wrists, the bruises on her face—none of Izzy's notes indicated Rowe had been abusive. And none of the Madigan siblings would have put up with that sort of behavior had they gotten so much as a whiff of it.

Fuck, how did he make the pieces of this puzzle fit? What was he missing? It was all there. He just had to figure out what tied it all together.

Hands on his head, he rotated slowly around the room, halting in front of the current investigation notes.

The explosives.

"That was your mission. You found something. Is that why Rowe killed you?"

They were connected to all this, and Hawes was doing everything he could to get the organization out of that business. Too much of a risk, too high a cost, he'd said last week. The definition of collateral damage.

No collateral damage.

"That's what you were." Not a mole, not caught up in a domestic disturbance. No, as far as Hawes knew, she'd been Rowe's girlfriend, and that night, she'd been in the wrong place, at the wrong time. "Unacceptable collateral damage."

Chris rushed the desk full of notes and began pulling sheets of paper and tacking them to the wall in a separate collage. Repositioned crime scene photos to go with them. The things that never quite added up. A Madigan company sedan at the scene, but no hair or fiber from Izzy or Rowe inside it. Tire tracks and skid marks that didn't match the sedan. That were more likely a van or truck. Like the van loaded with explosives that had tried to kill Hawes after Papa Cal's funeral. He snatched the bank record showing Amelia's deposit to Zander Rowe and added it to the story.

"Rowe was a traitor. Diverting a van of explosives. And you found out." The last report she'd filed—the night she'd died—was that someone else was trying to buy the explosives. She'd found out, and the neo-Nazi who died Tuesday was at the top of her suspects list.

No, the neo-Nazi who was killed. *By...*

"Hawes. He found out too."

Which would be unacceptable to the then prince. The potential for collateral damage—to his family, their empire, and his city— would be too high.

What'd he do, Dante?

Ice crept through his veins as the jagged puzzle pieces began to match up, began to fit into a picture that was still blurry, but which some inherent part of him knew he didn't want to see. Not the picture of home he'd been putting together. A nightmare instead, like the one Hawes suffered—*replayed*—nightly.

"He intercepted the van."

Not just ice anymore. A whole mountain of snow buried him in an avalanche as actions and words from the past week played through his mind.

Hawes's revulsion at the gun Chris had shoved in his hand. *"They kill too fast,"* Hawes had said. *"Without thought. It's too easy to make the wrong call."* In every fight, the assassin had used a different weapon—his body, a garrote, his words. Until Friday morning, when he'd picked up Chris's gun, and Helena had been shocked and terrified.

Why?

Chris guessed the terrible truth. "Because he hadn't touched one in three years."

Then he hunted for the evidence to disprove what he didn't want to believe. Rifling back through Izzy's files, he searched for pictures of Hawes from before Izzy's death.

A photo of him at MCS, dressed in one of his fitted suits, a visible bulge under his left arm.

On the yacht, a bump on his right hip under the hem of his sweater.

He used to carry.

Until he'd made the wrong call.

He flipped to the next picture in the file.

Hawes, in a fog-filled alley, a gun pointed at a man on his knees.

A Colt 1911.

The same type of gun on the ground next to Zander Rowe's body. The gun that had fired the bullet that killed Izzy. A gun that wasn't registered to Zander Rowe. That they'd never been able to trace. They'd thought it had been Rowe's, obtained illegally.

Whose was it, Dante?

Bile surged up Chris's throat, and he braced his hands on the wall, on either side of the ad hoc story he'd constructed. Of the assembled puzzle in front of him, the nightmare crystal fucking clear.

No indiscriminate killing. The last of Hawes's rules. Something a gun tended to do. The weapon Hawes wouldn't use. The rule and aversion the very opposite of the title that had been bestowed on him.

The Prince of Killers.

Why does he hate it so much?

"Because he thinks he killed his parents." Hawes had told him that story. How he'd been the one to give the order to pull the plug and take his parents off life support. But that wasn't the only reason. Those weren't the only deaths Hawes regretted. There was another one staring Chris right in the face. A truth that kept

Hawes up at night, that he and his siblings had tiptoed around in conversation, that Hawes had apologized for the other night, only Chris hadn't understood then.

He understood now. His gut burned, and his chest ached, ripped apart by another loss—his hope for a future, a *home*, bleeding out on the hardwood floor. Like Izzy had bled out that night in the street, murdered by the same man Chris had fallen for.

Who else did he kill, Dante?

Pushing past the pain, he spoke the truth that had eluded him for three long years. "You."

FIFTEEN

Chris ignored the vibrating phone in his pocket, same as he'd ignored the other umpteen calls today while he'd been adjusting his frame of reference. Rearranging the evidence into a picture that was indisputable. Replaying every interaction he'd had with Hawes Madigan.

Betrayal stung hot and deep. Fucking karma.

Until this morning, Chris had been sincere in his aim to help Hawes hold on to power. The direction Hawes and his siblings were taking the organization, the rules they followed, did result in less death. Only the worst criminals, those who'd escaped the justice Chris and the law doled out, met their end. As much as Chris wanted to believe the rule of law was enough, he wasn't a total fool.

But knowing the why now, knowing that Hawes had been undercutting Chris's primary mission at every turn, knowing that Isabella's killer had been staring him right in the face, kissing him, writhing under him, had sent Chris gagging over the toilet more than once today.

Disgust and damnable desire still churned in his gut, but anger fueled his footsteps up the stairs, two at a time, to Kane's office. He banged open the stairwell door, glimpsed the directional signage, and diverted. He wanted to check something else first. Another thing that didn't line up about that night.

He found the IT department, and Jax's platinum Mohawk was like a beacon, drawing him to their workstation. They spotted him several desks away and reared back in their chair. Chris slowed his gait and reined in his glare. He needed their help, but he was taking a gamble. Jax had only started at SFPD last year. He didn't think they would have been involved three years ago, but they were one of Holt's kids. There was no way to know for sure what they might have done off-book before joining the force. If nothing else, Chris was sure they would report this encounter.

"Agent Perri," they greeted cautiously. "What's going on?"

He pulled a flash drive from his jacket pocket. "Cue that up."

They gave him the same skeptical raised brow Holt had when Chris had earlier presented him with a flash drive. "It's SFPD's own footage, from a previous crime scene."

"If this has a—"

"No virus. I wouldn't know how anyway."

They still ran a virus check after inserting the device and before clicking any of its contents. That done, Jax opened the video footage and pressed Play.

And nothing. As frustratingly boring as it had always been. Just a recording of the rain-slick street that cut off before Isabella and Rowe ever appeared.

"I don't get it," Jax said.

"According to the police report, the traffic cam that captured this intersection cycled off two minutes before a double homicide occurred here." He tapped the screen. "Can you tell if that's the case?"

"It is," they answered immediately. "But it's been looped before that."

"Excuse me?"

"Right before the cutoff. It's a loop feed. A very well-executed one, but it's a loop. I'm red-green color blind." They pointed to a Golden State Warriors flag hanging over a shop door in the far-right corner of the screen. "That flag is royal blue and yellow to you. To me, it's navy and white, as in bright white, which really shows in the dark." Their fingers raced across the keyboard, and a second later, the picture was in monochrome "Take out the color saturation, and the details pop for you too." Indeed, Chris noticed it more clearly now. "You see it move?"

He nodded. "With the wind."

"The exact same way?" They rewound the footage, slowed it down, and sure enough, it was an exact replica. More like a blip than a nudge from the breeze. "And look at the reflection in the puddle." Of the neon red CLOSED sign in a storefront window, with a news ticker below, displaying the same line of text.

"Fuck." But it was still cut off before the incident. What had they hidden in those few seconds? The van coming into the scene? Someone else—Hawes—arriving there too? "Can you recover the altered footage?"

They shook their head. "Past the three-year archive mark. But I'm the best here at finding hidden code." Fingers flew again. "It's got to be buried here somewhere." Another two minutes in which Chris tried not to lose what little was left of his shit, and then they stopped typing abruptly.

Chris glanced at the screen, at the string of numbers that didn't mean a thing to him but clearly translated for Jax. "What is it?"

"Nothing. There's nothing here."

Chris grabbed the arm of their chair and spun them around to face him. "You're doing good work here. You've come a long way from the shelter. Don't risk that."

"I can't get the footage."

"But you know who made the change." He glanced at the screen. "Your mentor, Holt, I'm guessing?"

"Not exactly." They tapped a nail against the armrest, reticent to say more.

Which was more than enough for Chris. If it wasn't Holt, there was only one other person Jax would protect with their silence. And as luck would have it, he worked in this very same building.

Kane stood behind his desk, waiting at military attention. Legs spread, arms crossed over his chest, he didn't blink, didn't flinch, when Chris charged into his office and slammed the door behind him.

"What happened the night Isabella died?" Chris demanded.

"That was before I was chief."

"But you were here, on the force, weren't you?"

"I'd come on about eighteen months before."

Wasn't that convenient? The Madigans' pet cop showed up shortly after Hawes's ascension. Had they always planned it that way? Probably. Chris didn't think it was by chance.

He tossed the flash drive onto the desk. "You altered the surveillance footage from the night Izzy died."

Kane paled and dug his fingers into his biceps, but he didn't say a word to confirm or deny.

Chris stepped forward, thighs butting the edge of the desk in front of him. "You helped them cover it up."

"I don't know what you're talking about."

Chris scoffed. "Did you know they left a clue in the system?"

"There's no evidence—"

"Jax is a better hacker than you or Holt think."

Kane's brows dipped into a *V*, but he kept his lips pressed together, silent.

"Don't have your orders yet, do you?"

The chief of police, the man charged with upholding the law in San Francisco, took his cue not from the law, but from an organization of assassins. Twelve hours ago, Chris thought maybe that worked. That the delicate balance was needed. Not anymore. And judging by his locked-down, cold demeanor, Kane wasn't looking at Chris as an ally anymore either. In front of him stood Agent

Perri, the man who could blow apart his entire house of cards. Given what was at stake, and Kane's military training, this exercise was futile. He wasn't going to crack.

"I need to talk to Amelia," Chris said.

"She's already been transferred out."

Of course she had. Growling, Chris flung out an arm and whacked the candy bowl off the desk. The carpet prevented it from shattering, but caramel candies went flying, pinging off the walls and floor. "Then *you're* going to give me some fucking answers, or I'll—"

"You'll what?"

Chris whipped around to the woman who had the most impeccable timing in the world, and a knife in her hand, the razor-sharp tip now pressing into the tender spot beneath his last rib. "Haven't we been here before, Mr. Hair? Did you not learn your lesson about making threats?"

"Of course you're here."

Helena shrugged and pressed a measure harder with the knife, only a flick of her wrist away from drawing blood, or worse. "What was that threat you were about to make?"

Well, he'd needed to talk to her anyway. The day had gone sideways, and he'd lost sight of another of his priorities. Here was a chance to fix that at least. "Two things," he said to her. "One, I need a good family lawyer."

Helena tilted her head, eyes narrowed. "You?"

"My sister. Husband beat her up. Needs a TRO and a divorce."

No hesitation, no flinch. "Done."

"Two, did Hawes kill Isabella?"

That made her flinch, and it was as good a confirmation as any.

Fuck.

This whole time, his partner's killer had been right there in front of him, under him, in his arms, in his fucking bed. He stumbled back against the desk's edge and hung his head. "And I thought *I* was fooling *you all.*"

They'd fooled Kane too, judging by the man's muttered curse.

"You didn't know?" Chris asked over his shoulder.

Kane collapsed into his chair and covered his face with his hands. More than enough betrayal to go around it seemed.

"Hawes was fooled too," Helena said, drawing Chris's attention back to her. She'd stepped back and stashed the knife God only knew where. "He thought she was an accomplice, and then he thought she was an innocent. It's torn him up every day for the past three years, and then you show up and hammer that nail even harder. But she was neither of those things, was she? She was an agent, she knew what she was getting into, she knew the risks. Same as you. He was set up, just like the rest of us."

"He fucking shot her, and all week, he—*all of you*—let me think it was someone else."

"It *was* someone else," Kane said, and Chris whipped back around, glaring. "Do you remember what Amelia said? Whoever she's working for knew who you were before you got here. I'm guessing they knew who your partner was too. Helena's right. Hawes may have pulled the trigger, but someone put him and your partner there."

"Right now, that someone else isn't my fucking problem." He pushed off the desk and used his full height to loom over Helena. "Where is he?"

"Not a chance, Mr. Hair."

He shoved past her toward the door. "You better hope you find him before I do."

SIXTEEN

Helena had found Hawes first, or at a minimum, delivered a warning to him, because wherever Chris looked, Hawes wasn't there. The cold storage facility on the docks, the warehouse in South City, the company yacht. The South Beach condo, the family fort in Pac Heights, the ballpark. Chris had flashed his badge to get in and scouted the entire club-level concourse. Like a ghost, Hawes had vanished. Chris didn't think he'd left town, not with so much uncertainty hanging over his family and his organization. And he wouldn't leave Helena unguarded tomorrow, but he was apparently playing Casper until he had to show himself.

Probably better that way. Chris had a fucking op to prepare for, one that depended on the Madigans' cooperation, one that could save countless lives, but all Chris could focus on was the life that had been lost. And the man who'd stolen it. The man who'd stolen something else from Chris that left his chest aching, his gut twisted, and his entire being hollowed out and drifting, no longer at home in the fog. Suffocating under the weight of it.

Frustrated and empty-handed, Chris was in a mood that matched the night sky by the time he returned to his condo. Home. Didn't much feel like it anymore, just when it had recently begun to for the first time in a decade. Trudging up the steps,

Chris curled and flexed his fingers, itching to tear the place apart. To tear anything apart.

He opened the front door and got his wish in the form of a six-foot-two, blue-eyed, suited assassin standing calmly by his kitchen island.

With a gun in his hand.

Chris had misjudged him once again. Hawes hadn't been playing Casper at all. He'd come directly here to face the truth. What was it he'd said? He was done with this shit. Apparently so. Hawes squared his shoulders and lifted the arm holding the gun. Chris closed his hand around the grip of the backup weapon in his holster, but then released it when Hawes placed his—no, Chris's gun, from Friday—on the island next to a bottle of Crown Royal Rye, the same they'd shared at Hawes's condo. "I didn't mean to leave you defenseless."

Defenseless. Apt description. Sure, he had a gun within reach, but the absence of truth was far more deadly. Chris slammed the door shut, tossed his jacket in a corner, and stalked across the space between them. No more lies. "Why did everything change that night?"

Defiant, resigned eyes stared back at him, a winter storm swirling in their depths. "Because I shot Isabelle Costa."

Chris grabbed him by the jacket lapels, spun, and slammed him against the wall between the study and bedroom. "You killed her? Not Rowe?"

Despite the manhandling, Hawes didn't fight back and gave no sign of distress. "I did," he answered flatly.

Cold, untouchable. Now Chris got it. And it only amped up his anger, made it burn hotter. "You knew why I was here, what I was looking for, and you let the past week and a half slip by without a word."

"You were using me. I was using you."

Chris flattened his hands on Hawes's chest and pushed, slamming him against the wall again. "We're way past that, and you fucking know it."

"I think the same person behind the coup was behind that night."

Anger erupted at the deflection, at Hawes's ability to keep that cool, flat tone when Chris's world was coming apart at the seams. "You pulled the fucking trigger! Maybe you are a fucking curse."

Finally, a reaction. Hawes whipped his head to the side as if he'd been slapped. He stared out the back windows, Adam's apple bobbing erratically.

Chris cupped the side of his face, far from gentle, a thumb wedged under his chin, his fingers splayed over his cheek, the grip secure. "And after what I told you the other morning, about Ro, about how Izzy saved me, you still didn't tell me the truth. I trusted you. I lo—" Hawes tried to jerk free, and the pressure that exerted on Chris's hold tripped up his words before he uttered the last thing either of them needed. "Fuck!"

Hawes's response came out a hoarse whisper. "I still don't know who set her up to die."

Chris forced his face back around. "Does it matter? You pulled the trigger. You killed her."

Hawes lowered his eyes, long lashes brushing his pale cheeks. "I'm so sorry, Dant—"

"Don't! You don't get to use that name anymore." Not now that the spell was well and truly broken. He pressed his fingertips into the hollow of Hawes's cheek, demanding his gaze again. "It meant I mattered to someone again, to her. And she mattered too."

"She did."

Cold, hard metal pressed against Chris's stomach. He glanced down, then back up in surprise. In his anger, in the flurry of earlier movement, he hadn't noticed Hawes snatch the gun off the island, hadn't realized he'd been at Hawes's mercy this entire time. And now Hawes was at his, Hawes shoving the gun at Chris butt-first, barrel pointing at his own gut.

"She did matter," Hawes said, voice rough, his icy exterior shattering with each word. "And I'm willing to lose everything for her now. I pulled the trigger. I relive that night over and over. I did it, yes, but I want to know who put me and her in that position, who brought you to my doorstep three years later, who knew you'd be my weakness."

He pressed the gun harder into Chris's abs, waiting for him to take hold of it, and only continuing once he had. "I want to know the whole truth, and so do you. More than that, I want to stop it from ever happening again, and I can't do that alone. I went into this using you, but you're right—we flew way past that, and now I need you. Help me stop this, and then I'll turn myself over to you, on or off the books."

Chris moved the gun out from between them and eased his grip on Hawes's face, but he didn't step back, held there by truth and lies and all the gray space between them. "After the strike tomorrow."

Hawes nodded. "We shut this down, and then I'm yours."

SEVENTEEN

Chris found Wheeler in the war room, as expected. Tie gone, sleeves rolled up, he was shuffling through surveillance photos and street maps with one hand and tapping out a staccato rhythm with the pen in his other. "You've been trying to reach me," Chris said, making his presence known.

Wheeler's head shot up, gaze surprised, then furious. "For an entire fucking day." His temper quelled, though, at whatever he saw on Chris's face. He dialed it down from a ten to a tolerable five. "You haven't been answering my calls and you've been ignoring my voice mails."

"One, learn to text. Two, I was sorting some stuff out, which we'll get to in a minute." He lowered himself into the chair across the table. "But first, is this the tactical plan for tomorrow?"

"Yeah, based on our work yesterday."

Chris nodded. "Okay, give me the rundown."

Wheeler walked him through it, step-by-step—the pick-up, the approach, the convergence, the attack, and the seizure. Assuming all went according to plan. He had contingencies mapped out, multiple means of transport ready, and surveillance points and tactical check-ins every step of the way. He'd done good work, had coordinated with SFPD seamlessly, and all systems were a go for the operation. Chris intended to follow ninety-nine percent of the plan. He didn't think Wheeler would mind the one percent change.

"That's not exactly how the op is going to go down," he said.

Fury returned as Wheeler shot to his feet. "I'm sorry, *what?*" He expected Chris to override him, to scrap the tactical plan he'd lost God only knew how many hours of sleep over.

"Hear me out," Chris said. "I want the same thing you do."

"To secure the explosives."

"And to bring down the Madigans."

After the confrontation with Hawes, he'd walked the park for an hour, debating Hawes's offer. *I'm yours.* To kill, to fuck, to arrest, to walk away from.

To keep.

That last option had driven him here. He couldn't keep Hawes and get justice for Izzy. They were incompatible. Hawes had killed Izzy. Chris had to bring the ATF in on this because it was what she deserved, and because the temptation to do otherwise was a siren song he didn't know if he could resist, even through a hurricane of betrayal.

Brown eyes wide, Wheeler barely managed to aim his ass into his chair as he fell back into it. "Since when?"

"Since I found out who killed my partner."

"What did you find out?"

"That it wasn't a domestic disturbance, that the Madigans covered it up, and that the person who pulled the trigger isn't the only one responsible." He wasn't willing to turn over all his cards —Chris would only completely trust himself now—but Wheeler could help win the hand. "I want all of them, and the explosives are the common thread."

"I may have a lead on that." Wheeler bounded out of his chair, no longer unsure, and darted for the stack of files at the other end of the conference table. He dug out a manila folder, and from it, photos of their mystery man from the auction site. "He's not a building resident, but I used the surveillance time stamp and the building access logs to see which units were pinged for entry at the time he arrived. There were two, and when I searched each of those residents' social media feeds, I found this." He handed Chris a second photo, a screenshot of an Instagram feed.

This was why you wanted Scotty Wheeler on your cases. Never met a haystack he didn't like. "Karen Alexander," he said. "Unit 501."

Chris examined the photo.

The twenty-something blonde, dressed for a day of sailing, stood on the deck of a boat, the Bay Bridge in the background, their mystery man at her side. Chris read the caption, dated the morning of the op: *Thanks for the tug, GB. Dinner on me tonight?*

"Gilbert Baker," Wheeler said, beating Chris to the question. "He runs a tug and"—he curled his fingers in air quotes—"salvage operation out of China Basin."

"And by salvage you mean smuggler."

"Never charged officially."

"Of course not. Wouldn't be in business long if he had." Chris worked through this new development. "He's not high-level enough to be competition for the Madigans, but if you were in the market for explosives and needed to move them…"

"He would be your guy." A stack of stapled papers—a list— appeared under his nose. "The people he does business with."

Chris whistled low. It wasn't a short list, and many of the names—legitimate and otherwise—were recognizable, including one from Izzy's files. "Carl Reeves is on this list."

Reeves's front company, a shipping business, had contracts with MCS. Izzy had suspected there was more to it than supplying freezer units for his shipping vessels but had never gotten the evidence she needed to officially pursue the lead. She'd sniffed around, though. If Reeves had gotten wind of that, of Izzy, if he'd dug into those investigating him, maybe he'd learned who Izzy really was. Who Chris was. If they were looking for a player with the juice to move everyone around the board, Reeves fit the bill. And a hostile takeover of the Madigans would fit the bill too.

Vertical integration for his legit business. Trained assassins and a stockpile of explosives to protect his other enterprise. A force on land and on sea.

Wheeler lowered himself back into the chair across from Chris. "I'm guessing Karen's boat didn't just happen to have engine failure that day."

"Good guess."

Reeves would have seen the Madigans auction notice on the dark web and been looking for a way in, a way to set the trap. Gilbert secured entry and likely smuggled those explosives into the building.

"His contracts with the Madigans began to dwindle five years ago, then were completely terminated at the three-year mark."

"Because Hawes didn't want anything to do with him."

"Or because Reeves knew they'd been infiltrated. It's all tied together," Wheeler said with a nod. "I believe you."

And now Reeves was reaching out to Helena. Overthrowing the man who'd ruined his plan and installing a new queen for his empire. Chris had other ideas. "Check his connections to all the siblings and to Rose." The matriarch wasn't just sitting by. She had effectively run that meeting at the Buena Vista. Was she also running something on the side? Was she unhappy with the more restrained direction her grandkids were taking the company? "Let's be ready so when we catch him, all of them, in our trap, we can take them down."

Wheeler's grin was just shy of feral. "The King Slayer came to play."

Chris forced himself not to cringe, the instinct automatic. But the King Slayer was who he needed to be right now, to take down the man who wanted to be king and to get justice against the king who'd killed his partner. The King Slayer could silence the sirens, forget the picture of home they sang of.

"I'm assuming you can adjust the strike plan?" he said to Wheeler. "We secure the explosives, then we secure the targets. All of them."

"I need a couple more agents. Two, maybe three."

"Vet them." Chris did cringe then, reminded of Amelia's jab. He did sound like Hawes, but in this instance, their op depended on it. They couldn't have any leaks. "If they're clear, bring them in."

"Kane?" Wheeler asked.

Chris shook his head. "Compromised." Then almost laughed out loud at the pot-kettle irony of labeling Kane compromised when he'd been the one jerking Hawes off in an alley last night. But it wasn't Kane's partner Hawes had killed. Let the chief struggle with whether his loyalty lay with the law or the Madigans. Chris knew where his lay: with Izzy. "ATF only."

With a sharp nod, Wheeler rose and hustled toward the door. "Give me an hour. I'll call in who I need and have a revised tactical ready—"

Chris waved him off. "Sleep, Scotty. We can go over everything in the morning. The op isn't until tomorrow night."

Wheeler let out a breath and a tired chuckle and ran a hand through his rumpled hair. "I broke up with sleep a long time ago."

"Kiss and make up," Chris said. "It's going to be a long day tomorrow. I need you sharp."

"I'll try. And you too."

He didn't give Chris a chance to respond or to pass back the list and photo in his hand. Chris stared at the missing pieces to the puzzle of that night three years ago. He was so close to bringing Izzy's killers to justice. He kept that thought at the front of his mind, ignoring the kernel of suspicion in the back of it that this—targeting Hawes and his siblings—was exactly what the person who'd engineered that night wanted him to do.

One hour and half a bottle of whisky later, that kernel of doubt had turned into a whole field of corn. And Chris was fucking lost in it.

The confrontation with Hawes continued to play in his head, the *I'm Yours* no less loud. Nor was the image of a defiant yet resigned Hawes any less vivid. Shoulders square, jaw set, ready to take a bullet if Chris delivered it, tonight or a day from now.

Chris lifted the bottle of Crown Royal and took another swig. The fiery rye burned across his tongue and down his throat, but it failed to burn away the indecision that knotted his stomach, twisted his heart, and fucked with his head. Torn between what he wanted to do and what he should do, and the multiple options in each of those columns.

Fuck.

He capped the bottle and lay back on the narrow strip of grass he called a backyard, staring up at the dark sky that failed to give him any answers. He half expected Hawes to be lingering, to appear out of the fog at any moment, but so far, it was just Chris and the dark, unhelpful nothingness.

He closed his eyes, saw Hawes behind his lids, heard *I'm yours* in his ears, remembered Amelia's and Kane's words from the station, recalled Scotty's gleeful *King Slayer*, and the merry-go-round started again. Was he being manipulated too? Was he playing right into Reeves's hand? Did it fucking matter if he got justice for Izzy?

The spinning only stopped with the metal *clank* of the side-gate latch. Instantly alert, Chris rolled onto his side, adjusted his grip on the bottle, the only weapon he had at the ready, and cocked back his arm, preparing to hurl it at the late-night intruder. But then the burst of adrenaline sharpened into focus, and a tread as familiar as his own reached his ears.

Relaxing on his hip, he took another swig of whisky and waited for his sister to appear from around the corner. In the dark, with only the ambient light of the flat above them, the bruises on her face and neck weren't as glaring, but the way she moved was careful and measured, feeling the aches and pains of the fight with Dex. There was also a steely, encouraging set to her spine that had been long missing. And a helmet in her hands that made him grin. "You bring me a gift, Cee?"

"I brought you the thing that's required by law."

"You're such a mom."

"Shut it." She tossed her purse on the rusty, broken beach chair and lowered herself, cross-legged, next to him on the ground. "Lawyer called today. Wanted to say thank you."

"At midnight?"

"Another lawyer called. She said you might need someone tonight."

He raised a brow. "And you decided to be that person?"

She shoved the helmet at his chest, and he collapsed back, feigning injury. She laughed, a good, welcome sign, before snagging the bottle and taking a healthy swallow. "Neither of us has been there for the other like we should have been. Like we used to be. But you were there for me today, and I'm here for you now."

Warmth, the first since this morning, suffused his person and soothed a little of the ache in his chest, turned the chaos down a measure in his head. He ran a hand over the basic yet durable helmet, letting that calm him further too, thankful for the reprieve.

"You want to talk about it?" she asked.

"I found out who killed Izzy."

She covered his hand with hers. "Not the boyfriend?"

Fuck, he wished it had been Zander Rowe, wished he could rewind and tell the grief-stricken, vengeful Agent Perri of three years ago to let it go, to just accept the official cover version of events. It would have been a whole lot less painful, less complicated. "Not who I thought it was at all."

"And you're not happy about that."

He laughed, because what the fuck else was he going to do? Cry? He pushed himself upright, set the helmet on the ground, and reclaimed the bottle, taking another swig.

Gaze downcast, Celia picked at the shop grease under her nails. "Dex isn't who I thought he was either."

"Cee…"

"I know I have a blind spot where he's concerned, but we had some good years before the bad. He gave me two beautiful kids, but then he changed, and so did I." She sighed, heavy and tired. "But you know what didn't change? My responsibility to those kids, and I let them down. I should have left him years ago, for their sakes."

He'd seen the same play out before, in Jennifer's family and in the circles he'd infiltrated as an agent. He knew who was to blame, and it wasn't his sister or the kids. "That's not how abuse works, Cee."

"I'm not sure how a lot of things work."

"Except an engine."

She glanced up at him, a small, welcome smile flitting across her face. "That I do know."

"Dad taught us well. You better."

Surprising him, she reached for his hand. "But that's not the only engine he taught us about. Mom and Pop, they also showed us how to run the engine of a family and a job too. My kids, the shop, those are the things that keep me going. I'll focus on them, fine-tune 'em, and let that drive me. What's driving you, big brother?"

I'm yours.

He shook the thought away. "I'll sleep, then I'll get up tomorrow, and Special Agent Christopher Perri will do his job." One last time. For Izzy. For Ro. For this family. Complete his final mission and get out. He'd lost sight of that, blinded by a future he couldn't have. He remembered it now, and he'd let it drive him. He'd be done tomorrow, one way or the other.

EIGHTEEN

A black town car pulled into the drive of the Madigan family fort, headlights blasting the sage-green Victorian. Lights also beamed bright above, the house ablaze from the main floor all the way up to Holt's attic lair, giving the impression that the hacker was there. Not sitting behind Chris in the back seat of Kane's cruiser, parked in the shadows of the driveway across the street.

"Here we go," Helena singsonged, her voice echoing out of the cruiser's speakers. She leaned over and kissed Rose's cheek, the matriarch standing in front of the big bay windows, Lily in her arms.

"We've got you," Holt reported back as the red dot on the dashboard screen tracking Helena's movements headed for the door. "Keep your channel open so we can hear, but no further communication."

"Not a rook, Little H."

No, Helena definitely wasn't. Her posture was relaxed, her demeanor calm as she descended the porch steps, approached the town car, and stretched out her arms, allowing the driver to check her for weapons and devices. Unarmed and all clear, the same undetectable tech Chris had planted on Iris undetectable once more. The driver opened the door for her, and Helena slid into the back seat. She had no idea what she was getting into, who might be waiting for her, and yet the petite blonde clad in leather and cashmere didn't display an ounce of trepidation. Impressive was right, and confident in the fact that she was deadlier than a good percentage of the population.

Chris wondered, not for the first time since he'd squared off with her in Kane's office yesterday, how involved she'd been the night Izzy died. She'd clearly known what had happened and understood how the fallout had changed her brother. Had she been there? Had she left Izzy in the street? Been the one to tamper with the crime scene to make it look just enough like a domestic disturbance? With Kane then at SFPD, willing to cover for them, and the ATF silent, unwilling to disclose their presence, how much time and evidence had they lost? Maybe Chris would have put the pieces together sooner, before everything had become a jumbled mess.

"So, just me and you?" Helena's polite chitchat with the driver brought Chris back to the present. She was letting them know she was alone in the car as it started down the hill out of Pac Heights.

"Alpha on the move," Chris radioed the task force teams. "Tactical, hold for advance. Beta, go in sixty."

Exactly a minute later, a Benz crept out of the alley two blocks up, Avery behind the wheel, Hawes in the passenger seat. A blue dot appeared on Kane's dashboard screen, following a discreet distance behind the town car. "Beta on the move."

Kane waited another minute before easing the unmarked cruiser out after them. "Command on the move," Chris reported. "Tactical, hold another sixty, then commence advance."

As planned, Helena's response to the seller had insisted on visual proof. She wouldn't make any deal without clapping eyes on the entire lot of explosives. In reply, the seller proposed a meet, location undisclosed, making the task force's rolling tails one of the trickier aspects of the op. Never mind the twist Chris had planned for the end, assuming they secured the explosives first.

Toward that goal, they couldn't be seen before reaching the

destination. The teams moved in a grid pattern behind them. Wheeler, at the tactical helm, called out the cross streets every few blocks, and the teams checked in, confirming their locations. There were additional teams in the field, positioned near the half dozen possible locations Chris and Wheeler had scouted, but none of them had reported any activity. As they continued down Third, across King, and past the ballpark and arena, Chris began to understand why, started to suspect where they were headed.

He swiveled in his seat. "Is this another fucking setup?"

Judging by the pale faces beside and behind him, he guessed not. Holt shook his head. "We weren't expecting this either."

Confirmed by Hawes's "Fucking hell" over the comm as the town car carrying their sister turned onto the road leading to the pier where MCS's headquarters were located. "We're following," Hawes said.

"Beta and Command only," Chris radioed the teams. "Traffic is too light for all of us. Wheeler, shift the Hunter's Point tactical team to the pier here."

"On it," Wheeler said, then relayed the order down the line.

Chris tuned him out, trusting Scotty to do his job, and turned his attention to Hawes. "Do not go all the way to the gate, Madigan. Stealth approach. It's our best chance for salvaging this op."

"Fuck your op," Hawes practically growled. "I'm not letting my sister go in there alone. What part of trap don't you understand?"

He understood all of it, including the trap he had planned. He wasn't about to let this op go to shit either. "We devised a tactical plan for the pier down in Hunter's Point. We're shifting that team up here. By boat, they'll be here in ten minutes, max."

"Hena can stall at the gate," Holt said. "But that'll probably only buy us five minutes."

"Do it," Chris told him. "The other teams will get here in time for backup."

Holt relayed the request to Helena, who cleared her throat, signaling message received. Hawes smacked the dashboard of the

Benz, clearly frustrated, a loud *thump* sounding over the comm. They'd boxed him in, hadn't given him an opportunity to object. He ordered Avery to pull into the parking lot a building over from MCS, and Kane swung the cruiser in beside them.

Hawes bolted out of the Benz and immediately took up his pacing. Sympathy sliced through Chris's chest—he'd be going crazy too if that were Celia—and his heart, as much as it hurt for Izzy, as much as it still stung from Hawes's betrayal, traitorously itched to comfort the other man.

He reverted to agent mode and shut his insides down, ignoring the irrepressible attraction and the lingering doubts that maybe he too was walking into a trap. Work the tactical; that was the best way to avoid it all. And the best way to get justice for Izzy. "Do you have staff on-site?" he asked Hawes.

"Minimal. We're between shifts at this time of night."

"Because someone knows exactly how you operate."

"Another fucking mole."

"Do we think the explosives are really there?" Kane asked.

Holt flashed the countdown clock on this tablet. "Four minutes left and we find out, one way or the other."

NINETEEN

Four minutes and Helena's expert stalling gave their small team time to converge on foot. Kane waited in the cruiser, prepared to run point as tactical arrived, while Chris, Hawes, Holt, and Avery approached via the adjacent property. Hawes picked the lock on their neighbor's gate, its fence behind the parking lot and closer to the building, unlike MCS's fully gated yard, and Holt hacked their alarm system, on the police chief's orders of course. It was a risk to have Holt here too, all the Madigan siblings on-site, but he'd refused to sit on the sidelines this time, and they needed him for exactly these situations. No one knew the security around here better. They snuck inside and crept along the shadowed walkway between the building and the barrier separating the two properties.

As they neared the back, where stairs led down to the docks and water, Chris drew their group to a halt and spoke in a whisper. "We'll be too exposed down on the dock."

"I'll go over first," Hawes said, pointing up at the barrier wall that descended in a set of terraced levels.

Chris gestured at the wall itself. "If there's a hostile on the other side, you gonna shoot 'em?"

Hawes's jaw hardened, his blue eyes shining bright with defiance. "I don't need a gun to take someone down."

"I know that," Chris replied, straining to keep his voice low and calm. "But we need every second we can get, and a quick, relatively silent takedown is necessary."

"I'll go over first." Avery held up her pistol, which was fitted with a silencer. "Lighter and quieter."

"No," Hawes said, voice brooking no argument. "We don't know who's on the other side of that wall. We can't shoot first and ask questions later. That's not how we work anymore."

Admiration surged in Chris's chest until he remembered why Hawes had those rules, and all that unbidden warmth froze in his veins. Hawes stared back at him, some of the hardness in his eyes softening with regret, making the same connection Chris had, but he still wasn't giving an inch.

Helena's voice cut through the stalemate. "You took my phone," she said to the driver. "If I had it, I could call our IT guy and find out what's up with this gate."

"Nice try," the driver replied. "What's the number? And no funny business. Just relay the problem."

She rattled off a string of digits, which when dialed, rang directly to Holt's comm. He answered, not letting on who he was, pretending instead to be a groggy IT guy just woken from sleep. She explained the issue, and he returned a, "Yes, Miss Madigan, give me just a minute." He clicked off the comm and turned to Chris. "Boost Hawes over on the count of three."

Now Chris was the one boxed in without a choice, Holt tapping away on his tablet as Hawes stepped closer. Close enough for his breath to tickle Chris's cheek, for the smell of expensive aftershave to tease his nose, for Hawes's heat to warm the chill that had overcome him a moment ago.

"One."

Hawes put a hand on Chris's shoulder, heat magnified tenfold, intensified by the vulnerable tremble in his grip that Hawes couldn't hide from him. Fuck but Chris hated that hesitation, hated this ebb and flow of trust and distrust between them. Hated that Hawes was right to doubt him. They had to trust each other, at least for the next hour, if any of them were going to get through this alive. And the bearing walls were there to do that. Yes, the foundation was shaky, both of them lying about pillars critical to the other, but they'd worked well together when they'd thought their interests were aligned.

"Two."

Chris sank into a crouch, hands cupped for Hawes's foot, and Hawes's grip on his shoulder tightened. Glancing up, Chris's eyes clashed with Hawes's, and a flood of memories washed over him like the waves lapping at the dock below. Chris in a similar position the night he sucked Hawes off against the ladder. Their positions reversed when Hawes had returned the favor in front of the couch. Their eyes locked in his reading nook, in the alley, as they'd been unable to resist each other this week, coming together again and again. Hawes trusting him. Chris had fallen for that heady gift, those blue eyes and the man they belonged to, his descent starting the second he'd walked into Danko the first time and spotted him across the room.

The man who'd killed his partner.

Fuck.

But was Hawes the same man? Nightmares of that night plagued him, yet he got up every day and changed everything about himself, his life, and his organization so nothing like that night would happen again. To atone. For Izzy. To bring her justice.

Their interests were still aligned.

"Three."

Hawes put his foot in the cradle of Chris's hands and released his shoulder. Trusting him. Chris powered up and heaved the man who'd made a tangled mess of his insides, of his priorities over the wall.

A quiet *thump*, Hawes hitting the ground, was followed by a half-spoken, "Wha—" before the stranger's question was cut off.

Two quick slaps of skin on skin, hand-to-hand combat, then another *thump*.

"Clear," Hawes said, and Chris didn't want to consider his relief at that single word in the king's familiar, confident tone. "Send Avery over, then come around the wall. We'll unlock the gate."

They gathered again outside the loading docks on the south side of the MCS facility. Hawes was shoving an unconscious merc clad in all black into a storage unit.

Chris had barely gotten out a, "Good work," when Helena's startled, "What the hell is going on here?" echoed over the comm.

"Exactly what was promised."

Chris's stomach sank, Holt hung his head, and Hawes cursed.

"Fuck," Avery gasped. "They got to Zoe too."

Another, deeper voice entered the fray, speaking to Helena. "A chance at the future."

Holt's head shot up. "Is that—"

"Carl Reeves," Hawes said.

Chris measured his reaction, not letting on that Reeves had recently shot to the top of his suspects list. It was a risk, surprising Hawes and the teams in the field, but Chris hadn't disclosed it in advance, not wanting to risk Hawes or anyone else eliminating his best chance at confirming the puppeteer behind Izzy's death. "Was he on Rose's list?" Chris asked.

Hawes shook his head. "We haven't done business with him in years. We wouldn't consider him a competitor in either business."

"Why'd you stop doing business with him?"

"Wasn't comfortable with how he was using our products and services."

That euphemism was almost as ironic as assassins running a cold storage business. "Seems he didn't take kindly to that."

"But he went his way, and we went ours," Holt said.

"Or," Chris ventured, "he's been circling like a shark this entire time."

Helena asked, "And if I don't accept?" drawing their attention back to the showdown happening in the front yard.

"I push this trigger, and the past is erased," Reeves replied. "The future moves on without you."

Chris's stomach went tumbling the rest of the way to his feet. "The explosives are here." He clicked over to Kane's open channel. "Chief, you hearing this?"

"Just gave the order to keep the teams back at the perimeter." He cleared his throat. "Get them out of there, Perri."

Chris clicked off without replying, hoping the excuse of Helena speaking again would be reason enough for his nonanswer. "You think Hawes will let that happen?" she said.

"We're not worried about the prince," Zoe said, notably not referring to him as king. "His days are numbered."

Hawes's gaze snapped to Chris, and the kernel of doubt in the back of Chris's head ballooned—burst—sending a chill snaking down his spine and out to his limbs. They were all being manipulated, moved around the board to satisfy Reeves.

"And Holt?" Helena asked.

"Will, in the end, do whatever it takes for those he loves."

Across from them, the man in question hung his head and laid a hand over his right pec, fingers digging into the flannel that covered a lotus tattoo in honor of his daughter. For a second, Chris thought they'd lost him, but Holt lifted his dark, determined eyes, then lifted them even farther, up toward the command perch on the top floor of the facility. "I'm going up," he said. "Depending on how they've wired the explosives, I might be able to do something about them from there."

Hawes nodded. "Avery, go with him."

They took off as Helena continued to stall, demanding proof of the explosives. Her gulp a moment later was audible. "You wired the north wing." Where all the manufacturing took place. "That's a fucking tinder box."

Reeves must have shown her a live feed on a tablet. Good. Better even if the trigger was on it, because then Holt had a chance. And in case he needed more time, Chris and Hawes needed to move. Chris gestured toward the standoff at the front of the building.

"Let's go," Hawes agreed, falling in behind him. "Hena, we're coming to you. Keep them talking."

She didn't miss a beat. "That's a stockpile's worth of explosives."

"All of them," Reeves said. "Mine now."

"If you blow it, you won't have any left."

"I've got recruits," Zoe said, and by the shuffling of gravel behind them, she had a good many there on-site with them. "Soldiers who've done the dirty work, making and exploding them for years. They'll make more for us. We're not afraid to sell and use them."

"And the display will be powerful," Reeves added. "You should be a part of it."

"Why would I join you?"

"Why wouldn't you? There's nothing holding you to your current life. You could still live your life and do your job if you need to. We wouldn't care."

We. Was he referring to Zoe or someone else?

"She said you were the star, an asset the organization couldn't lose."

She.

"*Amelia?*" Hawes mouthed, brow raised.

Chris was likewise skeptical and mentally ticked through the options. From questioning Amelia, Chris didn't think she was the sort to heap praise on Helena. Zoe, while in the inner circle, didn't ever strike Chris as having that kind of worship for Amelia either. But Avery…

Pale-faced, Hawes had already reached the same conclusion and turned his gaze skyward, looking up toward his brother's office. It was dark, no sign of movement, but Holt would know not to turn the lights on, to operate under the radar as long as possible.

Wouldn't he?

If he ever made it up there.

Holt down wasn't necessarily contrary to Chris's objective, but fuck, he did not want the younger twin, who really would do anything for those he loved, his daughter especially, to go out that way. It was too cruel a fate for Lily and those who loved him, including Hawes.

"We're set." Holt's voice came over the comm, and both Chris and Hawes gasped out a held breath. "I'm tapped into their signal."

"Take these fuckers down," Avery added, proving her loyalty once more.

Hawes grinned, that wicked, beautiful thing that made Chris's blood run piping-hot and knotted his insides. He shouldn't want it, shouldn't want him, but he was irresistible. And that picture of home that had been shifting in Chris's head? It included this Hawes, the man he was now. The emptiness Chris felt after the auction, after almost losing him, knowing if he had lost him the puzzle would be incomplete, was proof enough.

I'm yours. And he was Hawes's.

And their common objectives—the explosives and the seller, and the person who may have set Izzy up to die, who may have set up Hawes to pull the trigger—were in their grasp.

Chris crept toward the corner of the building and fought off a full body shiver when Hawes put a steady hand to his lower back, no more trembling, trusting now, braced to enter the war with him.

"You forgot one thing," Helena said. "I'm loyal."

"To your family," Zoe said.

"Exactly. To my brothers."

"All teams, hold at the perimeter," Kane ordered over the comm. "Be prepared to go when the lights come up."

"You'll die for that loyalty," Reeves said, and pressed the button on the trigger.

Brightness exploded, but not from the bombs—from every light in and around the facility suddenly blazing to life.

The battle was on, and Chris and Hawes entered it, together.

For a few valuable seconds, everyone in the yard stood frozen, blinded by the lights and waiting for the blast that never came. It was the opening Chris and Hawes needed to bolt from behind the building and reach Helena, who expertly handled the Ka-Bar Hawes tossed her direction. It hit her palm with a *smack*, and it was like pressing Play on a recording. Everything around them snapped back into action.

At Zoe's signal, three soldiers rushed them. Chris introduced one to his boot, kicking clear his weapon. Momentum carrying him, he planted his kicking leg and swung the other around, delivering a round house kick to the soldier's head. The soldier crumpled in an unconscious heap.

"No promotion for that one," Hawes said, as he yanked back another soldier's elbows with his garrote, the angle unnatural, the *crack* of bones sickening. "No promotion for this one either." With a smooth flick of the wrist, Hawes withdrew the wire and the soldier's broken arms fell limp. Hawes kicked him in the kidneys and sent him flying face first into the pavement.

They turned in unison to Helena. Her back was to them, her knife dripping blood onto the downed soldier at her feet. He was breathing still but decorated in blooming red slash marks. "That all you got, traitor," Helena hollered at Zoe.

Hawes spoke to the other soldiers. "They've fooled you. Lay your weapons down and no retribution will come to you."

"Like Lucas, Jodie, and Ray?" Zoe countered.

"They made their decisions," Hawes replied. "Now I'm giving these soldiers the same choice."

Several fell back, but an equal number remained at Zoe's side. She didn't, however, send them in the next wave of attack. Mercs were more expendable than valuable soldiers. No shots were fired. They'd clearly been given the order to capture, not kill. Chris went hand to hand with one, and out of the corner of his eye, watched as Hawes and Helena worked in perfect tandem. Catch, slice, release. None fatal, but those hired guns weren't getting back up anytime soon. Neither was the merc Chris finally choked out with his denim jacket.

Helena looked on approvingly. "Double denim for the win."

The reprieve was short-lived, and Chris worried the next, larger wave of attack would be more than their trio could handle. Hawes recognized it too. He stepped closer, their shoulders brushing. "She's trying to wear us out."

"Call in the captains?" Helena said.

"No," Hawes said. "We need them in reserve."

"No need," Holt radioed. "Rest of the cavalry is here."

He'd barely finished speaking when the flash of blue and red lights reflected in the charging mercenaries' eyes.

"Break, Hena!" Hawes shouted.

She spun left, Hawes right, taking Chris with him. The maneuver put them outside the mercs charging into the middle, easier to handle just the few on the perimeter, while the others scattered in the wake of cop cars and cruisers setting up a barricade, officers and agents taking position behind them.

"We brought friends!" Hawes said.

"Cops and feds," Reeves said. "What happened to you?"

"I trusted the right people."

Warmth flooded Chris's chest, then fled at Reeves's next words. "They'll find the explosives and arrest you."

That had been the plan, but Chris had thrown that plan into jeopardy when he'd thrown Hawes over that wall. Tossed it out all together when Hawes had laid a hand on his back as they'd prepared to charge the yard. Together. At least for the duration of this battle. Longer, if he could figure out how to reconcile justice, his conscience, and his heart. He didn't think the answer in any scenario was the arrest or death of Hawes Madigan or his siblings.

As for the immediate challenge, Holt solved that problem for them. Zoe's and Reeves's own pre-battle words—claiming ownership of the explosives, the intent to make, sell, and use more—blasted out of the yard speakers.

"Sounds like those are your weapons," Hawes said.

"Which you intend to use in the commission of a crime," Chris added.

"With the intent to make and distribute more," Helena finished. "And you can bet we'll also be filing trespassing charges."

"And the bodies at your feet?" Reeves said.

"Not dead," Chris replied. "And if they were, self-defense." Beside him, Hawes chuckled. Chris likewise smiled at the irony of his words, the past week coming full circle.

"Stand down, Reeves," Kane bellowed through a megaphone. "It's over."

"Fall back!" Zoe ordered. Only two soldiers joined her and Reeves and the couple remaining mercs as they sprinted around the opposite side of the building and down the access ramp to the water.

"They're headed for the docks!" Hawes said.

"They'll run into agents that way," Chris said. The boat coming up from Hunter's Point, and Wheeler's three-man team who thought they were there to capture Hawes.

"I'll stay and manage the scene here," Helena said. "Go!"

Rather than following down the ramp, Hawes ran flat-out toward the front door, Chris in his wake. "We'll go through the middle," he said, as the doors opened for them. "Thanks, Little H."

They circled the security desk, cut through the break room and cafeteria, and hustled down the same stairwell they'd used last week. Hawes slammed open the emergency exit door to a hail of gunfire, and Chris acted on instinct, forcing him against the wall and covering Hawes's body with his larger one. Hawes could be pissed at him later.

Except he wasn't. He fisted the sides of Chris's shirt and held him tighter, closer, face buried in the crook of his neck.

"You hit?" Chris whispered in his ear. Hawes shook his head. Neither was Chris. He looked up and around. They were alone. Gunfire broke out again. "It's at the docks."

Hawes drew back enough to meet his gaze. "I'm sorry. I just needed a second."

Chris lowered an arm from over Hawes's head and palmed his cheek. "Steady, now?"

He nodded, confident once more. "Let's go."

Chris, however, held him firm. There was one more thing he needed to say, before they walked into the firefight. "You need to know—"

"That you intended to arrest me, if we survived this night."

Chris blinked, then smiled. Of course he knew. "That's not my intention anymore."

Hawes circled his wrist, fingers over his pulse point, and squeezed. "My promise holds. I'm yours, either way."

Chris knew which of the options he wanted now. But the ratcheting up of gunfire drew their attention and they were off again, running for the docks. The scene there was not good. Wheeler's team of ATF agents, plus the four-man team from the other boat, were now on Gilbert's salvage vessel, taking on Zoe, Reeves and their reinforcements. It should have been an easy win for the ATF, based on numbers, but while their orders were to capture, the bad guys had no qualms about killing or throwing LEOs overboard.

Zoe was directly engaged with Wheeler while Reeves and Gilbert stood out of the way by the helm, like this was not what they'd signed up for. Chris thought maybe they could use that. He and Hawes crept closer, almost to the boat. The view was good enough, the distance short enough, that when Zoe pulled her gun and shot Scotty in the side, right where the Kevlar didn't cover, she caught Chris's movement as his hand whipped to his side arm.

"Came to play, finally."

"Zoe, let's go!" Reeves yelled.

"He's not the one pulling the strings," Chris said under his breath.

As Chris made the observation, Zoe swung her gun arm around and shot Reeves, point-blank between the eyes. Gilbert screamed, which was the exact wrong move. Zoe's focus shifted to him, and he went down in a heap next to Reeves.

Her attention diverted, Hawes made a break for the boat. Cursing, Chris drew his weapon and ran after him. They got two steps onto the deck when Zoe brought them up short with a warning shot right between their heads.

"Reeves fits your criteria," she said to Hawes. "The smuggler too. Don't they?"

Hawes didn't take the bait. "Who are you working for?"

"The person who's always put this organization's interests first."

"You calling working with Reeves putting us first?"

"He was a pawn, like all of you." Her hazel gaze shifted to Chris. "Including your old partner. She knew."

Chris gasped. "What?" His knees would have given out from under him, if he hadn't stood braced against the waves already.

Zoe smirked, the same smug grin that Tamela had worn at the BART station. "So does your current partner. He came to us, just like Isabella did. But I'm done trusting feds."

She raised her arm, gun pointed directly at Scotty's head, and Chris didn't hesitate to draw his and fire. At Zoe. She crumpled to the deck, lifeless, and Hawes crumpled over, hands on his knees, expelling a giant breath.

Chris's head was spinning with the revelations of the past minute, but he kept himself upright by focusing on the man beside him, who was reining in what had to be an even bigger hurricane in his mind. He laid a hand on Hawes's back and circled to kneel in front of him. "She was going to kill him."

Eyes still closed, Hawes nodded. "It was the right move. The last thing we need are more dead feds."

So much for ignoring Zoe's words about Izzy. Was the lieutenant playing them? Or was there more to the story of Izzy's murder than Chris or Hawes knew? Chris was ninety-nine percent sure Izzy hadn't been dirty, but he couldn't say that with one hundred percent certainty. Tran believed she'd gone rogue when she'd gone dark right before her death. Chris didn't have an explanation for it, and now there were more questions swirling in that dark space. Questions that made him hold back that one percent. A one percent they needed to account for, and the person who could help them get answers— the person Chris had zero doubts about—was on this boat.

"Listen to me, Hawes." Blue eyes opened and locked onto his. "Scotty Wheeler is the last person—"

"I believe you." Hawes took a deep breath and straightened, and Chris moved to check on Scotty.

The agent was still breathing, and the blood loss was thankfully slow. The hit to his head when he'd fallen was probably what had knocked him out. Chris grabbed a deck towel, shoved it over the wound, and rearranged Scotty's vest to keep the towel wedged there.

"Got a tip earlier today that he was dirty," Hawes said. "More traps."

Chris stood and looked back and forth between him and Wheeler. "Then—"

"She needs to think I fell for it. And I need you to help me sell it."

Anger sparked brightest in the whirlwind of emotions, all of it spinning too fast. "What part of don't leave me out of the loop—"

Hawes cut him off and deflated his anger by stepping forward and putting one hand on his hip and the other around his neck. "Until twenty minutes ago, I thought you were going to kill me, not kill to protect my organization."

Chris closed the distance between them and rested his forehead against Hawes's. "Baby, I can't kill you. I think I might love you."

Hawes inhaled sharply, then smiled that wry grin that twisted and warmed Chris's insides. "Will you still love me when I throw you off this boat?"

"Fuck, I was afraid of that." He stepped back and looked over the side at the dark water, all thoughts of warmth fleeing. He couldn't look at Hawes when he asked, "Do you know who she is?" He didn't want to see the hurt in his eyes, didn't think he could bear it.

"I think so, and I think you do too. I can't believe my—" The hurt in his voice, though, was a million times worse.

Turning back to him, Chris put a hand over his mouth to stop the painful sound. "Don't say it, not until you're sure." He nodded at Wheeler. "I had my suspicions too. Had him check. That's probably why they flagged him, then tried to get you to eliminate him."

"Two birds, one stone."

"Same as they tried the night of Izzy's murder." Which was a thousand times more complicated now. "When he comes to, he's your best bet for confirming it. And Izzy's involvement."

"*If* she was involved."

Chris appreciated the consideration, what it meant that Hawes was willing to hold on to Izzy's innocence, and in doing so, his own culpability in her death. It spoke to the man he was, the man Chris had fallen for. The man who deserved his consideration. "We need to find out the whole truth." He glanced again at Scotty and sent up a prayer for forgiveness for tangling him up in all this. "Protect him."

"You know I will." Hawes ran a shaking hand through his hair, glancing back up the hill where shouts were growing louder and flashlight beams brighter. Kane and his men weren't around the corner yet, but any minute now… "If we're right, I may have to bend the knee."

Chris grabbed his hand and laced their fingers, hauling Hawes close once more. "We've been fighting this from the outside. We fight from the inside, if we have to. That might be the only way we find the truth."

"All of it," Hawes said, some of his confidence returning.

"All of it," Chris repeated, then shoved the butt of his gun in Hawes's middle, same as Hawes had done to him last night. "Sell it, either way." Chris swallowed Hawes's gasp, pouring everything into the kiss—admiration, love, trust—and getting the trust back that he so desperately needed. The trust that they would need to find their way home again, because that's what Hawes was to him. Undeniably. The picture was clear.

Gun in hand, Hawes drew back with a final, achingly sweet kiss to the corner of his mouth. "I think I might love you too."

Warmth flooded Chris from the center of his chest out to his fingers and toes, shielding him from the pain of the bullet that ripped through his shoulder and the cold dark water of the Bay that swallowed him whole.

Keep reading!
Hawes & Chris's story reaches its exciting romantic conclusion in
A New Empire!

A NEW EMPIRE

FOG CITY, BOOK THREE

A New Empire

Copyright © 2019 by Layla Reyne

Cover Design: The Book Brander

Cover Photography: Wander Aguiar Photography

Editing: Edits by Kristi, Keren Reed Editing, Susie Selva

First Edition

November, 2019

E-Book ISBN: 978-1-7341753-0-1

Paperback ISBN: 978-1-7341753-1-8

Content Warnings: explicit sex; explicit language; violence.

ABOUT THIS BOOK

The things that mattered were true.

Trust is a fragile thing.
Between a cop and a criminal, it's downright brittle.
But Hawes wants back in Chris's arms.
And Chris wants the home he's found with the Prince of Killers.

A home that's threatened by an enemy dangerously attached to the past.

Old ways that Hawes wants to leave behind.
But to do that, he'll have to bend the knee.
In the hope he can bend his enemy's will from within.

On the outside, a restless Chris must keep the faith.
Must do whatever it takes to ensure Hawes comes out the other side.
Including becoming a wanted man himself.

The King and King Slayer fight together in this thrilling conclusion to Hawes and Chris's trilogy!

ONE

The salvage boat, jacked as it was for smuggling, was more than fast enough to outrun the converging officers and agents. Hawes swung the boat around, gunned the engine, and disappeared into the night, the lights and shouts fading into the darkness behind him.

If only his conscience—his heart—was that easy to outrun.

Dante…*Chris*…was back there, shot and sinking in the cold, dark water. The only things that kept Hawes driving forward, kept him from yanking the wheel and turning the boat around, were the tracker he'd slipped into Chris's pocket, the flare he'd thrown into the Bay where Chris had gone under, and Kane's shouts as the chief had splashed into the water.

They would find him. It was a clean wound. He'd be fine.

And Hawes had another bleeding agent on deck to worry about. Not to mention the other bodies…

He withdrew two phones from his pocket. On the first, he texted Holt, alerting him to the tracker on Chris. Then he tossed that phone onto the deck, brought his heel down on it, and kicked the shattered pieces overboard. On the second, a burner, he texted an SOS to the single programmed contact. He had alerted her in advance and asked if she'd be willing to assist, in case he had to put certain contingency plans into motion. She was ready and waiting. Coordinates came back in less than a minute.

Ten minutes after that, Hawes maneuvered alongside a sleek yacht with Irish and American flags flying off the stern. He lowered the salvage vessel's anchor, killed the engine, and moved to greet the statuesque woman standing at the portside rail of the other boat.

"Went sideways?" Melissa Cruz asked, her dark eyes assessing the wreck of a deck Hawes had picked his way across. Bodies, blood, weapons.

"Sideways, upside down, briefly right side up, then underwater." Hawes tossed a mooring line to the former FBI Special Agent in Charge. In the private sector now, Mel handled security for Talley Enterprises and hunted down bounties on the side.

She secured the rope to the yacht's rail, helping to steady the two vessels so Hawes could extend a gangway between them. She was dressed down in jeans and a sweater, her dark curls piled in a bun atop her head, but casual wear did nothing to make her any less intimidating. Hawes knew of only one person who had ever bested Helena in hand-to-hand combat, and that person was standing across from him. "Sounds like an eventful night," she said.

"As expected." And unexpected in other ways—Reeves's involvement, Zoe's betrayal, Chris's change of heart, the unconscious agent Hawes now hefted into his arms. "We need to get him medical attention," he said, carrying ATF agent Scott Wheeler across the gangway to the yacht.

"I'm not set up here," Mel said, "but the *Ellen* has a full-scale infirmary. I can have a doctor meet us there."

"She's in dock?" Hawes was familiar with TE's shipping vessels, Madigan Cold Storage having custom-built or retrofitted the refrigeration units on most of them.

"Port of Oakland." She helped him get Wheeler situated. "They finished off-loading yesterday. Good timing."

That was about the only thing good right now. Hawes straightened, and his gaze strayed back to the salvage vessel. To Zoe lying dead next to Reeves and Gilbert. His breath caught, and heat stung the corners of his eyes, betrayal burning through him like a branding iron. So much betrayal littering that deck. Littering his life.

She.

The deepest cut, if he and Chris were right.

"What do you want to do about it?" Mel asked.

The cold night air swallowed Hawes's bitter chuckle. "You're gonna have to be more specific."

She laid a hand on his shoulder, squeezing, then nodded toward the other boat. "About that?"

The boat, the bodies, were evidence Chris and Kane and their teams could use. That maybe even Holt could extract valuable information out of. Hawes never put anything past his hacker twin.

"Sell it," Chris's voice echoed in his head. Sell the story they needed her to believe.

She would want it destroyed, would want all the evidence erased. *Clean up your messes.* That's what she'd taught him.

"Protect him," Chris had urged.

Hawes glanced over his shoulder at Wheeler. Burning the boat would accomplish that too. Would buy Hawes time to convince Wheeler to play along. To keep him safe. To fool her.

And that's what Hawes had to do. Fool her. Put on the best performance of his life. Because if he faltered, if he couldn't sell it, the lives of too many people, including those he loved, would be on the line. Hell, were already on the line. Losing them—losing any more innocent lives in the fallout—was unacceptable. It violated his rules. Rules he had fought too damn hard for, lost too damn much for, and he would be damned if he didn't see them to victory.

For the sake of his family, his heart, and his soul.

Sell it.

He righted his gaze and nodded. "We burn it."

HAWES FLIPPED THROUGH THE MORNING NEWS PROGRAMS. ON ONE, the woman he recognized as Chris's boss, Special Agent in Charge Vivienne Tran, was claiming victory for last night's seizure of a major weapons cache. Kane stood beside her, looking grim and uncomfortable in his uniform. Another local station showed predawn footage of the smoldering salvage vessel. A third featured exterior shots of MCS's headquarters. Business as usual there this morning, except for the cops at the gate, checking anyone going in or out. Three flips through each program and no other references to his company, his family…or Chris. Or the unconscious agent in the infirmary bed beside which Hawes sat. Tran didn't mention any loss of life in her remarks, focusing instead on the weapons seizure and case closure, the successful culmination of a long-term ATF operation. No acknowledgment of Christopher Perri's or Isabella Constantine's roles in that effort.

A wave of sympathy rolled through Hawes—for Chris's mission, for the agent's devotion to his partner, and for the difference Isabella had made in Hawes's life. For the better, even if it had led to the present chaos. Inevitable, if Hawes was being honest with himself. Change didn't happen without resistance. The new would always run up against the old. That was the way of the world—in business, in politics, in life, and in families, including his own…if he was right.

"You owe me two bounties."

Hawes muted the wall-mounted television and shifted his attention to the woman standing in the doorway. "Reeves's mercs?"

Mel nodded. "The price on their heads was high, but honestly, I'm not too cut up about it. Saved me the hassle."

Hawes slumped in his chair. "But brought you more."

She sauntered into the room and lowered herself into the chair on the other side of Wheeler's bed. "You know, I've watched you for years. I even considered recruiting you and your siblings into the FBI, but I sensed something different about you three. That maybe you'd be more valuable on the outside. When you came to me three years ago, torn up and ready to make a real change, and when Holt and Helena backed that play, I knew I had made the right decision."

"And now?"

"More sure than ever." Her dark eyes flickered to the TV, the press conference still going. "Just finish this, Hawes, and stop making life difficult for my family and friends."

"Christopher Perri one of those friends?"

The corners of her mouth tipped up, like she was fighting a smile. "He's what you needed, isn't he?"

One second, he was amused at her playing matchmaker. The next second, the full meaning of what she'd said sank in, and Hawes shot to the end of his chair. "You sent him to me?" He had thought it was Amelia who'd sent Chris the flash drive that had accelerated his appearance on the scene and in Hawes's life. There had been two folders on that drive. One full of pictures of Isabella's crime scene. The other with various surveillance shots of Hawes, a bull's-eye on each. Enough to pique the interest of the investigator with a personal stake in the case.

"Chris was already sniffing around," Mel said. "He's a good man, a good agent, and he was getting closer by the day. I wanted to make sure he ended up on the right side of this." She leaned forward and pinned Hawes with a look he was sure more than a few targets had been uncomfortably familiar with. Her husband too probably. The don't-argue-with-me-because-I-always-win stare-down. "With you."

He wouldn't argue *that* point. He liked having Chris on his side too, for multiple reasons—professional and personal—but there was a fact still nagging him. "How did you get into Holt's system?" They had been sure it was Amelia, who had a photographic memory and who had frequently positioned herself to spy on her hacker husband.

"She didn't," a voice said from the doorway. "I did."

Hawes didn't have to ask who the man standing in the doorway was. He wasn't Hawes's type—too clean-cut, too boy-next-door—but he was no doubt the handsomest, and tallest, man Hawes had ever seen. His wide, easy smile was as inviting and attractive in real life as it was on ESPN, as was his honeyed Southern accent. Thank fuck Chris wasn't here to see Hawes swoon. And thank fuck he was sitting down so Jameson "Whiskey" Walker didn't notice either.

Mel's bemused chuckle shook Hawes out of his starstruck daze. "Hawes Madigan, meet Jameson Walker. Jamie, meet Hawes."

Hawes started to stand, praying for steady legs, but Jamie waved him back down. "Don't get up on my account." He approached with an outstretched hand. "Nice to meet you, Hawes."

"Likewise. I think my brother would like to meet you too," Hawes said, returning the handshake. "Maybe also kill you."

Jamie laughed. "Sucks being second best."

"Don't let Lauren hear you say that," Mel chimed in.

"Correction," Jamie said, still smiling, "third best." The handsome man's grin dimmed, however, as he withdrew a flash drive from his pocket. "There's a reason Holt got this to us."

"Amelia's backup?" Hawes asked, and Mel nodded. Despite what they'd told Chris, Holt had found it earlier in the week, in a hospital lockbox registered to one of Amelia's nurse mentors who had recently retired. But finding it had been only half the battle. And Holt, after beating his head against the desk for days, hadn't been able to win the other. He had told Hawes he needed an assist. "You cracked it?"

"She used one of my older, more obscure protocols." Jamie handed him the stick. "Messy but relatively simple. Holt was overthinking it. I've made the same mistake too."

Mel rose to her feet. "We all have." From the look on her face, Hawes knew she wasn't only talking about the flash drive encryption. "It wasn't just you and your siblings she had evidence on."

"Her boss?"

Mel's expression shifted from bleak to sympathetic, and Hawes had his answer. Yes, they'd overlooked—or more accurately, willfully ignored—a messy but simple explanation. Hawes stood. Time to stop ignoring the mess and clean it up. "Got something I can play this on?"

"There's a laptop set up in the Talley stateroom, just down the hall," Jamie said. "It's the oldest of the videos. We didn't open the rest."

"Plausible deniability," Mel explained.

"I saved the decryption key on the drive so Holt can open them."

Hand to his shoulder again, Mel stopped Hawes in the doorway. "You might want to wait for Holt and Helena. I can get them here."

Hawes shook his head and averted his gaze, unable to bear the empathy and pity any longer. "I can't risk them," he forced out around the lump in his throat. "Not until I confirm what I *think* is in that video and decide how to play this."

"Okay." She dropped her hand. "We'll be here if you need us."

"Thank you," Hawes said, to both of them. This was more than they had to, or should, do. But this—these connections with good, decent people, people who had his, Holt's, and Helena's backs in the midst of an epic shitstorm, allies he trusted—was what he had to fight for. A better way to conduct their business and their lives. One based on trust, cooperation, and respect, not on fear and betrayal.

Two unsteady steps later, he paused and called after Mel, "Is our mutual friend okay?" He didn't mention Chris by name, preserving Jamie's deniability, just in case.

"He's at SF General," she said. "Out of surgery and in recovery. Stable condition. Kane will keep us updated."

An ounce of steadiness returned, and Hawes let it carry him the rest of the way to the stateroom. He counted his steps and measured his breaths until he stood behind the desk, flash drive in hand and laptop open. If he didn't know the *Ellen* was dry-docked, he would have sworn it was at sea, being tossed around by a hurricane. He lowered himself into the chair before the storm in his head took out his limbs. No swooning this time, just abject terror and despair at what he was ninety-nine percent certain he was about to see.

He plugged the flash drive into the computer. It lit up, as did the dark screen, the icon for the drive highlighted. Hawes closed his eyes and tried to breathe around his racing heart. He picked up his counting again—breaths, pulse, the nicks in the desk on either side of the leather desk blotter. But the counting didn't calm him; it only seemed to compound his rising anxiety. He needed to get steady. He withdrew the burner phone from his pocket and punched in Chris's number. Thumb hovering over Send, he glanced out the window, across the Bay toward SF General. Would Chris even be awake to take his call? Would he curse Hawes for contacting him—the fed Hawes supposedly tried to kill? For not selling it? She would doubt his loyalty, and Hawes was already up against a mountain of suspicion.

She.

Fuck it.

Hawes tossed the phone on the desk, double-clicked the flash drive icon, found the single decrypted file, and in the drop-down menu, hit Open. A video window appeared—dark—with a prompt to hit Play.

He clicked—another second of darkness as the video loaded—then his world exploded.

He thought he was prepared for it, all but certain of what —*who*—he was going to see. He wasn't wrong as to the parties on-screen: Reeves, Amelia, and her. But he wasn't prepared. He wasn't ready for the explosion that rocketed through him.

He smashed the keys as he desperately tried to pause the video, to pause the truth so it didn't blind him all at once. The playback froze on a picture of her. Gray hair perfectly twisted into a chignon, Chanel suit perfectly in place, her facial expression perfectly imperious. Hawes slammed his eyes shut, a million denials running through his head despite the truth on the screen, the truth he and Chris had already put together.

Chris.

Hawes scrambled blindly for the phone. He clutched it in a death grip, as if he could draw some steadiness out of the mere possibility that he could call Chris or his siblings.

Fuck, his siblings. What was this going to do to Holt and Helena? They were already fraying at the seams, and now this. To learn that the last remaining pillar of their family…

Hawes lost the battle with the storm, his insides surrendering to the riot of thoughts in his head and the pain in his heart. He shoved back from the desk and grabbed the nearest trash can, spinning so he faced away from the computer and door as he emptied his stomach. It didn't relieve the sour in his soul or in his gut, and the sting and stench of bile in his throat and nostrils only made it worse. He had to get rid of it, had to not look at the computer screen again just yet.

Had to deny the truth a little longer.

He stumbled to the en-suite bathroom, washed out the trash can and his mouth, then, back in the main room, made a beeline for the wet bar, aiming to burn away the remnants of the awful taste in his mouth. He shuffled around bottles until he found a whiskey, one that cost far more than his Crown Royal, but it did the trick, giving him a different kind of burn than bile and betrayal to focus on. He tossed back the rest of his first pour, then poured another two fingers' worth into the cut-crystal tumbler. He started back toward the desk but only made it halfway, stalling out at the end of the bed. It didn't, however, stop the scene from the video replaying in his mind.

Disregarding the people in it, the setting was familiar to Hawes. From the plate-glass windows overlooking the Bay, to the fluted plaster crenellations around the door and the metal seismic struts running to the roof, to his brother's command station visible through a connecting door. They were in Hawes's office at

MCS, formerly his grandfather's. And that's what the three people in the video had been arguing about before Hawes had paused it.

"*He's cutting me off,*" Reeves had said. "*Do you know how much this is going to cost me? This is not the agreement I had with Cal. We were supposed to do more business together, not less.*"

"*Have you talked to Hawes?*" Amelia asked.

"*He says MCS is going a different direction.*"

"*He is the CEO now.*"

"*And the other business?*" Reeves glared at the older woman behind the desk. "*It's not only official business I need the Madigans for. Cal understood that.*"

"*We expected some shifts,*" she answered. "*Some new ideas.*"

"*Do you expect his legacy—*"

"*He's not dead.*" The daggers of ice in each word were enough to cut, as were the daggers shot from the ice-blue eyes in her murderous expression.

That's where Hawes had managed to pause it. Where he needed to resume. Sitting on the end of this bed was not going to change what happened in the past. But facing the truth could change the future. He had to finish this—the video, and all of it. He downed the rest of the whiskey and stood. He grabbed the burner phone, clutched it tight, and situating himself in front of the computer again, pressed Play.

In the video, Reeves stepped back and raised his hands, palms out. "You're right. My apologies." He lowered his voice and continued, tone and manner deferential. "When he passes, will your family's empire survive? Because this isn't the way to do it. And I'm not the only one Hawes has cut off. You need to bring him in line."

"We're working on it."

"Why didn't you take over?"

"Because day-to-day operations has never been my role. And there are complications I'd rather not be tied to directly."

"Complications?"

"You likewise might be better off unconnected," Amelia said. "For the moment."

Reeves looked back and forth between them. "You've got a mole?"

"We're handling it," the other woman said. "And we'll handle Hawes."

A shiver ran down Hawes's spine, replaying how she'd handled him the past three years. The setup with Isabella, using him as a scapegoat. Conspiring with Jodie, Ray, and Lucas to kill him. With Amelia, Zoe, and Reeves to hijack the explosives. Going so far as to willingly injure herself. All to handle him.

"Rest assured, the ship will be righted, and you'll be there with us. With me." Her tone had melted from winter to spring, sweet enough to draw the bees into her garden. Like she had drawn so many people into her web over the years—business leaders, socialites, and politicians, all dirty enough to be leveraged. That's what she did best. That was her role. And she'd weaponized it against Hawes. "Can I count on your support?" she said to Reeves.

"Of course," he acquiesced, putty in her hands.

Because *she* was the queen. Because she was Rose Madigan, and Hawes had been a fool to forget his grandmother was the most dangerous of them all.

HAWES WATCHED FROM THE INFIRMARY WINDOW AS THE LATE afternoon fog rolled back in, snaking around Sutro Tower and through the city's skyscrapers, creeping toward MCS and the waterfront, across the Bay from where Hawes was still waiting on Scotty Wheeler to wake up.

The holding pattern, while frustrating, had also been valuable. It had given him time to process and plan. He was still working out details—contingencies if Wheeler didn't cooperate, if Helena or Holt didn't get on board, if Rose didn't buy his performance—

but he was more confident now than he had been last night or this morning. Granted, he still didn't have all the details—there were more files for Holt to decrypt—but Hawes had enough to go on.

He turned the flash drive end over end in his hand, started to clutch it like he had the burner phone, then stopped himself. The narrow piece of plastic wouldn't withstand the force, though even the phone hadn't withstood his anger. As soon as Hawes had been able to think straight after watching that video, he'd texted Holt: **Get Lily. She stays with you, Hena, or Brax at all times.** Immediately after, he'd powered off the device and hurled it against the wall, shattering it to pieces. The swell of anger, and its release, had felt good. He'd used that rolling wave to power through the rest of the day. Mel had checked on him periodically, bringing him food he forced down and updates about the investigation and Chris, who was still unconscious post-surgery. Chris's family was at the hospital, as was Hawes's. Hawes didn't necessarily like that Helena and Holt were in the same place, but at least Kane was there too, standing guard.

Now, if Wheeler would just wake up, Hawes could get the rest of his plan underway. On cue, a groan sounded behind him. Hawes turned and waited with his back against the wall, watching Wheeler grow increasingly agitated, as if caught in a nightmare. Hawes knew the feeling well and was sure when he got the chance to sleep again, the memories of shooting Isabella would be joined by fresh ones of shooting Chris. Torture all the same, no matter if the latter had been done with permission.

Mumbling from Wheeler brought Hawes back to the present. The sounds resolved into a name. "Sam… Sam, no…"

"Wheeler." Hawes stepped toward the bed. "Wake up."

The agent's breath hitched, and his body froze, surprised into wakefulness. The next instant, he visibly forced his breathing to even out, pretending to still be asleep.

"I know you're awake, Scotty," Hawes said, trying the nickname for more of a response.

Nothing.

Hawes wasn't going to pry—he didn't like when strangers pried into his nightmares either—but Wheeler wasn't giving him a choice. He had to do something to break this standoff. "Who's Sam?"

Another hitched breath, and then dark blond lashes fluttered up, the brown eyes underneath hazy but alert. "I don't know any Sam."

Yes, he did, and Sam, whoever they were, haunted the man's thoughts. Sympathetic to his plight, and having gotten what he wanted, Hawes let it go. "All right."

"Where am I?" Wheeler asked.

"On a boat."

"Captain obvious," Mel said, appearing in the doorway. "You're on the *Ellen*, Agent Wheeler. Talley Enterprises' flagship vessel."

Wheeler's eyes rounded, wide as saucers. "Agent Cruz." He struggled to push himself upright and winced. Hawes moved closer to help, and Wheeler jerked in the opposite direction.

Judging by that instinctive reaction and the wariness in his eyes, Wheeler still read him as an enemy. Hawes mentally recalculated his contingencies; he might have to put the first into action right away.

Or he could wait and let Mel work her magic. "Just Ms. Cruz now." Smiling kindly, she approached Wheeler's other side and helped him into a less vulnerable position.

He relaxed a measure and split a glance between them. "What happened? How did I get here?"

"You were shot," Hawes said.

Wheeler laid a hand over his side, over the surgical gown that covered the bandaged gunshot wound Zoe had inflicted. "By one of your people."

Hawes shook his head, covering the fresh surge of betrayal that made him want to wince too. "Not one of mine."

"Hawes brought you here," Mel said. "Got you medical attention."

"Why did you do that?" Wheeler asked, eyes narrowed.

"Because that's what Chris wanted." Hawes lowered himself into the chair he'd occupied for most of the past twenty-odd hours. Doing what Chris had asked. "He told me to protect you."

Lines formed in the agent's forehead. "You were working together?"

"Not exactly." Yes, they'd planned the strike together, but Chris had had another objective, which he'd then altered mid-course. They hadn't planned that part together, but it had worked out in Hawes's favor.

Wheeler tapped his thumbs against the bed rails, no doubt trying to sort out the tangled course of events. "But you are now?"

Hawes tilted his head. "Not exactly."

"So what, then?" Wheeler barked, growing impatient. Hawes had to admit, he kind of liked needling the agent. It was the first bit of amusement he'd had since... He couldn't remember. Wheeler, however, wasn't amused. "You're holding me hostage?"

"Technically, your agency thinks you're dead."

Saucer-eyes returned. "What?" Wheeler pushed back up, wincing but not stopping, until Mel put a hand on one shoulder and Hawes on the other. "I need a phone. I need to call—"

"Whoever you need to call," Hawes said, "if you want to keep them safe, if you want to see them again, you need to stay dead." He stepped back when Wheeler shrugged him off. "At least for a few days."

"And you expect me to trust you?"

"Chris did."

"Not a ringing endorsement," Wheeler said. "He's a wildcard. The whole agency knows it."

"You got on board with his plan yesterday."

"Because he's also one of the best agents I've ever worked with."

"I feel the same," Mel said. "And if that's not enough, then trust me."

As Wheeler considered that, Hawes played his ace, or what he hoped was his ace, while they had the opening. "I need you to take this to Chris." He held out the flash drive. "He needs to get it to Holt, who can finish the decryption. It's a copy of Amelia's backup."

"You had it all along?"

"We didn't know who we could trust either. Now I'm trusting you."

Wheeler took the flash drive, handling it as if it were a grenade. Smart man. "What's on it?"

Hawes tried not to shatter the bed rail where he gripped it, the anger lapping at the shores of his control again. "Evidence that my own grandmother has spent the past few years trying to overthrow me."

Wheeler's gaze shot to Hawes, but he didn't look surprised. Chris had mentioned that he had Wheeler digging into Rose. This was the other reason Hawes had needed him to wake up.

Hawes reclaimed his chair, crossed one knee over the other, and clasped his hands in his lap, ready for whatever revelations Scotty Wheeler was about to unload on him. "What else did you find out?"

Wheeler's gaze flickered to Mel, and at her nod, back to Hawes. "She has a separate trust set up for Lily. But you all have trusts set up for Lily, so I didn't think anything was odd about it. Until…"

"Until what?"

"I found trails of communication between Rose and former Madigan clients, including Carl Reeves."

"Did you check her travel and communications against Jodie's and Ray's? Against Lucas's and Zoe's?" The dead lieutenants who'd betrayed him. Hawes suspected they'd find her visiting the same coastal motel when Jodie, Ray, Lucas, and Amelia had. That she would have taken more meetings with Lucas and Zoe, probably at the off-site warehouse where the explosives had been stored. And stolen from.

"That search was running when I left for the op last night."

"Get those results"—he nodded at the flash drive in Wheeler's hands—"and that to Chris."

"How?" Wheeler asked, the confused expression back on his face. "You just said I'm supposed to be dead."

"Don't get seen." Hawes withdrew a folded slip of paper from inside his coat pocket and slid to the end of his chair. "Then go here to hide out after." He'd called in a favor from Shawn Gillespie, who, in return for Hawes having gotten, ironically, this particular ATF agent off his back, was more than happy to offer up one of his real estate projects as a safe house. "Don't tell anyone you're going there."

Wheeler gave the note a cursory glance, then folded it around the flash drive. "Why can't you take this to him?"

Hawes rested his elbows on his knees. "Because I have to go convince my grandmother I've seen the error of my ways."

"You're going in?" Mel said from across Wheeler's bed.

"There are answers we still don't have. Answers Chris and I, and the rest of my family, need. Inside is the only way to get those answers."

"How will you convince her?" Wheeler asked.

"I burned Gilbert's salvage vessel last night. I'll tell her you were on it. That I destroyed all the evidence against her. That and the fact I shot Chris should buy us a few days."

"You shot—"

"He's fine." Mel's hand on Wheeler's shoulder kept the agent from rocketing up again and doing more damage.

"But the ATF—"

"Has accomplished its primary objective," Hawes said, "according to your boss's press conference this morning. The explosives are secured. No mention of you or Chris, by the way."

"She plays things close to the vest," Wheeler said. "She was out for you and your family too. We can't be sure she's going to drop it."

"All I need is a few days to try and save what's left of my family, my organization, and my city." Hawes rose and stood at

Wheeler's bedside, not bothering to hide the plea from his voice or eyes. "Will you help me?"

"Why me? Why not Cruz?"

"Because trust is a two-way street." That's what he and Chris had failed to realize until it was almost too late. What his grandmother failed to realize was in their family's best interest going forward. Trusting Wheeler now would hopefully be further proof that Hawes's way forward was the better one. "Chris said to trust you. Now you need proof of my motive. So I'm trusting you."

"He said you were different." Wheeler closed his fingers around the piece of paper and flash drive and nodded. "Don't make him a liar."

TWO

Chris sensed eyes on him, multiple sets. Combined with the furious keystrokes and repetitive beeping, Chris felt like he was in an action movie, like there was a metronome counting each beat of rising tension. Counting down to some suspenseful event. He doubted opening his eyes would be all that exciting. Especially not when he was lying flat on his back in a hospital bed, judging by the beeping heart monitor, the lingering antiseptic smell, and the post-surgery ache in his shoulder. He opened his eyes, and, as expected, the sight of generic, white ceiling tiles was less than earth shattering. The relative dimness of the room, however, was curious. Had he beat the morning sun? He must have been rescued quickly. He'd seen the flare hit the water above him, and now here he was, alive, with sensation in all his limbs, including the arm pinned to his chest in a sling. Had they rushed him from the scene directly into surgery?

He rotated his head to the right, guessing the direction of the window based on the fading cone of light on the ceiling.

Celia's tired yet relieved face cut off his view. "Hey there," she said.

Cee, he tried to return, but his mouth was too dry.

Beside Celia, a second person appeared, her blonde hair atop her head in a messy bun. "Drink, Mr. Hair," Helena said, holding out a paper cup. Celia propped the pillows behind him, and Chris pushed himself up with his good arm. He took the offered cup and sipped through the straw, slurping loudly in the otherwise silent room.

Silence.

The typing had stopped.

And with that realization came another that made Chris's pulse jump.

Lily. He'd last seen her with…

The worry must have shown on his face because Helena's fell to match. Chris's heart skipped another beat. Until she lifted her gaze to the opposite side of the bed. Chris whipped his head around, faster than he should have—twin spikes of pain and nausea assaulting him—but at least his heart resumed its regular rhythm. The redheaded munchkin was safely tucked in a sling against her father's chest. The sight was comforting enough to even ignore the Toronto Raptors T-shirt Holt wore beneath his flannel.

"Hawes texted," Helena said. "After all that's happened, we're not in the habit of questioning him."

Chris took another gulp of water, then handed the cup back to Helena. "I need you to remember that."

"What's that supposed to mean?"

Chris eyed the woman beside her, and Celia scoffed. "I know that look," she said. "Shop talk, and not my kind." She lifted a hand, fingers spread. "Five minutes, for Mom and the kids to see you. They've been waiting all day."

"All day?"

"It's almost eight."

"In the morning?"

"At night."

"You've been out all day," Helena said. "Doc said your body was demanding sleep."

"Fuck sleep." He moved to sit fully upright, ignoring the pain that shot through his shoulder. They had to get out of here, find out what Hawes needed, how they could help him. "We've got to—"

Helena planted a hand on his chest. "You know I can take you healthy. I can fuck you up good like this." Her evil grin left no doubt as to the truth of that statement. "Doctor and family first."

"We don't have time—"

"It'll give us time to call Brax back from the cafeteria and to get Rose here."

Chris swallowed back a wave of nausea. "Just Kane."

The siblings exchanged a look, and the air in the room grew heavy, ripe with tension. As did Helena's hand still on his chest. Had they already discussed the possibility? Or did Holt and Helena still doubt his loyalty? The latter would be fair; he couldn't blame them. Either way, they let it pass for now. Holt nodded, and Helena removed her hand, after a little shove. "Always a negotiation with this one."

"Try growing up with him." Celia rolled her eyes for added effect, and the tension in the room eased.

And eased further with the parade of visitors that followed. The doctor on duty checked his wound—a clean through and through, no damage; Hawes had known exactly where to aim— and pronounced him healing well. Dischargeable by the end of the night, thank fuck. After the doctor left, Gloria barreled in with a box of mistletoe cannoli, Mia with a paperback for him, and Marco with eyes that kept straying to Helena.

"Too old for you, Plato," Chris said, and his nephew turned beet red as the rest of the room erupted into laughter.

Helena bumped his shoulder. "Don't take it personally. I only date folks older than me." Her blue eyes strayed to Celia, who was older than her.

Chris did not want to think about that. Better to think about another cannoli instead. They demolished the box of pastries, leaving only one for Kane, who, when he entered the room, moved to stand behind Holt and Lily. The chief made polite chatter, but his attention was mostly on Holt, who hadn't spoken other than to settle his daughter or mumble, "Thank you," when handed a cannoli.

Once his family finally cleared out, and it was just Helena, Holt, and Kane in the room with him, Chris asked, "How did you get the visiting hours relaxed?"

A pale Holt finally spoke. "They're used to us around here. Amelia…"

Chris could have kicked himself. Of course. Holt's wife had been a nurse here. The whole lot of Madigans were probably fixtures here too. They certainly had been over the past two weeks.

"All right," Helena said, taking up position on the windowsill. "Spill, Mr. Hair."

"Where's Rose?" he asked.

"At MCS, I assume. She's been holding things down there." Helena crossed her arms. "You didn't want her here."

"What's this about?" Kane asked.

There was no easy way to do this. Just rip off the Band-Aid. They didn't have time to waste. "We think she's the traitor."

Helena shot forward, bearing down on him. "*We?*"

"Me and Hawes, I think."

She stopped at the bed rail, barely. "You think?"

"We didn't get to work it all out, given the circumstances. I wanted to be sure before leveling that on him."

"But you'll level it on us? You could just be trying to tear this family apart. More than you already have."

So maybe that earlier tension had been about him, then, not Rose. "If you don't trust me, why are you here?"

"Because you had my back last night." Her gaze flickered to the door. "And your sister is kinda hot."

"Fucking hell." Chris scrubbed a hand over his face. "That's the last thing any of us need right now."

"I'm not good enough for your sister?"

"No, that's not it at all." He dropped his hand. "You're exactly what she needs, but after the bullets stop flying, please."

Helena shrugged. And fought a smile, poorly. "Fair enough."

"What proof do you have?" Kane asked, bringing them back on track.

Chris began counting off on his fingers. "She's the person with the juice to make this happen. The Madigan with the most connections." He lifted a second finger. "She and Cal built this empire, your parents fueled the fear and image of a killing machine, and now Rose doesn't like where your generation"—he split a glance between Holt and Helena—"is taking things." A third finger. "She's all about power. I saw that Wednesday night at the Buena Vista. She's intimidating as hell."

"Speculation based on circumstantial evidence," Helena said.

"Lawyer."

"Yes, that's my day job, remember?"

"And yet you"—Chris shifted his gaze to Holt—"don't look surprised."

The oldest Madigan in the room remained tight-lipped, and the tension ratcheted up again. Until Lily's soft snuffles turned into a wail, and everyone's attention momentarily shifted to taking care of the littlest Madigan. Helena fetched a bottle out of the diaper bag, and when Holt lifted Lily toward Kane, the chief took her and the bottle. He situated the munchkin in his arms and began feeding her like it was the most natural thing in the world. The surprising sight would have kept Chris transfixed, if not for Holt retrieving the laptop he'd set aside and turning it so the screen faced Helena and Chris.

"Reeves wasn't on Rose's list," Holt started, voice scratchy. "When he showed up at MCS last night, her omission was hard to ignore. I've been digging to see when and where their paths last crossed."

"Anything?"

"Almost all their contact went through Amelia." He pointed at the windows open on the screen. "Phone records, email records, and several reservations and other meetings. Same time and place."

"You said *almost*."

"There are instances of them at the same events, around town and whatnot. And he was a veteran too, so he was at those benefits with us."

"What else?" Helena asked, accurately reading her brother's caginess.

He turned the computer halfway back around, closing windows and opening others. "I also went back and looked at visitor logs."

Kane peered over his shoulder. "Are those for the hospice house where Cal—"

Nausea walloped Chris again, and Helena looked sick to match. "He was there?" she asked, voice barely a whisper.

Holt nodded, and Helena inhaled sharply, her knuckles white where her hands curled around the bed rail. Chris laid his good hand over one of hers and asked the question she couldn't. A question no kid or grandkid should have to ask, but that's where they were, and Chris hated Rose for putting them—and him—in this situation. "Did she have anything—"

"No," Holt said, and Helena exhaled her held breath. "I contacted the doctors. She had nothing to do with Papa Cal's death. Completely natural causes."

"But Reeves was there," Helena said, "plotting with her and Amelia to kill our brother."

"They were plotting it long before then," came a voice from the doorway.

If not for the Georgia-twang on the last word, Chris wouldn't have recognized the man dressed in Talley Enterprises coveralls, his face shadowed by a Giants baseball cap, beads of sweat at his temples. Scotty Wheeler leaned precariously against the door jamb, and his feverish brown gaze darted around the room, settling, to Chris's surprise, on Holt. The plastic stick he held up explained the direction of his focus. "I have proof, from your brother."

"Which one is that?" Kane griped gruffly, despite the nursing baby in his arms. "I'm getting tired of fucking flash drives."

Chris shared the sentiment, except there was a certain flash drive still at-large that held special interest for him. He had a feeling he was looking at it in Wheeler's hand. "Is that—"

"Amelia's backup," he confirmed.

Helena withdrew her hand from under Chris's before he could crush it. He tried crushing her with his scowl instead. "You had it all along?"

"Didn't trust you. Still don't completely." She shifted her icy glare to Scotty. "Trust you even less. What are you doing *here*, with *that*?"

"As I said, your brother gave it to me." He glanced nervously over his shoulder, back toward the hallway. "And I'm supposed to be playing dead, so..."

"Get in here, Scotty," Chris said with a wave.

Wheeler hobbled forward and collapsed into the chair on the other side of Helena. Once Kane moved in front of the door, Wheeler removed the ball cap, revealing sweat-soaked hair, and unzipped the coveralls partway, exposing a gray T-shirt that was likewise damp in places. He did not look good, and the hand he placed over his side, right where Zoe had shot him, did not make Chris feel any better about his condition.

He nudged the pitcher of water on the bedside table. "Get him some water," he said to Helena. He didn't want Wheeler to pass out before he divulged what had happened to Hawes. Chris had kept those worries at bay long enough to reassure his family, and to prepare Hawes's for the worst, but now he needed to know Hawes was okay.

Helena beat him to it. "How's Hawes?" She held a cup out to Wheeler, who took it and drank greedily, until Helena *tsk*ed at him. "Easy, or you'll throw it all back up."

Wheeler finished more slowly, then handed the cup back to her. "Your brother's not at all what I thought."

"Great, you're having an epiphany, but how—"

"I suspect it's been one of the worst days of his life."

Chris bit out a curse. He'd fucking slept the day away *here* while Hawes had been out *there*, somewhere, dealing with God only knew what, alone. Chris should have been there. Should have gone with him last night. "Fuck," he cursed again.

"That flash drive have something to do with it?" Helena asked.

Wheeler dropped the device into her outstretched hand. "You need to be prepared for what you're about to see."

"I briefed them in advance," Chris said. "About Rose."

"You were right to have me look into her."

Helena tossed the flash drive across the bed to Holt. "Cue it up, Little H." She was putting on a front for Wheeler, acting casual and unaffected, like she was unbothered and in control, but Chris had seen that control slip a moment ago, and he didn't miss how the wobble of her hand threw off what should have been a practiced toss.

Holt nevertheless caught the drive without issue. He plugged it in, then adjusted the laptop so it was visible to the room again.

"I'm going to step out," Kane said.

He made it less than a step before Holt shot out a hand and grasped his elbow. "I need you to stay."

Kane motioned with his arms, Lily still in them, toward Helena. "I can give her to—"

"You," Holt rumbled.

Wheeler watched the exchange like it was a tennis match, Chris like it was further evidence to support his suspicions, and Helena like it was a day that ended in Y. Holt and Brax, for their part, seemed to forget anyone else was in the room.

"I've got earplugs," Holt said, "if you need them."

Chris took pity on them. "There are two federal agents in this room. Plausible deniability is off the table."

Denial, however, was the emotion that invaded the room once they'd watched the video. Sitting on the arm of Wheeler's chair, Helena stared into space and clicked her nails together, a nervous tendency akin to Hawes's counting. By the window, Holt stood holding Lily, giving his head a shake every few seconds. Chin ducked, Kane waited by the door, arms crossed over his chest, keeping one eye on the floor, the other on Holt. Even Wheeler looked stunned.

For his part, Chris had absorbed all of Helena's earlier anger and was ready to explode with the force of it. Ready to rocket out of this bed, out of this hospital, so he could hunt down Rose Madigan and exact justice for what she'd done to the family in this room, to Hawes, and to Isabella. He was sure that's who Rose and Amelia were referring to in the video. Promising to "handle" both Izzy and Hawes. Setting the one up to die, the other to die or take the fall.

But Chris couldn't leave and couldn't do a damn thing about his anger because of the damn IV in his hand, the ex-soldier blocking the door, and the missing Madigan who had embarked on a dangerous solo mission. Exactly as Chris had told him to do. He fell back on his pillows and stared at the ceiling. It was the right call—fuck, the only call—and he'd suspected this much, but having it confirmed, knowing with certainty what Hawes was walking into, made his gut clench with fear for him.

"What are we going to do about this?" Helena asked after another minute of silence. Past her denial, then; she'd skipped right over the other stages of grief to acceptance and planning.

Impressive.

"Hawes is already doing something," Chris said, righting himself. "He's going back in."

Holt spun from the window. "He's *what*?"

"I told Hawes to sell it." He pointed at the gunshot wound to his shoulder. "I told him to shoot me, to protect Scotty, and to sell it. He's going to bend the knee."

Anger roaring back, Helena grabbed the paperback Mia had

left on the table and chucked it at him. "This is not a fucking fantasy novel."

He batted the book down, and it landed in his lap. "In a way, it is."

"Why would she trust him?" Kane asked.

"He shot me. By all appearances, he killed Scotty. He wielded a gun for the first time in three years. He'll pretend to abandon his other rules too, pretend to be the soulless assassin she wants him to be, so he can get inside and get the evidence we need."

"You're still after what happened to Isabella," Helena said.

"For what happened to my partner *and* your brother. Neither of them should have been put in that situation."

"And the ATF will play ball?" Kane asked Wheeler.

"I can't say. I'm dead." He curled his fingers in air quotes around the last word. "But that"—he nodded at the laptop—"is evidence your grandmother was the genesis of the current case. We get more evidence to prove that, then yes, I think the ATF will focus on Rose."

"Why are you helping us now?" Helena asked.

"Your brother could have let me die last night, but he didn't. And you have friends"—he tapped the TE patch on the coveralls —"who I trust and respect. They believe you're truly trying to make a difference. I may not agree with your approach, but in this case, we're on the same side." Wheeler was proving the faith Chris had put in him had not been misplaced. He'd admitted his mistake last week, realigned his approach to the case and the Madigans, and now they had another resource and friend.

"Glad you came to see that," Chris said.

He sheepishly shrugged a shoulder. "Turns out we should have been trying to slay the queen."

"And who's going to worry about Hawes?" Holt asked from where he sat propped on the windowsill. "Who's going to pull him back if he has to break his rules?"

"Me," Chris said without hesitation. "I'll pull him back."

"Why?" Helena pressed.

"Not gonna tell you," he said, "before I get to tell him, properly." *I think* wasn't good enough. Chris was pretty damn sure he *knew*, if his earlier anger and the ache in his chest were any indication. And he was damn sure Hawes would be the first to hear *those* words.

One corner of Helena's mouth tipped up. She knew the answer. He figured they all did. "How's that gonna work with you being ATF?"

"I won't be, after this is done."

Various expressions of shock filled the room, except from Kane, who already knew Chris's intentions. Wheeler's surprise faded first, the agent no doubt putting together the pieces. So Chris spoke to the two Madigans who still needed convincing. "I want a life and home with Hawes." Either at Hawes's condo or at his, and regardless of location, he knew who would be showing up, unannounced, to interrupt them, frequently. "And God help me, I want all of you to be a part of that future, with us."

THREE

"Are you done trying to kill me?"

The chair behind Hawes's desk swiveled, its occupant rotating to face him. In the otherwise dark office, the twinkling lights of the bridge, combined with the moon's reflection off the water, cast Rose Madigan in an eerie, foreboding glow. One Hawes had only ever associated with Papa Cal, one that others likely associated with Hawes, but in that moment, his grandmother wore it better than either of them ever had.

"Are you done disrespecting your grandfather's memory?" Rose countered, not bothering to deny the truth of Hawes's question. Her verbal knives were almost as sharp as her icy glare. "Your parents'?"

"That's not—"

She tapped at the in-desk controls, and the room lights came on. "They built all of this," she said, gesturing at their surroundings. "And our other empire. Both were running smoothly, thriving, until you started severing relationships. Started turning down work, making unwise alliances, and crusading for justice." She spat the last word like a curse. "What was wrong with the way they—*we*—did things?"

Life, work, companies had to evolve. *They* had to evolve. To keep up with technology, with the criminal landscape, and with the new and better tools law enforcement had to navigate their world. And *he* had to evolve. His conscience demanded it—demanded justice—ever since the night he shot a supposedly innocent woman.

He didn't say any of those things to his grandmother.

"I was taking steps to insulate us from the law."

"And now they're closer than ever."

She wasn't wrong, though the attention from law enforcement had started long before his ascension. Hawes remembered his parents' many absences, Cal and Rose's too, the closest scrutiny coming when Noah and Charlotte had died. Lying low, hiding from enemies and the law after particularly high-profile jobs, one of which had killed his parents. They operated an organization of assassins; attention from the law would always follow them. But it didn't have to be the kind they ran and hid from, and they didn't have to engage in side businesses—like manufacturing and trafficking explosives—that attracted even more attention. He would not put his niece and any future niblings, or if he was lucky enough, his own children, in the situation he and his siblings had been in as teens. Of being alone when they needed their family most. And yes, law enforcement was closer than ever—with Chris and Kane inside their circle, and Mel and her connections a phone call away. They were inside, yes, but working with them. Making their city safer. Crusading, maybe. Surviving, definitely.

He didn't say any of that to his grandmother either.

"I recognize my errors," he said instead, twisting deeper those knives she'd thrown. "I acknowledge them, they're mine, which is why I'm here. To clean up my mess, and I need your help to do that."

"I don't trust you," she said.

"I don't trust you either." No sense beating around that bush. And no sense appealing to familial ties; that was clearly a nonstarter, given her inference of disrespect. Deference, then. "But I'll answer your questions truthfully, here and now. And then maybe we can negotiate a way forward." He gestured to the visitor's chair. "May I?"

The blue-on-blue stare-down lasted ten long seconds before Rose nodded. His ass had barely hit the seat when the inquisition began.

"Where have you been the past twenty-four hours?"

"There was the small matter of evidence to destroy."

"I saw the news," she said. "No one mentioned any bodies being found on board the salvage vessel."

"Probably because they're still trying to identify them."

"How many?"

"Six." Lie one. "Reeves, Gilbert, Zoe, two mercs, and the fed."

"Which one?"

"ATF agent Scott Wheeler."

"The other fed lived?"

Hawes kept his face blank as he pulled Chris's service weapon from the holster nestled uncomfortably under his arm. He'd swung by his condo before coming here, for a shower and a change of clothes, and to dig the shoulder holster out of the bottom of his closet. After three years, carrying again felt unnatural, as had the several times he'd handled this particular weapon over the past two weeks. It was a relief to get it off him and lay it in the center of the desk. "I shot him, with his own gun, and he fell overboard into the Bay. That's the last time I saw him."

Rose flicked her gaze to the gun, then back up to him. Granted, she could pick it up and shoot him at any second, but she would have done that already if she was going to. "He doesn't seem to want to die," she said. "He's at SF General, recovering from surgery."

Hawes slid back in his chair and crossed one leg over the other. "I didn't intend for him to live." Lie two.

"And if I asked you to take that gun and kill him? For good this time?" She said it casually, as if asking him to do a small favor for her. Not like she was asking him to snuff out the flame that had burned through him the past two weeks, hot and bright. To kill the promise of what that heat might spark where there had been so little warmth for years.

"I would, if that's what it takes to win back your trust." Lie three. "Though I think that's an unwise move. He's too visible."

"He won't stop until he learns what happened to Isabelle."

"What did happen to Isabella?"

Finally, a flinch. Because he'd used the undercover agent's real name that Chris had drilled into him? Or because there was more there? "It's the past," she said. "We need to move on."

Not so fast. "I thought you wanted me to respect the past?"

"Yes, respect our decision on how that particular matter was handled."

There was that word: *handled.* Hawes wanted to rail. He didn't do that either, because there was definitely more there, which made the lies and restraint worth it. "He no longer has jurisdiction," Hawes said. "I saw the coverage too. The ATF seized the explosives and closed the case. His boss, SAC Tran, said so in the press conference. If Perri persists, we report him, and he'll be out of our hair."

"That's been taken care of already."

Hawes forced himself not to lurch forward in his chair. "Tran's in your pocket?"

No answer.

Fuck, the last thing Chris needed was someone inside his own agency gunning for him too. How had Rose gotten to an ATF SAC? How long ago? "Have you known what the ATF was up to all along?"

"No one was watching while *I* kept tabs. While *I* kept this family and its legacy as the number-one priority." Fire burned in her eyes, and a small smile turned up the corners of her mouth. Too reminiscent of Helena's when she had her target right where she wanted them.

A full-body chill raised the hairs on Hawes's arms. He waited for it to pass before speaking, not wanting his voice to waver.

"You have to give us that information, if we're to continue to carry on the legacy."

"I gave it to one of you. The one I trusted implicitly."

"Amelia."

"You want to prove your loyalty to me and to this family? Get Amelia back."

"We've gotten her the best attorney—"

She reached out and pushed the gun back toward him, her eyes piercing and determined. "That will take too long."

Hawes eyed the gun warily as he struggled to wrap his brain around the gauntlet that had been laid in front of him. This sort of extraction was not in their usual job description. "You want me to break her out?"

"I need her for the next phase." With her manicured nails, Rose traced the edge of the framed photo of Lily that Hawes kept on his desk. "And Lily needs to visit with her mother."

Hawes didn't disagree, though the implication that Holt wasn't enough rankled. As did the implication that Holt would somehow deprive Amelia of contact with Lily, even while Amelia was in prison. What rankled most, though, was Hawes's certainty that Rose's motive for getting Amelia back had more to do with needing her to hack something—again, lack of confidence in Holt —than with Lily's well-being.

"How do I know she won't kill me the instant I free her? That my death or my siblings' isn't a part of your next phase?"

"She has her orders. And you're going to have to trust me." When her gaze cut to the gun again, Hawes read the silent order and retrieved the weapon, securing it back in his holster. "You are my grandson. My blood. I love you. I don't want to kill you, or Holt, or Helena. But I will do what I have to to get this family and our businesses back on track. To see that Cal's, Noah's, and Charlotte's contributions don't go disrespected or wasted. We retain our power and protect it for future generations. That's how the Madigans survive and prosper."

Power, by force and might. Same as Amelia had argued. And what did power respect? More power. She'd perceived him as weak, so she hadn't respected his rule. He'd have to show power to earn back her respect and trust and to fool her into believing he'd returned to the fold. And then he'd give her a goddamn coup.

But there still had to be an escape route for the innocents. Her affection for Lily, he hoped, would make her amenable. "A show of trust, in return?"

Her eyes narrowed. "What do you want?"

"No harm comes to Kane."

"I thought you recognized and acknowledged your errors."

"I'm not asking for myself or because Brax is a cop. I understand that was an ill-conceived alliance. I'm asking because we've kept one member of this family relatively clean, and if anything happens to the rest of us, he's going to need his best friend to help him pick up the pieces. For Lily."

"That dependency—"

"Is something none of us can understand. We didn't live through what they did." While Holt had never told them exactly what had happened in his last year of service, Hawes was certain his twin wouldn't have survived at all if not for Braxton Kane.

Rose folded her hands in her lap. "All right. And in any event, if he becomes a problem, I can have his badge with a phone call."

"Just don't take his life."

"And you'll free Amelia?"

Hawes stood and buttoned his coat, as satisfied as he could be negotiating his life and those of his loved ones with his own grandmother. "I'll make it happen."

HAWES HELD IT TOGETHER LONG ENOUGH TO MAKE IT TO HIS CONDO. Just barely. He closed the door, activated the security locks, and flipped on the hallway lights. Propped against the foyer pole, he toed off his shoes and tilted back his head, staring at the ceiling and counting—wires, track lighting, sprinkler heads. Anything to calm the rapid breaths that had started in the Lyft. Once they'd crossed King, on their way to his place in South Beach, some part of his brain had judged him far enough away from MCS and his grandmother to begin to unravel.

And now the threads were slipping faster, while the pressure on his chest mounted, like a landslide of rocks burying him, making it hard for his lungs to expand and take in air. Pushing off the pole, he shed his coat and ripped out of the shoulder harness, tossing both at the loft stairs. He loosened his shirt buttons and staggered toward the open living area, toward more air.

Iris greeted him at the dining table, winding around his ankles. The weight on his chest eased a measure as he knelt and ran his fingers through her silky black coat. She *meowed* pitifully. "I know, girl. I'm sorry I haven't been around much. It'll get better soon, I promise."

She blinked her big yellow eyes at him, then, as if judging him a liar, she turned tail and scaled furnishings and cabinets, disappearing over the half wall to his lofted bedroom. Someone else he'd let down. Someone else whose trust he had to win back. Add her to the list. A list that was about to get even longer.

His windpipe constricted as more boulders piled on, stealing his breath and balance, forcing him to brace his hands on the table. He dug his nails into the weathered wood and willed steadiness and control back into his being. Didn't work. Frustrated at the weakness in his limbs, at his lack of control over this whole goddamn situation, at the losses suffered and those likely still to come, he lashed out, sweeping an arm across the table. A stack of cookbooks, a paperback, a water glass, and a leftover coffee mug tumbled to the floor, the latter two shattering.

He stole a breath. Finally.

Desperate for another, Hawes spun and searched for his next target. Desk. He kicked the rolling chair out of the way, then cleared the desktop with two satisfying passes of his arm. Papers, pens, and other home office detritus clattered to the floor.

Breathing came a little easier.

He uncuffed his sleeves, rolled them up, then launched himself over the couch. He flipped over the coffee table, sending a vase and remotes flying, on his way to tearing apart the media unit. By the time he was done, vinyl records, more books, and two broken game controllers littered the floor.

But he could breathe. Lungs finally full, almost to bursting, he ripped off his shirt and braced his hip against the panic room ladder, sucking in giant gulps of air and expelling them in choked huffs. Just this side of sobs. He closed his stinging eyes, saw his grandmother's cold blue ones in his mind, and when his windpipe constricted again, he shifted to kick the ladder. And only managed to hurt his foot, the ladder locked into place on its short track. But the pain was good. It provided a point of focus other than the knives still lodged in his heart, twisting and tearing him apart every time he remembered Rose's words. Her accusations. Her expectations.

Fuck, he needed something stronger than the twinge of pain in his foot. He bypassed the liquor cabinet, wanting cold oblivion tonight rather than the burn of whiskey. On his way to the kitchen, he kicked the closest metal barstool at the island, and the line of them toppled over, the crash loud and satisfying, dampening her words that played on repeat. The cool, crisp Pilsner he grabbed from the fridge, and drained, muted them further.

But it did nothing to mute the very real voice that came from overhead. "Feel better now?"

The empty bottle slipped through Hawes's fingers and would have shattered on the floor if he hadn't slowed its momentum with his foot. Hawes bobbled the bottle with his toe, nudged it toward the recycling bin, then lifted his gaze, and lifted it more, to the man whose head and torso appeared over the loft wall above the kitchen. The very last person who should be here. "What the fuck are you doing here?" he snapped at Special Agent Christopher Perri.

Not that he wasn't happy to see him. He was happy and so

fucking relieved—Chris was here, alive and breathing, his brown eyes alert and his long hair tied up in a messy topknot—but the two of them spending time together, here at Hawes's condo, was possibly the most dangerous thing either of them could do right now.

"Thought you might need to let go," Chris said. His gaze wandered past Hawes, to the open area behind him. "Did a fine job of that yourself."

Hawes looked over his shoulder at the mess he'd made… The mess… He shook away the nagging conversation with Rose and focused on the mess here. His eyes tracked to the far end of his unit, to the giant glass windows and balcony doors there. "If someone saw you or heard you…"

"We're clean for bugs."

Hawes opened his mouth to remind Chris of the clever bug he'd planted here a week ago, but the agent beat him to it.

"I even checked Iris," he said. "And no one saw me. I kept it dark, then came up here to stay out of sight." He nodded toward the windows, and hair escaped his wobbly bun. "And because lying down is easier on this." He cringed as he shrugged his bandaged shoulder, ignoring the sling that was clearly supposed to keep it stable and still.

Breathing became difficult again. "Fuck, I'm so—"

"I told you to shoot me. Did it work?"

"Maybe. I don't know." Resting back against the island, Hawes curled his fingers over its edge. He closed his eyes and hung his head, reality heavy as fuck again. "My own—"

"We'll talk about that after."

Hawes blinked and lifted his head. "After?"

"Get up here, Madigan."

His small inviting smile made Hawes's stomach flip, in a good way. Made Hawes want to sprint down the hallway and up the stairs to the loft. He forced himself to do the opposite. To pick up the beer bottle, wash it out, and toss it into the recycling bin. To right the barstools. To grab his coat and gun holster off the stairs, to hang up the first and secure the latter in the closet safe, before finally taking the closet-side stairs one at a time up to the loft.

Chris, in jeans and nothing else, was waiting in the center of the bed, stretched out with Iris on his bare belly, scratching her behind her ears. Maybe she hadn't been abandoning him earlier but rather returning to her new favorite human. Hawes would be jealous if not for Chris's heated gaze tracking his every step as he moved to the side of the bed.

"I'm a little offended it took you so long to get up here."

Hawes reached out and pushed back a strand of hair that had fallen across Chris's face. "I was trying not to seem desperate." He lingered there, tangling his fingers in the hair at Chris's temple.

Chris's gaze raked down his body to the erection tenting Hawes's slacks. So much for not seeming desperate. Smile wicked, Chris shooed Iris off his lap and off the bed. Sitting up, he swung his legs around to hang on either side of Hawes's. His molten gaze burned back up Hawes's body, as did his right hand, up the back of Hawes's thigh and over his ass, kneading a cheek possessively. "You desperate, Madigan?"

Stepping forward, Hawes wove both hands into Chris's hair, loosening the hair tie so the strands fell loose through his fingers. He cupped the back of Chris's head, tilted his face up, and stared into his dark eyes as relief pushed balance and steadiness back into him. So much relief. Chris was here, alive, and he was letting Hawes touch him like this, after everything. "More desperate than you know," he said, voice rough with need. "But we should talk. So much has—"

"We'll talk, but I don't think that's what either of us needs right now." Hand tightening on Hawes's ass, Chris drew him closer and nuzzled his belly. "And I know about desperate." He opened his mouth, and warm breath seared Hawes's skin. "Fuck, baby, I know."

Hawes's stomach more than flipped, and his right hand did a fine imitation of its somersaulting, flitting above Chris's left shoulder. "But your injury."

Chris captured his hand and pressed it lightly against the bandages. "This," he said, then using Hawes's hand in his, pulled Hawes onto the bed with him, and once they were stretched out, dragged Hawes's hand down to his crotch. "Has nothing to do with this."

Hawes curved his fingers over Chris's dick, stroking it through the denim. Hard as Hawes's, and from the groan that rumbled out of Chris, aching just as badly. "Are you—"

Chris surged up, cutting him off with a kiss that silenced anything and everything but Hawes's need to be with him. His need to taste every corner of Chris's mouth, to bury his nose in the crook of his neck and inhale the scent of eucalyptus, to feel every inch of his body against—inside—his own.

Need that was reflected in Chris's words when they next broke for air. "I'm sure I need to be back inside you as fast as I can get there." Chris lifted his right hand and cupped Hawes's cheek. "As long as you're sure too. But if you need to talk now, we will."

Hawes muffled his strangled, bitter laugh in Chris's palm. He was the one who'd murdered Chris's partner, he was the one who'd lied time and again this past week, he was the one who'd shot him, and yet, Chris was here, in his bed, hard with want and handling him with care. If there was no doubt in Chris's mind, there was certainly none in Hawes's. He'd gotten over any doubt about where Chris's heart lay during the night they'd shared at Chris's place, and over any doubt about his allegiance last night when Chris had shielded him from flying bullets. Hawes's heart and mind were in the same place—with Chris.

He kissed Chris's palm, then reached across him to the bedside table and retrieved a condom and lube from the drawer. "I'm good with after." Rising on his knees, he finished undressing them, and once stripped, rolled the condom down Chris's dick. Chris shivered under him and bucked as Hawes stroked his erection, covering it in lube. Then Hawes reached behind to ready himself. "What's easiest?" he asked on a panted breath as he worked himself open. "With your shoulder."

Red streaked across Chris's cheekbones as he eyed Hawes hungrily. "Ride me. Unless you need more, and then I'll make it work."

He would always need more, but he understood what Chris was asking. If he needed Chris to exert more control so Hawes could let go, he'd find a way. Like he'd been doing the past two weeks. Tonight, though, there was only one thing Hawes needed. Ready, he snagged Chris's hand and brought it to his hip. "Keep me steady."

Chris fanned his fingers over skin and bone and squeezed. Hard. "Always."

Hawes covered the weightlessness that overwhelmed his insides by bringing his weight down on Chris, slowly sinking onto his cock. "Dante," tumbled from his lips, and Chris groaned, his fingers digging into Hawes's hip. Chris's sling-trapped hand splayed on his own chest, scrabbling for purchase, and Hawes reached down to tangle their fingers together. He reached his other arm over Chris's head, grasping the headboard, then rammed back down onto Chris's dick.

"Fuck yeah," Chris cursed, grip tightening in both places he held him. "Let go for me, baby."

And Hawes did, filling himself over and over with Chris, the taste of his mouth and skin, the scent of his sweat and sex, the thick fullness inside him, deep inside him, and the lightness it brought to every other part of him. Both lost and found in the fog of lust—and love—that wrapped tightly around them.

He dragged his mouth over Chris's scruff-covered jaw, to his ear. "I don't just think," he said between grunts, the speed and force of their thrusts violent almost, their orgasms near. "I know, Dante."

Chris lifted his hand off Hawes's hip, and Hawes cried out from the loss, until Chris brought the hand to his cheek. Handling him so gently while his cock pounded inside him, pegging his prostate with unerring accuracy. He ran a thumb over Hawes's cheekbone, drawing his gaze. Hawes saw the same flood of emotions reflected there, then heard it in Chris's wrecked voice. "I know too."

And after that there was nothing left to see. Hawes's orgasm barreled into him, blinding him to everything but the gentle hand on his face and the strong, hard body climaxing beneath him, the man who was lost in pleasure—and love—with him.

FOUR

"I'm not sure this is the best thing for your gunshot wound."

Chris tightened his good arm around Hawes's bare chest and kissed the shoulder freckle he'd been worrying with his teeth. "That's why I'm sitting behind you"—he tapped his foot against Hawes's at the far end of the soaking tub, splashing the shallow water—"with my bandaged shoulder wrapped in towels and my upper half out of the water."

Hawes had left the bed to toss the condom and get them washcloths, and Chris, remembering a certain fantasy he had involving this tub, had followed him down the loft stairs to the bathroom. Approaching from behind, he'd snuck a hand over Hawes's hip and down to his dick, teasing and tempting as he'd made his demand for a bath known. Hawes had conceded, as had Chris, allowing the turban of towels around his bandaged shoulder.

Hawes lolled his head on Chris's other shoulder and nipped at the underside of his jaw. "You gonna do more than just tease?"

Chris trailed his hand down Hawes's lean, chiseled torso, under the warm water, and circled Hawes's cock, giving it a tug and relishing the quake of the body in his arms. Thanking all that was holy for the chance to be here again with Hawes Madigan. Touching, teasing, together. "Eventually," he said. While Hawes was seemingly ready to go again, Chris's recovering body needed more time, and his brain needed to fill in some blanks from the past twenty-four hours. One more stroke, then he withdrew his hand, chuckling when Hawes muffled a whine in his neck. "I promise," Chris assured him, looping his arm back around Hawes's chest, holding him lightly. "But first, we need to talk."

"So this was a trap," Hawes said, even as he closed his eyes and relaxed into Chris's embrace.

Ridiculously pleased at that sign of trust, at the small victory in an otherwise raging war, Chris hid his smile in the divot of Hawes's collarbone. He swirled his tongue in the groove, and Hawes squirmed, stretching like a cat seeking more. He spread his legs, stiff cock breaching the water's surface, and Chris, his own dick reawakened, reconsidered whether they really needed to talk first. But then Hawes righted his gaze and tensed, seeing something Chris didn't.

Chris drew back and nuzzled behind his ear. "What is it?"

Hawes lifted a long leg out of the water, and with his big toe, traced the tile sun framing the faucet. "This was one of the last things he remembered how to do."

Chris didn't have to ask who Hawes was referring to. All he had to do was look around the bathroom, at the yellow and white tiles that brightened the otherwise enclosed space. At odds with the condo's sleek modern design, the tile work had obviously been done after Hawes had bought the place. By a master...or his apprentice; by a king...or the prince. A touch of home, of family, that Hawes had brought with him. "Papa Cal helped you lay this?"

"No, but he told me how." Hawes inhaled sharply. "Asked about it every time I visited." Another short, shaky breath. "He didn't always remember who I was, but he remembered I was the one laying tile in a bathroom." His breathing grew ragged, like before when he'd torn apart the living area.

It had torn Chris apart to wait in the loft while Hawes had let go without him. But Hawes had needed that then, and Chris would have been no help with his own anger and bum shoulder. Now, though, unwound, Chris could help cushion Hawes's landing as he suffered the hard fall back to reality. Chris pressed his chest snugly against Hawes's back. "Breathe with me," he said. "In." He inhaled, lifting his chest and relaxing his arm as Hawes's chest expanded. "And exhale." He deflated back to neutral, his hold steady but light.

In and out, together, until Hawes's breathing returned to normal and he slumped back into Chris's body. "Thank you."

Chris kissed his temple. "Time for that talk."

Nodding, Hawes curled his hands over Chris's forearm, holding him there. "You saw the video?"

"Scotty brought it to us."

A big relieved sigh. "Good, he made it to you."

"Barely," Chris said. "But yeah, he got there. We got him an IV before he left again. Said you'd arranged a safe house."

"One of Gillespie's properties down on the Peninsula."

"Fitting bit of irony."

Hawes tilted his head and flashed him a smirk. "I thought so."

"Thank you for keeping your word and protecting him."

"Thank you for trusting me," Hawes said, before his contented expression was replaced with a pained one. His voice was strained to match. "Fuck, Chris, my own grandmother."

"I'm sorry I wasn't with you when you had to watch that." Holt and Helena had taken it hard, and they weren't the ones who'd been directly targeted, the ones Reeves had directly blamed, the ones Rose had promised to "handle." Chris couldn't imagine what Hawes had gone through watching that truth unfold, digesting it alone. Chris's chest ached, and he held Hawes tighter.

"Puked," Hawes said, "then washed my mouth out with fifty-dollar-a-glass whiskey." He moved out of Chris's arms but only to run a splash of hot water and wet a washcloth. "I came by here after, showered and changed, then headed to MCS."

"Earlier, you said you weren't sure it worked."

"Neither of us trusts the other, and she's so fucking cryptic. Always has been." He scooped water into the rag and scrubbed his face. "I suspect she bought it as much as I buy that she won't try to kill me again. Or use me as a fall guy if things go sideways."

Chris removed the rag from his hands and set it on the ledge. He shifted Hawes between his legs, as much as the tub allowed, and curled a hand around his neck, turning his face to him. Pale skin red from the hot water and emotion, the ends of his light brown hair wet, his blue eyes damp with sorrow, Hawes looked far removed from the thirty-three-year-old king of corporate and criminal empires. "You don't have to do this," Chris said. "We can find another way."

Hawes shook his head, drops of water falling from his hair onto the back of Chris's hand. "That's time we don't have." Determination shoved aside the misery in his eyes. "And I don't want to be on the outside. Not if she's trying to get her hands on those explosives again. I can't risk what she might do with them. Or what she might do, period."

"You think that's what she's after? The explosives?"

"She wants me to break out Amelia." He fiddled with the towels around Chris's shoulder. "Given their obsession with power, I'd guess the explosives are involved somehow. There's the sheer power of them, plus the message it'll send, if they can steal them back from the ATF."

Chris shook his head in frustration and dismay. "Quiet power is far more frightening."

"I agree. Case in point, Helena, who strikes silently but is deadly. We don't need the explosives, or the guns for that matter, but that's not how Rose sees it. I'm hoping she's so blinded by her need for loud power that I can get to Amelia and leverage her."

"For?"

"The truth about Isabella." Hands flat on Chris's chest, Hawes had to feel Chris's galloping heart. Hawes's was likewise working overtime, pulse hammering under Chris's hand around his neck.

"Was there anything else on the flash drive?" Hawes asked. "About her?"

"Holt was still decrypting files when I left, but he didn't think so. There was evidence to implicate all of you, like Amelia had said, but nothing else about Izzy. You think Amelia knows more?"

Hawes shifted forward, ran another splash of hot water, then rested back against Chris's chest. "She's been Rose's right hand this entire time. Maybe Papa Cal's too. She was in that video with Rose and Reeves from years ago, and it had to be Isabella they were talking about. If she made one video, then…"

"Stands to reason she made more." Chris snagged the washrag and soap and began skimming them over Hawes's torso in a light wash. "I can deputize you. Transfer her into your custody."

"I'm not supposed to be working with you."

"And Tran would probably never go for it."

Hawes laid a hand over his, stalling its motion. "We need to be cautious. Rose said something that made me think Tran could be dirty."

"For real? Or was Rose playing you?"

"Either way, it's worth looking into. And worth our caution." He released Chris's hand, and as Chris resumed the light scrubbing, he rested his head back on Chris's shoulder. "We don't know the full scope of Rose's reach."

"All right, I'll get Scotty digging into it first thing. And we'll proceed with caution. What else do you need?"

"Get a message to Holt and Helena. They need to appear to fall in line, but behind the scenes, Helena should rally the captains for when we're ready to make a play."

"I'll haul them into the station for more questioning. Or make it look like that." Chris smiled, despite the complicated maneuvers they were discussing, despite all the complications this conversation was bringing up. Because despite everything, it felt good, natural, being here at home with Hawes and strategizing with him. Like partners.

"What's that grin about?" Hawes asked, looking up at him.

That only made him smile wider as he pushed a damp flyaway off Hawes's forehead. "I like working with you, not against you."

"Me too." Hawes nipped at the underside of his jaw, but then grew quiet. His hard swallow echoed in the silence, and Chris cuffed his neck in comfort, as if he could steady the words for Hawes, make them come easier. They did, after a moment. "There's something else," he said. "I need you to help me minimize collateral damage. That's off the table for me now."

No, there was no *easier* way to deliver those words. The pain they brought was evidenced in Hawes's strangled voice and in the way Chris's insides knotted in sympathy. "Hawes…"

Blue eyes blinked up at him, pleading. "Help me make it so it doesn't reach the table at all. I have to be able to come back from this."

Chris drew up his left knee, forcing Hawes to turn into his chest and allowing Chris to wrap his right arm more fully around him, nestling him in. He dipped his chin and rested his forehead against Hawes's. "No matter what, I will wait for you on the other side of the fog."

"Why?" Hawes whispered against his lips. "I killed your partner."

Chris opened his mouth to say what had been swirling in his head during the strike at MCS, and later, what had crystallized as he'd lain there in that hospital room.

But Hawes beat him to it. "We have to talk about that too," he said, starting to draw back. "Until last night, I thought you were going to kill me."

Chris halted his retreat, hand palming the side of his face and drawing him back in. "I know you." He kissed one sharp cheekbone. "I know you love your family, all of them, even the ones who betrayed you." Kissed the other. "I know what you are and what you want your organization to be." Kissed the crease that formed between his brows. "You could have pulled that trigger against me the morning I revealed myself, but you didn't." Kissed the tip of his nose, and then his lips, lightly. "You wouldn't, just like I know, given the choice, you wouldn't have killed Isabella that night either."

"I'm sorry, I didn't—"

"I know now you didn't mean to kill her."

Hawes covered his hand with his own, leaning back enough to lock their gazes. "I want justice for her too. Everything I've done since that night has been about righting that wrong."

"I know that." Chris slipped his hand out and kissed Hawes's palm. "I'm sorry I almost destroyed your family to figure that out."

"We were all played. Everything I did… It wasn't enough." He closed his eyes, defeat stealing over his features again.

Chris could commiserate. The same weariness infused his bones from driving himself into the ground, and driving his family away, these past three years. Hell, the past ten. But over the past couple of weeks, he'd seen the path back from that dark place to a renewed closeness with his family and a home with the man in his arms. If they were going to get there, though, he needed to resurrect the man who'd time and again walked into a trap and turned it around on the fool who'd thought him weak. The strongest man Chris had ever met, who'd turned Chris's world upside down, for the better.

His king.

"Listen to me, Madigan." He gritted through the pain of pulling his arm out of the towel sling, because dammit, he needed two hands for this. He framed Hawes's face, holding his gaze, his attention, their world, steady. "The organization needs you. Your family needs you. I fucking need you."

"Why?" Hawes choked out.

"Because I don't just think I'm falling for you. I fell, baby, the minute I walked into Danko and saw you across the room, your head held high like you fucking owned the place. The second you called me Mr. Perry." He gave him a little shake for emphasis. "*I know.*"

Hawes closed his eyes, and Chris's heart skipped a beat, until they opened again, full of resolve. Of that same confidence he'd fallen for. "I fell for you that night I walked into my condo and saw the box of mooncakes. You got it. You got me. *I know too.*"

"Then we'll get her," Chris said, heart racing now, with love and hope for the future. "And we'll get justice for Isabella, for our families, and for us."

"And then?"

"And then we'll rebuild the empire, by your rules, better and stronger than ever before. Together."

The king smiled—wicked, deadly, and fucking glorious.

FIVE

Chris grabbed a cold pack out of his mom's freezer and laid it atop the assortment of foodstuffs he'd tossed into the cooler. Snacks for Mia and Marco on the drive up, everything his mom and sister needed to make the family lasagna once they reached their destination, and a bottle of wine for all the trouble Chris was causing them.

He zipped up the cooler and carried it to the dining table, where Mia glanced up from her e-reader. "Is this really necessary?" Despite her griping, Chris's niece was ready to go, her bookbag and duffel on the floor by her feet, while the rest of the family was still upstairs packing.

"Are you really complaining about a week in Tahoe?"

She shrugged a shoulder, insolent teenager in full effect.

"Let me guess," Chris said. "This has to do with the guy."

"Ethan," she supplied. "And no. Aunt Ang was supposed to teach me the mistletoe cannoli recipe this week."

"Fuck, Mia," Chris said, genuinely apologetic. "I'm sorry to make you miss that."

"Language," Celia said as she crossed the family room toward them. She dropped Marco's duffel next to Mia's, then kissed the crown of her daughter's head. "And I'll teach it to you this week at the cabin."

Gasping, Mia swiveled in her chair. "You've known this entire time?"

Celia shrugged, and Chris laughed at the similarities between mother and daughter. His smile lingered at seeing the spark back in Celia's eyes. He hated asking his sister to drop everything at the shop, and likewise interrupting Gloria's, Mia's, and Marco's lives, but he needed them safe, which meant far away from the shit going down here. At least Celia had a solid garage staff to cover for her, and the kids would get a nice midsummer vacation on the lake. Chris wished, more than a little, that he could join them. Maybe also bring—

"Chris, grab the cannoli ingredients and add them to the cooler," Celia said, snapping him out of his daydream.

Mia whirled back around, glaring at him. "You too, Baelish? Traitors, the whole fucking lot of you."

"Language!" Celia chided again, but the accompanying laughter belied her scolding. "I'm going back up to herd the others."

She disappeared up the stairs while Chris made several trips to the fridge and pantry, gathering cannoli ingredients and adding them to the cooler. "We're all taught the recipe, right around your age. But there's usually only one in a generation with the patience to make them."

"I can't wait to learn," Mia said, eager in a way she wasn't about most things at her age. "I've got the muffins down and the cookies too. Cannoli would be an awesome way to end the summer."

Chris figured he knew who'd be second in command at AB's before long. More immediately, though, there was another piece of family history he needed Mia to protect. From his saddlebag, he retrieved the weathered Sendak book which had been his daughter's, Rochelle's, favorite.

"Why do you have that with you?" Mia asked.

He lowered himself into the chair next to her. "I need you to keep it safe for me."

Worry overtook her expressive features—dark brows drawn, the darker eyes beneath them wide, her upper teeth worrying her bottom lip. "Why's it not safe at your place?"

He opened the book to the picture of Ro tucked between two pages. "I'm probably being overly cautious." His condo was between two other units in a three-story Mission Dolores Edwardian. A property-destroying attack was unlikely, but he couldn't be sure with the way things were escalating. And he had to be sure with this. "I can't let anything happen to this piece of her." He closed the book, picture tucked safely back inside, and held it out to Mia, who'd been Ro's biggest fan and best friend. "Can you do that for me?"

Eyes glassy, Mia took the book and tucked it into her bag.

"Thank you," he said, extending his good arm for a hug.

She tipped sideways into him. "Thank you for trusting me with it."

Trust went hand in hand with family, or it should have. Chris couldn't help but think of Hawes and the betrayals of trust he'd suffered lately. His grandmother, Amelia, his lieutenants, Chris.

Chris hoped he'd done enough last night to convince Hawes he could be trusted, but Hawes would still be within his rights not to trust him. And vice versa. But at least they were moving toward the same goal. Hawes and Rose weren't, which Chris feared would undermine any trust the one was pretending to have in the other. Which would in turn lead to God only knew what kind of chaos in the coming days.

A series of *thunks* on the stairs drew Chris out of his thoughts and up from the table, hurrying over to help Celia with the suitcases. "We're about ready," she said. "Lake Tahoe, here we come."

"How *did* you magically make a cabin in Tahoe appear?" Mia asked.

Chris tossed his badge onto the table with a grin.

"Didn't your mom teach you not to lie, Mr. Hair?"

Chris glanced over his shoulder to find Helena, dressed in riding leathers, strutting across the parlor, arm in arm with his mother.

"Of course I did," Gloria said. "Can I get you a coffee, dear?"

"That'd be lovely, thank you."

Chris waited until Gloria was out of earshot before murmuring, "Way to invade my family."

Helena shoved her helmet at him and shook out her hair. "You invaded mine first."

Celia snorted. "Nice to see someone throwing it back at him for a change."

"Hey!" Chris protested, but neither woman seemed to notice him.

"You have something to do with this impromptu trip to Tahoe?" Celia asked Helena.

"My brother, but I'm gonna make sure you get out of town safely."

Celia's blush knocked five years off her thirty, until the flirtatious grin fell from her face and she turned fretful eyes to Chris. "Are you—"

"I'll be fine, Cee."

Gloria rejoined them and handed a steaming mug to Helena. Her words, however, were for Chris. "We just got you back."

"And I'm not going away again that easily," he told the three Perri women staring at him with the same skeptical eyes.

"Mom!"

Saved by the screaming preteen upstairs.

"Duty calls," Celia said, then to Helena, "Hold him to that."

"Count on it."

Celia nudged Mia up from the table, beckoning her to help Gloria take the first load of luggage down to Celia's SUV in the garage.

"You shouldn't be here," Chris said, once it was just him and Helena in the room.

"No one saw me."

He set her helmet on the table. "You don't think anyone will see you escorting them out of town?"

"If anyone sees anything, it'll look like I'm tailing them." She sipped from the mug, then judging it worthy, gulped less cautiously. "Do you trust anyone else to do it?"

Of course he didn't. "Thank you."

"You need to focus." She finished her coffee and moved to the kitchen to wash out the mug. "And they need to be safe for that."

He leaned a hip against the counter next to her. "Well, this does save me the hassle of hauling you and Holt into the station."

"Why were we coming to the station?"

"It was supposed to look like we're cutting ties."

"As a front for what?"

"Planning Amelia's jailbreak. Hawes met with Rose last night. She demanded a show of loyalty and her right hand back in play."

"Fuck." Her confident nonchalance disappeared, and she braced both hands on the counter, shoulders hiked and head hung between them. Loose blonde strands hid her expression, but Chris could guess at it well enough. He covered her hand closest to his, as he'd done before at the hospital, giving her quiet support as she gathered herself. She kept things buttoned up, same as Hawes, but where his control manifested as chilly and untouchable to outsiders, Helena played the family spitfire, strategically aiming all that fire in the courtroom or in dark alleys. Or in a well-timed caustic barb. Which made these quiet moments even more stunning, same as the woman.

She inhaled deeply, relaxed her shoulders, and lifted her head. "How is he?"

"Better." Chris tossed her a goodwill match. "After I spent the night with him."

She scoffed and rolled her eyes, and when they righted, he was glad for the mischief and gratitude sparking in them again. "Thank you for being there for him."

"He needs all of us now."

"How does he want us to play this?"

"How do *you* want to play this?" Chris knew Hawes's plan, but it wasn't a bad idea to solicit a tactical perspective from the deadliest of the Madigan assassins and the person who spent her days testing the limits of judge and jury. She was a master tactician in her own right. Chris also wanted to see if the siblings were on the same page.

"We need to look like we're falling in line. Like Rose's takeover succeeded. At the same time, we work behind the scenes on a takeover of our own. Turn this whole shitshow back around on her."

Confirmation of Hawes's strategy and of the sibling synergy Chris admired, at least with respect to Hawes and Helena. But as to Holt… "Your other brother feel that way?"

"Let's find out." Helena withdrew a phone from her pocket and laid it on the counter.

A call was connected to a number Chris didn't recognize. The voice, however, he did. "I'm onboard," Holt said. "Helena can rally the captains."

Chris shifted his gaze between the phone and Helena. "He's been listening the entire time?"

"Yes," Holt said, "and Helena will give you the encrypted burner I sent with her as long as you shut up about your night with Hawes."

"Seconded." Helena dug another phone out of her other pocket and handed it to Chris. "You're both assuming I can rally the captains."

"Listen," Chris said, clasping her shoulder. "While it was your brother I fell for—"

"Oho," Helena said, brow cocked. "You're saying it now?"

Frustration and amusement warred. "Can I please finish paying you a compliment?"

Her manicured brow lowered, and the opposite corner of her mouth hitched up. "Proceed."

"You are damn impressive, Helena Madigan." He gave her

shoulder a squeeze. *"That's* why Rose wanted to recruit you. The rest of the shit Reeves said—"

"Is true." Her gaze flitted to the garage stairs.

"Hena," Holt said gently. "What Reeves said has nothing to do with why the captains haven't broken ranks. *You've* kept them in line because *you* inspire loyalty. They'll continue to stand behind you."

She smiled softly. "Thanks, Little H." Then she tightened her jaw as she returned her attention to Chris. "Is that what Big H wants too?"

Didn't matter. "Is that what *you* want?" Chris asked instead.

"Yes," she answered without hesitation. "The rules Hawes put in place have made us better. We need to keep going in that direction."

He was relieved she recognized that. Now she just needed to recognize in herself what everyone else did. "Then use your power to make sure they, and all of us, survive."

CHRIS CHECKED THE REARVIEW MIRROR FOR THE UMPTEENTH TIME IN forty minutes. He didn't spot any tails other than the motorcycle several car lengths back. While Chris knew the bike was there, the casual observer wouldn't think anything of it. Just another vehicle on the road. The rider did a good job blending in. Not as good as Chris would have done if he were on his bike, but good enough to make Chris jealous. With one arm still in a sling, he wasn't about to risk the Hog, so he'd borrowed his mom's CR-V for this quick errand out of the city.

Another mile south and his exit appeared. Chris signaled to exit the freeway, without his tail. The motorcycle would continue on ahead, down 280 to the next exit, as they'd arranged. Following the map Hawes had drawn, Chris wound along Skyline for a few miles, crossed the intersection with Highway 92, then veered onto Cañada Road. As the Crystal Springs Reservoir glimmered to his right, he rolled down the windows and let the warm afternoon air inside, thawing him out from the city fog he'd left behind. He rounded a bend between two marshes, and then, as cypress trees rose on either side of the road, he came upon two weathered driveway posts. Chris turned onto the gravel drive, which sloped down toward the water. At the bottom of the hill, on the shore of the man-made lake, he came upon a collection of Cape Cod style buildings—cedar shake siding, pitched gabled roofs, and huge picture windows—all in various states of renovation. He parked in front of the largest of the three structures and was unloading tote bags from the trunk when the front door opened.

Chris almost dropped the bags. "I didn't think you owned any denim."

"Not mine," a dressed-down Scotty Wheeler replied. "There was a stack of clothing and first-aid supplies waiting for me when I arrived." He plucked at the untucked hem of the Gravity Craft Brewery tee he wore with a pair of Levi's. And no shoes. "Fits well enough."

"Casual looks good on you," Chris said, even if the rest of Wheeler looked rough. Wheeler was a pale guy to begin with, but the near-translucent pallor of his skin was worrisome. As were the dark circles under his bloodshot eyes. Chris reached the top of the porch steps, next to where Wheeler stood leaning against a post. "How you doing, Scotty, for real? Hiding out and playing dead isn't worth it if you actually end up dead." Collateral damage was collateral damage, and Chris wouldn't let Wheeler fall into that category with Izzy.

"Thanks, I think," Wheeler said with a half smile. "And I'll manage. It's more lack of sleep than anything. It's too quiet here at night. No bugs making a racket, and way the fuck out here, no city noise either. I was up all night, jumping any time the windows or floors creaked, and—" He cut himself off and ran a hand down his weary face. "And now I'm rambling because tired and too much coffee. Sorry."

Chris grinned, concern banked in favor of amusement. "You know your Southern accent gets thicker when you're tired and rambly?"

"I'm aware." He sounded as annoyed at himself as he was at Chris for mentioning it. Chris chuckled, and Wheeler gave up being perturbed. Smiling, he nodded at the sling. "How about you?"

"It's more of a hindrance than anything." Like not being able to ride his bike and not having two hands to juggle the tote bags, which he lifted again one-handed. "Let's get these inside. Groceries."

"You didn't need to do that," Wheeler said, holding the front door open. "The clothes fairy stocked the fridge and pantry too, though there was a shocking amount of Dunkin' Donuts. If they weren't so damn good, I'd be offended on behalf of LEOs everywhere."

Before Chris could inform him that it was likely the local FBI ASAC who'd delivered the clothes and food, they were interrupted by the crunch of gravel and rumble of an engine. The motorcycle that had been tailing Chris pulled into the drive behind the CR-V.

"What's this?" Scotty asked.

"Something else you need," Chris said with a wink. The driver dismounted, removed their helmet, and ran a hand through their platinum Mohawk, fluffing it back to life. "You remember Jax?"

"Agent Wheeler," the IT specialist greeted. "Glad to see you're not dead."

"Scotty, please," Wheeler said. "And thank you."

"You mind some company?" they asked. "Agent Perri said you might need some help."

"With the investigation," Chris added, before Wheeler could object, correctly, to Chris's ulterior motive, namely not wanting Wheeler recovering out here alone. "No such thing as too many hackers."

Jax waited at the bottom of the steps, two saddlebags in hand. "And I make good coffee."

Wheeler narrowed his eyes at Chris, onto the truth, but his smile for Jax was grateful and polite. "I'd be happy for the help and the coffee. But fair warning, this place is spooky as fuck."

Wheeler wasn't lying. Once they got everything inside and unpacked, and Jax was setting up their computer workstation at the half-finished kitchen bar, Chris surveyed the large open floor plan. With most of the sparse furnishings covered in sheets, the new mantle above the stone fireplace bare and unstained, and no blinds on the still-stickered plate-glass windows, he got the spooky-as-fuck vibe all right, even in the middle of the afternoon. It was eerily quiet, eerily desolate, and eerily half-finished.

Chris swept his gaze from the sunken living room to the raised dining area, and to the long, wooden table covered in files and papers. "You've been working?" he said to Wheeler.

"Like I said, it's fucking spooky here. Can't sleep."

From what Chris had seen last week, the man didn't sleep much to start with. "What have you got?" Chris asked as he circled the table.

"Based on my conversations with you and Hawes, I'm focusing my efforts in two places." Standing across from Chris at the middle of the table, Wheeler stretched an arm out to the right. "Connecting Rose to current events, namely the explosives and the related incidents over the past couple of weeks." Then to the left. "And connecting her to past events, including the night Agent Constantine was killed."

Not died; *killed*. Chris nodded at Wheeler for that acknowledgment, then moved toward the collection of evidence on present events. He spied a receipt for a private air charter, from San Francisco to Monterey, the closest airport to the remote coastal inn where the lieutenants who had betrayed Hawes had met and plotted the coup. "The dates line up?" Chris asked.

Wheeler nodded and handed him a copy of a page from the mayor of Monterey's official calendar. "She was on the mayor's agenda that day to discuss a fundraiser for Alzheimer's research. I called to verify the meeting. Rose cancelled at the last minute."

"Because she never intended to go. She was only using it as cover." He noticed a highlighted phone record next and slid it closer. "Rose's call log?"

"Yes. As I mentioned, she's been in contact with ex-Madigan clients. Those are the top three. Reeves, the Neo-Nazi who died in the sting last week, and Elliot Brewster."

Jax gasped. "The Madigans worked with that asshole?"

"He was the first person Hawes cut off when he assumed control."

"And one of the first people to reach out to Rose." Chris tapped at the earliest highlighted entry, only a few weeks after Cal stepped down and Hawes took over.

Chris wasn't surprised that Hawes had cut Brewster off, or that Brewster had tried to use Rose to get back in the Madigans' good graces. He was a dealmaker, legit and otherwise. He fronted as a commodities trader, but in reality, weapons were his most profitable items of trade. He'd been on the ATF's radar for years. He also had a bad habit of treating women like objects to be traded too. He was presently on wife number four and had twice been accused of domestic violence. No charges either time, of course. It was almost as if he used the news generated from those incidents to cover his other illegal dealings. He hadn't been mentioned in any of Izzy's files, but that just meant he was more careful than Reeves. Or that Callum and Rose shielded contact with him particularly well.

"The arms dealer that was killed in the sting," Chris said, "was he affiliated with Brewster?"

"A competitor, from what I can tell."

"Hawes said he had contracts on each of them."

Wheeler pulled a bank ledger toward them. "Paid for by this entity." He pointed at a highlighted entry. A generic holding company name Chris didn't recognize. Didn't mean it wasn't connected to Brewster. Or Rose. "I didn't get very far before hitting a privacy wall."

"I can help with that," Jax said.

"Keep digging," Chris said. "This could be our way in. If it traces back to Rose, see where else her money goes, and comes from. She can't have funded all of this with Madigan money or else Hawes would have noticed. We need an independent money trail."

Chris strolled to the other end of the table, to the collection of crime scene photos and case files he knew all too well. And yet, had only just gotten a fuller picture of. "I can fill in more details about this night."

By the time he was done, Jax was silent, and Wheeler had collapsed into a chair, his elbows propped on the table, his head held in his hands. "How are you… How can you… Aren't you angry at—"

"I'm fucking furious," Chris bit out, letting loose a little of the anger he'd kept locked down. "And that anger almost cost you your life and almost cost me my family and my future." He shuffled papers and yanked out Izzy's ATF headshot. "It almost cost us any chance of getting her justice." He took a deep breath, reined the anger back in, and laid the picture down. "Because my anger was focused in the wrong direction. Hawes isn't the problem. Rose is the culprit. Hawes was just trying to protect his family, his company, and his city. He thought he was acting in self-defense. And maybe he was. We still don't know what happened during those few days before Izzy's death. She went dark. Amelia and Zoe both implied there's more to this." He turned his attention to Jax. "Can you help with that too?"

"I'll do what I can."

"Thank you." Chris stepped back from the table. "And make sure he also gets some sleep."

"I'm a hacker, Agent Perri," they said. "Not the best at that either."

"Take shifts, then," Chris said, turning for the door. "And check in regularly."

Wheeler followed him out onto the porch. "You still don't trust me."

Nothing could be further from the truth. "Why do you think that?"

"Because you're not telling me everything." Despite the increasing paleness of his skin and the sweat dripping down his temples, Wheeler stood tall, demanding to be taken seriously.

Chris pointed back at the door, toward the table full of evidence the agent had already assembled, even operating at half-strength. "That case you're building in there is the key to shutting this down, once and for all, and getting justice for Izzy. You are the best agent I've worked with when it comes to the details, which makes you the best person for this task. Hawes and I need your focus here. Trust us that we're covering the other bases."

Wheeler held his stare one beat, two beats, then deflated. He rested back on the patio rail, head hung. "I'm sorry. I'm just not used to this."

"Used to what?"

"Someone wanting me on their team."

Chris clasped his bicep. "We do, Scotty. Don't forget that."

"Thanks." He cleared his throat, then lifted his head again. His gaze bounced around, landing anywhere but on Chris. "Listen, um, has the agency made any official announcement…about me?"

"Still listed as MIA. No official statement."

Wheeler tapped his thumbs against the rail, the rhythm rapid and irregular.

"Is there someone—"

"No," Wheeler cut him off. "Perri—"

"I think you can call me Chris."

"Chris, this job is all I have." His wandering gaze drifted back toward the house. Toward his work. "I don't want to lose it."

"Just trust me a little longer."

"We at least need to brief Tran, before she makes any further statements."

Chris looked away then. "About that…"

"Fuck, did Rose get to her too?"

"Hawes thinks it's possible. Add her to your dig list."

Wheeler ran a shaky hand through his dirty-blond hair, mussing it up more than it already was, the unstyled strands longer than Chris had realized. Despite the circumstances, casual and disheveled was a good look on Scotty Wheeler. "How big is this, Chris?" Wheeler asked. "When's it going to end? *How's* it going to end?"

"With us getting justice for our colleague and making this city a safer place." Chris had to believe that, on both counts, given the number of people depending on him. And if he and Hawes were to have any hope for that future—that home—Chris wanted. "That's our job, isn't it?"

"But is it going to get us killed?"

Chris sure as fuck hoped not, but he couldn't answer *no* with any certainty.

SIX

Blue eyes blazing, Helena squared off across the dining table from Hawes, every sharp line of her body taut. "You're throwing it all away, just like that?"

Was she putting on an act, or was this for real? It sure as fuck looked real. Same with Holt, who sat at the head of the table, bottle-feeding Lily. His expression vacillated between blank despondency and anxious fear. Either way, he hadn't liked what he'd heard; that much was real. But was it a surprise to him? Hawes's SFPD sources had reported that Chris was at the station today, but neither Holt nor Helena had been summoned for questioning. Did they know this had been in the works? Had Chris gotten the message to them? Did it matter when Hawes was certain Rose was eavesdropping from the kitchen? He had to sell this either way.

"What am I throwing away? A two-week fling with a federal agent?"

Hawes fought not to flinch at his own lie. *Fling* was too small a word for the hurricane that had upended his world, but in the midst of the storm, he'd found something he thought out of reach for himself. Something his brother had shared with Amelia, for a time; that his parents and grandparents had been lucky to find. A steadying rod, a lover, a partner. Yes, it had only been two weeks, but Hawes knew. Chris was it for him, not just some *fling*.

"A mode of operation that's held us back."

Another lie. Hawes's rules had kept them clear of the law. Had made both their operations—legal and illegal—cleaner and easier. Less risk of life and livelihood. But that's not what Rose needed to hear.

"Let's talk about what we'd be gaining back," he argued against himself. For her benefit. "A ready-made weapons stash. Stability for the organization, inside and out. Our sister-in-law."

"The mother of my child." Holt glanced up from Lily and her bottle, his warm brown eyes both anxious and angry. "If we do this and we get caught, she could go away for even longer than what's on the table now. How does this work out for her? For me and Lily? Why not let Oak handle it? They've got Reeves on tape as the responsible party. Oak will find a way to get her off or at least reduce the charges."

It didn't work out for Amelia or for her immediate family. That realization had settled into Hawes's gut as he'd failed to fall asleep in Chris's arms last night. Amelia was just another pawn for Rose to manipulate. The only way this worked out for Amelia was to cooperate with law enforcement, which he and Chris had agreed on in the wee hours of the morning, before Chris had left the condo. But again, with Rose listening, that was the last thing Hawes could say.

"We don't have time for that. Rose needs Amelia—"

"What can Amelia offer that I can't?" Holt countered. "I'm a better hacker. Whatever Rose needs, I can do it without risking Amelia."

"You'd do that for her?" Rose entered from the kitchen, revealing herself. Tulip and Daisy trailed behind her as she rounded the table to Holt's side. "After she betrayed you?"

He aimed the same worry and ire at their grandmother, equal opportunity it seemed. And not to be cowed where his family was concerned. "She's the mother of my child."

"I need both of you."

"I can—"

"She has a part to play. She knows that." Rose squeezed Holt's shoulder. "I will protect her, I promise." Then let her hand drift lower, to run her fingers through Lily's auburn fuzz. "This is all for Lily, and I won't cause her mother, or you, any harm."

Maybe she did actually believe that, but Hawes wasn't willing to take the risk. He'd done what he could to pave an easier road for his brother's family. But even then, he wasn't taking a chance.

"And we'll have her back in custody before anyone realizes she's missing," Hawes said.

"How's that going to work?" Helena asked.

"By taking a page from your favorite movie." He retrieved two tote bags from under the table and dumped their contents out on top—brown hair dye and matching wigs. As serious as the matter was, he couldn't hold back a smile. This had been something he and Helena had talked about as kids. A heist they'd dreamed about pulling one day. He'd never thought it would be his sister-in-law they were stealing, but Hawes couldn't deny the rush that came with knowing they were actually going to do this.

Seemed Helena was feeling the same way, one side of her mouth quirking up. "We're going to *Thomas Crown* this shit?"

Hawes nodded. "She's being brought to the courthouse tomorrow morning to be arraigned on additional charges connected to the incident at MCS. We'll make the switch while she's in the Federal Building."

"We have soldiers who look close enough to make the disguises work," Rose added.

"A couple captains too," Helena said.

Hawes's stomach sank, the momentary rush skidding to a halt. If Helena was willing to bring the captains in on this, had Chris failed to get the message to her?

Motion at Helena's side, the one away from Rose, caught his attention. Five fingers spread, once, twice. *Five by five*, a saying from Helena's favorite *Buffy* character, Faith. A secret code he and

Helena had picked up, which their parents and grandparents had never caught onto. She'd gotten the message, loud and clear.

Hawes's smile returned. "You going to play along?"

And Helena's grin grew wider. "We've waited our whole lives for this. Fuck yeah, I'm in."

The only one not smiling was Holt. Two steps closer and Hawes knelt beside his brother, hand on his knee. "She's the mother of your child. We don't do this without your okay." Fuck Rose. On this, Hawes would not compromise.

"You promise to protect her?" he asked Hawes. Not Rose or Helena. That trust his twin still had in him was more of a rush than any heist they were planning to pull.

"I promise, Little H. This is all about protecting your family."

Holt's big mitt came down on top of his. "Our family."

⸻ ⣤⣤ ⣤⣤⣤ ⸻

FCI Dublin was a short walk from the ATF's Northern California division office. That was the only explanation Chris had for why Vivienne Tran was climbing into the back of the transport van where Chris waited for Amelia. He was at a complete loss, however, to explain away the signs that Tran hadn't come from the office—black jeans, gray T-shirt, leather jacket; hair loose, out of its usual bun and cascading down her back and around her face in glossy black sheets; eyes as far from flat as Chris had ever seen them. They were liquid tar, the angry heat in them dangerous, a trap for anyone who tread too close.

He scooted the opposite direction on his bench seat. "SAC Tran—"

"Save it, Perri."

The familiar bark quelled some of Chris's dissonance, but not enough that he was willing to disclose more than he had to, especially in light of Hawes's suspicion that Tran might be dirty. "Save what?" he hedged.

"The lie you're going to tell me about simply escorting Amelia

Madigan to the courthouse." She slammed the doors shut behind her and claimed a spot on the bench across from him. "That's the marshals' job, not yours."

"Given the nature of the case—"

"I said save it. We don't have time."

A swerve from what had sounded like the beginning of a dressing down. So what was this, then? Even more unsure of her motives, Chris held his cards close. "Time for what?"

She shifted forward, forearms resting on her crossed knees. "Time for me to explain how this jailbreak is really going to go down."

Chris pushed back with his heels, sliding down the bench seat while drawing his gun, leveling it, two-handed, directly at his traitorous superior officer. "You're working with her?" His voice came out a rough growl, from the blistering heat of betrayal and the blistering pain in his shoulder.

Tran didn't flinch, at his voice or actions. "Yes."

"Why?"

"Because she killed my wife, and I will see her pay for that."

"Who—"

Tran twisted a finger in the bullet chain around her neck, drawing up the weight that hung below the collar of her shirt. Two rings, both coiled serpents, one studded with amethysts, the other with rubies.

Chris gasped and lowered his gun, pain temporarily sidelined by surprise. He'd seen that amethyst ring more times than he could count. On Izzy's finger. He'd never known it was a wedding band, much less that Vivienne Tran had one to match.

"Izzy was your wife?" How was that possible? Tran wasn't listed in any of Izzy's records. But given the way Tran longingly regarded the rings in her palm, Chris didn't doubt the truth staring him in the face.

"We couldn't do it officially, under the law, for too long, and then because of the agency. I was her superior, technically. We had a private commitment ceremony." She closed her eyes, and her fist around the rings, holding them to her chest. "She was my wife here, and in all the ways that counted."

While Chris's head still spun, she delivered another blow. "She'd gone dark for three days and then resurfaced only for me to be in a fucking meeting. She broke cover to leave me a voice mail. Said the mission was going to shit. I tracked her phone, but I was too late, by five fucking minutes. I got to the scene, and Hawes Madigan was on his knees beside her, where I should have been." She cast her gaze aside and swallowed hard. "Maybe if I'd gotten there in time, if I'd just answered the call, I could have saved her."

Dots connected that never had before. "That's why you covered it up. Because you wanted vengeance too."

"Vengeance… and absolution." She let the rings fall back below the collar of her shirt. "This has been the longest three years of my life, Perri. But we're so close now."

Chris reholstered his gun as he sought to connect more dots. "How did no one see you at the scene?"

"I didn't get to be SAC without some skill."

"Except Rose found out you were there," Chris speculated. There had to be some sort of leverage that connected them.

"Only because I told her," Tran said, shooting down his theory. "I went to her, told her who I was to Izzy, and told her I wanted vengeance, against Hawes."

Not leverage, a common goal. Chris peeked beneath his collar to check the bandages around his shoulder. Something mundane to counteract this wobbly reality. Except he'd gone without the sling today—he needed the extra mobility for the tasks ahead— and now his shoulder ached from the quick draw, a stark reminder of the reality of the past two weeks. Of the full weight of what Tran was saying. "You let me walk into this."

"Because that's what Izzy would have wanted. She said you were the best, and you've proven it, even if you are a giant pain in my ass. And now we have Rose right where we want her."

"Rose? Not the rest of the Madigans? You said you wanted to bring them all down. That Hawes was a target."

"For her benefit," Tran said. "She needed to think I was on her side. That the ATF was after Hawes and not her."

"So Hawes—"

"I was *there*, Perri. I saw him that night. He was on his knees, in the rain, crying as he tried to stop Izzy from bleeding out. Helena had to drag him away from the scene. He regretted what he did, immediately. It was a terrible accident, engineered by his own grandmother."

Fucking hell, she'd known the entire time, and she'd still sent him in to infiltrate the Madigans. She couldn't have known he'd fall for Hawes, but she'd kept those details secret, from everyone. Part of him was angry at her for that omission. But another part of him understood that she couldn't disclose those details without disclosing her relationship with Izzy. Understood that those details could have compromised his cover. Understood, all too well, the lengths a person would go to to avenge the ones they loved. In any event, none of that mattered because she was right. They were so close now.

"All right," he said. "What's the plan?"

She briefly confirmed the details of the bait-and-switch plan he'd also received an encrypted message about in the wee hours of the morning.

Then Chris filled her in on his conversation with Wheeler and their suspicions about Elliot Brewster.

Tran nodded. "Rose thinks Brewster is her best bet for shoring up power. But she also hates him, even more so after the last DV charge. She's surrounded herself with powerful women, and he is a slap in the face to all that. Which is why we're going to give her an alternative."

"And now we're back to 'how this is really going to go down'…"

Tran smiled, and Chris thought maybe he'd slipped into an

alternate reality. Until another blast from the past surprised him back to this one as she said, "Remy Pak."

"We have her?" Remy Pak ran guns for the Russian mob and had been a supplier for the gang Chris had dismantled in Seattle.

"We've been on her since you hauled her in," Tran said. "She slipped up about six months ago, and she's ours now. She'll pretend to have the means to help steal back the explosives, and Rose will get the added satisfaction of double-crossing Brewster. We'll catch Rose red-handed."

"And we need Amelia to facilitate," Chris said, anticipating the play.

Tran drew two folded sheets of paper from her coat pocket. "This," she said, handing him the first, "is the signed order officially transferring Amelia into your custody, should you need it." She held out the second. "And that's the name of one of Remy's captains who was in lockup with Amelia. She just has to tell Rose that Remy reached out and wants to play ball." Tran sat back, legs crossed. "I'll drop a bug in Rose's ear too."

"What's in this for Amelia?" Chris asked as he glanced at each sheet of paper. He tucked the first into his coat pocket and kept the second out, tapping the folded crease against his knuckles. "We have to offer her something."

"Besides not extending her sentence for trying to break out of jail?"

"She was as much, if not more of a pawn than anyone," Chris countered. "She had no family before Cal brought her into the fold. Rose treated her like a grandchild, elevated her above her biological ones. And she married Holt and had the first great-grandchild. If she went against Rose, she could have lost all that."

There was a commotion outside the van. A horn blowing, voices calling for gates to open, the *clank* of metal and *whir* of gears. Amelia was on her way.

"Did she drink the Kool-Aid? Yes," Chris continued, raising his voice to be heard over the racket. "Did she have a choice? Not really."

Tran considered him a moment, dark eyes assessing, then stood. "Her cooperation won't go unnoticed."

"How much do I tell her?"

"You haven't made a wrong step yet, Agent Perri. Do what you think is best." The voices were right outside the van now. "You work your Madigan contacts, I'll work mine." Tran turned and hustled out the front of the van, disappearing from sight just as the back doors swung open.

Amelia, standing between two marshals, spotted him, and her green eyes widened. But that was the only part of her that looked alive. Despite the designer threads and heels she'd changed into for her court appearance she looked like she had aged five years in the mere five days since Chris had last seen her.

She climbed into the van, and the marshals entered behind her, long enough to attach her shackles to the hook on the floorboard and to toss Chris the key. They backed out and shut the doors behind them. A transport driver slid into the front cab, checked that they were all set, and then secured the interior doors between the cab and the back of the van, leaving Chris and Amelia alone.

When they got moving a minute later, Amelia was the first to speak. "What's going on? Anything to do with why they let me change first?"

Chris considered again his question to Tran. How much to tell Amelia? If the past few days had taught him anything, it was that the truth got him a lot further than lies. And right now, with the way Amelia kept rubbing her right hand over her right shoulder, where he remembered she had a water lily tattoo that matched the one on Holt's chest, Chris believed that Amelia would do just about anything to get back to her daughter. She needed to trust that Chris wanted to get her there too, and that he wanted to protect her family.

Breaching the distance between them, he held out the second slip of paper Tran had given him.

Amelia took it with her chained hands. "What's this?"

"That's the key to saving yourself and your family. I'm

trusting that's what you want most now." He leaned forward, making sure, even in the shadows of the van, that she could see the sincerity in his eyes. "I need you to trust that's what I want too. And that I can help you get it."

She stared down at the paper for a long moment, then green eyes lifted to meet his, and while there was a truckload of apprehension in them, there was also a spark of hope. "How?"

Chris could work with that.

SEVEN

"You know you're half a foot shorter than her, right?"

A very sharp stiletto dug into the top of Hawes's foot, hard enough to sting through the brushed leather of his loafers. "That's what these five-inch Louboutins are for," Helena said. "And you're a fool if you think I'm gonna sit this one out."

He decided not to remind her that Amelia would be in similar heels, thereby obliterating her advantage. "You have a bigger role in this," he said instead. This whole plan would fall apart if she failed at either of her two critical tasks. Which was why Hawes only trusted Helena to accomplish them.

She removed her heel from his foot and buttoned her tailored suit coat. Black, same as the tailored pants and designer heels, with a simple beige top completing the outfit. All of it chosen to blend in and be easily replicated. "Don't worry, Big H. I'll take out the Klimt."

"And…" Holt prompted over the comm.

"And switch out the Renoir."

"Good, because it's showtime."

Hawes peered around Helena, out the long narrow window next to where they stood on one of the lower floors of the Federal Building. A prison van was backing up to the rear entrance, the one that led directly to the secure elevators used to transport prisoners and witnesses to the various agencies and courtrooms in the building.

"Monet on the move," Helena said, and Hawes righted his gaze in time to observe Victoria, one of their captains, striding past them toward the main bank of elevators. The doors opened to a packed cab going up, and Victoria, wearing a suit similar to Helena's, her long dark curls straightened for the occasion, slid inside.

"Cézanne on fifteen," Alice radioed. "Inside Judge Riley's chambers." Which were located directly across from the witness and prisoner holding rooms used for the federal courtrooms on the same floor.

Alice, the blonde captain with a passing resemblance to Helena, was likewise pulling double duty, first posing as Helena to get into the secure area, then donning a wig for her next role, to come shortly.

The real Helena hip-checked Hawes. "The artists are a nice touch."

"It was your idea." Decades ago, before they knew their prize or the very real complications involved in this heist. But it was the least he could do to show his appreciation for his sister, who always had his back, especially in this, their future.

She rose on tiptoes and kissed his cheek. "Thank you for remembering." And then she was gone, skirting past him toward the stairs. "Van Gogh on the move."

"Don't lose an ear," Hawes added, and chuckled at the middle finger she shot him as she disappeared into the stairwell.

"Eyes on Renoir and da Vinci," Holt reported, and Hawes snapped his gaze back to the window, to the man and woman exiting the van outside. Mostly to the man. Had it only been thirty hours since he'd lain in those arms? It felt like a lifetime. And with no idea when he might get the chance again, a lifetime felt like fucking eternity. But they couldn't risk it, not until this was over, which meant this heist had to go off without a hitch. They needed to move on to whatever Rose planned next so they could set the final trap for her. So they could be done with this and Hawes could get back to the life, to the future, he'd just begun to think possible.

As the van pulled away, a Madigan soldier, Eva, dressed in the same black suit, with her normally dyed bright hair now a sedate brown, appeared and passed close by Chris. Their hands brushed, too passing a touch for a casual observer to notice. "Munch has made the handoff," Hawes said.

Eva continued on to the sidewalk, while Chris and Amelia made their way to the entry doors, Chris rubbing at his right ear. A moment later there was a *click*, and Holt confirmed, "Da Vinci is live."

Chris grumbled, "Very funny," and Hawes had to stifle a laugh with his hand.

"Well, we couldn't use Dan—" Helena sniped, only to be cut off by Holt. "Da Vinci and Renoir are in the elevator."

"Rembrandt on the move," Hawes said, forestalling any further verbal sparring. He'd spotted his mark—one of the federal judges' clerks. The chambers access badge Hawes needed hung from the pocket of the hipster's corduroy jacket, right where Helena said it would be. He followed the clerk into the crowded elevator, and ninety seconds and a little pickpocketing later, exited onto the fifteenth floor, the rectangular piece of plastic in his palm. "Access secured."

"Monet, Gauguin," Holt said. "You're up."

With federal courtrooms on either side of the expansive lobby, jurors, attorneys, press, and even a tour group filled the high-traffic area. And among them, half a dozen brunettes in the same dark suit, slipping in and out of courtrooms, like any other legal or court personnel. Hawes had to concentrate to track each one, to catch the do-si-do two of their operatives, Gayle and Sue, executed, before they headed in opposite directions. It was masterful, and Hawes regretted Helena wasn't here to see all the moving parts in action, including Victoria and Elisabeth—Monet and Gauguin—break out into an argument in the middle of the lobby. As intended, the escalating altercation drew the armed guard off the door marked Authorized Personnel Only.

Hawes approached the door—not too fast, not too slow—not wanting to redraw the guard's attention and giving Holt time to blind the eye in the sky, the black bubble cam right over the door.

"Countdown for Rembrandt," Holt said, and Hawes took a step closer with each tick. "Three. Two. One. Clear."

Hawes flashed the access card, the lock turned green, and he pushed through like he had every right to do so. Again, less likely to draw attention. The door had barely shut behind him when a deep, surprised voice sounded over a comm. "Amelia, what—"

Oakland Ashe's words died, a *thump* followed, then silence. They had ten seconds, at most, before their timing was shot. It only took five. "Klimt is down," Helena confirmed.

"Excuse me, sir."

Hawes's gaze shot up, meeting that of the bailiff at the end of the hallway closest to the stairs.

"You're not supposed to be back here," the older man said.

Behind the bailiff, the stairwell door banged open and Helena emerged, looking more like herself with the dark wig gone. "Sorry, Jimmy," she said, laying a hand on the big man's arm. "Hawes knows the rules but getting him to follow them is a full-time job."

Hawes reached into his coat, dropped the access card into his pocket, and withdrew a photo of Lily. "Just wanted to give this"— he stepped closer and held up the picture—"to my sister-in-law. It's her daughter."

The drawn *V* of the bailiff's brows eased as he looked from Helena to the photo to Hawes, then deepened again when he looked past Hawes to the lobby door. "How did you—" And then deeper still as his gaze skittered farther down the hall to the opening elevator doors. "You're not the usual marshal."

Chris held up his badge one-handed, his other hand over Amelia's cuffed wrists at her back, as they stepped into the hallway. "Special Agent Christopher Perri. ATF. Relieved the marshal as she's our prisoner. I have the paperwork, if you need it."

Amelia looked like hell. Pale skin, limp hair, dark circles under her dull green eyes. Hawes worried maybe this wouldn't work, the surface appearances not close enough, but the way Amelia still carried herself—proud and alert, shoulders back, chin held high, and eyes darting around the hallway—would be the things a stranger recognized first. Those mannerisms were replicable, and the rest was close enough. Assuming Amelia, who was clearly assessing escape routes, didn't make a break for it and fuck this whole operation. And assuming Chris had been able to convince her to help them, not Rose.

Either way, they were out of time, Holt giving the next order. "Monet, Cézanne, go."

Between where Hawes stood and where Chris and Amelia had halted, Alice, dark wig on now, appeared out of Judge Riley's chambers, and across from her, the lobby door opened again, admitting Elisabeth. The operatives bumbled into each other mid-hallway, a few feet from Chris and Amelia, and with the three women similarly styled, and Chris also in black jeans, a black leather coat, and his long dark hair loose, it was a virtual traffic jam of sameness. If the bailiff's face were an emoji just then, it would have been the head-exploding one.

Helena pounced, stepping closer to him. "So, Jimmy, about that offer you made on the Ducati. I might be willing to consider it." Suddenly, she had all the big man's attention.

And in that instant, in a blink, Amelia's freed hands dropped to her sides, she spun one way, Elisabeth the other, and in the next blink, Elisabeth was beside Chris in Amelia's place, hands behind her back.

And Amelia was free. Her eyes cut to the lobby door, and it took everything in Hawes not to step her direction, to trust that Chris had come through and that Amelia would put her daughter first.

His trust was not unfounded.

Alice struck up a conversation with Amelia as if they were besties, and Amelia played along, looping an arm through Alice's, and together, they exited back out to the lobby. The door shut behind them, and Alice reported through the comms, "Renoir secured."

Helena didn't miss a beat, shifting the bailiff's attention back to the people in the hallway so he wouldn't dwell on the two who'd just left it. "Seriously, Hawes, you have to go."

Chris stepped around him and handed Elisabeth over to the bailiff. "Transferring her into your custody."

Jimmy did a double take, eyes narrowing. Before the bailiff's suspicions could take form, Hawes handed Elisabeth the picture of Lily and leaned in to kiss her cheek. "Holt wanted you to have this. They miss you."

Elisabeth's eyes filled with tears, and she lowered her chin, hair falling forward and obscuring her face. Preventing further examination. Hawes made a mental note to elevate her to lieutenant.

"Shall we?" Helena said, gesturing toward the courtroom.

"You're representing her now?" Jimmy asked. "I thought Oak—"

"Had a family emergency. Just filling in." She handed him a sheet of paper. "Temporary substitution of counsel." It had been a stipulation of the retainer when they'd hired Oak to represent Amelia. If for some reason Oak couldn't make a court date, or was removed from the case, Helena would be able to step right in. An emergency measure. This wasn't the emergency any of them had had in mind, but it was an advantage they were willing to use under the circumstances.

"I'll need to clear this with the clerk," Jimmy said.

"Of course," Helena said. "We can finish discussing the Ducati while we wait. Inside?"

Interest piqued again, Jimmy moved for the door, then paused, glancing back at Hawes. Chris was already at his side, hand on his arm in an official-like capacity. "I actually need to question this one in our offices." Just a couple of floors away in the building.

Jimmy bought it. "Thank you, Agent."

They walked to the stairwell door, slow enough to be sure Jimmy admitted Helena and Elisabeth into the courtroom, and slow enough for Holt to confirm the stairwell cameras were still under his control. Once inside, Hawes slumped against the wall and exhaled. The next instant, a warm body crowded his, surrounded him, and he inhaled eucalyptus, leather, and coffee, and tasted the man he'd been craving.

Tongues and teeth clashed, and Chris slid his hands down Hawes's arms, caught his wrists, and hauled them up above his head. Pinning him to the wall, their bodies stretched and aligned, almost as close as they could be. Hawes grunted his agreement and hitched a leg around Chris's, closing that last bit of distance, bringing them hard dick to hard dick, and thrusting. Letting go and letting Chris hold him up, burn him up. Fuck, he needed…

"You two cannot fuck in a public stairwell," Holt grumbled over the comm.

Hawes tore his mouth from Chris's long enough to bark, "Stop fucking creeping."

Chris shook with laughter, his brown eyes alight with desire and humor. "As much as I want to fuck you right now, he's right. And if I keep my left arm up here like this, I won't be able to help you move that tree."

"Plus, bogeys five flights away," Holt said. "So cut the make-out session short and move it."

Chris trailed his hands down Hawes's arms, making him shiver, then stepped away. Hawes pouted as he peeled himself off the wall. "Do we have the Renoir?"

"Renoir clear," Alice said. "On our way to the mountain."

"Copy that." Hawes removed the comm from his ear and motioned for Chris to do the same. "Do we really have her?" he asked Chris.

"I hope so."

Not the answer he wanted. "Hope isn't good—"

Chris curled a hand around Hawes's neck, thumb coaxing Hawes's tightening jaw to relax again. "I'm trusting so."

Better answer, and Chris's confidence went a long way to reassuring him.

"Do you trust me?" Chris said.

Hawes kissed him in answer, stealing one more taste, before reluctantly returning to the task at hand. "Let's go move a tree."

EIGHT

Hawes navigated the SUV up Fassler, routinely checking his rearview mirror for tails. None that he could discern. Only a few cars straggled around him on the winding road up from the Pacific Coast Highway and into Pacifica's canyons. He reached up and angled the mirror down, checking on the VIP immediately behind him. Thumb in her mouth, Lily remained fast asleep. She'd been fussy the last time they'd brought her out here, the twists and turns tough on her tummy and the climbing altitude no kinder on her ears. But all the activity this morning—a surprise trip to Uncle Brax's place, then a few hours at MCS—must have tuckered her out.

"She's good," Holt said from the passenger seat beside him.

"What did you tell Brax when you picked her up?"

Holt continued to tap and swipe at his tablet. "Same as I told him when I dropped her off. That the three of us were needed in court and that her godfather was the only other person I trusted to keep her safe."

"Maybe we should have left—"

"I'm not keeping her from Amelia."

"It's not Amelia I'm worried about." Granted, Hawes's sister-in-law could still change her mind—God only knew what Rose had told her in the hours since she'd escaped custody—but given how shaken Amelia had looked under her put-on poise, and how confident Chris had been in her cooperation, Hawes considered her more likely than not to side with them. And he had zero concerns about Lily's safety during this visit. Amelia just wanted to hold her daughter again; that much was obvious, the signs of separation anxiety written all over her face.

No, the one Hawes was worried about was Rose, who would no doubt ask why they were keeping Lily from *her*. What more would she ask of them? Another scheme that risked their lives and freedom? A job that required them to leave Lily with her while they did her dirty work? Hawes clutched the steering wheel, knuckles white, as he summoned his control and steeled himself for the conversation ahead.

"The name Chris gave you checks out," Holt said. "She's a captain for Remy Pak and was Amelia's cellmate, for a night. I doubt they talked much, but Rose won't know that."

"And Pak?" Hawes had heard of the Russian mob lieutenant, but she was relatively new in San Francisco's criminal circles.

"Her bosses brought her in to try and get a bigger piece in the weapons trade here. She's got reach."

Holt held up his tablet, screen toward Hawes, so he could take a quick peek. Hawes whistled low. On-screen, red dots were scattered up and down a map of the West Coast.

"That's everywhere her name is mentioned on the dark web in connection with *explosives* and similar words."

"Does the ATF really have her?" Hawes asked.

"She was hauled into the Seattle field office about a year ago."

"When Chris was there?"

Holt nodded. "She was tangled up with the gang he busted up there. Suspected of dealing AKs and other weapons to them."

"So this will also look like vengeance against him." Or maybe it was actual payback too. With a wildcard like Pak, Hawes couldn't discount the possibility, regardless of any cooperation she promised the ATF. "Business adjustments since the bust?" Hawes asked, from his own experience.

"Not then," Holt answered. "Six months ago, though, she set up a trust fund for someone named Samantha Smith. Next day, Pak left San Diego, where she'd been since leaving Seattle."

"Samantha Smith. Relatively generic." Though something about the name tickled the back of Hawes's mind. Something familiar.

"Alias?"

"Likely," Holt replied, then lapsed into silence. The quiet, however, only lasted a few minutes, long enough for them to crest the hill into Park Pacifica and turn onto Grand Teton, their destination imminent. "If Perri and his boss are wrong," Holt said, "we could be giving Rose exactly what she wants. A dangerous new ally."

"I trust him." Hawes thought back to their too brief respite in the Federal Building stairwell, to the trust that had flowed between them, to the steadiness it had provided in a sea of swirling chaos. "I know it doesn't make any sense—I've only known him for two weeks, and he's a fucking fed—but the way you trust Brax, that's how much I trust Chris."

Surprising Hawes, Holt let out a short, sharp laugh. "I trusted Brax the second I stepped off that army transport in the desert, and I had no idea who he even was. He was just some captain in a uniform at the bottom of the plane's stairs, but when he lifted his shades and introduced himself as our unit leader, I knew I was going to be okay. So I get it." He tossed his tablet onto the dash and angled toward Hawes. "But it's not Perri I'm worried about," he said, repeating Hawes's earlier words.

And the sentiment applied the same, though in this case, it wasn't only Rose. Tactically, they also had to worry about Pak, Tran, Brewster, and their soldiers, whose allegiance was still unknown for the most part. There were multiple wildcards, and yet only one viable play on the board. "It's the best option we've got," Hawes said. "But the tip has to come from Amelia. Rose won't buy it otherwise."

"I'll talk to Amelia, if she doesn't come through."

Hawes slowed to a stop in front of the fixer-upper Holt had purchased earlier that year, and put the SUV in park, turning the wheels toward the curb. He unbuckled his seat belt and shifted to face his twin. "Are you ready for this?"

Holt's gaze drifted out the window toward the house. "I thought we'd fix this place up and it would be our home. Something Amelia and I could call our own. A nice place in a nice neighborhood to raise a family. And now…"

The dejection in his broken voice and the slump of his giant shoulders made every part of Hawes hurt. Made him grieve for his brother and for the happily ever after that Hawes himself had aspired to. "Holt…"

"She befriended me at a time when all I wanted to do was push people away, and she made me laugh. It was only the second time I'd been attracted to someone, the only time I'd fallen in love, and she didn't think that was weird. She took me to the shelter, introduced me to a demi friend of hers, and for the first time since I'd come home, I didn't feel alone. I didn't feel invisible. But now I don't know how much of that to believe. Was she actually attracted to me—did she love me—or was she just following our grandparents' orders? Was she just humoring me and my sexuality?" With every question, Holt's voice grew louder, more strained, fear, despair, and anger riding him hard. Hawes wanted to reach out and comfort him, but before he could get in a word, Holt was speaking again, the rising anger reddening his cheeks under his beard. "And while she was bettering my life, for real or not, she was ruining Max Bailey's, convincing him to drive that van that almost killed you. I was his sponsor! How can I ever trust her again? She lied to me for years." His last word was barely a whisper, fury having run its course and despair taking over. Holt dropped his gaze to his lap, where he clasped his shaking hands. "I'm scared," he rasped out.

"I'm scared I won't find that connection again, with her or anyone."

Hawes covered his brother's hands with one of his. "Don't count Amelia out. Chris wasn't who he said he was at first either."

"But he was, Hawes. Underneath it all, Perri was who he said he was. I don't know who Amelia is, other than the mother of my child."

Hawes squeezed his hands, then unbuckled his brother's seat belt. "Then you focus on that."

"But what she did the week before last—" Holt's words cut off as he got tangled in the seat-belt strap, the man too big for his own good. Freeing himself, eventually, he let the strap fly with a huff, and the buckle clanked against the window.

Hawes couldn't help but laugh, and after a moment, so did Holt, the tension in the vehicle eased by the unexpected, mundane battle. Behind them, Lily snuffled as she began to wake. Hawes retrieved the tablet off the dash and handed it to Holt. "Focus on what Amelia did today and how she helped us last week."

They unloaded from the car, Hawes bringing Lily in her carrier around to Holt and trading off for the diaper bag. They walked up the cracked cement path to the front porch, and Hawes opened the door, ushering Holt and Lily inside. Holt stalled in the foyer, and Hawes nearly ran into his back. Glancing around Holt's shoulder, he spotted Amelia at the top of the split-level stairs. The smile that graced her face, the happiness that lit her eyes, was all Hawes needed to see. They'd made the right call trusting her, and Chris.

From the lower level, someone cleared their throat, demanding his attention. Helena waited at the bottom of the stairs, her barely contained fury the polar opposite of Amelia's joy. She mouthed, *"Get down here,"* and Hawes hustled to comply.

Hanging the diaper bag over Holt's shoulder, Hawes nudged his brother up the stairs and cringed as they groaned under his weight. The entire house needed structural reinforcement, the decks on both levels needed to be totally rebuilt, and as Hawes descended the rickety stairs into the very unfinished lower level, he thought, for the umpteenth time, about telling Holt—*again*—to just tear it all down and start over. Busted ductwork and insulation hung from the open ceiling, the Sheetrock on the walls was intermittent, errant wires hung low, and the slab floor dipped and rose under Hawes's feet. The only light in the dank space came from the two windows in the far wall and from the standing lamp in the adjacent room, visible through the gaps in the Sheetrock. Rose sat in the halo of its golden glow, a single folder on the table in front of her.

Helena fell into step beside him, and they moved toward the room where Rose waited. Unfortunately, all the open walls made it impossible to ask what fresh hell Rose had planned for them next. "Any complications?" he asked his sister instead.

"None," she said, then under her breath, "Until five minutes ago," before leading him into the room with Rose. "Elisabeth is in local lockup until tomorrow afternoon. The ATF helpfully indicated they may need to question her further. We'll have to make the switch back before the transport leaves for FCI Dublin at three."

"Phase two, then?" Hawes said to Rose. "We freed Amelia as you requested, but time is tight."

"I have another job for you first." She pushed the folder across the table toward them. "Nicholas Ferriello's birthday party is tonight at Club Sterling. In attendance will also be Antonin Volz and Patrick McKennie."

"Three of our active targets." Helena tried not to seethe and failed. Whether because of Rose or the targets, Hawes couldn't say. This obvious test when they were on the clock was ridiculous. And the three targets were targets for a reason. A ruthless merc whose playboy ways got people killed, a prickly German arms dealer with zero scruples about whom he traded with, and the Irish mob's racist blowhard and hit man of choice.

"You didn't have any problem taking out targets at that auction you engineered last week," Rose said. "You wanted to make a show of power then. I want to make one now, for our *entire* family."

In a popular nightclub, full of innocents. This was dangerous; the potential for collateral damage was enormous. None of that mattered to Rose. But why didn't the more effective show of power—stealing back the explosives—matter more?

"Why are we really doing this?" he asked.

"We have an opportunity," Rose said. "A potential new ally, but given the recent upheaval in our organization, she requires a demonstration."

"And you want to test us." Helena didn't hide the affront in her voice. "Again."

"Can you blame me?" Rose countered. "None of you even trust me with my great-granddaughter. You don't trust me, and yet you expect me to trust you again with this organization."

Hawes shared his sister's indignation, and his concern for Lily was at the forefront of his mind once more. But also there, with the anger and anxiety, was a burgeoning sense of victory that had Hawes clutching his hands behind his back, controlling the urge to fist-pump. He had a good idea where this was headed, and it was the direction he wanted. "How did this new ally come to us?" he asked Rose, seeking to confirm his suspicion.

"I can answer that," Amelia said, appearing over the threshold with Lily in her arms. "One of her captains was my cellmate at Dublin."

"Who did your cellmate work for?" Hawes asked.

"Remy Pak."

Hawes nearly crushed his fingers to keep from smiling.

HAWES SECURED LILY'S CARRIER IN THE CAR SEAT BASE AND TUCKED her diaper bag on the floor. When he straightened and turned, he found himself caged in, Helena standing at the open door.

"What am I missing?" she demanded.

"Keep it down." He ducked under her arm and circled to the rear of the SUV, an incensed Helena on his heels. Resting against the bumper, he positioned himself and Helena so that he could keep an eye on the house while also preventing Rose from having too close an eye on their conversation. "Remy Pak is in the ATF's pocket."

To her credit, Helena schooled her features, not expressing the surprise that colored her voice. "You sure about that?"

"Can we ever be sure with people in our business?"

"Accurate." Helena began tapping her nails, and Hawes discreetly knocked her hand. He needed this convo to appear casual, not nerve-racking. She cursed, and Hawes thought it was directed at him, until she crossed her arms so her hands were tucked. "At least she's a better option than that asshole Brewster."

"That's why Chris's boss put Pak in Rose's path."

Face angled toward him, she arched a brow. "I thought this came through Amelia?"

"Through her, yes, but planted by Tran, whom Rose called to confirm that Amelia and Pak's captain had in fact shared a cell."

"Chris's boss is Rose's mole at the ATF?"

"Not exactly." Hawes laid a hand on her biceps, ready to stop her if surprise sent her flying off the bumper. "Tran was Isabella's wife."

Beneath Hawes's hand, Helena strained to hold still as she muttered a, "Holy fuck."

"Accurate," Hawes parroted back.

Helena lifted a hand, started to run it down her face, then corrected, lifting the other and pulling her hair into a ponytail with the elastic around her right wrist. "This op has disaster written all over it. Putting aside trying to figure out who is playing who, the potential for collateral damage at Sterling is massive."

That had been his first thought too, until he'd considered the upsides. How they could roll this morning's victory into an even bigger one. How they could swing the momentum their direction. "Yes, it's risky, but we can use it to our advantage."

Helena side-eyed him. "You've got that look. The same one you had when you thought flying solo at that auction was a good idea."

"It worked out in the end." To their advantage professionally and to his personally, resulting in a fight that led to a breakthrough—and blowjob—with Chris. Hawes could make this job work out for them too, professionally at least. Handling the personal aspect with Chris would be tricky—he would no doubt protest that it was too risky—but Helena was the person Hawes had to convince first. "Rose won't be at the club. We'll be out from under her nose. Let's use this op to take care of some other business. To shore up our forces."

"You want to meet with the captains."

Hawes nodded. "Those involved this morning were spectacular. They deserve to hear that, from both of us, and they need to know what our plan is going forward. Most importantly, they're the only operatives I trust to minimize collateral damage at the club."

"While also showing Rose what she needs to see."

"Exactly."

"Speaking of..." She flicked her gaze toward the house, and Hawes shifted for a better view. Rose, Holt, and Amelia, with Lily in her arms, had emerged onto the porch. The tension between Amelia and Holt was apparent, but so was the fact that they were standing together...and apart from Rose.

A good sign.

"I'll get the captains ready," Helena said, then pushed off the bumper and strode toward the sedan where Holt was leading Rose. Amelia carried Lily to the SUV, and Hawes opened the rear door on the side with the car seat.

"Thank you," Hawes said, "for helping us."

"I'm helping my daughter." Amelia buckled Lily into the seat. "And Perri said my cooperation would be repaid."

"If he doesn't make it happen, I will."

She kissed Lily's head, then righted herself, turning sharp green eyes on Hawes. Assessing him, like she'd done in that court hallway this morning. Thankfully, she came to the same conclusion. "Thank you," she returned as she softly, reluctantly closed the car door.

"You'll be okay here?" Hawes asked.

"Are you asking if I'll run?"

"No, I'm asking if you'll be okay here. It's not exactly a livable structure yet."

"It's got power. I'll manage. And I have work to do."

Hawes caught her by the elbow before she started back toward the house. They hadn't had a moment alone together until now—he didn't know when they might have another—and there was another dangling thread on his mind. "We found and decrypted your backup. It didn't contain any information on Isabella."

"Who's your priority, Hawes? Perri or your family?"

Same thing, or as near as, with respect to his future, but that wasn't the answer Amelia wanted to hear. She wanted the answer that best protected her daughter. "My priority is putting all of this to bed so our family can move forward, and as far as I can tell, the situation escalated to the point of no return the night Isabella died."

"You uphold your end of this bargain, and I'll cooperate, fully."

Meaning she had more to tell. The whole truth was still out there, and Hawes would do whatever it took to get it, for Chris and for all of them.

NINE

Two hard raps on the front door drew Chris's attention from the Club Sterling blueprints spread on his kitchen island.

"You expecting company?" Tran asked from across the island. "Madigans?"

Chris checked his personal cell first. No texts from his family. He flipped over the encrypted burner. No messages from any of the Madigans either, not that they ever bothered to knock when showing up unannounced. "No idea."

More hard knocks echoed down the hallway.

"Whoever it is," Tran said, "get rid of them. We're on the clock."

She wasn't wrong. T-minus two hours until showtime.

Adjusting the sling he'd put back on, Chris strode down the long narrow hall and opened the door to Braxton Kane. Eyes hard, face drawn, the chief looked stressed out and pissed off. He didn't wait for Chris to invite him in. He pushed inside and rounded on Chris as soon as the door closed behind them. "What the fuck is going on?"

"Plausible—"

Chris's words died as his back hit the wall, Kane's forearm

shoved under his chin. "Fuck plausible deniability. This is my family."

"How's that, Chief Kane?" Tran asked.

Kane's gaze whipped to the side, and his hazel eyes widened, round as dinner plates. Chris had probably looked much the same that morning when he'd first glimpsed this stripped-down version of Vivienne Tran.

"Your last name's not Madigan," she said. "You're no blood relation. Leave, while you still can."

Chris was fairly certain Kane couldn't leave at this point either, but he offered him the out anyway. "Still want to fuck plausible deniability?" he croaked out around Kane's forearm.

Kane stepped back, but he didn't turn for the door. He lifted his chin and gritted out, "Yes."

As Chris expected. Kane was too invested, same as Chris. Readjusting the sling, Chris followed the chief into the kitchen.

"What are these?" Kane asked, eyeing the floor plans on the island.

"Blueprints for Club Sterling," Tran said.

"Where a Madigan op is going down tonight," Chris added.

"The explosives?" Kane asked. "Surely they aren't there. Rose isn't that reckless."

"It's another test," Chris said, and proceeded to fill Kane in on the details Hawes had shared with him that afternoon. "And an audition for a potential new ally."

"Who?"

Tran gave a single shake of her head, sharp enough that glossy black strands escaped her ponytail.

Chris ignored her. He wasn't changing his approach now, especially not with one of the few people involved in this mess whom he trusted completely. "Remy Pak."

Fuming, Tran yanked the elastic out of her hair, the rest of it falling free, as she stalked away from them, toward the back of the condo, muttering "insubordinate fucker" curses and "fire his ass" promises.

"Pak runs weapons for the Russian mob," Kane said, continuing to track Tran with his gaze. "She hit our radar when she flew into SFO. I do not want her in my fucking city, and she is not a player we want in Rose's corner."

"She's working with the ATF," Chris said, and Kane's gaze snapped back to him.

"So this is an ATF op tonight? Why wasn't SFPD notified?"

"Because," Tran said, pacing back their direction, "SFPD will not be involved tonight. And neither will the ATF, except to observe."

"We're going to let this play out," Chris explained.

Kane shoved the blueprints aside and planted a hand on the tiles, facing Chris directly. If he'd been pissed off before, he was fucking furious now. "Remember what I told you a while back? I do not want a bloodbath in my city, and I do not want my family dead in its streets."

Tran came at them like a tornado, shoving Chris aside and getting right in Kane's face. "My family did die in these streets, and you"—she jabbed Kane's chest with an accusatory finger—"helped cover it up."

Gasping, Kane wobbled back a step, and Chris shifted to avoid a collision. He'd had that fire directed at him before—Tran having chewed him out on the regular—but never had it been so scalding or so personal. It made him doubt the trust he'd put in her. While he understood Rose was the architect of Izzy's death, he wasn't sure Tran wouldn't shoot Hawes given the chance.

"Fuck," Kane muttered, recovering his voice. "Isabella?"

"They were married," Chris replied when Tran didn't; then, as another wife came to mind, his gaze slid sideways, avoiding Kane's.

The top cop caught the dodge. "What else aren't you telling me?"

Chris took another step back, out of reach of any punch Kane might throw. "Amelia's back in play."

If Chris had thought the chief's eyes dinner-plate wide before, they were the size of turkey platters now. "She's not in custody?"

"Do you really want me to answer that question?"

"This morning, Holt dropped off Lily…"

Chris didn't nod or shake his head.

Kane figured out the answer easily enough. He turned away, his motions stilted as he skimmed a hand over his head. "For once, I'd just like to not be the last person to know everything."

"They're protecting you, Brax."

"But I'm the cop." He sounded weary, as close to broken as Chris had ever heard him. "I'm the one who swore to protect and serve. I've protected him…them…"

Chris laid a hand on his forearm, noticing for the first time the intricate tattoos there. They were usually covered by his shirt sleeves, which now that Chris thought about it, were never rolled up. He shook away the momentary distraction. "Let them protect you for a change."

"It's your day off, Chief Kane," Tran said, resuming her position on the other side of the island. "Go home and forget this conversation ever happened."

Kane's defeated daze only broke when they reached the front door. "Should I expect babysitting duty tonight?" he asked, one foot over the threshold.

"No, Rose will keep an eye on her." The words sounded as wrong to Chris as they must have felt to Kane, who lurched forward and grasped either side of the doorframe.

"Why the fuck would they do that?"

"She was suspicious about why they were keeping Lily from her. Why Holt brought her to you this morning instead."

"But what if she—"

What if she kidnapped Holt's daughter, Kane's goddaughter? It was the same fear that had gripped Chris when he'd woken up in that hospital bed on Saturday. The worry was no less acute now, and the risk was even greater. Which was why Kane couldn't be at the club tonight. He had someplace more important to be—

on a stakeout to protect their most vulnerable family member. "I think you know where you need to be tonight."

"Fuck." He pushed off the doorframe and stalked a frustrated circle on the porch, before turning back to Chris. "I'll stake out the house, call if she moves. I'm counting on *you* to keep the rest of them safe."

For a split second, Chris felt as weary as Kane looked, but then Chris remembered Hawes in this condo last week—how he'd made it feel like home again for the first time in years—and answered without any further hesitation. "Trust me."

HELENA CLOSED THE DOOR BEHIND VICTORIA, MUTING THE THUMPING bass of the club music downstairs. Normally, Hawes didn't mind the deafening racket of a packed club. He loved dancing, loved getting lost in the music and the sea of swaying bodies. Aside from sex, it was one of the only other times he let his control slip. But he couldn't let anything slip tonight. So he let the rumbling vibration of the music steady him instead, imagined the rhythmic beat was that of the heart of the man on the other end of the burner phone in his pocket. There if Hawes needed him, always keeping him steady.

He perched next to Helena on the edge of the manager's desk and eyed the captains spread around the room. Despite their seemingly relaxed positions—Alice and Malik on the chaise, Austin and Grant on top of a low filing cabinet, Gayle, Sue, and Connor at the round table in the corner, and Victoria on the arm of the chair where the lone lieutenant, Avery, sat—all of them were alert and ready for the op. And all of them but Avery regarded him cautiously, their eyes frequently darting to Helena for their cues. Which was why Hawes, after commending the captains involved in that morning's operation and elevating Victoria and Alice, and the absent Elisabeth, to lieutenants, turned the floor over to his sister.

A ripple of surprise swept the room, cresting before the wave crashed into Helena. Her confused blue eyes landed on him, and Hawes hoped she saw in their reflection all the confidence he had in her. The people in this room trusted him only so far, but they trusted Helena implicitly. That was the loyalty they needed tonight. He would prove himself through his actions; his sister already had. They needed to hear the plan—the orders—from her. "You're the impressive one."

She cast her gaze aside and inhaled deeply. Hopefully, as he'd intended, she was recalling the conversation they'd had after Papa Cal's death. That day in the garden, she'd called Holt the brave one, him the strong one, and herself the scared one. All true, except all three of them were scared, unsure of what the future would hold and scared for their loved ones. But despite that fear, she'd held it together and held their coalition together too.

Impressive.

He scooted closer, enough to give her a subtle hip check and draw her gaze back to him. Love, loyalty, and appreciation shined in her eyes, and he would have wrapped her in a crushing hug if not for their present circumstances. A smile would have to do, and he didn't bother hiding how wide or full of pride it was. He wanted the captains and lieutenants to see that too.

She returned the grin, then straightened and stepped forward, shoulders back and arms loose at her sides. Confident, like she could spring and kill at any second. "You have a choice to make tonight: the past or the future." She addressed the team like she addressed a jury, the lawyer in her coming out as she made her opening statement. "You're all aware of the recent tension in the organization."

"Because he slept with a fed," Connor said.

"No," Helena said. "Because our grandmother had a fed killed."

"He pulled the trigger," Victoria said.

Hawes internally winced at the mention of that night—the mental film reel of it impossible to pause—but the identity of the speaker did not give him pause. He respected Victoria even more for voicing it, despite the promotion he'd just bestowed on her. He wanted independent thinkers, not blind followers.

"I did," Hawes said. "And I've tried to do better every day since."

"I've seen it," Helena said. "You've all seen it. No indiscriminate killing. No collateral damage. No unvetted targets. Hawes's rules have kept us safe. Kept us as clean as we can be in this business."

"So why does Rose want to get rid of them?" Alice asked.

"Power. Profit she thinks we're leaving on the table. A notion that the old ways are better."

"Sometimes they are," Connor replied, and the twitch of Helena's hand reflected the niggle of worry swirling in Hawes's gut. Connor was their most junior captain, promoted earlier that year. Had Rose and Amelia recruited him while he was still a soldier?

In any event, Malik shut him down. "Usually they aren't."

"Our city, our world, is changing," Helena said, taking back the reins of the conversation. "We have to change with it. That's what my brothers and I are trying to do."

Hawes braced as Connor opened his mouth to speak again. "Why were we sidelined?" the captain asked, and Hawes better understood the young man's simmering resentment. Was relieved by it, as it was something they could work with, to their benefit.

Helena was on it already. "That was Rose and Amelia's decision," she told Connor. "They manipulated the other lieutenants and soldiers."

"And left me out," Avery said, "so I know how you feel."

Hawes recalled the chart on Chris's wall, thought about where Rose and Amelia had struck within their organization—at connections that were either long established, meaning the lieutenants, or not established enough, meaning the soldiers. "They left you out, Avery," he said, "because you were the most recent captain promoted. They left all of you out because you were not as easily influenced as soldiers nor as tied in as longtime lieutenants. You are the independents."

"And you outnumber us, up and down," Helena said. "This is as much, if not more your organization than ours. You make this call."

"What are we being asked to do?" Victoria inquired.

"Our grandmother's ultimate goal is to steal back the explosives seized by the ATF. Then she wants to sell them to the highest bidder, which is currently Elliot Brewster."

Curses and scoffs bounced off the walls, and disgusted faces were had by all. Hawes's earlier pride in his sister expanded to each of their colleagues in this room. They'd picked their people well, and Rose and Amelia had done them the favor of weeding out the bad apples.

"That's the past," Helena said.

"And the future?" Alice prompted.

"Wants nothing to do with explosives. We don't need them. We're assassins. Explosives look powerful, but they aren't the source of our power. They aren't our primary skill." Helena reached behind her, lifted her leather jacket, and withdrew her Sig. "We don't need these either." She set the gun on the coffee table in front of the chaise.

Pride and affection swelled for his sister, but Hawes worried it was too much of an ask, given the sudden quiet among the others. "Hena, you don't have to—"

Helena, however, pushed on. "There's another potential bidder. One we prefer, though it is not our intention to actually go through with the heist and sale." She didn't go so far as to name Remy, or to indicate she was an ATF plant, or that they were working with the ATF, but she didn't need to to make their point to this audience. "The new bidder requires a demonstration, as does Rose. But I want to do it on our terms. On the path we"—she gestured at herself and Hawes—"want to take into the future. The question is, are you with us?"

Malik didn't hesitate. He rose from the chaise and set his gun beside Helena's. "The past is rarely ever the right way to go."

Avery was fast on his heels, her loyalty already proven. Victoria and Alice were a tad slower to follow, but once they'd made their allegiance known, the rest of the captains fell in line. Everyone except Connor, who instead came to stand in front of Hawes and Helena.

"I trust you," he said to Helena, handing her his gun. His dark eyes shifted to Hawes. "I'm not sure how much I trust you."

Hawes surprised him by clasping his shoulder. "I have to earn back your trust, that's fair. But your trust in Helena is enough for now."

TEN

It had been years since Chris had stepped foot inside the building that now housed Club Sterling. Back then, it had been some generic seafood place. From what Chris recalled, the drinks and views had been better than the actual food. Situated on the Embarcadero, in the shadow of the Bay Bridge, the cavernous space boasted floor-to-ceiling windows that provided unparalleled vistas of the Bay and the bridge.

Now, as a high-end nightclub for San Francisco's rich and powerful, legal and otherwise, the location, space, and sleek, modern decor were likewise unparalleled—from the polished-wood bar at one end, to the dance floor that stretched out in front of it, to the brick wall at the far end where a steel staircase led to the mezzanine. Under the mezzanine overhang, polished steel and leather booths provided main floor seating and more gleaming surfaces to reflect the club lights out onto the water.

Club *Sterling* was right. And Chris sure as shit didn't have enough sterling in his bank account to be let in here. But he did have a shiny badge that got him past the bouncer, and once inside, he was grateful for the black dress slacks and collared shirt he'd dug out of the back of his closet. He was getting plenty of looks, but none of them were the you-don't-belong sort. They were the sort he might have returned for a chance at a quick fuck a few weeks ago, but now he ignored them and made his way to the bar instead.

"What'll it be, handsome?" the bartender asked, also giving him an appreciative once-over.

Fernet would be appropriate in a place like this, but he couldn't stand the bitter liquor. "Stout. Gravity, if you got it."

"I've got it," she said with a wink. "Be right back."

She headed to the other end of the bar, and Chris did a slow shift, from his left hip to his right, surveying the space, cataloguing the exits, and noting any variations from the blueprints he'd studied earlier.

"Here you go," the bartender chirped behind him.

Rotating back to the bar, Chris wondered at the items left on the napkin. The bottle of beer was correct, but the pair of eyeglasses next to it were unexpected. "I don't—"

"You left them last time you were here." She pushed the items closer and tapped a barely there bump under the napkin.

"Thanks for holding them for me," he said, acknowledging what was said and unsaid.

"No problem. Let me know if you need anything else."

He waited for her to move on to another customer before he slipped on the tortoiseshell frames and lifted the bottle. Pretending the napkin was stuck to the bottom, he cupped his hand beneath it and caught the tiny comm unit. Bottle in one hand, he used the other to push back his hair and, in the process, tucked the comm into his ear.

"Good evening, da Vinci," Holt greeted.

Chris took a swig of beer, then with the bottle in front of his mouth, hiding its movement, whispered low, "We're sticking with that?"

"Efficiency."

"And the glasses?"

"Disguise, and the camera in them gives me a better view.

Club floor is packed. I can't see everything through the security cams."

"So you're using me?"

"Yep," Holt said, not sounding the least bit contrite. "You're the designated observer."

"Where are you?" Not in the manager's office, Chris guessed. That would effectively put all three siblings in the same place. Too risky. But Holt would be close.

"Fire station." A building over, close but protected. "Now stop worrying about my twenty and do your job. Give me a good look around."

Chris took another swallow of the stout and repositioned himself, back to the bar, elbows resting on its rounded edge. He slowly panned the dance floor, giving Holt the requested look. It was hell on Chris, not focusing all his attention on locating Hawes, but the careful survey gave him the opportunity to locate several other familiar faces in the crowd—the Madigan captains from that morning and those he'd only ever seen on his office wall. They blended in expertly. If Chris didn't know any better, he'd think they were like the rest of the hipsters filling the club, young, rich, and out for a night on the town. But knowing what he did, Chris recognized their positioning for what it was—a Madigan operative on each exit and one in each quadrant of the dance floor.

And where the four corners met in the center of the room, Helena and Avery were putting on a show. Dancing close but with enough club light between them to be decent, barely. They moved in sync, with each other and the music, and their sexy show was drawing eyes from all over the club, including from Patrick McKennie.

"Van Gogh, Degas," Holt said, "you've caught the Irishman's eye. Up the ante."

The taller Avery draped her long brown arms over Helena's shoulders, bare above Helena's leather bustier, while Helena dove her hands into the back pockets of Avery's jeans, hauling her closer. Ante upped, indeed, and so much for decency. And so much for McKennie's date, assuming that's who the woman was in the booth next to him. His gaze was locked on Avery and Helena, eyes widening as Avery wove her fingers into Helena's long blonde hair, tilted back her head, and nuzzled her neck. That was the tipping point for McKennie, who brushed off his date and slid out of his booth. He wove through the crowd toward Helena and Avery, exactly as they'd intended. Chris hid his smile behind another drink from his bottle.

"Nine o'clock," Holt said.

Chris shifted his attention toward the wall of windows. Antonin Volz had his beefy arms slung over the shoulders of two girls, neither of whom looked a day over twenty-two, barely old enough to be in here at all. And definitely not old enough to realize the level of asshole they were flirting with. One of Volz's soldiers opened the terrace door, ushering Volz and his unsuspecting prey outside.

"Cézanne, Monet, you're up as soon as Matisse intervenes." On cue, Volz's rearguard got tangled up with Sue on the dance floor, which gave Alice and Victoria the chance to duck out after Antonin's party.

"Where's Rembra—" Chris didn't finish his question. Didn't need to. He'd swung his gaze forward and found the man he'd been searching for. Finally. Only he suspected everyone else had found him too. Dressed in combat boots, dark jeans, and a black tailored suit jacket, no shirt on underneath, Hawes slowly descended the stairs from the mezzanine. Like he wanted every set of eyes on him, like he owned the fucking place. The king in all his glory, no matter what anyone said. Top strands moussed for maximum volume, the sharp lines of his face were accentuated, as was the blue of his eyes, practically glowing in the club lights. Beautiful and dangerous, the picture of control, in his movements, his appearance, and his sway over the room.

Chris nearly choked on the need to shove his way through the crowd and meet Hawes at the bottom of the stairs, to claim the man as his, to give him the release from the control that Chris knew was costing Hawes so much when he had so little left to give. It ached—in his gut, in his chest, in his dick—to be even this far away from him.

"Stay at the bar," Holt said, as if reading his thoughts. The surprising snap of command in his tone shocked Chris back the step he'd taken toward Hawes. "Get it together."

Cursing, Chris drowned his instincts with the rest of his beer. "That's not exactly discreet."

"He's not meant to be. He's the distraction."

Fuck. Chris recalled what Hawes had said to him last week after the auction: *"If that's what it took to keep my family and city—you—safe."* He'd been willing to sacrifice himself then, same as he was willing to do now. So the rest of his team could do their work, and so he could prove to Remy Pak that he could still control a room. She was leaning over the mezzanine rail, watching as Hawes snaked through the crowd, pretending to eat up the attention, to respond to the hands on him and the propositions whispered in his ear. Hawes smiled indulgently at every suitor, and moved each one exactly where he wanted them, disguising his intentions with dips and sways to the music. Moving, with each interaction, closer to Ferriello's gathering. He caught the eye of two of Ferriello's men, who after a quick word with their boss, started toward Hawes.

"They're on him," Chris said, setting the empty bottle on the bar.

"Just wait," Holt warned. "Remember, he's the distraction."

And boy did Hawes play up his role, drawing Ferriello's men in with hungry eyes and a sexy smirk. Chris couldn't say if their initial interest had been business or pleasure, but Hawes's confidence, the sex appeal rolling off him, made the latter impossible for Ferriello's men to resist. Positioning one on either side of him, Hawes danced with the two men, dividing his attention equally, keeping them both on a string. Leaning his body into the one who wrapped an arm around his waist, under the flaps of his jacket, while turning his face toward the other, who was grinding on his hip. Keeping each soldier's holstered weapon on the side facing away from him and out toward the crowd, where a Madigan captain could quickly divest them. It was masterful, it was frustrating, and it was sexy as hell.

"Jesus Christ," Chris muttered, rotating back to the bar and flagging down the bartender. "Something stronger."

She smirked, sensing his conflict as any good bartender would do. Or she'd seen him adjusting himself. "You were the hottest piece of ass in here," she said, setting the generous shot of amber liquid in front of him, "until he walked in."

"No shit." Chris tossed back the shot of whiskey and let the burn refocus him.

"Feel better?" Holt asked.

"Marginally."

"Good. Now show me something else. Status on the other targets."

After a quick check on Hawes, who still had the undivided attention of Ferriello's guards, Chris searched out Avery and Helena. They were dancing on either side of McKennie, kissing over his shoulder until McKennie insisted on getting in on the action. They took turns kissing him, and by the time Helena was done with him, he was wobbly. And not just in the near-coital kind of way.

"They gave him something."

"To make him more pliable on the way to his long farewell," Holt said as Helena and Avery led McKennie toward the stairs.

"They've picked up a tail," Chris reported, tracking a McKennie guard on their heels.

"Remy's on him," Holt replied, and Chris looked up to find Pak making her way to intercept the guard. "Showstopper appearing on your six."

From the kitchen doors behind the bar, Victoria and Alice emerged, now in server uniforms, carrying trays of champagne and cake. They made their way along the perimeter, heading for Ferriello's two party booths at the end.

"He getting a farewell present too?"

"His will be much shorter."

"Not if he doesn't eat or drink," Chris replied, watching with a sinking feeling as Ferriello brushed off the champagne and cake, his gaze instead trained on Hawes. "Looks like someone was too good a distraction."

Ferriello scooted out of the booth and made a beeline for Hawes, who was now sandwiched between Ferriello's guards. "Backup plan?"

"My brother is more than capable of handling this on his own."

"I know he is, but he shouldn't have to," he bit back. "I'm his partner, dammit!"

Silence greeted him, and the gravity of his words, the truth of them, sank into the center of his chest. It could have thrown him for a loop, but it focused him instead, put this operation into tactical terms his brain could use to muffle his possessive heart.

"There are at least four other crews in this club," Chris said. "All of them with eyes on Hawes. And Ferriello is carrying."

"We have our operatives," Holt replied.

"None of whom are carrying, am I right?" He'd seen no telltale signs of holsters or guns on Alice and Victoria when they'd passed close by a moment ago, nor on Avery and Helena as they'd climbed the stairs with McKennie. He assumed the other captains had likewise foregone the firepower.

"You're not wrong," Holt confirmed.

A show of support for Hawes that Chris both appreciated and cursed. "Those other four crews are not as ethical."

"You're only there to observe. You don't have a gun on you either."

He didn't, but that was hardly the point. "What part of partner didn't you understand?" Chris dug a twenty out of his wallet, slapped it on the bar, and began cutting a path through the crowd to Hawes.

As if sensing the volcano about to erupt, Hawes lifted his chin, and his gaze shot past Ferriello's guard grinding against his front, past Ferriello himself, who was five seconds from ripping his guard out of the place he wanted to be, and clashed with Chris's.

Chris froze mid-step, a monolith as bodies jostled around and into him. He hardly noticed them, having a silent conversation with Hawes instead. Partners—in life or work—trusted each other to make the right call. If Hawes wanted to handle this himself, Chris had to trust him. This was his call.

Hawes made it, with a come-hither smirk and inviting tilt of his head.

Chris answered the call. Coming unstuck, he forced his posture and his carriage into the casual, loping swagger that had started all of this. Tonight was another of those occasions when he needed to be Dante Perry, not Special Agent Christopher Perri. And thanks to Tran, who'd wisely not mentioned his name or flashed his picture at recent press conferences, no one seemed to recognize him as he cut across the dance floor.

"He's got a pill. Inner jacket pocket," Holt told him. "Five minutes, once it hits saliva."

"Copy that."

Two more steps and Chris was close enough to overhear Ferriello say to Hawes, "Rumor has it you've returned to the dark side."

Grinning, Hawes slung his right arm over Ferriello's shoulder. "Don't believe everything you hear, Nicky."

Eyes flicking to Chris, Hawes made a circling motion with the hand behind Ferriello's head and tilted his own head slightly back. A signal. *Come around behind me.*

Chris continued to listen in as he moved into position.

"If it's true," Ferriello said, "we could fuck some shit up together. Wouldn't mind having some fun with the Prince of Killers."

Hawes shuddered, and Chris recognized the reaction for what it was—disgust and revulsion, a moniker Hawes hated but used when he had to, like in the present instance. Hawes smiled, playing his shiver off as attraction and excitement. "Not ruling it out," he answered coyly. "But that's not the kind of fun I'm looking for tonight."

"Aw, come on, Madigan," Ferriello said. "I wasn't around before you got all pious and shit."

"Oh, Nicky," Hawes cajoled, running a finger along the merc's jaw. "I'm a long way from pious."

Chris stepped directly behind Hawes and grasped his hip, spreading his fingers and squeezing, the gesture theirs, letting Hawes know it was him. "I can attest to that," Chris said, loud enough for Ferriello to hear. He cast a cursory glance at the other man, then nuzzled behind Hawes's ear.

"What's this?" Ferriello snapped, defensive at being challenged for Hawes's attention.

"*Who*, Nicky, and this is Dante Perry."

Chris smothered his grin in the crook of Hawes's neck. Partners, indeed.

"You with him?" Ferriello said.

"I am," Hawes answered.

"He is," Chris echoed, stretching his good arm around Hawes's shoulder, over his chest, and inside the opposite lapel of his jacket. A possessive gesture, and one that also gave him access to Hawes's inner pocket and the pill inside it. "I heard mention of some fun tonight. I'm game."

Ferriello's dark eyes flared. Definitely interested. Chris knew he and Hawes looked good together, knew they would be a temptation a playboy like Ferriello wouldn't be quick to dismiss.

Chris tempted him some more. "What else do you want to do with the Prince of Killers?" He drew Hawes firmly against his chest, then uncurled his arm from around him. Once clear, Hawes, with his arm still over Ferriello's shoulder, dragged the merc closer. Chris then skated his hand up Hawes's neck, using it to angle Hawes's face.

"This maybe?" he said to Ferriello before tilting Hawes's face and kissing him. Gentle and seductive at first, a show for Ferriello, then hungrily, craving the taste he'd missed since morning, the heat of Hawes's skin, the way that sharp body melted against his. Hawes groaned, acknowledgment and want, and an opening for the pill to slip from Chris's palm into Hawes's mouth. Officially on the clock, Chris reluctantly pulled back and found their audience hooked.

Olive skin flushed, breathing rapid, Ferriello stepped closer, a leg on either side of Hawes's left thigh. "Yeah," he panted, skating a hand up Hawes's chest and neck in a motion that mirrored Chris's. His eyes roved over Chris. "And I want you to watch."

Chris braced his right leg on the outside of Hawes's and wrapped an arm around his middle, under his jacket, flattening his hand against Hawes's tight stomach. "I'm not going anywhere," he said, moving their lower bodies to the music.

Ferriello swayed with them and brought his mouth to Hawes's.

Jealousy flared, hot and sharp, in the pit of Chris's stomach, but it was quickly doused by observation and admiration. Hawes didn't respond to Ferriello's kiss the way he had to Chris's. His skin didn't heat, his weight didn't shift, his breath didn't quicken. No, this kiss was all tactical and executed to perfection. He toyed with Ferriello, giving him several light, teasing kisses that made Ferriello chase for more, before, hand in Ferriello's hair, Hawes sealed their lips in a deeper kiss. And transferred the pill from one mouth to the other.

Ferriello jerked back. "Hey, what's—"

Hawes slapped a hand over his mouth. "Just a little something to make it extra fun."

"Two incoming on your six," Holt radioed, and Chris drummed his fingers twice against Hawes's belly.

Hawes removed his hand and cupped Ferriello's cheek.

"Heard you liked to have fun, Nicky. Consider it a birthday gift." He leaned forward and nipped Ferriello's ear.

Pretending to be dancing still, Chris shifted them so the incoming guards were at Ferriello's back, not his and Hawes's. "Have fun with us, Nicky."

"Boss!" a guard called out.

Ferriello lifted a hand and glanced over his shoulder. "I'm fine," he told his men. "We're just having fun." They moved a few paces back, not as far as Chris would have liked, but he didn't have time to dwell, his attention drawn back to Ferriello, who was pushing up on Hawes. He dragged his mouth along Hawes's neck to his ear. "I cheeked the pill, assholes," he said, then sharp eyes on Chris again, spit the pill at his chest. It bounced off Chris's collar, against Hawes's shoulder, then onto the floor at their feet. "Poison," Ferriello scoffed. "Fucking woman's weapon."

Hawes righted his head and sank back, more fully into Chris and separating them from Ferriello. "The strongest people I know are women."

The merc smiled, smug like he knew the best secret. And apparently couldn't keep it. "You know, Hawes, one of those women still wants you dead. A two-million-dollar contract went up tonight, on your head." He slid his hands up Hawes's chest, going for his neck. "And guess who's close enough to pull it off."

Holt's "Bitch" echoed Chris's "Fuck." Rose had set them— Hawes—up again. But there was no time to wallow in the anger of betrayal, not with Ferriello going for the kill. Knocking aside his hands and wrapping both arms around Hawes's torso, Chris yanked him back, out of Ferriello's immediate reach. Ferriello raised a hand to signal for his guards to converge and reached the other inside his suit coat for his gun.

"Lift!" Hawes shouted, and Chris shifted his own weight, planting his feet, lowering his center of gravity, and leaning back, lifting Hawes off the ground in front of him. Hawes swung his legs up in a scissoring motion. The first kick knocked the gun out of Ferriello's hand, the second knocked out Ferriello. The merc sank to the floor like a rag doll, which brought every guard's gun up on Hawes and Chris. And every one of them found their gun kicked away from behind, a Madigan operative having snuck up on them.

At which point, panic at the disco broke loose. The Madigan and Ferriello crews were engaged in hand-to-hand combat, McKennie's men caught on to their missing boss, and Volz's muscle scurried for the exits, thinking their boss gone already and not wanting to get caught in the melee.

Hawes sprang forward, out of Chris's hold, and spun to face him. "Go!" he shouted.

"Are you fucking kidding? I'm not leaving you."

"I can't keep you clean if you stay."

"And I can't leave my partner!"

Everything around them was chaos—people shouting, glass breaking, bodies hitting the ground—but Hawes's smile in that moment was radiant. It silenced the swirling chaos and any remaining conflict between Dante and Chris in Chris's head. They weren't separate entities. They were both here, right where he was supposed to be. With Hawes.

"Let's have some fun, then," Hawes said, giving him a quick, hard kiss, before spinning back around and engaging the nearest Ferriello guard. Chris fought at his side, working with Hawes to take them down in pairs, until, after they'd dropped their third set, they turned to find only Madigan operatives standing. The club had cleared out, what was left of McKennie's crew was cornered in a booth by Helena, Avery, and Victoria, and the rest of the dance floor was littered with Ferriello's guards.

Applause erupted from the far end of the space. "Well played," Remy said, descending the stairs with several of her soldiers behind her. Her gaze zeroed in on Chris as she approached their group. "And you, Agent Perri, willing to get your hands dirty now, I see."

He looped an arm around Hawes's waist. "Just needed the right incentive."

"Well, then, consider me incentivized too." Her playful tone vanished, as she shifted her attention to Hawes. "I'll get this cleaned up, and then I'll be in touch." She extended a hand to him. "I look forward to doing business with you, Mr. Madigan."

"Likewise," Hawes said, shaking her hand. "Until then."

She nodded, and Hawes signaled for the Madigan operatives to retreat. They scattered different directions—Helena, Avery, and Victoria out the exit beneath the stairs, a group out the terrace doors, another out through the kitchen. Chris and Hawes exited via the front door, side by side, and as soon as it shut behind them, he grabbed Hawes by the wrist and hauled him down to the shadowed promenade. He tossed the eyeglasses into the water, the comm units in after them, then pressed Hawes against the railing, caging him in. Hawes's relieved sigh was music to Chris's ears.

"Better?" he whispered against the skin of Hawes's neck. He kissed a path to the sharp hinge of Hawes's jaw, flattening his tongue over it and soothing away the last of the tension there.

"Almost," Hawes breathed, then conversely pushed him back.

A spike of worry hammered Chris, until Hawes used the space he'd created to unbutton his jacket and boost himself onto the railing. Jacket open, knees spread, eyes molten ice, Hawes was an invitation Chris hurried to accept, closing the distance between them again and capturing Hawes's lips in a searing kiss. Hawes wrapped him up in arms and legs, and Chris was awash in possibilities. Warm, sweaty skin to run his hands over, a hard cock to rut against, the mouth he wanted to feast on until the sun rose behind them.

"You in those glasses tonight about did me in," Hawes mumbled.

Chris spread his hands over Hawes's chest. "Says the man wearing no shirt under his tailored jacket." He coasted a hand up, into Hawes's hair, and dove south with the other, cupping Hawes through his jeans and pressing the heel of his palm against the erection there. It swelled in his hand. Fuck, all he wanted to do was yank open Hawes's zipper, go to his knees, and put his mouth on Hawes, suck him off right here under the stars, with the waves of the Bay lapping behind them.

"Fuck, Dante." Hawes pressed up into his hand, cock straining the fly of his jeans. "Need you to get me home and fuck me."

Chris didn't think he was going to make it that far, and he wasn't the least bit ashamed about that fact. He wanted Hawes, now. "I don't need to get you home to make us come." Curling a hand under Hawes's thigh, he hiked the leg higher, shifting their angle so he could rut against Hawes's taint while Hawes's cock ground into his abs. "Come for me right here, baby."

Their hips rocked faster, driving them higher, so close to the edge. And then a ringtone cut through their ragged, grunted breaths, piercing the otherwise quiet night.

Not just any ringtone.

Braxton Kane's.

Lily.

Chris ripped out of Hawes's arms, panic freezing lust in its tracks. Hawes, equally alarmed, jumped off the rail and struggled to get his phone out of his pocket, his trembling hands making the task difficult. This—seeing Hawes shaking with fear for his niece—made Chris ache almost as badly for him as he had in the club, but it was a different sort of ache. The need to comfort and support his partner. He curled a hand around Hawes's neck and gently knocked his flailing hand away. "Breathe, baby, then try again."

A deep, shuddering breath later, Hawes managed to get the phone out of his pocket. Chris steadied his hand, the two of them holding the device together as Hawes hit Accept and put it on speaker. "Is she moving Lily?" he asked, voice cracking.

"No," Kane replied, and they each released a held breath. Only to have it stolen again at Kane's next words. "But Amelia just showed up at the house, with a bruised and bloodied Scotty Wheeler."

ELEVEN

"It was all a fucking diversion."

"Not completely true," Helena said, shifting in the passenger seat of the SUV. "It was also a show for Remy."

"An unnecessary one." Hawes stared out the rear window as the city flew by, Holt racing to get them to the house in Pac Heights. After getting a similar call from Kane, Holt had come barreling out of the fire station in the SUV, squealing to a stop at the curb to pick up Hawes, then a few blocks down the Embarcadero, Helena.

Traffic noise blared from the speakers, Chris switching off mute. "It wasn't unnecessary," he agreed. "Not to sell this."

"How the fuck am I supposed to sell that I kept Wheeler alive?"

"She respects power. That's how you have to spin it."

"Fuck!" Hawes braced his elbows on his knees and raked his hands through his hair, flattening the mousse-stiff strands. His hair was fucking ridiculous. This whole thing was fucking ridiculous. When were they ever going to get ahead of Rose? Was it even possible? Every time he thought they had the upper hand, Rose yanked the rug out from under them again. He'd had wins tonight: securing the captains' allegiance, Remy's cooperation, and Chris's declarations. But learning that Rose had put a contract out on him and that she'd kidnapped Scotty were two massive losses.

"When you get to the station," Holt said to Chris, who'd taken off in the opposite direction, "I want a report on Jax."

"Kane said they were fine. They weren't at the house when Scotty was taken."

"That doesn't mean they're fine," Holt replied. "Shelter kids are sensitive to things being taken from them. Wheeler being snatched out from under their nose might trigger some of those same fears."

"Got it," Chris said. "I'll make sure they're okay."

"We're at the house," Helena said as they rumbled onto the driveway pavers.

Hawes lifted his head, glancing out the front windshield at his childhood home, fearing it like he had haunted houses as a kid. Not that this house was dark; every main floor light and Holt's lair lights were blazing, but it was spooky—deadly, even—for other reasons.

"Kane still there?" Chris asked.

Hawes swiveled in his seat to look out the back window, to the same spot where they'd waited the night of the MCS showdown. The same dark cruiser was there now. "Yeah, he's still here."

"Tell him I'll meet him at the station," Chris said. "And keep me posted."

"Ten-four," Holt said, then clambered out of the car, heading Kane's direction without a second thought.

Helena exited at a more human speed, and Hawes took an extra minute to slip a T-shirt and loaded holster on under his jacket. How fucked up was it that he was fine walking into a club full of armed gangsters without a weapon, but he was unwilling to walk unarmed into his family home? He had no idea what surprises awaited him in there, and he wasn't willing to risk his siblings' or niece's lives. He composed himself, then climbed out of the car and waited with Helena at the back bumper.

Her attention was on their brother, who was leaning against Kane's driver's side door, speaking to the chief through the open window. "Should he—"

"It's fine," Hawes said. "Kane's safe."

Her attention swung to him, a brow raised in question.

"Part of the deal I made with Rose." Granted, their grandmother wasn't holding to the rest of the truce, but Kane's role was independent of Hawes, which Hawes hoped insulated the chief. But they couldn't push her too far. "His presence here tonight, though, is one more thing I have to explain."

She gestured toward Holt and Kane. "That one's easy, *if* she noticed." Then she pointed up at the house. "The other one, not so much."

"Chris is right. We'll spin it." He rested back against the bumper. "But how did she fucking find him?"

"Mr. Hair must have missed a tail. Or Jax."

Hawes shook his head. "I don't buy it."

"Neither do I."

"Do you have a file on you?"

"Do I look like a manicurist?"

Hawes held out his hand, palm up. She didn't go into an op without knives, as in multiple. Sure enough, she dug the blade out from between the seams of her bustier. "Thank you," he said, tucking it up his sleeve.

Across from them, Kane's car came to life, engine cranking and lights flashing on. Holt double tapped the hood, and Kane drove off, down the hill toward the station.

"He good?" Helena asked, once Holt had rejoined them.

"Not in the slightest, but he's Perri's problem tonight." He glanced up at the house, then back to Hawes and Helena. "How are we gonna play this?"

Hawes pushed off the bumper. "I have a starting point, spinning it as Chris suggested. We'll improvise from there."

"Haven't you improvised enough tonight?"

"Only as much as we had to to accomplish the mission *she*

gave us. Which we did. No more tests. She wants to force our hand with Wheeler, then we'll force hers. I want this done."

"Agreed," Helena and Holt said together.

Did they still agree with him, however, once they reached the lair and got their first look at a tortured Scotty Wheeler? The agent was strapped to a chair in the middle of the room; Rose stood menacingly behind him.

"You want to explain to me why the dead fed is still very much alive?" she demanded.

"I needed information," Hawes answered. "From what Perri told me, Agent Wheeler is the best at finding it."

Rose circled the agent enough to see his face. "You agreed to help him?"

Narrow slits of brown, barely visible between bruised and puffy lids, shifted between Rose and Hawes. "I thought he was working for the good guys."

Hawes approached, risking Rose's striking distance to squat in front of Wheeler. And to drop the file on the floor by his left foot, out of Rose's eyesight. "You should have gone with that first instinct of yours."

Wheeler closed his eyes and gulped, selling it for Rose, as he moved his foot over the file.

"You were getting me the info I needed," Hawes continued, "and now we have a federal agent as leverage."

"As a hostage."

"I was trying to be kind."

"Fuck you," Wheeler spat.

"Was anyone working with you?" he asked, knowing Rose would if he didn't.

"No," Wheeler answered. Too fast. He was a desk jockey, not a field agent. How had he even survived Rose's torture this long?

Hawes peeked at Amelia out of the corner of his eye. She was sitting in Holt's chair in front of the bank of computers, Lily in her arms. Was she still on their side? How much had she told Rose about what she'd seen at Gillespie's property? She cuddled Lily closer. Was that a sign? Was she willing to play ball for the good guys if it got her more time with her daughter? Chris would tell him to trust her. Trusting him, Hawes squarely settled his gaze on Amelia. "Was he alone?"

"Yes."

Hawes slowly let his held breath out through his nose. Also seemingly satisfied with Amelia's answer, Rose headed for the couch. "What did you need him to find?" she asked him.

Hawes stood. "Information on the competition. And on Elliot Brewster."

Rose's steps faltered. He'd actually managed to surprise her. He followed her to the seating area and claimed an armchair. "You were willing to work with Reeves," he said, "to initially steal the explosives and move or sell them. When Reeves was eliminated, you moved on to your other partner. I wanted to know who that was, and you'd already been working with Brewster."

"You were supposed to trust me and do as you were told."

Not if he ever wanted her respect, or at least enough of it so she'd stop trying to kill him. Time to flex some of that power. "I don't blindly take orders, from anyone. Not when the lives of our family and our people are on the line. We make decisions together."

"And this decision, regarding Brewster… Do you disagree with me? With the direction?"

"I do disagree." Before she could object or let her speculation run rampant, Hawes carried on. "Because there's a better option on the table, and she's game. We passed your test and hers tonight. Now let's move the fuck on."

"What about the fed?" Rose said with a nod to Wheeler, who sat trembling in his chair. "You've got the information you needed."

"Doesn't mean he's not still leverage."

"And if I asked you to kill him?"

She'd posed that same question to him before, only then it had been about Chris, and Chris hadn't been in the same room. He couldn't answer differently now without giving away the ruse. He shifted in the chair and withdrew his gun, leveling it at Wheeler.

The agent's eyes widened, as much as they could before he winced, caught between fear, confusion, and pain. "Please, no."

"I'll do it," Hawes told Rose, "but I don't think it's the right call. Are you sure you can trust Tran?"

"She's the one who told us where he was."

Hawes was glad to be angled away from Rose right then. It covered his surprise. Whether it was a good one or a bad one, he wasn't sure. Either Tran had purposely sent him in, or Tran was actually dirty. And Wheeler couldn't signal him either way without signaling Rose. Didn't matter, though. Hawes's response to Rose was the same either way. "Holding him helps keep her in line. She hasn't said a word about him—missing or dead—for a reason. And he can give us more information on Perri, if we need to neutralize him."

"I think it's the right play," Helena said.

"Same," Holt added.

"Amelia?" Rose said.

His sister-in-law's green eyes flickered to him, then over his shoulder to Rose. "Holt and I can hack all day, but the fed can give us a more concrete direction to go in."

"All right," Rose said, after what felt like the longest five seconds of Hawes's life. "We'll play this one your way. You've earned that much."

Hawes allowed himself two seconds to fume over the back-handed compliment before he lowered his gun and rotated back around in his chair. "Thank you. Now, can we talk about how to finish this?"

"Interesting choice of words."

"I want to be finished with the doubts, and with the ATF, so our family can move on and thrive. Same as you."

She rose, and Hawes worried for a moment that he'd over-played his hand. But then Rose held a hand out toward the stairs. "I've got the plans for the next phase laid out in the dining room."

He hadn't overplayed his hand at all. He'd played it just right.

CHRIS BEAT BOTH KANE AND TRAN TO THE STATION, BUT NOT JAX. Their bike was parked in the back lot, the fender still warm to Chris's touch. The duty cop riding the night desk confirmed they'd arrived five minutes ago, and Chris hung a right at the top of the stairs, toward IT instead of Kane's office. He crossed the threshold and spotted Jax at their workstation, hanging their leather jacket on the back of their chair. Before he could speak, though, the burner in his pocket vibrated. He dug out the phone, read the text from Holt, and cursed.

"Guessing that wasn't good news," Jax said.

Chris glanced first at Jax, then at the other IT officer in the mini bullpen. His glare, fueled by the anger Holt's message had sparked, was enough to send the young man scurrying. Once he was out the door, Chris closed it behind him.

Jax collapsed into their chair. "Is it about Scotty? Is he okay?" They looked worn out and torn up, like they hadn't slept for days, and yet the nightmares had still caught up to them.

Remembering what Holt had said, Chris sat in the chair across from them and scrubbed the simmering anger from his voice. That ire was reserved for Tran, not Jax. "Hey, this wasn't your fault."

"He's a nice guy. I left… I didn't think…" They picked up a pencil and began bouncing the rubber end against the desk.

"Tran did this, not you. That's what Holt texted. That Tran was the one who sent him in."

His words seemed to make the guilt plaguing Jax worse, the pencil bouncing faster. "I think," they said, "that Scotty actually did this."

Chris shot to the edge of his seat. "He *what*?"

"We found a series of suspect cash transfers, but we need to be hooked directly into the Madigans' system to access the most recent ones, which is the last piece we need to tie Rose to Brewster and the explosives... And to Isabella."

Fucking hell, *now* Scotty wanted to play cowboy?

"I'm sorry," Jax said. "I should have realized and stopped him."

"Listen to me, Jax. This isn't your fault. He went in with his eyes open. That's good."

"She could still kill him."

Chris reached out and laid a hand over theirs, stilling the pencil. "We'll get him back. For now, we're gonna have to trust Hawes, Helena, and Holt to keep him alive. You trust them, don't you?"

"I'd trust them with my life."

"Then trust them with Scotty's."

They took a deep breath and laid down the pencil. "All right."

Before either of them could say anything more, Chris's other phone buzzed with a **Where are you?** text from Kane. He tapped back an **On my way** as he stood and turned toward the door. "Let's go fill them in and plan a rescue."

"Wait!" Jax said. They rounded the desk, a flash drive in hand. "This is everything we found about the night Isabella died, including the missing footage from the scene." They held out the flash drive, and Chris took it warily, as if it might bite. And then they went and doubled the fun, holding out a second flash drive, this one with a sheet of paper folded around it. "And I think maybe this is the last piece of the story."

He recognized the slip of paper. On the outside, in Tran's handwriting, was the name of Remy's captain. Except, as he unfolded it from around the flash drive, he saw the writing on the inside too. *I'm trusting you, Dante,* in a different hand.

"Where did you get this?" Chris asked.

"It was on the table when I got back to the house and Scotty was gone."

Amelia had been the one to bring him to the house in Pac Heights. Chris wasn't familiar with her handwriting, but he guessed he was looking at it right then. She was trusting him to do what? The right thing with whatever was on this drive? Or more than that? Her note was on this paper for a reason. She was trusting him to uphold the bargain they'd made in the transport van this—yesterday—morning. To do right by her and her family for her cooperation. And what? She was giving him the rest of the answers now? On this drive?

"Did you check what's on it?" he asked Jax.

They shook their head. "It was clearly for you."

The urge to log on to any of the dozen computers in here to see what was on the second drive was damn near irresistible.

Wait for Hawes, Izzy said in the back of his head, her voice returning from wherever it had disappeared to the past few days. *Watch it with him.*

She was right. If whatever was on this flash drive was anything like the video on the first one of Amelia's they'd found, he didn't want to watch it alone. He'd seen Holt's and Helena's immediate reactions after watching that one and Hawes's reaction at the condo when he'd nearly torn it apart. Hawes shouldn't have been alone the first time he'd watched it. Chris wouldn't be alone this time. And he wanted it to be Hawes with him.

He folded the paper back around the second drive and pocketed it. "Is there anything on here"—he held up the first drive Jax had handed him—"that Kane and Tran shouldn't see?"

"No, it's mostly financials and the incident footage," Jax said, gathering up their laptop and files.

"All right, then. Let's go."

They reached Kane's office and found the chief squaring off against Tran. "You didn't think to tell us you were sending him in?"

"Agent Wheeler called me," Tran said. "He told me he needed inside the Madigan compound, and I had an hour to extract him."

"Amelia would have been closest," Chris said, announcing their presence.

Kane hardly acknowledged them, his wrath still directed at Tran. "Why did he need inside?"

"I can answer that," Jax said. They opened their laptop on Kane's desk and logged on to a secure server. "Right now, we only have Amelia directly tied to the explosives, and she's not our ultimate target. So Scott—Agent Wheeler—and I were following the money, trying to connect Rose more directly to trafficking in explosives, as that's the ATF's jurisdiction." They opened an account ledger. "We flagged this separate trust account Rose set up for Lily. There were irregularities that stood out from the other trust accounts set up by Hawes, Holt, and Helena." They toggled to side-by-side spreadsheets, one showing deposits, the other withdrawals. "We back traced the account that made these deposits into the trust." They highlighted those green. "And the account that received these payments." They highlighted those red.

"Payments, from the trust account?" Kane said. "Lily's eight months old. There shouldn't be any payments."

"Exactly. And they're all going, through a series of transactions, to the same entity, which has an account set up at the same offshore bank we previously flagged."

"That's gotta be Rose," Chris said.

"And the numbers match," Tran noted. "The money came in and went back out in the same amount."

Chris connected the dots. "She was using the trust account to funnel the money for her coup."

Jax nodded. "Separate from any other Madigan accounts."

"And that's why she needed Amelia. To disguise the transactions and hide the money trail."

"How do you know it's connected to the explosives?" Tran asked.

Jax clicked on several of the green-highlighted deposits, then on the amount cells of the first two. "Add these two up. Does that sum ring any bells?"

"Yes!" Kane said, tearing apart the stacks of files and papers on his desk. His prize was a thin manila folder near the bottom. He opened it, revealing a single sheet of paper—the ad for the dark web auction. Kane pointed at the buy-in amount. "It's the sum."

"Exactly," Jax said. "Now, that money came into the trust from this entity, which also made these two other deposits." They clicked on the other green entries they'd highlighted.

"Let's assume this"—Chris pointed at the entity making the deposits—"is Brewster."

"We're ninety-nine percent certain it is, given the account's other activity and the corporate formation documents. We just need a warrant to get the Account Control Agreement."

"Give me everything you've got on this account and on Rose's," Tran said. "I'll take care of the warrants."

"Thank you," Chris said, then asked Jax, "Are there matching payments out for these deposits?"

Jax toggled over to the payment screen again. "For three of them."

Three of them, Izzy prompted. *Not four.*

Why not four? Chris reread each highlighted line.

What's important about those amounts? Izzy asked.

The first two were the same—together, the total auction amount—and then the other two were the same, albeit significantly larger sums. Two sets.

Installments.

Made how often?

The dominos began to fall in Chris's head. "Look at the dates," he said, reaching an arm over Jax's shoulder. He tapped the date on the auction deposit. "That's the down payment for the auction." He pointed at the same payment a day later. "And that's the rest of it, for getting the job done."

"But Hawes didn't die in that auction," Tran said.

"He didn't," Chris conceded. "But he removed one of Brewster's competitors, and Rose proved she had the explosives."

"So then this"—Kane tapped at the earlier, larger installment on the date of Callum's funeral—"is the first payment for the explosives?"

Chris nodded. "When Rose first stole them."

"And that's the second," Tran said, identifying the last. "Made yesterday, for when she delivers them. But she hasn't paid it back out of the trust account yet."

"Because of Remy?" Kane asked. "Because she's not sure she'll deliver them to Brewster now?"

"Or," Jax said, "because there's a delay in the bank showing it. They're down for maintenance at this time of night, but if we're in her system…"

"You can see if the action has been scheduled," Chris said, putting it all together. "And if she's still planning to proceed with Brewster." He rounded on Tran, another realization hitting him. "We could have not risked Scotty and trusted Amelia to confirm this."

"I didn't," she said. "And I wasn't taking any chances. That's why the timing was imperative. Rose has been paid for the job. If that money is paid out, she'll steal those explosives right out from under their—*and our*—noses."

"No *if* about it," Jax said. "Scotty just sent us a message."

All eyes swung to them, and to the text box open on their screen.

Two words: **payment scheduled.**

TWELVE

"That's the plan," Hawes said, looking up from the break room table he stood beside. It was covered with maps and satellite photos, a route marked on each. Five hours from now, just after rush hour, an ATF transport driven by Tran and Chris would travel that route, moving the seized explosives from evidence lockup to a controlled detonation facility, ironically only a couple of miles from where they now stood, in the warehouse where the weapons were manufactured and stored. "Everyone understand their roles?"

Various points along the route had been circled. The plan Rose had laid out for him, and which Hawes had relayed to their operatives, included locations where the Madigans were supposed to intercept the transport, where a third party might beat them to the intercept and attempt a rip-off, and where they were supposed to transfer the explosives to Remy.

Hawes, together with Chris, Tran and Kane, had subsequently added locations where a handoff to Brewster was more likely to occur, where Rose might try to steal the explosives for herself, and where SFPD and the ATF would have secondary teams. Law enforcement would be less than a quarter mile from each other identified location, ready to converge on their signal. They would allow the handoff to occur—either to Remy, who had made a verbal agreement with Rose for the weapons, or to Brewster, whose account agreements would show he'd paid for them—thereby solidifying the trafficking charge against Rose. If she tried to steal them for herself, with force, they'd have her on grand theft robbery, plus theft of evidence, obstruction of justice, and a whole host of other charges. Either way, once criminal action was taken, law enforcement would move in, seize the weapons, and make the arrest. Hawes had no delusions it would run so smoothly, but at least it was an elegant plan. Especially considering it had been conceived on no sleep at three in the morning.

"All set, boss," Avery said. She'd be driving the car with him in it, trailing the transport van.

Connor spoke next. "And I'll back up Kane on Rose." Rose and Amelia, who was supposed to be back in custody by mid-afternoon, would be at the house in Pac Heights, operating as base command. "We'll make sure she doesn't slip free."

That had been Hawes's one alteration to the assignments Chris had originally suggested. Kane was supposed to be the LEO on Brewster, but Hawes had shifted him to Rose. He was the one LEO in the least danger from her. Though Hawes couldn't be certain she'd keep that promise, so he wouldn't leave Kane without backup.

Across the table from Hawes, Alice snapped pictures of the maps and photos, then handed the phone to Victoria. She quickly scrolled through them. "We're good," she said with a nod. "We'll get orders to the rest of the captains."

Hawes braced his hands on the back of the plastic chair in front of him. "Last chance," he said, meeting the gaze of each operative. "I'm giving you the same choice I did at the club. You and the other captains outnumber the four of us." Chris and Helena stood on either side of him, and Holt was listening in by phone. "Do you want to do this?"

"She put us through a needless test at Sterling," Victoria said. Before explaining the tactical, Chris had filled them in on the accounts Jax and Wheeler had discovered, the proof that Rose still intended to sell the explosives to Brewster. "She lied to us."

"So did I," Chris said.

Alice tilted her head toward Hawes and Helena. "They didn't." Her blue eyes landed on Hawes. "You made your rules clear."

"And you fought with us tonight," Connor said to Chris. "For Hawes."

"I intend to keep doing so." His hand landed in the center of Hawes's back, and Hawes felt its heat through the cotton of his tank, imagined it chasing away the chill that had gripped him since that call from Kane.

Connor nodded. "We know who we're standing behind."

"And what we're standing for," Victoria added.

"All right, then." Hawes straightened, and Chris's hand drifted to his lower back, settling there, settling him. "Go home. Get a few hours of sleep if you can."

The operatives exited the break room into the main warehouse, Hawes and Chris trailing. Their steps boomed in the cavernous building, the sparse furnishings—the table and chairs in the break room, desks in the handful of offices, workbenches with scattered parts down the center of the A-frame's open space —doing little to muffle the echoes off glass, steel, and concrete. It reminded Hawes of a fucking tomb. He bet the storerooms where they had kept the explosives were even more creepy. Good riddance to that inventory, if only Hawes could actually be rid of it.

"Change of plans," Helena said from behind them. "I'm on the primary intercept team."

Hawes spun, nearly knocking Chris over in his haste to shut this idea down as fast as possible. "No fucking way."

"Why not?"

"Because when this is done, you're the fucking queen." The words were out before he could stop them. Before he could consider the full weight of them or discuss them with Chris. Not that they weren't true. Not that Hawes's thoughts hadn't been headed this direction already. Not that the overwhelming sense of pride and relief in saying them aloud hadn't suffused him with as much warmth as the hand at his back.

Helena caught her balance against the nearest workbench, her big blue eyes staring back at him, shock and no small amount of fear swirling there. She looked much the same as she had in that courtyard after Papa Cal had died, except now the dark surrounded them instead of sunlight. And here again, it was as fitting a coronation as Hawes could imagine.

Hawes pointed toward the door where the operatives had left the building. "They were here because of *you*. Same as they were in the club. They trust *you*. They follow *you*."

She shook her head, not wanting to believe what he was saying. He half expected her to cover her ears with her hands. "That's not what I was after."

"I know," Hawes said, and Chris gave him a slight nudge forward. Taking the cue, Hawes reached out and squeezed his sister's shoulder. "And that's why it should be you leading them when the dust settles."

"What are you going to do?" She shrugged off his hand, some of the litigator fighting back and infusing her voice. "Fuck off with him somewhere?" she said with a flick of her hand at Chris. "Because that's not how this works. You, Holt, and I run this company, and the organization, together. That's what we've been fighting for."

"I might fuck off for a week with him, to fuck," Hawes said, trying to lighten the mood and earning the eye roll he wanted. "But after that, I'm back by your side," he assured her. "You're right. We do this together, and someone is going to have to step into Rose's role, making the social and political connections the company and organization need to survive."

Her lips rounded into an *O*, finally seeing what he had. The more natural fit for him in the evolved Madigan empire. "The alliances you've made…"

Hawes nodded. "Let me do what I'm good at, positioning us externally through the company and otherwise. You do what you're good at, which is organizing and leading us internally. And Holt will continue to be the technical engine that keeps us running."

She crossed her arms and furrowed her brow, contemplating, which was better than outright refusing. "We'll need to clear this with Little H."

Heat hit Hawes's back as Chris reached an arm around him and set his burner phone, face up, on the nearest bench, the call to Holt still connected. "Let's see what he says."

Helena gasped. "You kept him on the line?"

"Your own trick."

"It's the right move," Holt said. "Every aspect of it makes sense."

"And what about you?" Helena asked Chris.

"Seems your organization is the sort that could use a private investigator." His hand returned to Hawes's back, and Hawes never wanted to go without that touch. Chris's suggestion made it all the more possible. "I'm with him, in whatever capacity you all need," Chris said.

Helena's gaze shifted between them and the phone, as if she could somehow see Holt through it too. Eventually, she conceded, fighting with her topknot as she did. "I'm definitely not going to sleep tonight."

Hawes gently lowered her arm and cupped her shoulders. "One step at a time, Hena. You're not intercepting the truck, agreed?"

"Agreed, but if you need back up, I'm far away."

"Fair enough. We'll get through this op, through today, and then we can worry about the day after," he said, desperately hoping there was a tomorrow for all of them.

"He puts on a brave front, but—"

"But he's barely holding it together," Chris said, finishing Helena's sentence. He had witnessed Hawes's shaking hands during Kane's call, had heard the cracks in his voice after, had felt the tiny trembles that continued to intermittently ripple through Hawes.

Helena slung a leg over her Ducati. "Take care of him."

"Count on it." The helmet was just over her head when Chris recalled something else he'd meant to ask. "Why does he think Kane is safer on Rose?"

"Not totally. Connor is providing backup."

"That doesn't answer my question."

"He made a deal with Rose," Helena said. "It was his condition for breaking out Amelia."

"Because of Holt."

She nodded. "You hear from your family?"

"Safe and sound at the cabin," he said with a smile, translating *family* to *Celia*. "Thanks for taking care of them."

She couldn't get the helmet on quick enough to hide her smile.

Chris's grin lingered as he walked back into the warehouse, until he glimpsed Hawes's solitary form at the far end of the space. Right arm braced above him, he was leaning against the windows, staring out at the Bay. Except as Chris approached, as Hawes's reflection in the glass resolved, Chris saw that Hawes's eyes were closed. Above them, his brow was pinched and his forehead wrinkled, and below them, his lips were pressed together in a thin line. Distress was similarly reflected in the tense curve of his spine and the fingers he dug into his hip, knuckles white.

"Hey," Chris said softly, warning of his approach. Hawes's eyes opened, the harsh lines of his face easing. Chris slid a hand under his, picking it up off his hip and holding it in his own as he wrapped Hawes in an embrace from behind. "You put on a good show just now, but you can talk to me."

Hawes didn't dodge the comment; further evidence of his exhaustion. "I don't want it to all be for nothing."

"No one fights this hard for nothing."

"I didn't really expect my grandmother to ever trust me again, but to have it confirmed like this…" Hawes lowered his arm and leaned fully back into Chris, head resting on his shoulder. "Forced into a battle of wills, of power, that could cost people their lives. I just want to do right by my family, by my city, by my people." He buried his face in Chris's neck. "And by you and the past."

By me, Izzy supplied, and Chris stiffened, remembering the flash drives in his pocket.

Hawes turned in his arms and reversed, thinking Chris's tension was something he'd caused. "What is it?"

Chris didn't let him get away. "Scotty and Jax didn't just find information on Rose's current activities."

"Her past ones too? Her involvement with Izzy's death?"

"Jax thinks so, and they recovered the video footage of the incident."

Face awash with remembered pain, Hawes did escape this time, wrenching out of Chris's arms and pressing himself back against the windows. "Did you watch it?"

Chris shook his head. "I didn't need that distraction right now. Which was the same reason why I didn't hand it over to Tran." He withdrew the second flash drive from his pocket. "Or give her this one."

Hawes paled impossibly further. "What's on that one?"

"Amelia left it for me when she took Scotty. After her last present, seeing what it did to you and your siblings, I didn't want to watch whatever's on here alone."

Hawes's gaze skipped toward the adjacent offices. "There's a computer still in one of those." He made no effort to move in that direction, though.

Neither did Chris. Instead, he crowded Hawes against the window, front to front, his right forearm braced over his head, not letting him escape. "I'm not sure we can handle what's on that drive on top of everything else."

"What if it's something we need to know?" Hawes whispered, like it was the very last thing he wanted to ask but had no choice.

"What if it's something meant to throw us off?" Chris countered.

"I thought you said Amelia is on our side."

"Can we be sure of that?"

"Of course not." Hawes closed his eyes and rested his head against the glass, fatigue overwhelming him once more.

Chris wished he could alleviate it, wished he could fast-forward through the events to come later that morning and be done with all of this. Arrest Rose now and skip the risky part altogether. But those were not the cards they'd been dealt. The best they could do was solve one problem at a time. The best he could do, in *this* moment, was try to ease Hawes's distress. He brushed the falling top strands off his forehead. "Let's not add more pieces to the already crowded board."

Chris glided his hand down, cupped Hawes's cheek, and Hawes nuzzled into the touch. "But isn't this the battle that matters most to you? What this has been about for you all along?"

Chris lightly grasped his chin and righted his gaze. Hawes opened his too blue eyes, and they were a cyclone of regret, weariness, determination, and desire, spinning so fast it would drown Hawes unless Chris could give him some peace in the storm. "This stopped being about vengeance for me a while ago."

"She deserves justice."

"And she'll get it, when we put Rose behind bars."

"Is that enough for you?" His Adam's apple bobbed as he swallowed hard.

Chris soothed it with his thumb. "You're enough for me."

"Even after the hell my family has put you through, is still putting—"

Chris silenced the rest of his words and the self-recriminations bubbling up from the floor of Hawes's emotions. Showing him instead what this had become about for him. The lips under his, the tongue sliding against his own, the sharp, stubbled jaw beneath his palms, and the tight, hard body between his and the window.

The heart beating in time with his.

Breaking the kiss, Chris rested his forehead against Hawes's, the other man's face in his hands. "You made me feel at home for the first time since Ro died."

"Dante."

Chris smiled so wide, it hurt his face. "And then there's that."

"I don't understand how, after what I did."

"You say it like you're lucky, like you think you still don't deserve it." Chris traced his thumbs through the wetness under Hawes's eyes. Through the evidence of the assassin's soul. "You do, baby. You make your family better, this city better, me better. And I want to make a home here, with you."

"You hardly know me. I've lied—"

"So have I." He hadn't denied it to Hawes's operatives, and he wouldn't deny it to the man himself. But it wasn't the entire story. "We've both lied, but the things that mattered were true." He removed a hand from Hawes's face and laid it over his heart. "I know you here." He trailed the hand lower, over his cock, which had stiffened against Chris's thigh as they'd kissed. "And here."

Chris stroked up and down Hawes's erection, which grew harder in his hand. He knew he was playing dirty, but he was on the cusp of winning this debate—the last time he wanted to have it. He needed Hawes confident going into this op, feeling like the king he was, and the fact that Chris could give that to him, that truth, mattered too. That part had never been a lie.

"That night in your condo against the ladder, when you gave me control of you, what mattered more—that you hardly knew me, or that I could give you this?" Chris pressed harder against Hawes, pinning him to the window, shoving his thigh between Hawes's legs.

Hawes keened. "Fuck yes."

"Or the times we've been together since. In my condo when I fed you my cock. The other morning in your bed." Chris kissed him, slow and deep, until they were both panting. "Does it make any difference to you that I don't know what your favorite color is? Or what your favorite food is?" Chris slowly sank to his knees. "Or does it matter that I make you feel steady?"

"Oh God," Hawes groaned, thrusting forward as Chris worked open his fly. "I need you."

Chris yanked Hawes's jeans and boxers down and breathed against the cock straining toward him. "I need you too, baby. In my mouth, in my home, in my future." He shifted back on his haunches and stared up at a lust-drunk Hawes Madigan. Hands on Hawes's hips, Chris pressed Hawes's bare ass against the window, breaking his daze enough to make him loll his head forward, gazing down at Chris. "Do you want that too, with me?"

"Fuck yes," Hawes moaned again. "All of it."

"Then trust me. Trust this as much as I do."

Chris expected an *okay*, an *I do*, a *yes*. He didn't expect Hawes to step out of his jeans and boxers and slink down the window onto his knees, bringing them front to front. To give Chris a long, claiming kiss, the best of Chris's life. He didn't expect Hawes to draw gently back with a "thank you" and then lie back on the floor, completely open for the taking.

Trusting.

Chris rewarded that trust. Teasing his cock and balls with licks and kisses. Nipping his way back up Hawes's body as he rid him of his tank, flattening his tongue over his nipples, sucking and biting and making Hawes's spine bow. Spreading Hawes's legs and ass cheeks and working him open with his tongue. And once Hawes was good and slick, writhing and begging for more, pumping his fingers in and out as he jacked Hawes's cock with his other hand. Leaning over and catching the eruption in his mouth as Hawes's chants of "I love you, I love you, I love you" echoed off the walls.

Then, once Hawes had caught his breath, Chris falling onto the floor next to him and trusting Hawes to handle him with the same care. Arching his back and scrabbling at the unforgiving floor as Hawes mercilessly teased, kissed, and licked, then shouting as Hawes swallowed him down without preamble, confident and in control. Returning the chorus of "I love you, I love you, I love you" as his king sucked him off to the light of the morning sun streaming in through the windows and brightening their world.

THIRTEEN

Elegant only lasted as far as the San Mateo Bridge. They had just crested the mid-rise and were coming down into Foster City when not one but two tails fell in behind them.

"We've got company," Hawes said. "Two bikes behind us."

"Bogey at the turnoff," Chris radioed. He was a few car lengths ahead, riding passenger in the transport van while Tran drove. "Black Jeep Trackhawk. Tinted windows. Can't detect the number of bodies inside."

The tails were unexpected, the bogey was not. This was one of the third-party rip-off spots they had anticipated. A spot where highway patrol frequently hid to speed-trap drivers who hadn't slowed down after coming off the bridge. A spot where someone aiming to highjack the van full of explosives could dart right out of.

Fuck, they weren't even going to get to where Alice and Sue were supposedly hijacking the transport. Someone else was doing it first.

"Intercept four," Holt announced to the rest of the team, deducing the same. "Initiate traffic break at 101 and on the bridge at the rise. No more traffic coming through. Perri, slow enough for the traffic around you all to clear out."

But not so much that the tails behind them would catch up. It was a tricky balance. Avery, driving the vehicle Hawes was in, slowed to keep pace. At least whatever hell was about to break loose would be contained to this stretch of only a few miles. Didn't make the knot in Hawes's gut loosen much. Yes, he was ready to get this over with. Yes, he'd directed other complicated ops before, including the one last night. But none of those ops had this much riding on it—the lives of those he loved, the future of their organization, his family's legacy. He'd be a fool not to feel some apprehension.

"Clear of surrounding vehicles," Holt said.

Beside Hawes, Avery stepped on the gas, moving closer to the transport van. And Chris.

"Any idea who?" Hawes asked.

Holt, who was operating remote command in a Jax-driven van a mile ahead of the transport, was tapped into the traffic cams, full access courtesy of SFPD. "Can't get a read on the bikes' plates. Will get the Jeep's plates as soon as it hits the freeway."

Was this a true third-party rip-off, or Remy or Brewster springing early, or Rose trying to take off with the explosives while keeping Brewster's money? All options were on the table. Any of them could hijack the van, keep driving west on 92, hit 280, and be home free. Which was why they had planned for this scenario as well. They were ready.

More than ready. Fuck it. "Faster, Chris. Let's get this done."

Chris had the gall to chuckle. "Your patience is for shit."

"For this, it is. We've controlled the variables as much as we can. Let's do this, on our terms."

"Roger that."

Hawes heard the lingering smile in his voice, and it steadied him, even as the bikes behind them grew louder, speeding up too. "You ready to drive like our lives depend on it?" he said to Avery.

Her grin was positively ecstatic. "Always, boss."

"Three minutes out," Helena said over the roar of her Ducati.

"Hena," he warned, a reminder of their conversation last night.

"Backup only, I know."

"Victoria, Malik," Holt said, "confirm position."

"In position," Victoria replied. They were waiting just past the turnoff, in a parking lot near where the mileage sign overhung the freeway, a hole cut through the wire fence so the SUV they were in could plow through and enter the freeway if needed.

"Bogey is on the move," Tran said.

As were the bikes behind them, drawing up on either side of Hawes's rear bumper. "Faster, Avery."

Chris started the countdown ahead. "Passing the intercept point in three...two..."

"Fuck!" Holt shouted. "I've lost eyes on!"

And on the heels of that report, Chris bit out, "Jesus Christ!"

Hawes whipped around in his seat, looking ahead to where the bogey had charged onto the freeway right in front of the transport. The van swerved to avoid hitting the Jeep but clipped its back fender and sent it spinning. The van careened the opposite direction, teetering on two wheels, then came down hard, one tire blowing out with a bang.

Hawes caught sight of Chris's wide brown eyes for a split second before Avery shouted, "Incoming eastbound."

Hawes whipped his gaze to the other side of the freeway. Two sedans were drifting across the lanes, sliding so they'd align right on the other side of the dividing barrier. It would be a short hop over the concrete half wall and across a lane of traffic to where the transport had shuddered to a stop.

Hawes pointed ahead, to the gap. "Get between them."

"Can't go that direction. Bike's between me and the wall." Sure enough, the tail on their left had drawn up alongside the back door. And they were both closing in too fast on the van to just smash the bike into the wall. They wouldn't fit.

Hawes drew several knives out of the bag at his feet. Wrapping his nonthrowing arm through the seat-belt strap, he leaned out the car window, aiming for the bike on their right first, eliminating the other rider's cover. Two knives—one into the driver's chest, the other into his front tire—and the bike and rider went down. He climbed farther out, ass on the window frame, and aimed toward the other rider. The first throw ricocheted off the rider's shoulder, slowing them down enough that Avery drew ahead, and Hawes got enough distance to hit the rider center mass with his next throw.

No sooner had he let the knife fly than Avery yanked him back into the car. He fell into his seat, and he could swear his right hand scraped metal as Avery drove them into the gap, swerving and wedging them to a grinding halt. An added barrier for the unrecognizable mercs climbing out of their cars.

"This way!" Knife in one hand, Hawes threw open his door with the other, and Avery climbed out after him, her door jammed against the barrier.

A shot flew overhead, Hawes and Avery ducked behind their vehicle, and then the roar of a bike Hawes knew well sounded not just over his comm. "I'm on them," Helena said.

Hawes turned, looking back through the window, and watched as a knife flipped end over end, lodging in the chest of the merc half over the wall. Helena didn't even slow, just kept bearing down on the other merc, who was now running the opposite direction.

Toward where two more cars were careening over the mid-rise of the bridge.

"Holt!" Hawes called. "We need eyes, ASAP! They keep coming! Malik, get back there for rear support!" He needed to get to where he could hear Chris and Tran engaged in combat, but he couldn't leave them exposed back here.

"On my way," Malik replied, while Holt continued to curse.

"She's fucking locking me out."

"Who?" Hawes said.

"Amelia! I can recognize my own code."

Hawes's blood ran cold.

This was Rose. Again.

Except these were hired mercs attacking them. Not soldiers.

He glanced again at the car descending the rise. Eva's. And was that another soldier in the passenger seat? Were they coming to attack or support? Helena's tires squealed, smoking, as she wheeled back around. Leaving her back exposed to the incoming cars. Because she knew who those belonged to. Who they were loyal to.

Same as the sirens that now joined the cacophony of noise. The cavalry was closing in too.

They had the numbers.

They had Rose.

And Hawes was so done with this shit.

Knife at the ready, Hawes stood and stalked across the freeway toward Chris, who was engaged in hand to hand with another merc. Catching sight of him, Chris kicked his attacker back, right into Hawes. Looping an arm around the merc's chest, Hawes sliced the knife across his throat, dropping the merc.

There was a merc at Tran's feet too, but her focus was on the Jeep. "There's another one in there," she said, holding her gun at the ready. "I'm on it."

Hawes took his eyes off Tran for one second. One second to sweep his eyes up and down Chris, to check for any injuries, and in that one second, a shot rang out.

Tran's body spun, the force of the bullet sending her to the ground. "Tran's hit!" Chris shouted as he grabbed Hawes and yanked him behind the van.

"Victoria," Hawes called. She was the operative closest to Tran. "Get her clear."

"On it."

"We need to see who's in that car," Chris said, and Hawes nodded. Chris signaled to Avery to cover them, and he and Hawes approached together, Chris in front with his gun at the ready.

"ATF. Get out of the car."

Chris took another step toward the Jeep and a shot flew out the open back window. Hawes grabbed Chris by the back of the shirt and hauled him down, just in time.

"It's Scotty!" came Holt's panicked voice over the comm. "It's Wheeler in the car!"

"Are you sure?" Chris said.

"Amelia's blocking my eyes, but she sent me a message in the code."

Hawes hardly heard them, their back and forth no match for the blood rushing in his ears. Déjà vu of the worst kind washed over him, his worst nightmare come to life again. He saw the scene through his eyes of three years ago, something he'd fought to block out, same as he fought to control the variables in this op today, three years later.

Today was different. Light instead of dark. Dry instead of rainy. No gun in his hand, versus the Colt 1911. Yet it was the same. His future, his life, versus an innocent's.

The back door of the Jeep swung open, and bloodied wrists appeared, a gun in Scotty's hands, the bracing one missing a finger.

Calm resignation—and acceptance—washed over Hawes. It had never really been over, but it would be today, one way or the other. "Chris, back up."

"Hawes, no!" Chris shouted as Hawes moved in front of him.

Scotty wobbled on unsteady legs, tears streaming down his face as blood dripped from his wrists and hands. "I don't want to shoot you."

"I know," Hawes said, taking another step toward him.

On his periphery, Hawes saw Chris lower his gun and raise one hand. "Scotty, put down the gun."

"I can't! She caught me sending that message. Caught me trying to leave." He wheezed between heavy, labored breaths. "And she knows about Sam. She knows where Sam is! She's going to..."

"We won't let anything happen to Sam."

"You can't know that."

"Scotty," Hawes said calmly, drawing the agent's attention off Chris. He pointed at his chest.

Chris grabbed at his other arm. "Hawes, no, please."

"It's all led back to here, Dante."

"What part of don't sacrifice yourself—"

Hawes glanced over his shoulder, meeting dark, terrified eyes. "I understood. All of it. I also understand this can't end any other way." And it would seal the charges on Rose. No one in his family would ever be hurt again.

"Hawes, please." Barely a whisper, the last word cracking and cracking open Hawes's heart with it.

"I love you," he said. "Now trust me." He held Chris's gaze as he tugged his arm free.

Chris let it go, like making his fingers unclench was the hardest thing he'd ever had to do, and Hawes supposed if it were him in Chris's position, it would be for him too. "I love you too." Chris lowered his gun the rest of the way, and Hawes turned back around to Scotty, pointing again at his center mass.

"I'm sorry," Scotty said, aiming for his chest and pulling the trigger.

The lack of a good brace, owing to the missing finger, sent the bullet searing through Hawes's shoulder. It burned, like fire, and the force of the hit spun Hawes, like it had Tran, and he fell to his knees.

Behind him, he heard the gun hit the ground, then Scotty's body hit the side of the car, collapsing back against it with heaving sobs, Helena trying to quiet him.

Then Chris was in front of Hawes, helping him down onto his side, face pale with worry.

"I sold it." Hawes patted his breastbone, or rather the Kevlar over it, underneath his dark dress shirt. "But he was supposed to shoot me in the chest."

Chris heaved a half sob, half-relieved chuckle. "It wasn't your head, so I'll take it."

Speaking of his head, Hawes's felt woozy, light, like the whiteout from the pain was spreading through the rest of his body.

Chris scooted behind him, holding his body up, a wad of fabric pressed to his shoulder. "Hang on, baby."

"Give the order to Kane," Hawes said to whoever was still listening. "Take Rose into custody, and tell him to add conspiracy to commit murder to the charges."

"On it, Big H," Holt said.

"Good," Hawes mumbled as pain and exhaustion grew heavy, too heavy to hold his eyes open against any longer. Once he heard Kane's, "You're under arrest," over the comm, he turned his face into Chris's neck, smelling eucalyptus and leather. "It's over."

"It's over," Chris said, his warm lips pressed against Hawes's temple, easing him into the darkness. "The empire is yours."

"Ours," Hawes said, then for the first time in three years, he rested.

FOURTEEN

Being on this side of the hospital bed sucked, maybe even worse than being the one in it, which Chris remembered all too well as it had been him there only three days ago. Hell, the surgeon who'd worked on Hawes's GSW was the same one who'd mended him. Once Hawes was in post-op, she'd insisted on checking Chris's injury and wouldn't let him into Hawes's room until she'd wrestled his arm back into a sling. But that had been hours ago, and while Chris's arm did feel better, his heart and head worried over the too still form in the bed.

He scooted closer and reached out his good hand, laying it on Hawes's hip, hoping this time, unlike the dozens of others, it would wake him. It didn't. Hawes's injuries weren't life-threatening. The GSW was a through and through, no major arteries hit, but as with Chris last week, Hawes's mind and body had suffered more than just physical injuries. He needed time to recover. And as long as he was here, Chris would be too.

His head had just hit the bed next to Hawes's hip when a soft knock sounded against the door. He was halfway out of the chair when Tran slipped inside and waved him back down. She didn't come any closer, though, leaning against the wall next to the door. A safe bet, as Chris's anger still simmered. It hadn't exploded yet

—he was too tired for that—but it was there, bubbling beneath the surface.

"Rose is in custody," Tran said. "We picked up Brewster too."

The former Chris knew about, the latter was welcome news. "That's good."

When he didn't say anything more, she nodded toward Hawes. "How's he doing?"

"Doc says fine. He just hasn't woken up yet."

"Payback's a bitch."

If not for his anger, if not for the exhaustion, Chris probably would have laughed at her attempted joke—something he'd never thought he would hear from Vivienne Tran—but as pissed and tired as he was, the weak attempt at humor fell flat. He cut to the chase. "How's Scotty?"

"Sleeping, which is better than him being awake and in a world of hurt."

Chris was afraid of that. Wheeler had looked like hell on the scene, and it had only gone to shit from there. "How bad?"

"Broken ribs, punctured lung, head trauma. And there's risk of sepsis and gangrene from the GSW he was still recovering from."

"And his finger?" Chris asked, a phantom pain making his pinkie finger tingle in sympathy.

"Still missing."

Chris picked up Hawes's left hand, held it in his, thumb running over the knuckles of all five fingers. "At least it wasn't his dominant hand."

"He shouldn't have been injured at all." Sighing, she collapsed into the chair on the other side of the bed. "That's on me. I should have trusted you."

"Not me. Amelia. She's the one you should have trusted. She came through for us, multiple times."

"You're right." She drove a hand into her hair, grabbing a huge hunk of it and tugging. "Fuck, this could have been worse than Izzy's murder. That was the last thing I wanted."

Her voice vibrated with frustration, resignation, and anger, more than enough directed at herself. She didn't need Chris's piled on top of it—she knew she'd fucked up, she admitted it—and that was enough to cool Chris's bubbling fury. "You wanted justice for your wife," he said. "Things got tangled up. You didn't want to chance that."

Her dark eyes rose to meet his. "You didn't get tangled up."

"Oh yeah, I did," Chris said. "You just missed that part."

The corners of her mouth tipped up, but only for a moment, before her expression turned inward again. "How'd you find your way out of it?"

He closed his hand more firmly around Hawes's. "I chose to trust him and that what I felt for him was real. The rest flowed from there."

Her gaze drifted to the window while her fingers toyed absently with the chain around her neck. Chris wondered if she realized she was doing it, if she realized she was this far from her usual locked-down self.

"You'll find it again too," he said. "Someday."

She let the chain go and gathered up her hair, all of it this time, and secured it in a bun at the base of her neck. Putting herself back together. "Your instincts were right, Perri," she said as she stood. "About Hawes, about Amelia, about this entire operation. Which is why I'll be recommending you to a field leader position. You earned it."

Chris didn't hesitate to tell her, "I'm out."

She froze mid-zip of her leather jacket. "You're out?"

"Of the agency," he clarified, even though her response indicated she'd understood him just fine. "Once we tie up all the back-end work on this case, I'll be resigning, officially."

Her gaze darted to Hawes, then back to him. "They're out of the explosives business. They're no longer the ATF's concern. It's not a conflict of interest, as far as I'm concerned."

"It is for me, with what I want for my life. I want to be here, in our city." He glanced out the window, then at Hawes. "With him, his family, my family, and maybe *our* family in the future."

"You're a damn fine agent, Perri."

He stood and met her at the end of the bed. "And I was a damn fine private investigator too. Think I might give that a try again."

"You know..." The hint of a smile from earlier returned, growing wider this time. "Izzy once told me you were wasting your talents at the ATF, but she liked working with you too much to tell you that."

He chuckled. "Sounds like her."

Tran placed a hand on his forearm, and his laughter died. "She'd want you to be happy. I hope the PI gig—all of it—works out for you." She removed her hand, the personal connection fleeting, then vanishing completely as she held the same hand out to him, purely professional. "If you ever want to come back, I'll make it happen."

He shook her hand. "Thank you."

Help her, Izzy pleaded as Tran turned to leave.

"Vivienne," Chris said, startling her to a stop. "She'd want you to be happy too."

Tran rotated back to him, expression bleak as she tumbled the wedding rings in her palm. "Moving on from the love of your life is harder than the books and movies make it seem. I hope you never have to."

She left him with that painful thought, with the memory of the pinches of it he'd felt twice now—after the apartment explosion when he thought Hawes dead, and after Hawes had been shot today, even though he'd known the latter hadn't been fatal. He couldn't imagine what it would feel like to have Hawes ripped away for good, his heart torn out from his chest.

"I hope so too," came a scratchy voice from behind him.

Chris spun, finding Hawes awake, finally. Blue eyes tracked him all the way to the side of the bed. "Is this for real?" Hawes asked.

"Yeah, baby." Chris leaned down and dropped a kiss on

Hawes's cool lips, so very relieved to feel them moving beneath his again. "This is for real."

HAWES HAD DRIFTED IN AND OUT OF CONSCIOUSNESS MOST OF THE afternoon. Familiar voices and the drugs in his system had kept him in a comfortable state of mostly asleep, until Tran's relatively unfamiliar tone had caught and held, dragging him out of the fog. But he'd kept his eyes closed, pretending to sleep. He didn't want to interrupt. Chris and Tran's conversation had seemed important, for both of them, and for Hawes. He'd almost ruined the ruse and gasped aloud at Chris's verbal resignation. Granted, Chris had mentioned he was out when this was over, but telling it to friends and family was one thing, to his boss was another.

Staring at him now, Chris's dark eyes full of love, conviction, and relief, Hawes knew he meant it. No question. This was for real.

Chris gave him another too brief kiss, then handed him a glass of water. "How you feeling?"

Hawes sipped through the straw and swirled the cool water in his mouth, coating the parched surfaces. "Better than Scotty, sounds like."

"You were listening?"

Hawes took a longer swallow, then handed the glass back to Chris. "In and out."

"His recovery is going to be tough," Chris said, lowering himself into the chair next to the bed. "But he'll make it. How about you?"

Hawes tried to move his immobilized right arm and winced, pain like an arrow through his shoulder. Fuck, that hurt. "Believe it or not, this is the first time I've been shot."

"I believe it." Chris smiled, sly and heated. "No scars anywhere else I've seen, except the knife one here." He pushed up

Hawes's sleeve, running his finger along the jagged, raised scar on his left shoulder. Goose bumps rose all over Hawes's skin.

"Helena," Hawes told him.

Chris chuckled, the sound warm and more comforting than the drugs. "That I also believe. But you still didn't answer my question."

"It's sore," he admitted. "And I won't believe you if you say yours isn't still." He fiddled with the matching strap across Chris's chest. "I think maybe we should both take some time off to recover."

"Agreed." The smile that had teased Chris's lips faded, the lighter mood too ephemeral to hold on to.

Hawes coasted his fingers farther up the strap of Chris's sling, close to the spot where Hawes had shot him three days ago. "I can't relive this again." He dropped his hand. "And we still need to talk about the first time I lived it, with Izzy. You need to know what happened, see it for yourself, before you upend your life more than you already have."

"The future means more to me than the past. It's not going to change—"

Hawes stilled Chris's shaking head with a hand on his cheek. "I hope it won't." Correction. "I'm trusting it won't." Chris calmed, though his eyes remained wary. "But as we go on from here, if you're the only one without the full story, that's not fair. That'll breed resentment, feelings of exclusion, and that's the last thing I want between us."

"You're talking about the video from the night Izzy died."

He had been, but that wasn't the only problem they had to tackle. "So it was a video on the other flash drive Amelia left?"

Chris nodded.

"We need to watch that too, then. I need to know how deep my grandmother's treachery ran. And Izzy deserves justice. So do we."

Chris averted his gaze as he picked up Hawes's hand and entwined their fingers. "We can wait—"

Hawes squeezed his fingers. "Now, please. I don't want this hanging over us any longer."

"All right." Chris stood, untangled their fingers, and fished a flash drive out of the coat hanging on the back of his chair. "Holt consolidated and made backups," he explained, plugging the chip end of the drive into his phone. "Screen's not ideal."

"It'll do." Hawes pushed himself up and over, making room on the bed for Chris to sit next to him. The warm body pressed alongside his was another comfort, one Hawes desperately hoped would remain there after they watched these videos.

He had to trust... But it was hard once Chris clicked on the file labeled the day before Hawes's thirtieth birthday. Harder still as a picture appeared of that dark, rain-slicked street, as the phone speaker emitted the squeal of tires, the shouts between him and Zander Rowe, then the gunfire. The hardest when, after those few awful seconds of quiet, the truck door banged open and gunfire erupted again.

Chris's body jerked, and Hawes held his breath through his own recorded cries, the argument with Helena, and the fading roar of her Ducati. He hadn't even realized he'd closed his eyes and turned away until Chris's "Look at me" rumbled into the present silence. Like thunder, it was dark and ominous, and Hawes feared the accompanying lightning, what it might strike and destroy, how it might blind if he obeyed that order and looked at the man he loved. Did that man still love him? Hawes wanted to trust that promise so badly, but...

Rough fingers grasped his chin, no longer giving him an option. Hawes wasn't surprised by the tears on Chris's face or the anger in his eyes. But the words he spoke, "You didn't murder her," made Hawes inhale sharply.

"I pulled—"

"In self-defense."

"She was beaten and tortured, like Scotty." Hawes would never forget the marks around her wrists and the bruises on her face. He'd noticed them too late. Because he'd noticed the gun pointing at him instead. "She was just trying to escape."

"Maybe," Chris said. "But in order to do so, she had to kill you. Same as Scotty was set up to do today."

"Chris, what—"

The fingers gripping his chin eased, becoming a caress along Hawes's jaw, soothing him, soothing them both. "She was my partner, Hawes. We weren't in the field a lot together, but it was enough that I know what she looks like when she's frightened versus when she knows exactly what she's doing. She was more composed than Scotty was today."

Hawes's pulse raced, reflected in the rapid *beeps* of the heart monitor. "Are you saying this is the latter? Like Scotty?" He had never considered this scenario. The evidence to the contrary had seemed so cut-and-dried. But none of them knew Isabella like Chris did.

"I have no reason to lie. I'd already forgiven you, when you thought you'd murdered her. And I don't need to protect her either."

Hawes lifted a hand and brushed away the tears at the corners of Chris's eyes. The wetness was cool, but the eyes themselves were burning with fury. Despite Chris's gentle touches, that fire in his eyes had only mounted as they'd talked, as they'd analyzed with fresh eyes what they'd seen on that video. "Then why are you so angry?"

"Because my partner was going to kill you, then and today, because of something Rose held over them."

Hawes took Chris's hand in his, some instinct telling him to hold on tight. "You didn't know me then."

"If she had succeeded with Izzy, I wouldn't know you now. And Izzy would have never forgiven herself." Chris squeezed his hand so tight Hawes thought his fingers might break. "Rose would have taken you both away from me."

It was everything Chris could do not to bolt out of that hospital room and go straight to the station where Rose had been taken after her arrest. Only Hawes's hand wrapped in his and the investigator side of his brain kept him on that bed. Kept him wanting to know what was on that video dated the day before the one they'd just watched. It had to be the reason Izzy set out that night to kill Hawes. And Chris was sure that's what she'd meant to do. Her hold on the pistol, despite her injuries. The sharp angle of her clenched jaw. The desperation and determination in her eyes. In only a few seconds, Chris had recognized the danger, as had Hawes, who'd instinctively reacted to defend himself.

But why were they in that position at all? Rose had to have had something on Isabella, and as far as Chris could reason, it was one of two things: a case asset or himself. This had to be why she'd gone dark in the days before her death. Because Rose had taken her, worked her over, and forced her hand. Like she'd done Scotty. Fuck, if they had watched this before the op this morning could they have anticipated Rose's manipulation? Scotty's appearance on scene? Hawes had wanted to, but Chris had said no. He'd had his reasons, but if things had gone wrong this morning, if it had cost Hawes his life…

"Christopher." His full name, in Hawes's command voice, snapped him out of his spiraling thoughts. Hawes shifted closer, his eyes anxious and full of concern. "You've got enough on Rose already. Maybe we just forget that other video exists."

Chris knew what he was trying to do. Protect him, protect them. But Chris was too far into this—three years of his life into it —to turn back now. "I want to know the whole truth. I have to."

"But what if it's something you can't come back from?" A shiver wracked his body, belying the control he'd injected into his voice.

Chris inhaled deeply, calming himself, and slung an arm around Hawes's shoulders. "I think I need you to do that for me this time. I need you to keep me steady."

A long stare-down ensued, but Chris wasn't giving in. Hawes

eventually realized that and relented. Removing his arm from around Hawes, Chris retrieved the phone and held it between them once more. Hawes wound his good arm around Chris's waist, and Chris pressed Play.

An image filled the screen, and Hawes held him tighter.

Izzy was tied to a chair, arms wrenched behind her, feet secured to the posts. Her face was mottled with bruises, her nose was bleeding, and her shirt was dappled with spots of red.

"That's the warehouse," Hawes said. "One of the storerooms where we kept the explosives."

Amelia entered the picture behind Isabella. She dug into a pressure point on Izzy's back, and Izzy struggled in her restraints. Tears leaked from the corners of her scrunched-closed eyes, and her upper teeth chewed at her bottom lip. She didn't speak. Didn't make a sound.

"Enough," Rose said. Calm, like someone telling a waiter that was enough water.

Amelia backed off, and Izzy slumped in her chair. Head falling forward, she added tears and more blood to the canvas her shirt had become.

Rose stepped into the frame, immaculate in a designer suit, pearls on her neck and ears, not a hair out of place. "Let's try this again, Agent Constantine."

Izzy's eyes widened, too tired and tortured to hold back that tell.

Rose caught it. "We know you're not just a secretary. You're an ATF agent. A good one too. You almost succeeded where others have failed. You figured out to whom we were really going to sell those weapons. You even had an admirable plan to intercept them. But no one received it. We cut off your communications three days ago. No notes or contact. You've gone dark. Do you know what the feds think about agents who go dark?"

"I'm not dirty," Izzy seethed.

"I think they'll see it differently, especially with you in that truck with Zander tonight."

"I'm not—"

"You will." Rose stepped closer, daring Izzy to make a futile move from her position. "Or I will have your partner murdered."

Izzy lurched forward, and so did Chris. Amelia hauled Izzy back, a grip on her collarbone that made her scream. Hawes hauled Chris back, an arm around his chest and a kiss on his shoulder that made him whimper. Helplessly trapped in the now as he watched his best friend, his partner, being tortured in the past.

Izzy tried to disavow him, but Amelia rattled off all his pertinent details. Real name, badge number, address—real and undercover. "He's not here now," she said. "But he's got a niece that checks on his condo."

Fucking hell, Rose and Amelia had known all along. Who he was, where he lived, where his family lived. She still knew it.

On-screen, all the fight drained out of Izzy, her body folding in on itself as much as the bindings would allow. "Fine," she conceded. "Just leave Chris and his family alone, please."

"You do what I ask," Rose said, "and no harm will come to them."

"Why not just kill me?" Izzy asked. "Rowe can deliver—"

Rose shook her head, smile patient, like she was indulging a toddler. "This is the part of the plan you didn't know. Why I need you there too. Zander's not going to deliver those weapons tonight. He's going to die. By my grandson's hand."

"Hawes?"

"And once Hawes kills Zander, you're going to kill him."

Izzy paled, making the bruises and cuts on her face stand out in sharp relief. "Unless he kills me first."

"If he does, then he goes to prison for murdering a fed."

Except Holt and Kane had made sure that didn't happen. They'd erased the incident footage, erased all evidence of Hawes's presence at the scene that night, and Rose's coup had been put on hold for three years.

Hawes took the phone from him as the video finished, the

room going dark and Izzy's cries the only sound left. "She said she would handle us," Hawes said softly.

Chris's voice was not. "And now I'm going to handle her." The investigator side of him satisfied, neither Hawes's hand nor his body were enough to stop Chris any longer. Not when he was powered by pure fury.

"*Dante, no!*"

He ignored the twin shouts, from Hawes on the bed and Izzy in his head. Instead, it was something Scotty had said that rang loud in his mind.

Time to slay the fucking queen.

FIFTEEN

Kane was waiting for him around the corner from the holding rooms where Rose, according to the desk officer, had just met with her attorney. "Perri, you don't want to do this."

"Yeah, Brax, I do." Chris charged forward, intending to barrel right past him, and much like in his hallway yesterday, Chris found himself with his back to the wall and Kane immobilizing him with an arm across his chest. Chris struggled to wrench free and got nowhere. Even with both arms free, his sling discarded in the hospital parking lot, he was no match for the lean and wiry chief. Twenty plus years in the military, doing God only knew what, then a career in law enforcement, had taught Kane a maneuver or two.

"I'm trying to make sure you don't hurt yourself," Kane said. "Or those we care about."

"That's exactly why I'm here," Chris said. "She used me as leverage, against my own partner and best friend. Then she did the same to Scotty. We can't let her do that again."

"Who's to say she will?" Kane countered. "She could have called in my badge or had me attacked at any time this past week, but she didn't."

"Because that was the condition of Hawes's deal with her. He'd do her bidding, and no harm would come to you."

Kane's hazel eyes grew wide. "Me? Why?"

The press of his arm slackened, the surprise distracting him, but not enough for Chris to fight free. Chris figured his answer, though, the truth none of them spoke but all of them knew, would do the trick. "Because if she hurt you, Holt would either fall apart or kill her himself. Hawes was protecting both of you."

Kane staggered backward like he'd been punched in the gut. Chris shot off the wall and hauled ass toward the holding rooms, throwing over his shoulder, "She's fucked with all of us for the last time."

Lost in the rising tide of anger, Chris rounded the corner and nearly ran into Holt, who wore a stunned expression. His massive form was impossible to get past, as were his questions.

"Is that true? What Hawes did? The deal—"

"Why would I lie about that? And was he wrong?"

Holt's gaze drifted past Chris, toward the corner. "He saved me."

Chris didn't think he was talking about Hawes. But Hawes's future was on the line here, as was Kane's. "And now I'm asking you to save both of them."

Holt's eyes snapped to his, gazes clashing for a long moment in which Chris wasn't sure what the big man would do, and then he stepped aside.

To Chris's right, a door swung open. Amelia stood over the threshold with Lily in her arms, and behind her, Oakland Ashe, Melissa Cruz, and the local US Attorney sat at the table.

Fucking hell, if Cruz and that ex-SEAL prosecutor got out here and got ahold of him, there'd be no escaping. Not wasting another second, Chris ran flat out to Rose's holding room, darted inside, and slammed the door shut behind him. He had just gotten a chair wedged under the knob when a *thump* hit the other side of the door, rattling it and the observation window in the adjacent wall.

"Agent Perri," a cool, calm voice said behind him.

Chris turned to face the devil herself. Or at least the devil that had been fucking with him for the past three years. What he hated most was that he fucking owed her at the same time. He would have never found Hawes had she not set all of this in motion. But in doing so, she might have taken him forever, along with Izzy. Might have taken Scotty too.

"Perri!" Kane shouted through the intercom, along with more banging on the door and on the observation window. Chris ignored it, flipped off the intercom, and claimed the chair across from Rose.

"I won't be Agent Perri for much longer."

"You did seem to wear Dante better." She smiled, like she had at Izzy in that video, and Chris wanted to wipe the smug look off her face. Mostly because she was right.

"I'll give you that," he said. "Your ability to read certain aspects of people. What makes them tick. Otherwise, you wouldn't have been able to move us around your board for so long. Wouldn't have been able to leverage me against Izzy."

"Ah, so that's why you're here," Rose said, folding her cuffed hands in her lap. The guard had neglected to secure them to the loop in the table. Intentional? Or just too stupid to realize this seventy-something woman was the most dangerous person in the building?

It made his next move even riskier. He made it anyway. Reaching inside his jacket, he removed his service weapon from its holster and set it on the table. Banging on the door and window intensified. Chris raised his voice to talk over it. "You manipulated all of us, over and over again,"—his gaze flickered to the gun—"because of that."

"My actions had nothing to do with a gun."

"But they did, didn't they? That was the final straw. That was the final weakness you couldn't abide. That your grandson chose to do his job as ethically as he could, without the symbols of power you knew. The guns, the explosives, contracts with clients who lived in the past with you. Outdated symbols, outdated methods and ideas that create too much collateral damage and cost innocent lives." Chris shook his head. "Moving beyond all that wasn't weakness—it was strength."

"Then why are you brandishing a gun now?"

He leaned forward, forearms on the table. "To end this."

The supposedly dead speaker crackled, and Hawes's strained voice filled the room. "Dante, don't, please."

Holt, Chris suspected, had overridden the electronic controls.

And given Rose a last playing card, or so she thought, judging by the Cheshire cat grin that stretched across her face. "He knows you wore it better too."

"Except it's not one or the other, Rose. It's both. It's me."

"Chris, please," Hawes begged. "Remember what you said. The future means more than the past."

"Hawes," Chris said, splitting his attention between his partner on the intercom and the threat across the table, "do you trust me?"

Hawes answered without hesitation. "Yes."

"Do you trust me to do the right thing here?"

"You're angry—"

"Do you trust me?"

"Yes." No more equivocation.

He shifted his attention fully back to Rose. "As well as you read people, that right there is what you never understood. Trust. Your grandchildren do. I do. Hell, even Amelia does. That's where our power, our strength, comes from. I don't need a gun for that. I don't ever want to touch one again." Hawes's sharp inhale echoed through the speaker, his own philosophy taken up by Chris as well. The banging had also ceased, a sign of their observers' shared trust. Confident, his team at his back, Chris smiled as he carried on. "All I need to be strong and powerful is your grandson, the rest of his family, and mine. People I love and trust to have my back. That's all any of us need. And if you ever come for us again, if you ever think to leverage one of us against the other, all that power will be directed against you. Do you understand?"

She shifted in her chair, a first sign of discomfort, but she lifted her chin, grasping at her last perceived straw of control. "He's lucky to have found you. Or rather, lucky I gave him to you."

"Bullshit," Hawes bit out. "You didn't do that. Isabella Constantine did."

And just like that, the last weight lifted off Chris's chest. Hawes was right. The connection he'd discovered with the man on the other end of the intercom wasn't owed to Rose. It was Izzy who had brought them together. Chris's anger vanished, snuffed out by love and appreciation for his old partner, who'd helped him find his new one. "Turns out Izzy saved my life, not once but twice. You don't get to steal that from her—from us. And you don't get to steal the Madigan legacy from your family. All you've stolen is your own chance to watch your grandchildren take that legacy, update it, and thrive. Maybe one day you'll understand that." He stood, reclaimed and holstered his weapon, then pushed in the chair. "And make no mistake, that's my legacy now too, and if you ever threaten us again, I will defend it at my partner's side."

Blue eyes met his, and they were just as cold as when Chris had walked in there. But the ice couldn't touch him, not with Hawes's "I love you" from the intercom warming every part of him and carrying him out the door and into his future.

SIXTEEN

Four Months Later

Chris was late, and his sister was gonna kill him. He'd been the instigator of this idea, and then when the date had finally arrived, he couldn't get here on time. Not that she didn't have half a dozen other hands helping her plan and prep, but still, he was gonna catch hell. Even if it wasn't his fault his flight was delayed. He pushed open the heavy glass door at Restaurant Gary Danko, and a chorus of *"Happy Birthday"* reached his ears.

"Mr. Perri," the hostess greeted with a warm smile as she took his coat. "I don't think I need to show you to your table this time."

Chris returned her smile. "I'm pretty sure it's all of them." They'd bought the place out for a double birthday party—Mia's and Lily's. Lily's first birthday landed two days before Mia's sweet sixteen, a reason to celebrate for both of them and their families. Granted, Lily, asleep in her father's arms, wouldn't remember any of this, but Mia, holding court at the center table in the half of the dining room they were using, seemed to be having the time of her life. She wore a "Sweet Sixteen" tiara and, with help from Gloria and Jax, was passing out cannoli and birthday cake to the Perris and Madigans gathered to celebrate.

"Perri," someone called from behind him.

Chris turned to find Scotty Wheeler emerging from the shadows of the empty half of the restaurant. It had been more than a month since Chris had last seen him, when they'd presented to the judge at Rose's sentencing. She had pleaded guilty to avoid a trial, but the federal prosecutor had not gone easy on her in sentencing. They'd laid out all the evidence Scotty and Jax had assembled against her, detailed Scotty's captivity, and each provided statements as to the events that had led to Rose's arrest.

Scotty had looked half-dead the entire time they'd been working, surviving pot of coffee to pot of coffee, and avoiding Chris at every opportunity. Gone was the newly found friend, replaced with a robot who just wanted to work in his own office with the door closed.

Now, "half-dead" was being generous. Scotty's hair was overlong and tousled, his eyes puffy, red-rimmed slits of brown, and his pale cheeks were rough with stubble. The thrown-together outfit was also uncharacteristic—jeans that fit too loosely, a wrinkled dress shirt, and an overcoat buttoned unevenly. He looked barely any better than when he'd checked out of the hospital, against medical advice.

"What did we say about calling me Chris?"

"Shit. I'm sorry, Chris." He fiddled with the wrinkled collar of the shirt, smoothing it down like he'd just realized it wasn't pressed. "And I'm sorry to crash."

"Scotty, you look…"

He gave up on the collar and scrubbed his hands over his face and into his hair. "Like I haven't slept for four months? Because that's about right." He dropped his hands, opened his mouth to say something else, but then from behind them, Hawes called, "Chris, is that you?"

Chris rotated sideways, enough that Hawes caught sight of the person he was talking to and his steps faltered. Chris suspected more from shock at how haggard Scotty looked than at his presence here or from some leftover animosity. Hawes carried none of that, but Scotty still suffered the guilt from it. "I'm sorry to crash," he repeated to Hawes. "I just wanted to apologize."

Hawes reached Chris's side, sliding an arm around his waist as he addressed Scotty. "You have nothing to apologize for. We've told you that."

"I shot you," he said to Hawes, then to Chris, "I wasn't a good partner."

"You were the best partner I had since Isabella."

"I was the only one you had since Agent Constantine."

"Because I wouldn't work with anyone else."

"And you shot me," Hawes said, "because you didn't have a choice."

"I keep replaying it…"

"Are you seeing someone? A therapist?" Chris asked. "The agency has resources."

Scotty nodded. "I've been going, weekly, but I'm leaving. The Bay Area. I'm taking some time off, now that my work on the case is done and the doctors have cleared me to travel."

"Scotty," Chris said gently, "your Southern is showing." He was tired and rambly, and the Southern drawl was coating his words, thicker than Chris ever remembered hearing it. It was attractive as hell, but he knew Scotty wouldn't think so. "Stop a minute and breathe."

That won a small smile. "Before I left, I needed to apolog—say thank you."

"Is there anything we can do to help?" Hawes said.

Scotty raked a hand through his hair, tousling it more. "I'm not sure anyone can help me right now."

The blunt admission of helplessness would have made Chris stagger if Hawes hadn't been holding him steady. As it was, it temporarily robbed him of a response. But not Hawes.

"Sam, maybe?"

Scotty's gaze, which had drifted toward the door, shot back to Hawes.

"Where are you really going, Scotty?" Hawes asked.

"There's more than one nightmare I need to sort out."

Recovering from his surprise, Chris stepped forward and tugged a startled Scotty into a hug. "When you do need us, call. We'll be there."

At his side, Hawes clasped Scotty's shoulder. "We're family, and we will always be there, for whatever you need."

Scotty sniffled a little. "Thank you both."

"Thank you," Hawes said. "For trusting me, and us."

Scotty smiled, stronger than the one before. "I'm glad he was right about you."

They shared another round of smiles, of hugs and handshakes, and then Scotty disappeared out the door. Chris's worry, however, didn't disappear with him. "Remind me to have Holt put a flag on him."

"Monday," Hawes said with a pat to his ass. "When you're officially back at work."

Chris turned into him, dipped his face, and gave Hawes the kiss he'd turned his lips up for. "Sorry I'm late. Flight was delayed." Chris stole another kiss, making up for the two weeks they'd been apart while he'd been at Glynco, then in DC, officially retiring from the ATF.

"You made it," Hawes said. "That's what matters."

"Celia feel that way?"

Hawes took him by the hand and led him toward the party. "She's too pissed at my sister to be pissed at you."

That was news, proven by the two women very obviously, and very intentionally, sitting on opposite sides of the room from each other. Which was the opposite of how they'd been acting the past few months. Chris had it on good authority that Helena was the shop's best new customer. "What's that about?"

"Helena's icing her out for some reason. And they're not the only ones." He jutted his chin toward the table where Chris had first spied Holt sitting with Lily. Kane was hovering nearby, but he wasn't sitting at the table with them, which in a group of family and friends was unusual.

"The visit with Amelia today at Dublin?" Amelia was still at FCI Dublin but serving a reduced sentence in minimum security in exchange for her cooperation on the investigation and for assisting Melissa Cruz on some open bounty matters.

Hawes shook his head. "No, that went fine. She got to spend time with Lily on her birthday and signed the separation papers. But those two"—his eyes flickered back to Holt and Kane—"have been off since everything went down."

Chris felt more than a twinge of guilt for contributing to the wall of tension between the two friends. It had been there since the day Chris had confronted Rose, when he'd told Kane and Holt about the deal Hawes had made to keep the chief safe. Chris wondered what would happen when the tension between them finally reached its breaking point.

"I never thought I'd be the most settled of the three of us," Hawes said, and Chris's guilt faded in light of the happiness he shared with Hawes.

"They'll sort it out." He nuzzled behind Hawes's ear, inhaling the scent he'd missed. "At least Lily is oblivious to it, and Mia is having a good time. That's all that matters tonight."

Chris couldn't agree more, and he didn't think he could be any happier either. His old family and his new one, together, and all of them healthy and for the most part happy. And he was back here with them, for good now. Home. He rested a hand at the small of Hawes's back, then slid it around to his hip. "Thank you for helping make this happen."

"Our family deserved to celebrate something good after the past several months."

"*Our* family. Sounds good." He kissed Hawes's temple, unable to get enough of him. "I'd like to show you how thankful I am."

"Later." Hawes's blue eyes sparked with mischief. "I promise to give you something else to celebrate."

"It's Saturday," Chris bemoaned. "You're not supposed to be at work."

Hawes held the front door at MCS headquarters open for his partner. "How many Saturdays have I worked since we've been together?"

"All of them."

"Then what makes you think that's gonna change now?"

Chris grabbed him from behind as they waited for the elevator. "It's almost midnight." Kissed the groove of his neck. "I've been gone for two weeks." Nipped his ear. "Let's go home and fuck." Shoved his cock against Hawes's backside.

As tempting as all that sounded and felt, Hawes had something else he wanted to give Chris more. And he was fairly certain it would result in Chris's dick in his ass even faster than if they went home.

The elevator doors slid open, and Hawes tugged Chris inside. "This is my favorite time to be here," he told Chris as the elevator climbed to the third floor. Second shift on Saturdays was their last of the weekend. As the factory quieted, and as Saturday slipped into Sunday, it was like the whole world slowed down. When he was a kid, his parents or Papa Cal would use the time to catch up on paperwork, if they weren't on a job, and Hawes would tag along with them to MCS. While they worked, he would lie on the floor and stare out the windows, counting the stars in the sky when the fog allowed, or when it didn't, the stars in the water from the lights on the boats.

As an adult, he sat in the chair behind the desk and did the paperwork but still spent more time than he should staring out the windows. He enjoyed the time to unwind, to summon back the control the week had sapped away, to steady himself so he could do it all again. Except he had something even better than that now. The man pressed against his back, feeling him up and nuzzling behind his ear. "This that other celebration you mentioned?"

"Maybe..."

One of Chris's roving hands passed over where he'd been shot, and a shiver rolled through Hawes. Chris held him tighter, and before Hawes's mind could rewind too far, Chris's words pulled him back to the present. "Might have to fuck you first," Chris tempted, a hand lightly clasped around his neck and the other one not so lightly clasped over his cock. "Still haven't gotten the chance to fuck you in your office." He stroked Hawes's cock, and the friction through layers of silk about killed him. "Haven't been able to get that image out of my mind since the first time you brought me here. How I'd spread your arms and legs and bend you over, face first. Pin you down by the wrists and cover your body with mine. Ram my cock—"

Fuck, he was going to come too soon if he didn't shut the too tempting man up. He thrust back against Chris's dick, returning the torture, and tilted up his face for a kiss, demanding it.

Chris obliged, tongue down his throat, until the doors opened on the executive floor. "Been sittin' on that fantasy for months," Chris said as Hawes led them out of the cab.

Hawes stopped in front of the reception desk. "I want to make one adjustment."

"What's that?" Chris pushed him back against the polished wood. "On your back instead? Watch me as I fuck you?" He hitched up one of Hawes's legs. "Or do you want to ride me as I sit in your chair?" He grabbed Hawes's aching cock. "Or maybe you want to be the one fucking me?"

"Yes," Hawes gutted out, right at the edge again. "All of the above, but I want you to fuck me in *your* office."

Chris froze. "My office?"

Hawes slunk out from between the desk and Chris, took him by the hand again, and led him past Helena's and Holt's offices. He stopped in front of the new door in the line—four now where before there had been only three—and opened it for Chris.

Chris was silent as he walked into the new office, created from the more than extra space in Holt's and Hawes's offices. Hawes grew more nervous as the silence stretched on, to the point he felt compelled to fill it with words. "You've given me a place in your home." He'd moved into the condo in Mission Dolores last month. So Hawes had made room for Chris at MCS too. "Now I'm giving you a place in mine."

Chris paused beside the desk and tapped the pink box on the corner. "Those what I think they are?"

"Mooncakes, yes, for celebration, I hope." He pointed at the mini fridge in the corner. "And there's champagne in there."

Chris continued on around the desk and inhaled sharply, his gaze landing on the framed pictures on the window ledge. Hawes crossed the room to stand beside him, to look again at the pictures of Ro, of Chris and his family, of Chris and Izzy at Glynco, and of them enjoying a couple beers after moving Hawes into the condo. "Gloria helped me with the pictures."

Chris lifted a hand and covered this mouth, whispering through his fingers, "Hawes, this is…"

Hawes looped an arm through his. "I didn't mean to presume, but you're out of the ATF now, working as a PI for us and for clients Mel refers. It makes sense for you to be here."

Chris shifted to face him, a brow raised. "Makes sense?"

"I want you with me, my partner at home and at work." He laid a hand on Chris's chest, over his heart that beat strong beneath his palm. "I never thought I'd have that, and a part of me is afraid it'll disappear one day, carried out by the fog."

"No, baby," Chris said, laying a hand over his. "The fog rolls in and out each day, but the Tower, the Pyramid, the Bridge, they're all still there before and after." He grasped Hawes's hip with his other hand, squeezing in that place Hawes considered his. "And I will be too, every day."

"So that's a yes, to the office?"

"It's a yes to everything with you." Chris hauled him into a kiss that stole Hawes's breath, that wrapped him up so completely he startled when his ass hit the desk, Chris having picked him up and set him on the smooth surface. He shoved Hawes's legs apart and stepped between them, their bodies brushing, cock to cock, lips to lips. "And it's a yes to fucking you on my new desk before I cover it with work."

Hawes hitched his legs higher, drove his tongue deeper, and claimed the life that was his, that he never thought he would have. Then he gave himself to the man he wanted to share the rest of that life with. Lying back on the desk as he had in that warehouse four months ago, as he had against the ladder in his old condo during their first encounter. Arms spread, at Chris's tender, ruthless mercy, and feeling like the most powerful man in the world, like a king, as he let go and got lost, trusting that Chris would always be there—on him, in him, with him. By his side. A lover, a partner, the steadying force Hawes needed as he and his siblings rebuilt their new empire, this new legacy, one Hawes was proud to call their own.

Want more Helena & Celia?
Read their opposites attract story, *Queen's Ransom*!

Want more Holt & Kane?
Read their best friends to lovers story, *Silent Knight*!

For all the latest updates on new projects, sneak peeks, and more, sign up for Layla's Newsletter.

Reviews are an invaluable tool when it comes to spreading the word about great reads. Please consider leaving an honest review for *Fog City: The Trilogy* on your favorite review site.

Thank you for reading!

A NOTE FROM LAYLA

Dear Reader,

Thank you for taking this *Fog City* journey with me. I hope you enjoyed Hawes and Chris's story as much as I did. And I hope you'll forgive me the cliffhangers as we made our way to the final page. I so wanted to do a project that was 100% me—an homage to the city I love and the action movies and episodic television I grew up on, including the dreaded to some, much beloved to me, *To Be Continued*. Thanks for your patience and support as I brought that dream to life in a series that I couldn't be more thrilled with.

So thrilled that this is not the end of the Madigans and Fog City. While Hawes and Chris got their happily ever after, we've got the other two Madigan to take care of still.

Also on that note, it wouldn't be a bad idea to check out my Whiskey Verse books in the *Agents Irish and Whiskey* and *Perfect Play* series, as you'll see more of those characters weave their way into the lives of our *Fog City* characters. The reading order and links for the complete Whiskey Verse are just a few pages over and also available at www.laylareyne.com.

Finally, reviews are an invaluable tool when it comes to

spreading the word about great reads. Please consider leaving an honest review for *Fog City: The Trilogy* on your favorite review site.

Thank you,

Layla

ALSO BY LAYLA REYNE

For the most up-to-date list of titles and a helpful reading order, please visit www.laylareyne.com.

Agents Irish and Whiskey:

Single Malt

Cask Strength

Barrel Proof

Tequila Sunrise

Blended Whiskey

Angel's Share

Trouble Brewing:

Imperial Stout

Craft Brew

Noble Hops

Final Gravity

Fog City:

Prince of Killers

King Slayer

A New Empire

Queen's Ransom

Silent Knight

What We May Be

Perfect Play:

Dead Draw

Bad Bishop

King Hunt

Best Play

Redemption Inc.:

The Accidental

The Bounty

The Martyr

The Boss

Soul to Find:

Icarus and the Devil

Jason and the Storm

Paris and the Reaper

Atlas and the Traitor

Table for Two:

The Last Drop

Dine With Me

Blue Plate Special

Over a Barrel

The Sweet Spot

Sigh of Relief

Changing Lanes:

Relay

Medley

Freestyle

More Contemporary Romance:

Barn Burner

Eyes on You

ABOUT THE AUTHOR

Layla Reyne is the author of *What We May Be* and the *Agents Irish and Whiskey*, *Fog City*, and *Perfect Play* series. She writes sexy, intense LGBTQIA+ romance featuring competent adults in kitchens, sports arenas, car chases, and other high-stakes situations. Whether it's adrenaline-fueled suspense, rival athletes, vampires and shifters, or love mixed with mouth-watering foodie goodness, queer folks finding happily-ever-afters is guaranteed.

You can find Layla online at laylareyne.com and at the following sites:

BB bookbub.com/authors/layla-reyne

facebook.com/laylareyne

instagram.com/laylareyne

tiktok.com/@laylareyne

bsky.app/profile/laylareyne

www.ingramcontent.com/pod-product-compliance
Lightning Source LLC
Chambersburg PA
CBHW070150310726
48976CB00001B/46